HEART'S EASE
THE NORTHWOMEN SAGAS

SUSAN FANETTI

THE FREAK CIRCLE PRESS

Heart's Ease © 2016 Susan Fanetti
All rights reserved

Susan Fanetti has asserted her right to be identified as the author of this book under the Copyright, Design and Patents Act 1988.

This is a work of fiction. Names, characters, places, and incidents are a product of the author's imagination. Any resemblance to actual persons, living or dead, events, or locales are entirely coincidental.

ALSO BY SUSAN FANETTI

The Northwomen Sagas:
God's Eye

The Night Horde SoCal:
Strength & Courage, Book 1
Shadow & Soul, Book 2
Today & Tomorrow, Book 2.5
Fire & Dark, Book 3
Dream & Dare, Book 3.5
Knife & Flesh, Book 4
Rest & Trust, Book 5
Calm & Storm, Book 6

The Pagano Family Series:
Footsteps, Book 1
Touch, Book 2
Rooted, Book 3
Deep, Book 4
Prayer, Book 5
Miracle, Book 6

The Signal Bend Series:
Move the Sun, Book 1
Behold the Stars, Book 2
Into the Storm, Book 3
Alone on Earth, Book 4
In Dark Woods, Book 4.5
All the Sky, Book 5
Show the Fire, Book 6
Leave a Trail, Book 7

and

Nolan: Return to Signal Bend

PRONUNCIATIONS AND DEFINITIONS

To build this Viking world, I did a great deal of research, and I mean to be respectful of the historical reality of the Norse cultures. But I have also allowed myself some creative license to draw from the full body of Norse history, culture, and geography in order to enrich my fictional representation. True Viking culture was not monolithic but instead a various collection of largely similar but often distinct languages, traditions, and practices. In The Northwomen Sagas, however, I have merged the cultural touchstones.

My characters have names drawn from that full body of history and tradition. Otherwise, I use Norse words sparingly and use the Anglicized spelling and pronunciation where I can. Below is a list of some of the Norse (and a few Estonian) names and terms used in this story, with pronunciations and/or definitions provided as I thought might be helpful.

NAMES:
- Åke (*AW-kyuh*)
- Åsa (*AW-sah*)
- Birte (*BEER-tuh*)
- Bjarke (*BYAR-kyuh*)
- Jaan (*YAHN*)
- Jakob (*YAH-kob*)
- Kalju (*kahl-YOO*)
- Knut (*kuh-NOOT*)
- Leif (*LAFE*)
- Oili (*O-ee-lee*)
- Rikke (*REE-kya*)
- Solveig (*SOL-vay*)
- Vali (*VAH-lee*)

TERMS:
- Hangerock—an apron-like overdress worn by Viking women.
- Hnefatafl—(*NEH-va-tahpl*) an ancient Viking strategy game, vaguely like chess.
- Jul—(*YULE*) Norse celebration of the winter solstice (there are many spellings of this throughout Scandinavia; this one is Swedish).
- Karve—the smallest of the Viking ships, with thirteen rowing benches.
- Kullake—(*KOOL-a-kuh*) an Estonian endearment, like sweetheart or dear.
- Skause—a meat stew, made variously, depending on available ingredients.
- Skeid—(*SHIED*) the largest Viking ship, with more than thirty rowing benches.
- Snekkja—(*SNEH-kya*) the most common Viking warship, with twenty rowing benches.
- Thing—the English spelling and pronunciation of the Norse *þing*. An assembly of freemen for political and social business.
- Völva (*VUHL-va*)—a seer or mystic.
-

For my grandmother, whose strength was quiet and gentle, yet unbreakable.

And thanks again to Lina Andersson, for her help, and that of her wonderful friends, in getting Vikings right.

PROLOGUE
WATER

THE WAY THAT WAS

"He should have the tea each time before he takes food." Olga held out a small pouch, and Johanna took it. Cupping her hands around the girl's, she added, "Two big pinches. Brew it like I did today, until it's nearly black but not cloudy. Then it will be strong enough to give him ease."

"Thank you. Will he get well?"

Olga considered the old man sleeping fitfully on the bed near the far corner of the hut. "Your grandfather is an old man, Johanna. The tea will make him comfortable and help his food stay to nourish him. But his time above the earth is nearing its end. He should come in from the shore, and so should you."

Johanna had twelve years. She had not yet had her womanly blood, but she might at any time; her breasts had begun to bud. Olga worried about her here in the fishing village. The fishermen were a rougher sort than the farmers in the inland village, and Johanna was one of only two young and unattached women residing near the shore. With no family but her weak and ailing grandfather to shield her, Johanna might well find herself used roughly by at least one of the men here.

Olga knew well a plight like that, and she would not wish it on another, certainly not a sweet, pale flower like Johanna.

The girl pulled away from her and went to tuck the pouch into an earthen jar. "He wishes to be near the scent of the water, and he is still able to tie the nets most days, when he feels well. He won't leave, and I cannot ask him to make himself unhappy when he is so close to leaving me."

She came back and took something from her pocket—a small, polished stone. "This is the last piece of my mother's necklace. Is it enough?"

Olga folded Johanna's fingers over the stone. "Keep it, *kullake*. I need no payment today. But I will take all the herbs you can gather and dry. You know which are best. When you have a basketful, send word. Or if you or your grandfather need anything, send word. I will come."

Johanna bowed her head. "Thank you, Olga."

Olga tucked a loose strand of fine, light blonde hair behind the girl's ear. "Be well, child."

Taking her leave, she stepped out into the sunshine of a late-summer morning. She stopped a moment and looked up, enjoying the caress of the sun on her cheeks. She closed her eyes and sighed; she was tired today.

She had left her tiny hut in the farming village before the dawn, catching a ride at the castle with a cart traveling to the fishing village. The cart carried supplies to the fishermen and would later carry a load of fish and other food from the sea back to the castle.

Among the supplies the cart carried to the village that morning was salted fish; the fishermen were not allowed to keep any of their catch for themselves. Prince Vladimir, the holder of the lands on which their villages rested, and their lord and master, took all of the yield of ocean and land and rationed a tiny portion back to the men and women who had caught and reaped that bounty.

It was a hard life, but it was the way of things.

Olga's life had been harder. She'd once had a husband; she'd been taken from her family and given as wife to a favored officer in Prince Vladimir's guard. She had then had more to eat, but her life was harder in other, private ways. When he'd died in one of the many battles among warring princes, she'd been turned out of the soldiers' quarters.

Now she made her way on her own, as a healer and a midwife, like her own mother, bringing what comfort she could to her people. Though her belly was sometimes empty and she was alone, she finally knew some ease in her life, if not in her heart.

A chill danced over her cheeks, and she opened her eyes. White clouds moved over the sun, chased by a northerly breeze. There would not be so many more warm days; already the dawns were crisp and the breezes brought chill. On the horizon, Olga saw the clouds darken to a soft grey. There might be some rain in the afternoon. She took a deep breath through her nose, inhaling the scents around her. Yes. Evening, perhaps, but rain before the night went black.

"Olga!" A weathered woman in a faded red headscarf trotted awkwardly toward her. "Olga!"

"Hello, Maret. Is there trouble?"

"It is Heino. A hook tore at his leg a few days ago. Just a small wound, but since yesterday, he cannot walk, and he is hot with fever. Will you look?"

When she came to the fishing village, even when she was called to see a particular person, as she had been on this day, she always brought a basket stocked with salves and herbs and other supplies. Someone else always needed her help.

"Of course." She followed Maret back to the hut, just across the way from Johanna and her grandfather.

Before she had knelt at the side of the bed, Olga knew that Heino had a life-threatening corruption in his wound. His breath was light and shallow, and his face was red and dry with fever. She laid her hand on his forehead and nearly drew back as if she'd been burned.

She folded the cover back. Heino was dressed in a sleeping shirt, and his legs were bare.

"Stoke the fire, Maret. I need hot water and clean linens." She opened her basket and lifted a small, wickedly sharp knife out.

Maret hissed at the sight of the blade. "You must cut him?"

The break in the skin itself was small, Olga could see—not even the length of her own smallest finger. But she could imagine the filth that had covered that hook, filth that was now growing robust in the warm wet of Heino's body. His lower leg was swollen to at least twice its normal size, leaving the skin taut and shiny, and mottled red and blue and green—and white around the cut.

"I must clear the corruption out, if he's to have any chance to save this leg. This is only a few days?"

Heino, insensible, groaned as she palpated his leg. Behind her, Maret hesitated in answering her question.

"Maret, how long since he was hurt?"

"The day after Mabon."

The celebration of the end of the reaping. The villages came together on that day to make what feast they could. Olga stopped and looked behind her. "That is almost two weeks."

The woman dropped her eyes, and her cheeks, dark and leathery from a long life in the sun and sea air, colored crimson. "He would not let me send for you."

"Boil water. I will try to save this leg, but the corruption is deep in the meat." Maret nodded and went to the fire and the pot.

"Then let me die," came a weak rasp from the bed. "We die if I cannot fish."

Olga turned back to her patient and laid her hand over his. "It is not time for that talk yet, Heino. Let me try to clean and drain the wound. I have good salve, and I can stay and apply poultices."

"We have nothing to pay." He closed his eyes and seemed to drift from his sense again.

Though he couldn't see her, and might not hear or feel her, either, she smiled and patted his hand. "It is not the time for that talk, either."

~oOo~

Once opened, the leg drained foul fluid, with a stench so strong Olga could only take measured breaths. She massaged around the long cut she'd made with her blade, working all the corruption out that she could, and she steeled herself to Heino's agonized groans and Maret's fretful fidgeting. A healer often had to cause pain to bring health.

She was not so sure health could be brought in this case, but she would do all she could.

When the swelling was noticeably lessened, and she was finally satisfied that no more could be drawn from the wound by hand, Olga covered it with a drawing poultice. The linen had been boiled and was still hot, and the herbs inside it had a healing bite. Heino groaned in his restless, sick sleep, but did not wake or fight.

When she was done for the moment, she covered him and went to the bowl and washed her hands. Maret stood near the bed and stared at her.

"Will he die?"

Drying her hands on her skirt, Olga turned. "We all go into the earth, Maret. But this could speed his way, yes. I should have been sent for many days ago."

"Such a small cut it was. And we have no payment. He would not seek help with no way to make a balance." She sighed. "I will starve if he dies."

Olga went to the woman and took her hand. "You will come to the inland village if that happens, and you will not starve. No more quickly than the rest of us, in any case. Let us take one step before we take another, though. He will need to eat soon for strength."

That perked Maret up. "Yes. I can…yes. Will you eat as well? It is only fish soup, but there is bread, too, and mead."

Often, the only payment Olga could expect for her healing was a seat at a table. It was enough. She nodded. "I would be happy—"

Her sentence was cut off by a harried shout from outside. Olga and Maret went to the open door together. Peeter was running over the rise, coming from the shore, screaming at the top of his voice, with such force and volume that the word he repeated over and over was distorted, and it took a moment for Olga to understand him. When she did, she felt a chill in the deepest part of her soul.

"RAIDERS! RAIDERS! RAIDERS!" the boy screamed, running through the tiny village. "RAIDERS! RAIDERS FROM THE SEA!"

~oOo~

Northmen. Barbarians.

Monsters.

Olga knew of the horde of animals who landed in long ships carved with dragon heads and plundered the coast. This village had been attacked three times that she knew of since she'd come to Prince Vladimir's lands. They would jump from those strange ships and charge in, killing and raping and stealing everything of any kind of value. Then they'd charge back to their ships and sail away, leaving quaking destruction in their wake.

The last time, when there had been little of value left to take, they had taken slaves instead—all of the young men and women, those old enough to work and at the peak of their strength. They had left the old and the very young.

Johanna and her friend Helena had been gathering in the woods, and so only they two were left among the young women, and only Peeter, now shouting a warning, was left of the young men. He had been on a cart to Mirkandi, the trading town, that day.

Then the wild-haired giants had burned the village to the ground, laughing and roaring as the people they had no use for ran from the fire.

Prince Vladimir wanted his fish, however, so he sent men from the inland village, and they rebuilt the coastal huts a few miles from the shore. Many then stayed to fish. Now the fishermen had to carry their boats to the water at the beginning of the season and back at the end, and they stayed in tents at the shore most of the season, coming back to their families at the village only one day each week.

Olga knew all this because she was a frequent visitor to the coast, and because the villages shared so much family that they were all of one. But she had never before seen one of the monsters from the stories.

Today was the week's day of rest; all the men were on land, at home in the village.

She stood a few steps beyond the door of Heino and Maret's hut and watched the men and some of the women running for weapons—fishing spears and massive hooks, even nets. No man here possessed a warrior's sword or more axe than that fit for firewood and building lumber, but they clutched what they had in resolute fists.

Olga turned to Maret, who stood gaping. "What do you have that can be a weapon?"

The terrified woman blinked and shook her head.

"A weapon, Maret!" She pushed past her, back into the hut, and searched, finally grabbing a small boning knife from the table. Then she took the poker from the fire and thrust them both at Maret. "Take these and stay with Heino. Fight, Maret. Fight!"

"Where…where are you going?"

As the raiders roared into the town and the screams began, Olga grabbed her blade from the table by the bed. She didn't answer Maret; she simply ran past her, back toward Johanna and her grandfather.

Already the village was in chaos, and Olga ran across the rutted dirt path, expecting any moment to feel the blade of a barbarian axe in her back. But she didn't.

The door to the hut was open, and Olga raced in. She was too late. Johanna's grandfather was dead, his chest sopping with blood, and Johanna was bent face-first on the table, screaming, a creature in furs ripping at her clothes.

These raiders weren't like the stories she'd heard of those who'd come before—these beasts were killing and raping indiscriminately. No, not indiscriminately. It was more horrible even than that. They killed with intention. They seemed bent on total destruction, on killing every one of them and on taking their enjoyment of the women before they did.

And the girls. Johanna was yet only a girl. Just a girl.

Olga shrieked and raised her knife over her head, held in both hands. She buried it in the savage's back. But his furs and leather were thick, and her knife was short, and she knew as it sank in that she had done him little damage.

He roared, though, and reared back. Johanna slid to her knees and crawled under the table, trying to cover herself again. Her eyes were round with fear and shock.

Keeping her knife with her, Olga sidestepped, wanting to stay close to Johanna and also find something to put between them and the monster.

He turned on her, snarling like a wild thing. His head was shorn but for a strange tuft on the top of his head, and his face and head were painted with horrible red smears. Olga wondered if it was blood he'd used to decorate himself.

She brandished her little knife before her, but the raider laughed and swung his axe, hitting her arm with its side. Pain sang through her bones. Her blade, and her hope, went flying, and as thick, rough fingers grabbed her throat, she prepared herself for what would happen next.

"KNUT!" a deep voice shouted from the door. Expecting a greater horror, Olga glanced in that direction and saw a broad-shouldered beast with flowing blond hair, his face splashed with blood. He turned to her, and his eyes—deep blue and wild—met hers and lingered. "Leave them for now. Soldiers approach."

Though she had never before seen one of these men, Olga knew some of their language. Her older brother, Mihkel, had left the village of their youth and gone adventuring, crossing sea and land alike. It had been long since she'd had word of him, and she believed him dead. But on his few visits home, he'd taught her some of the things he'd learned out in the world.

She had an agile mind and remembered all the things she saw and heard and experienced. So she understood the golden giant, and as the red-smeared savage stepped away from her, she knew she and Johanna had a brief reprieve. A chance to run.

When the raiders left, she went for her knife, then grabbed Johanna's hand and pulled her toward the door.

But there was nowhere to run. The raiders and soldiers swarmed the village, and bodies had fallen everywhere. Bodies of people she knew. The smell of death filled the air.

Johanna's knees gave out, and Olga barely kept hold of her. The girl was too afraid; they could never get through that murderous throng and find safety.

"Come—we will tuck away and wait for our chance." She pulled the girl back inside, found a knife near the fire, handed it to Johanna, and then dragged her to the farthest corner of the hut, behind the bed on which her grandfather's body lay. His blood dripped steadily onto the rough wood of the floor.

"Perhaps the soldiers will win," Johanna whispered.

"Perhaps they will." Olga doubted that; Prince Vladimir would not send many soldiers to die for a mere fishing village, not even one less than half a day's ride from the castle. He would keep his good fighters close and protect what he valued. The raiders would win and take their plunder.

Olga held her knife and knew that she should open Johanna's throat with it. There was no escape for them, and what awaited was a greater horror and a more painful death. It would be a mercy to end the girl's life now, before she experienced the world as it truly was.

Olga knew that was true, but she couldn't do it. The girl clung to her, taking comfort from her. She felt safer with her, and Olga could not face the betrayal she would see in Johanna's eyes as her lifeblood left her young body.

She was not strong enough to save Johanna or herself.

The women huddled together, their knives clutched to their chests, and listened to the village die.

PART ONE
EARTH

1

The barbarians won the village and all its meager spoils.

Eight women had been spared from death during the scourge and claimed as slaves, Olga and Johanna among them. Johanna's young friend, Helena, was also dragged away, bound by wrist and neck with hempen rope.

They were dragged farther inland, where the raiders made camp. A pen was made to hold the women, as if they were nothing but livestock. Olga understood enough of the talk around them to know that they were less than livestock to these strange men—and women, there were women among the raiders, bearing sword and shield and stained with blood as much as any man.

Four men—three fishermen and one soldier—had been held alive as well. The soldier was blindfolded and bound to a tree. The others were working to build the camp.

Some of the women were dragged away from the pen, and some were beset where they were, still tied to the post in the center by the rope around their necks.

Johanna was one who was dragged away. She screamed and clutched backward for Olga, her fingernails gouging deep into the flesh of Olga's arm, until the barbarian hit her in the face and threw her over his shoulder.

For her part, Olga was taken in the pen, thrown face-down in the dirt, the rope tugging at her throat.

It was not the first time she had been taken in this way. She knew the pain of it, and she knew that men who could take this pleasure would take more pleasure in her suffering, so she bore the pain quietly.

She could hear the screams and wails of the other women and the girls, and she spoke clearly, as calmly as she could. "Be strong, sisters. Your pain and fear feeds them."

Their anguish was too great, however, and they could not heed her.

Roaring fetid breath into the side of her face, the raider completed and left her. Before she could push herself from the ground, another was on her. She bore that, too.

And the next.
She did not resist; she lay as still and malleable as she could be, and she let it happen, because it would happen no matter her struggle, no matter her pain. It was the way of things.

Then she was left alone, as were the others in the pen. And then those who had been taken were returned. None of the women were unscathed; they showed ill use, and several had only scraps left of their clothing.

The raiders seemed to have burned off their savage need and were grouping now near a large fire, from which the smell of roasting meat wafted. They had a new appetite, and the women had a reprieve.

Johanna had been dropped near the pole and tied again to it. She made a weak cry and curled her body into a tight coil. Olga stood and went to her, ignoring the pains of her own body. Helena, bruised and battered herself, left wearing only a torn blouse, her bottom nearly bare, knelt over Johanna, sobbing; Olga nudged the girl to the side.

"Let me see, *kullake*. Let me see." At Olga's gentle urging, Johanna relaxed her body enough for Olga to examine her.

Blood had soaked through Johanna's skirt, turning the red wool black and shiny. Olga turned to use her hands behind her and pushed the skirt up, over skinny, bare legs, pale but for the vicious bruises blossoming red and purple over the young flesh. And the blood coming from her woman's place. Running freely. She had only twelve years. Only twelve, and the first blood to come from her womb should not have been this blood.

The sun still shone through pale clouds, and a light, cool breeze made leaves dance and sing on their branches. It seemed too light and gentle a day to hold such darkness.

The quantity of blood foretold that Johanna would die on this day, in this awful place, so close to her home, and yet a world away. She would die in agony, when all around them were herbs for healing and comfort. Barely more than an arm's reach away was bed of mouse-ear, which could slow the blood and give her comfort. And there were mushrooms that could take her away from this place. That could take them all away.

A certain kind of mushroom, and Johanna need never know pain again.

All of it, almost close enough to reach. But she was tied to a post, and her hands were bound against her back. In powerless frustration, Olga cast her eyes about the camp, as if there might be some help for them among the monsters making this nightmare.

Walking near their pen was the golden giant who had stopped the raider in Johanna's hut. He had washed the blood from his face and hands. Olga had no cause to think him less terrible than any other of these barbarous creatures, except that he had met her eyes in the hut, and she had seen in his something other than the rapacious hunger of his blood-smeared fellow. And he had not come for the women. Not in the village, and not here in the camp.

She stood and walked the length of her rope.

"*Palun!*" she called, and then remembered herself and sought the word in the raiders' tongue. "Please!"

He stopped and cocked his head but didn't speak.

Olga swallowed, and the rope rubbed against her throat. "Please." She searched her mind for the words her brother had taught her. "Girl is bad hurt." A nod toward Johanna on the ground would, she hoped, suffice to fill in any gaps in her words.

"You speak our tongue." He stepped to the rope fence that bounded their prison.

"Little, yes. A plant at woods. Golden flowers?" She didn't know how to say 'mouse-ear' in any other way. "It help her. Please."

"You are a"—he said a word she did not know, and she shrugged and shook her head.

"I not know this."

He paused as if he were thinking and then said, "You make people well?"

"Yes. I try."

The raider pulled a knife from a sheath at his back and came into the pen. Olga ran backward, away from him and what she was sure was her bloody death. She tripped over her feet and had no way to correct or catch herself, with her hands bound behind her. She would have fallen, except that the raider caught her, his massive arm sweeping around her waist.

He was even more enormous up close. Olga felt sure he could have snapped her in two, and she was sure he was about to do just that. Instead, he set her on her feet and used that knife to cut her rope free from the pole. They had the complete attention of the other women, all but Johanna, who was curled again and moaning.

"Please. She suffers. More than we others. She is girl only." Her mind raced, seeking all the words she knew of this strange tongue, which did not fit in her mouth very well.

He turned and looked down at Johanna, and, again, Olga saw something softer in his eyes. "How old is she?" When she couldn't quite make sense of the question and didn't respond, he asked, "How many years?" With that, she understood the first question, too.

"Twelve."

His eyes closed. When he opened them, he turned them on her. They were deep blue, like twilight sky. "You can be of use. If you will work and do no harm, I will unbind you." He shook the rope. "Understand?"

She understood most of his words, but she struggled to make sense of the change in her circumstances. Even if only temporary, it seemed an unthinkable boon. "I help girl?"

"If our healer can use your help, then yes. You will have run of the camp, and may see to the other slaves if you like. But if you make trouble, I will slit your throat." Brandishing his knife, he asked again, "Understand?"

Olga nodded. "Understand." She understood enough—he wanted her to work, and he would let her help Johanna. Perhaps the others as well. And he would unbind her.

He cut the rope from her hands and her neck, then sheathed his knife. With a huge hand wrapped completely around her arm, he led her from the pen and into the camp. Over her shoulder, she called to the other women in their own words, "Be strong! I will bring help!"

She hoped that was a truth.

~oOo~

The barbarian healer was another large man—they were all so big—though smaller than the blond, with bushy red hair and beard. He gave the blond one a long look and then nodded.

"You speak our language?" he asked of her.

She kept her eyes downcast; she knew well the role of the subjected. "Yes."

"You know how to care for wounds—battle wounds?"

Running that sentence through her head as quickly as she could, translating the words, she nodded. "I am healer." She used the word the blond one had used and thought she now understood its meaning.

There was only one wounded man in the tent. His face was covered in bloody bandages.

"I have no need of her now, Leif, but she can be useful," the healer said to the blond one. Leif. His name. She looked up at his face and found his eyes on her.

"I will have her tend to the thralls, then. Some of the women are already ill used and will not be of much more use if they aren't tended to."

Olga's head ached from trying to understand the raiders' words, but sense was already coming more easily to her. "Please," she said. "I help girl." Too much time had passed already.

The blond one—Leif—nodded and took hold of her arm again.

But then a horn blew somewhere, and instead of leading her out of the tent, he pushed her back toward the redheaded raider. "You stay with Sven." To the red one, he said. "Keep her here."

And he was gone.

~oOo~

"Usch," the redheaded healer—Sven—muttered under his breath again, while battle screamed and clanged outside the tent. "Usch."

He went to the tent opening and stood looking. Olga could not see around him, but she didn't need to; she had seen enough of battle in her lifetime. She had seen enough horror in this one day to last more than one lifetime.

She knew that she would be no help to Johanna now.

Sven turned back to her, a fierce scowl warping his features. "What are you called?"

"I..." She had not expected him to address her. "I..."

"Your name, girl! I am Sven." He slapped his chest.

"Olga."

"Olga. Fine. I have use of you after all." He waved a hand at the corner of the tent. "Lay out the mats and furs. I will prepare. We will have wounded. There are always wounded. Understand?"

She nodded and went to the place he'd shown her. His voice called her attention back, and she turned to him again.

"If we are beset, get behind me. Understand?"

Again, she nodded. Though the soldiers, if it was they who had attacked the camp, were ostensibly on her side, she had no trust that she would be rescued by anyone attacking the healing tent.

His eyes traveled the length of her body, one eyebrow cocked in appraisal. "You are the size of a child. There had better be more strength in those skinny arms than a child's."

Olga said nothing. She was small among her people, and slim, but not child-size. These giant beast-men seemed hardly human to her.

He turned and crouched before a chest and dug into it, then threw something at her. Of instinct, she caught it. Cloth.

"Cover yourself."

He had tossed her a tunic made of rough-spun wool. Olga looked down at herself and saw, for the first time, that her own blouse was rent down the middle. Her breasts were all but exposed.

She pulled the tunic over her head and rolled the too-long sleeves until her hands were clear.

"Let us prepare for our work." Sven said, and then proceeded to ignore her.

Olga got to work.

~oOo~

Four men and two women—Olga marveled again at the idea of women warriors, with leather breeches and blood-spattered faces, wielding swords that seemed as long as she was tall—were brought into the tent. One of the men and one of the women were soon carried out, after Sven looked them over and then shook his head.

The other four, and the unconscious man from before, made up their charges. A raider who had carried in some of the wounded stayed and began to help the healing, lifting heavy bodies and stripping armor from bloodied limbs.

Surrounded by work to do, work she knew, Olga focused on her tasks. After a short time, Sven seemed to understand her skill and to trust that she would do no harm, and he left her alone to work. When she said she needed a certain herb, using pantomime to bolster her faulty language and make herself known, he even sent the raider out to gather it.

Beyond the tent, the sounds of battle became the sounds of aftermath. Olga did not need to see outdoors to know that, again, the raiders had won.

Then there was a new commotion outside the door, and a crowd of raiders—four of them—barged in, nearly tearing down the tent in their hurry to be in it. They bore a blood-washed monster in their arms, a man bigger than any Olga had ever seen. A man so big he dwarfed Sven and the others.

They carried him face down, and Olga saw instantly why. He appeared to have been nearly sliced in half. A long, wide gash split his back from shoulder to waist, and as the men carried him and laid him on a pallet far shorter than he, the gash widened, and Olga saw the ladder of his ribs.

She watched and waited for Sven to shake his head and the men to carry the giant out again. But this man must have been special somehow. Perhaps he was truly a giant. Sven knelt at his hip and dug his fingers deep into the wound.

Then he brought his hand to his own mouth and sucked the blood.

"Clean. Thank the gods. Get out and let me work." The men who'd borne the giant into the tent all nodded and took their leave, and Sven began to clean the blood from that massive back.

"I help?" she asked, quietly.

Turning intent green eyes on her, Sven answered, "You help by seeing to the others and leaving me to this work. Dan"—he nodded to the other raider, who had stayed to help—"will help you. Understand?"

"Understand." Olga ventured to ask more. "This one is important?"

Sven stopped and looked at her directly. This time, she did not look away. "Yes. He is important. A good man and a legend."

"Sorry. I not know...*le-gend*."

The other raider, Dan, now standing at her side, answered. "Our people tell stories about him. Do you know *stories*?"

"Yes, I know. We have stories. Of great men. Strong."

"Vali Storm-Wolf is such a man," Dan said. "The best of us."

Olga thought even the best of men like these could not be so great a man, but she was moved nonetheless.

~oOo~

The rain that Olga had seen in the sky in the morning, long hours and a lifetime ago, crashed over them in the dusk, not long after the raiders' legendary giant had been carried into the tent. Olga turned and studied the opaque sheet of water beating down into the mud outside the tent, she listened to the deafening roar of rain pelting the tent roof, and she thought of the women tied to the post.

Without ever meaning to, she had abandoned them. She knew that by now Johanna was dead, and perhaps others as well. Hours since Leif had taken her away, and Olga had been so wrapped up in the work here that she had barely spared them—her friends, her own people—a thought. And now she was dry and protected, and they were alone, exposed to the elements and countless horrors.

The giant was conscious, but barely. Sven had begun to stitch the terrible wound closed, and a hoarse groan erupted from his patient every now and then, when the bone needle went into the tattered flesh.

In Olga's opinion, Sven was causing more pain for no sound reason. No mortal being, not even a legendary giant, unless he was made of something more than flesh, could survive such a wounding.

The tent shook as someone came in, and Olga turned quickly, her heart racing. She did not like these raiders coming up behind her; she expected each time to be grabbed or stabbed.

It was a woman, a warrior, drenched from the storm but still covered head to toe in blood. She was tall, more than a head above Olga.

She took note of the people in the tent. When her eyes turned her way, Olga saw how strangely lovely they were. Two different eyes in the same head. The left eye was a shade of blue, light and deep like a cloudless sky. Pretty, but not unusual. The other, though, was a marvel. Olga had never seen its like. Without thinking, she narrowed her focus, trying to see all there was to see in that right eye. The candles in the tent burned brightly, and Olga saw green and blue and amber swirled together in the woman's eye. More fascinating than that were the streaks of brown, almost like something drawn over all that color.

The warrior woman cocked her head, and Olga realized she was staring and dropped her eyes. She was sorry to do so.

"How is he?" the woman asked Sven.

Sven seemed shocked that she had spoken. He didn't look up at her. "There is no offal in his blood. He might yet live if the bleeding stops."

"See, Brenna God's-Eye?" the giant gritted the words out. "We are fated to save each other."

Vali Storm-Wolf and Brenna God's-Eye. Olga almost smiled. There was something strong between these two. A true bonding. Olga could sense the way their life forces mingled and became something new, something singular and unified, and she thought she understood the raiders' word.

Legend.

~oOo~

Vali Storm-Wolf's wound might have been clean of offal, but it had not been clean of filth. The next day brought fever and swelling, and Sven and she had worked long to draw the corruption from him.

The warrior woman with the strange and beautiful eye came to sit with him again. Brenna God's-Eye. These people must have thought her eye more than strange. They seemed all to fear it, and her. All but the giant, Vali.

Olga's people had no gods. They believed that what lay on the earth, and in it, and above it, and beyond it, was all of a piece, that life rolled like a wheel through it all, and that balance in all things was the only true reverence. They celebrated the solstices, the longest and shortest of days, and the sowing and reaping, because those days were days when balance was most clear.

They treated beasts and trees and plants, and earth and sea and sky, with the respect due equals, holding no thing above another.

The nobles, perhaps, saw balance in another way, but neither Olga nor any of her people saw nobles as part of them. They were merely raiders of another sort. The sort that never sailed away and left them alone.

A horn blew again, and Brenna left Vali's side. Shortly thereafter, a large party of the raiders left the camp on horseback. Sven stood at the tent opening, muttering under his breath.

Olga waited until he sighed and turned back to his patients before she asked if she might finally go to the women.

~oOo~

Johanna had died. The other women had tended her body as well as they could, but she yet lay tied to the post.

The storm and the night, and the raiders, had been hard on them all. They were all of them nearly or entirely naked, and they huddled together in the chill, trying to keep warm.

Olga, fully dressed and recently fed, knew deep guilt, and saw the condemnation on the faces of her friends.

But she had brought round loaves of flat bread and two skins of water, and a bundle of herbs gathered from the camp edges, and she did what she could to ease their way. They tore the bread and water from her hands.

With no way to prepare properly the healing herbs she had found, she made the best adjustments she could. After she treated the women's open wounds with a quickly-prepared healing paste and gave them herbs to eat to thicken their blood, she handed small bunches of wild mushrooms to each of them. "These will make it easier when the men come. I will ask to take Johanna away, and I will try to bring you cover. I am sorry I can do no more."

"It is the way of things," Lagle said and took a bunch of small, long-stemmed mushrooms. She stared at her hand. "If we eat these all at once?"

Olga understood what Lagle was asking, and she shook her head. "That will make you only ill and hurt more. I cannot go far enough into the woods for the right growth to do more than that. Forgive me."

There was commotion at the camp head; the raiders were riding back. "I must go. I will come back as quickly as I can." With a last, lingering glance at Johanna's small, broken body, Olga hurried away from the pen, back toward the healer's tent.

~oOo~

Olga left the tent later, needing to relieve herself. Though many of the men frightened her, they did not accost her and had not since Leif had removed the rope. It was as if word had been passed to leave her alone.

Only Vali was left to heal, and he had fought off the fever and corruption. Olga thought the giant would live. He must indeed have been something more than mere man.

Brenna, the warrior woman—Olga had heard a word several times, *shieldmaiden*, and she believed that she had parsed out its meaning—was sleeping in the healer's tent, stretched out at Vali's side. Indeed those two were bonded, though Brenna did not seem to know it. A strong aura of peace rose up around them when they touched. There was so little of peace in this place that Olga could not help but notice, and she could not help but take from it some small ease in her heart as well.

Coming back from the tree behind which she'd crouched, Olga heard something and stopped to make it out. A beast in the woods?

No, a man. Either in distress or in pleasure. The sounds some men made were similar in any extremity.

Distress. It was distress—the long, deep, wrenching groan of true pain. She had earlier heard the screams of a soldier being tested, but this could not be a captive, beyond the edge of the camp. It must have been a raider making such a dreadful noise, and Olga considered ignoring it and returning to the healer's tent. Now that Vali was recovering and alone in the tent, perhaps Sven would consider helping the women.

Or he could decide that he no longer needed her and send her back to the pen. Either way, she wondered how much the private pain of one of the monsters merited her attention.

Except that she was coming to see them as more man than monster. She was coming to *like* Sven, and Dan. And Vali and Brenna. Hidden away in the healer's tent, doing the work she knew and being treated as one who had skill, she had seen more of these people as humans than the women in the pen, tied to a stake, could see.

And she could not ignore pain when it was so close and so obvious. She headed in that direction.

Leif was sitting on a large rock, his back to her. She recognized his leather and fur, and the long, loose mane of golden hair lying over it. He was folded over, his face buried in his hands, and he roared into his palms, again and again, a sound of pure misery.

This was, indeed, private pain. Deep and harrowing. He wanted to be alone. Meaning to turn and leave him before he knew she was there, Olga's feet instead went forward, until she stood nearly at his side. He took no notice of her until her arm stretched out and her hand touched his head, stroking the length of his hair. Soft and straight, like spun gold.

He jerked from her touch and stood, his big hand gripping the pommel of the sword at his hip. His body was tensed to fight, but his face showed every shard of the anguish his voice had conveyed.

"You," he said, but there was no accusation or malice in the sound. Only surprise.

"You have pain."

His shoulders relaxed. "None that any healer can ease."

Not knowing why she did so, Olga took the steps between them and laid her hand on his chest. "Pain of heart, then. Sadness."

Leif stared down at her hand for a moment, and she felt the rise and fall of his breaths. Then he brought his own hand up and wrapped it around her wrist. He pulled her touch away and released her.

Again he said, "None that any can ease," and he turned and walked back toward the heart of camp, leaving her in alone in the growing dark.

2

The captive woman's touch seemed to linger even after Leif had left her, like a burn over his heart, although her skin had been many layers from his own.

She was small, so small. When she had come up to him and put her hand on his chest, that hand had been as high as her face. And delicate—her collarbones arced between her shoulders like an archer's bow, and her limbs were long and slender. Her eyes were big and deep brown, like a doe's, and her hair was likewise dark. It had been bound in a knot at the nape of her neck and wrapped in a scarf when Leif had first set eyes on her, but the trials of the camp had taken the scarf and unbound the knot, and the braid that remained dangled below her waist.

She seemed almost like a creature of Alvheim, beautiful and sensual, and not meant to dwell in this rough world of men.

He was glad to have saved her from further harsh use by his clansmen, but he could not save her completely. Calder would kill all the captives when they sailed. Even were he or his father inclined to traffic in slaves, and they were not, their plunder from the castle would be far too great to leave room for more than the raiders themselves.

At his thought of the castle, Leif's mind returned to its place of horror and outrage, where it had been spinning when the woman had come upon him. He again saw Einar, his young son, the only surviving of his children, of his family—he saw his boy's head displayed on a bed of greens, set out on a platter, his dead mouth and eye sockets stuffed with fruit.

He had but fourteen years. Leif should not have allowed him to join this raid, the boy's first. But Einar had his arm ring. He was a man, not a boy, and he had made his choice. By the time Leif himself had had fourteen years, he'd been a year married and a new father.

That first child, and now all six of his children, and his wife, and the child she'd been carrying inside her—all were dead. Leif was alone.

Theirs was a brutal world, one of violence and early, gory death. It was the kind of death a warrior strove for—bringing with it entrance to Valhalla. Leif had been under no illusion; he knew well that Einar might lose his life on this raid, his first. Any of them might. Live by the blade, die by the blade. It was their way.

What the prince had done, however—that was a foul thing.

Prince Vladimir had thought it a grand jape to draw the raiders into the castle and insult and shock them with their young scouts, Einar and Halvar, arrayed like the main course of a feast.

Now the prince and all his nobles were dead, and the raiders held his castle and his lands.

But what Leif had done—he closed his eyes, but that only brought the memory into greater detail. Not the memory of the act; he had no memory of the act beyond the flex and pull of muscle and the sound of his own roaring agony. But he remembered the aftermath, the bodies of men and women—and children, young children—tumbled at his feet like so much dross.

They were his enemies, the people of the prince, and it was not he who had brought women and children into an arena of ambush. But it had been his blade, to great extent, that had opened young and vulnerable bodies.

Leif was sworn to Calder's father, Jarl Åke, and he considered the jarl and his grown sons family. His only family, now. He had been close with the brothers all his life. Åke kept no prisoners beyond the encampment, and felt no compunction about the pain of those they attacked. Leif understood this to be the way of their people, and he made no judgment of any but himself.

In Åke's service, Leif had killed hundreds of men and women. He had killed boys wielding blades too heavy for them to swing. And he had taken his plunder in raids. None of this caused his heart strife.

But he had left the raping of women and the killing of children to others with stronger stomachs and harder hearts than his. Bloodlust charged his body like any warrior in a fight, but for him, it diminished when the clang of metal ended. He could expend what was left with a simple warrior's shout. He had no need to force himself on a terrified woman or slice open the babe in her arms to burn off the last of the rage.

Today, though, with the image his son's abased head—all that remained of him—vivid behind his eyes, Leif had known a rage and a need greater than he could now recall.

And now he was alone, the last of his children dead, and the blood of other young ones on his own hands.

The pain in his heart could not be eased.

He would have to bear it.

~oOo~

Unable to sleep, Leif spent most of the night near the central fire, finally drifting off as the sky began to brighten.

He seemed to have closed his eyes for only a moment when he felt a nudge at his thigh and opened his eyes to see Calder standing above him. At least an hour had passed; the sun was not yet up, but the sky had turned to the grey that meant sunrise was near.

"Where is the God's-Eye?"

Leif had seen her enter the healer's tent the evening before, when they'd returned from the castle. Knowing that there was only one patient still in that tent, and knowing that the God's-Eye had spent considerable time there, Leif sought something else to tell his friend.

Calder despised Vali Storm-Wolf. His father had allied with another jarl, Snorri, for this raid, and, though it had been agreed that Calder would lead the alliance, Vali was Snorri's most trusted man. And he was a legend, an Úlfheðinn, known for superhuman strength and ferocity and for a steady and loyal heart. Leif knew him also to have a quick mind and an agile way of speaking. He had Leif's respect.

Though the jarls were allied, the history between them was full of conflict, and Calder had struggled to conceal his contempt for Snorri's men. Vali, Calder's chief competition—and, Leif thought but would never say, the greater warrior—bore the sharp focus of his enmity.

Jarl Åke had a legend of his own: Brenna God's-Eye, a mighty and valiant shieldmaiden, whom Åke and his sons believed had been given to them by Odin himself. Her strange right eye was said by their people to be Odin's own, that which he'd given to Mimir in exchange for wisdom, and most people believed her to be a favored vessel for the Allfather himself. It was why no one dared look on her for long.

Leif knew the God's-Eye well, perhaps better than most. He had trained her in the ways of the warrior. He knew her to be a solitary young woman, one who thought herself alone in the world and held loneliness before her like a shield. Though he had fewer than ten years more than she, Leif bore her fatherly feelings—not that she would perceive that or, if she did, welcome it.

If she had found a bond to another, even with a man who had once been and might again become an enemy, Leif was loath to interrupt it. And he certainly did not want to turn Calder's suspicion in her direction. Calder was Leif's oldest and greatest friend, but he had been raised by a hard man and taught that hardness was strength.

Leif loved the jarl, and he loved the jarl's sons. He loved them for their good, but he did not pretend they were without their ills. Neither Åke nor Calder were temperate when they perceived a challenge or a threat, and they saw both in every dim corner.

If Leif told Calder that Brenna God's-Eye had been keeping company with Vali Storm-Wolf, there might well be blood in the camp. So he said instead, "You know the God's-Eye. She likely is off in the woods on her own."

Calder grunted and looked out over the camp. "Walk with me, friend. I must speak today, and I would work out my thinking on your wise ear."

Leif stood and went with his friend.

~oOo~

"You don't seem surprised," Calder noted after he'd explained his thinking.

"I am not. When we landed here, knowing that Finn's raid took this shore not long ago, I assumed there was more than plunder you wanted. I would be more surprised if I am the only among us who considered that you intended to take the castle." Leif took a breath and added, "I am surprised you thought it necessary to keep the knowledge close."

"I mean to make a settlement here, and I mean to claim this all in my father's name alone."

Leif drew up short. Half of the raiders were sworn to Snorri. Taking claim of and credit for the spoils of the raid would break the alliance and be seen as an act of war. It had been Åke who'd sought the alliance in the first place. "Then why ally at all?"

Calder didn't respond, and Leif stretched his mind for an answer. Before he could find one, Calder gave him an affectionate slap on the back. "Do not fret, my friend. All will be made clear. The seer has shown my father that the gods are with us. I tell you now so that your surprise is between us only, and so that your judgment will shape the way I speak with the others."

Understanding what Calder needed of him, and what he expected of him, Leif considered his words. "Breaking the alliance here in Estland would tear the camp apart, Calder. Be temperate. Your father is jarl. If a move is to be made, it should be he who makes it."

"But he is not here. It was *my* blade that washed Vladimir's blood over the earth."

Calder had grown impatient over the past few years to step out from his father's great shadow. Leif saw that impatience at work now and sought a way to allay it.

"And you will have that glory. Return to Geitland and your father with laden ships. If we fight among each other here, we will take losses, and you will diminish the greatness of your return."

After a long, heavy silence, Calder nodded. "You are wise, Leif. You see reason when I can only feel need."

Such had always been true. Though Calder was the older of them, Leif was the wiser.

The men embraced and returned to the camp.

~oOo~

After the meeting, Calder stalked off on his own. Leif stood at the God's-Eye's side and watched him turn into his tent. The fabric shook as he drew the walls closed; his friend was angry.

Leif had not planned to volunteer to stay behind in Estland and hold the castle. But then Vali Storm-Wolf and the God's-Eye had both volunteered, and Leif saw the trouble there. Besides, nothing and no one awaited his return to Geitland. The last of his family, his last son, was in this earth—what little of him they'd reclaimed. He was not ready to leave him behind.

"You should go to him," the God's-Eye said. "Make him see that it is right to leave strength behind." She turned and stared at the healer's tent, into which Vali had just returned.

Everyone, Calder perhaps especially, had been shocked to see the great man standing on his own power at the meeting, and speaking with a strong, true voice. Vali had challenged Calder's claim and changed his intention, and Leif had seen the killing urge light his friend's eyes.

But Leif believed the meeting had gone as well as it could have gone. A balance of both jarls' raiders had volunteered to stay and hold the claim. At least in Estland, the alliance would remain intact, and Leif would do all he could to ensure that remained true.

As for home, Calder would return victorious, and Snorri's fiercest warrior and strongest voice would not be there to dispute the credit. If Åke had some other plan, some dark purpose, then Vali's absence at home would weaken Snorri and further Åke's cause.

Leif was sorry for that; it sat hard on his shoulders to think that oaths had been made in bad faith, but he had made no such bad oath. He was sworn to Åke, and his allegiance rested in Geitland.

The God's-Eye walked away without a word, headed toward the healer's tent again. Leif watched her for a moment and then turned his attention to Calder's tent. Brenna God's-Eye was right. It could be only him to make Calder see that his position was still strong.

Leif could not foresee, and he could not control, what consequences might fall from these choices. He was neither a seer nor a leader. He was only a warrior and a friend.

~oOo~

After two days and four trips, the raiders had taken from the castle all the bounty the ships could carry back, even with their load lightened by about thirty who had volunteered to stay for the winter.

The camp was struck, and raiders carried gear and chests of precious metals and jewels back to the shore. Calder stood by the black ring that had been their central fire and surveyed the work. With a slow, satisfied nod, he turned to Knut. "You and Viger—kill the captives." Knut nodded and turned to find Viger.

"Hold!" Leif spoke, strongly, before he'd thought, and Calder gave him a narrow look.

With the camp struck, they had a clear line of sight to the pen. The healing woman—her name was Olga, he had learned—had been returned to her fellows that morning and bound again as they'd begun their preparations to leave this site. Leif did not think any woman had been beset that day; there had been too much to do to take such a distraction.

He hoped that was true. He should have paid closer attention. Now, though, he had to answer Calder and explain why he'd contravened his order in that way.

"The healer. She knows our language. She can be a help to us at the castle."

Calder smirked. "You like her look, my friend?"

Leif didn't answer, and Calder's smirk grew into smugness.

"Fine." He waved at Knut. "Bring my friend's pet to him. Kill the rest."

~oOo~

He would have wished Olga brought to him first, but Viger and Knut had a different idea.

When Viger handed the end of the rope tether to Leif, Olga was spattered with the blood of her friends, and those deep brown eyes were round with fear and shock.

"I am sorry," he said as he cut her bonds. "I would have spared you that if I could."

"Is—is way of things," she answered, her silky voice shaking. When her hands were free, she rubbed her wrists. "I not free. This right?"

Never before had he thought long about the plight of the slave. Slaves were the vanquished; their freedom was simply another thing that they had lost. But he felt a pang of compunction now.

"No, not free. We will bring you to the castle. We need you to ease our way with your people. And Sven is returning home, so we might have use of your healing. So we cannot let you go. But I would leave you unbound if you will stay without the rope. You understand?"

With her face turned up, she studied him, her eyes scanning back and forth over his. "You can keep men away?"

"I can." And he would. He felt an investment in this small woman, a protective urge. He knew not from where it came, but it was strong.

"Your word is good?" she asked, her eyes narrowing.

"It is." That was true as well. He did not make promises lightly, even to a slave, and he bore their consequences willingly. His word was the most valuable thing he had.

"Then no rope."

~oOo~

Strong though he was, Vali barely made it to the castle. Mere moments after they'd entered the hall, while Leif was still standing with his eyes closed, battling the memory of his son's head dressed like a meal, the mighty Storm-Wolf crashed to the stone floor, unconscious. Brenna God's-Eye took two quick steps toward him and then pulled up as if she had surprised herself.

When they pulled his fur from him, they saw that his back was soaked in fresh blood; he had reopened at least part of his wound.

Leif found Olga's eyes. "We have need of your healing before we will have need of your words, it seems."

She crouched at Vali's side and pulled up his sopping tunic. Examining his back, she spoke a long string of words Leif did not understand, and then she sighed and looked up at him. "Get him to bed. I find"—she said something else in her own language and sighed again—"things I need."

Leif nodded and turned to the raiders. "Let us get our friend into one of these royal beds."

It took four of them to carry the big man up a winding stone staircase, trying not to bend his back, but they found him a bed and got him into it.

~oOo~

Later, after Olga had tended to Vali, and Leif had spoken with him, Leif found the God's-Eye in the stable, combing her fingers through the lush, creamy mane of the mare she seemed to favor. Leif had long known her to prefer the company of animals—any animal, from the goats and fowl that ran loose in the Geitland hall to a magnificent beast such as this mare.

She glanced up briefly as he came to her side, but she didn't speak. She rarely did except in necessity.

"He is awake and asking for you."

No response or reaction.

"You are important to him, I think."

At that, she scoffed quietly.

"You are not?" Leif didn't believe that. It was obvious to any who cared to see it. Too obvious, he thought.

Brenna God's-Eye paused and looked up at him, her eyes meeting his. Like any other of their people, Leif felt the urge to drop his eyes. He did not fear her or her eye, but there was something unreal in it, something so intense that he felt as if she were seeing too much of him when she looked him dead on.

He meant to hold her gaze, but he blinked, and then she broke away. "He seems to want something of me, but I don't understand."

Leif fought back a smile. He knew the God's-Eye to be naïve in many things—most things, in fact, that didn't have to do with war and battle. It was said that she might steal the will, and even the soul, of any man who coupled with her, and he doubted any had ever tried.

If he read Vali right, then it seemed the Storm-Wolf thought to try. Despite his concerns, Leif hoped he was successful. This brave, lonely woman deserved to know some happiness.

But there were serious concerns to be managed if there were a strong bond between these legends.

"Be careful, Brenna God's-Eye. Know where your allegiance lies and keep true to it."

She frowned at him. "Now I don't understand you, either."

"Forgive me," he chuckled. "Go and see him. If there is nothing you want of him, then tell him so. If there is something, tell him that. But know your heart and your mind. Every choice carries its own burden."

"I like it better when no one talks to me," she grumbled and turned back to her horse.

3

Often of a morning, when Olga came to awareness and opened her eyes, finding herself nested in a cozy bed in the shelter of the castle proper, she felt a heady disorientation. At the hands of the monsters from the sea, she had found herself in a position of unfamiliar power and comfort.

The same men and women who had killed every inhabitant and visitor of the fishing village, except her, who had enslaved and beaten and raped her and the few other women they had not simply murdered on sight, who had seemed to leave oceans of blood and mountains of bodies everywhere they went—those same monsters had, within a mere few weeks of inhabiting the castle, improved Olga's life and the life of all of the people who'd survived their claiming.

It was as if they'd sent the monsters back to the sea on their strange dragon ships and left the human beings behind.

They had opened Prince Vladimir's stores to the villagers. People who had lived whole lives with the barest enough now knew plenty. The savages in bloodied leather had proved themselves more noble than any titled gentleman in gold chains and brocade.

Olga was no longer a slave; Leif and the others had freed her within days of moving to the castle and had left her to her own choice. Leif had asked her to stay and take charge of the running of the castle, and to ask other villagers to stay on and work for them as well.

He had *asked* her to stay. No person with power over her had ever sought her opinion or preference before.

When she'd said that she had never had the charge of something so great as a whole castle before, he'd laughed and said that neither had he nor any of his fellows. They would all be learning together, he'd said, his blue eyes alight.

She had agreed. Now they treated her as their equal, and she found that running a castle for people who knew nothing of them, and thus had few expectations, was not such difficult duty. Her work amounted to making sure that people were fed and comfortable. It was not so different from her healing—identifying a need and meeting it.

Their need of her as translator was harder work. Her mind whirled all the day, trying to keep two languages close at hand every moment, translating in both directions and trying to teach the raiders' language to those of her people who wished to communicate on their own.

They did not all share the same accent. Sometimes, the words they said sounded little like the words she knew, and her brain scrambled all the harder to make sense.

Of the raiders, so far, Leif was the only who wanted to know her language. He sought her out often to take a lesson. Those meetings were the best part of Olga's day.

Her own facility with the raiders' tongue had grown quickly with so much use, so that she hardly had to pause to find a word she wanted, though she still struggled to make the sentences flow gracefully. Sometimes words came at her very quickly, in both languages, and sorting through that cacophony made her head ache.

Sitting at the massive table in the main hall of the castle now, with Leif, and Vali, and Brenna, and several others of the raiders, and villagers, too, Olga clenched her hands in her lap. These meetings were among her hardest duties. Much rested on her making sense among people who could not understand each other. It was one thing when they were discussing the village and making plans for supplies or simply meeting to learn about this place. Today, though, three scouts the raiders had sent out—Tord, Sigvalde, and Viger—were reporting on the threat presented by the two princes whose lands bounded these.

If Olga misunderstood what was said, or if she used a wrong word to translate it, she might cause a war. She felt that responsibility like a leaden weight pressing on the back of her neck.

"The farthest is a hard day's ride northeast," Viger said. "A blue flag with a white beast."

Olga knew that flag to be the colors of Prince Toomas, the most powerful of the princes. He and Vladimir, who had been his equal in strength, had fought many times, moving the boundary between them back and forth. She translated what Viger had said to the villagers at her sides, focusing especially on Jaan. Although he was young, he was smart and perceptive. None of the villagers knew much of war but how to die in it, but Jaan noticed things others didn't bother to see.

Jaan nodded and turned to the men. He was trying to learn the raiders' language. "Toomas," he said to Leif, who was the leader of them all. He put up his fists as if to fight. "He..." Jaan faltered and turned to Olga. In their own tongue, he said to her, "I don't know how to tell them that Toomas is dangerous. In Mirkandi, we stay clear of his men—soldiers and villagers alike. They'd kill us coldly."

Olga nodded and turned to Leif and the others. She wasn't completely sure, either, but she tried. "Toomas make much war here. Jaan say in town men know to be..." She paused, seeking the way to describe the men's wariness. "Apart them?" That wasn't right enough, so she pantomimed a separation, drawing her hands away from each other.

Brenna nodded first, understanding. "He was Vladimir's foe?"

Such a strange thing for a woman to be sitting at a table like this. Olga understood her own place; she was the only among them who could hope to bridge the language gap for them all. But Brenna and another woman like her, another *shieldmaiden*, Astrid, sat here as if their opinions about matters of war and defense were relevant. More than that, they were wanted.

Olga was getting used to this interesting parity, but Jaan was still surprised that a woman had spoken. He turned to Leif, as if he could not bring himself to discuss such a matter with a woman, no matter her place among the others.

"Yes. No…friend here." He darted a glance at Olga, who smiled. He'd said it well enough.

"That is not encouraging," Vali said. "He wants this land and is likely to be ready to make war."

"The castle was not busy." It was the first time Sigvalde had spoken at this meeting. "There was no war making there—but it was already snowing. If they plan an attack, it won't be until summer."

"And the other? Ivan?" Leif seemed to be thinking hard. Olga had noticed that when a thought took him over, he ran his hand over his beard. A flick of a thought entered her head, an image only: her own hand smoothing over that golden fur, while his eyes stared down at her. Her belly twitched, and she blinked, forcing herself to focus on the words she must interpret.

Just then, Jaan nudged her, and she whispered a translation of what Sigvalde had said, as well as she remembered it.

"Straight south," Sigvalde answered. "The land is small and weak. We could take it, too. This Toomas is the danger."

Olga's heart skittered in her chest. She had been born on Ivan's land. Her family—her father and two younger brothers—still lived there. Since she had been taken from them, she had seen them only once or, rarely, twice a year, but her love for them had never dwindled. The boys, Anton and Kalju, were young men now, sixteen and fourteen years. Ivan would make them fight for him.

She had seen what war looked like for these raiders. She did not wish to see her own blood in a memory like that.

"Please," she said, seeking out Leif's eyes. They met and held hers. Around her, she could sense that everyone else's eyes were on her, too. "Will you make war south?"

Jaan nudged her again; this time, too intent on Leif's answer herself, she ignored him.

With a glance, Leif surveyed the raiders around him, then shook his head. "No. Sigvalde's meaning is that Prince Ivan is not a danger. The winter has our attention, and we will make ourselves strong here."

Relief suffused her, and she smiled, her eyes nearly filling with tears. Leif cocked his head at her, but he did not ask, and Olga dropped her head and worked to control her emotions.

~oOo~

"This is a wonderful country." Leif smiled at her. "How would I say that?"

They sat on the ground, at the top of a low hill overlooking her village. Winter was nearly upon them; the fields were fallow, and most of the leaves had fallen from the trees that would shed them, but on this day the air was warm and the sun golden. Perhaps one of the last of the warm days. All the signs pointed toward a harsh winter, bitter and long.

Weeks had passed since Leif had assured her that they would make no war her brothers would have to fight. Brenna God's-Eye and Vali Storm-Wolf had claimed their bond and would be wedded within the week. Olga's heart had warmed to see them grow close.

"*Eesti on imeline maa,*" she answered Leif's question.

He repeated it, but lost a syllable in the middle.

"*Eem-ah-leen-ah,*" she corrected.

"*Imeline,*" he pronounced properly. "*Eesti on imeline maa.*"

"*Jah. Hea.*"

He beamed at her praise like a young boy. Then he turned back to the view, and Olga studied his profile. Her first thought of him—in that life before, when he'd stood in the doorway of Johanna's hut and saved them, for the moment, from Knut, a man she now knew and did not fear—was that he was a golden giant. Still, it was her first thought upon seeing him, but now it meant more than his size or fair coloring. To her, Leif seemed to have a glow about him, a brightness, even though he seemed often shrouded in something dark—that pain she'd once witnessed in the camp. He pushed it away, but sometimes it crept over his shoulders and dimmed him.

He was a kind man and a good one. Not all the raiders were; though she had found her place among them, as had the other villagers, some of the men were rough and resented that there were no longer slaves left to their whim. But Leif and Vali—and Brenna, too—were quick and firm in their leadership, and the women who wished to be left alone were.

Olga wished to be left alone. For the most part.

"*Kas Sulle meeldis siin?*"

He focused on her again. "*Kas Sa saaksid seda korrata?*"

He'd asked her to repeat her question. "*Kas Sulle meeldis siin?*"

"*Anna andeks. Ma ei saa aru.*"

In excellent syntax and accent, he'd asked her to repeat herself, then apologized and told her he didn't understand. They were questions he had learned and that he used often, but his accent and flow had improved much. "But that is good! All that is good. I asked if you like it here: *Kas Sulle meeldis siin.*"

"Ah. *Jah. Ma olen…rahulik?*" He lifted an uncertain eyebrow, and she nodded.

"Peaceful? Yes. *Rahulik.*"

"*Ma olen rahulik siin,*" he repeated the full sentence. He was peaceful here. Serene.

"And you are not at peace at your home?"

Leif let out a long, slow breath, his eyes never leaving hers. In his own language, he said, "I am a warrior, Olga. We do not know peace. We know loss."

"Then why make war?"

"It's our way, and what I know." He put his hands before him and opened them so that the palms were up, side by side. "My worth is in my hands." He made two fists. "To live as a warrior is to seek the next life. Valhalla, where the brave dead dwell among the gods. Do you know of it?"

She shook her head. Her brother had told her a few stories of the Northmen's capricious gods, but they were not of her ken. "No gods live here. Only earth and sea and air, fire and flower, man and spirit. Here, all is one, and we know this life only until we go into earth to...to make balance. Understand? No seeking. Only living. Is life made of war..." She paused, seeking the proper way to express herself. "Is it not very tiring?"

Leif chuckled. "It is, yes. And invigorating as well. I am not unhappy in my life. But the calm I know here, it's new to me. A respite."

His fists were yet held out before him, and he had not shifted his gaze from them. Olga reached out and set her hand over them. His hands were large, seeming even larger coiled into fists as they were, and she felt the aura of his great strength all around her.

"Where there is always striving, always there is strife as well. Sometimes to be in one place is good. To be still."

Leif stared down at her hand over his, and Olga said no more. Since she had first seen him, she had thought him different from the others. Now, she knew them all not to be monsters but men and women, good and ill in portion like any other, but Leif was still different.

Olga had never known sensual love. She had not been loved in that way, and she had not felt that feeling for anyone else. She had been used by men, more men than the raiders. She had been forcibly married and used liberally and harshly by her husband, and on two drunken occasions by his soldier friends. When she was free of him, she had been glad to have become a widow, beyond the notice of men. She had never wanted the attentions of another.

But sitting at Leif's side, feeling his gaze on her fingers like true heat, Olga felt a stirring—and it was not the first time she'd felt it while with him. When he unfurled his fists and lifted her hand to his lips, she gasped. The brush of his golden beard against her skin made her fibers and sinews go taut.

Still holding her hand, he turned to her and brushed the fingers of his other hand over her cheek, then folded those fingers under and brushed the backs over the same path. She closed her eyes and savored that gentle, genuine touch. Her heart seemed to slam against the sides of her throat.

"*Ilus*," he murmured. The word in her language for beautiful. She sighed.

If he had come closer and kissed her, Olga would have welcomed it. She wanted that beautiful, kind mouth, that full beard. But his hand left her face, and nothing more happened.

She opened her eyes. He was watching her, as if waiting for her to come back to the moment.

"Leif?" Her hand reached to stroke his beard, but he caught her wrist and held her away.

"You are a good woman, Olga. Beautiful and kind. I think you are much of my calm in this place. But this is not my home. You have been too harshly used already. I will not take you and leave, and I cannot stay." He leaned in and pressed his lips to her forehead. "I cannot."

Too stunned by the strength of her reaction, both to her need and to his thwarting of it, Olga could not find the words to argue.

~oOo~

Olga pushed Vali aside. "I cannot work with you like a wall between."

He stepped back, not far, but enough to make room so that Olga could lay a cool compress on Brenna's still forehead.

"Why won't she wake?!"

Olga reached back and grabbed hold of Vali's hand—it was a massive, hard block of flesh. "Here. Feel this. Gently." She dragged his fingers close and set them on the lump at the side of Brenna's head. "She struck something when she fell. But she breathes steady and deep. She will wake. Let her rest, Vali. Calm is what she needs."

He drew his hands over his face and beard and walked away, to the end of the bed. "It has to be more. She is ill somehow. They said she dropped from the saddle. It is unlike her."

Olga thought she knew. She had noticed over the past few days that Brenna was pale and cross—more cross than usual—in the mornings, and she had stopped taking a morning meal, then seemed more well later in the day. She and Vali had been married several weeks. Weeks of punishing winter storms, where there was little to keep busy in the castle. Frankly, Olga was surprised that Vali had not thought of it himself.

Satisfied that Brenna was as well-attended as she could make her, and that she needed only rest before she woke, Olga turned and settled her hands on her hips. "Leave us, please, Eha," she said in her language to the village girl who had brought a full water jug. The girl nodded and left the room.

Vali watched her go, then brought his intense, worried blue eyes back to Olga. "Something is wrong. Tell me."

With little hope that he would have an answer—men were absurdly squeamish about such things—she asked, "Do you know her cycle?" Since she was speaking in his tongue, his blank look told her that he had no clue what she meant for other reasons, so she rephrased. "Do you know when she bleeds? Woman's blood."

"Ah. I think yes. She bled just before we were wed, and this morning, she said she thought she was ready to do so again."

She was impressed that he knew that much. But they had been wed nearly two months, and in her examination of Brenna this evening, she had seen no signs of her blood. "None since? You are sure?"

The giant's cheeks went pink, and Olga smiled. What would it be like to know love like their love? It was not her fate to know, it seemed. For the first time since she was a girl, she wanted physical, earthly love, but she could not have it, not as she wanted it. Leif refused to see her as more than a friend. They saw each other, spent time alone together, every day, but since that last warm day on the hill, before Vali and Brenna were wed, he had barely touched her except in passing.

She could still recall in vivid detail the sensation of his lips and beard and breath on her skin—on her fingers, her forehead. And the skim of his callused fingertips on her cheek.

The low rumble of his voice when he'd called her beautiful.

As much as she'd grown to care for Vali and Brenna, as pleased as she'd been to watch their love blossom and grow, Olga knew real envy of them, too.

"I would know," he said. "We…enjoy each other."

"I am sure. Why did she think her blood was coming today?"

That pink deepened. "She was…sore. Her breasts."

Unwellness at the morning. Dizziness. Lack of appetite. Sore breasts. No blood for two months. Yes, it was as she'd thought. "Vali, I believe that there will be a child."

The color dropped from his cheeks. "What?"

"Brenna is with child. This is why she fell. The early months are weak months. She will feel stronger—right and well—in time, as her belly begins to grow."

"A child?" He looked down at his sleeping wife, and a smile grew to take over his full face. It changed his look completely. "A child. Of course! Haha! This is great news!" He turned to Olga again. "When?"

After some quick figuring, based on what Vali had told her, Olga answered, "Midsummer, I believe." Her heart sank a little at the word. Midsummer. When her new friends and this particular life would be gone. When Leif would be gone.

But that was the future, and time had not turned so far as that yet. Only this moment, this present, mattered.

In this present, she had friends, and they had joy. Olga smiled and did not resist the crush of Vali's exultant embrace.

4

The winter had held on long—longer than it should have—but after months of brutal storms, they were finally seeing the signs of summer dawning. The day before had been warm enough to turn the land to mush and swell the river until it nigh burst its banks, but this next day had risen colder and hardened the earth again.

Still, the sun was bright and the air had the brisk scent of good weather not far off. The people of the castle and the village were in generally good spirits. Vali, riding next to him on this northward patrol, had been smiling all day, jesting with their group.

His friend was a man who seemed to have everything—a great love, good friends, and a child due in the nearing summer. He was at peace and seemed unconcerned about the precarious point on which all he had was balanced. On that point stood likely disaster and certain strife: Jarl Åke Ivarsson would not simply let Brenna God's-Eye go.

The jarl would have no choice; Brenna was wedded and with child, and, even if Vali were to abjure Snorri and swear to his wife's jarl—which Leif knew he would not do—Åke's claim to her was lost. Unless Brenna herself declared otherwise, her husband had the greater claim.

Åke would see it as a betrayal—in truth, it *was* a betrayal of her sworn oath—and he was not a man who stood by and allowed loss to happen. There would be consequences when the ships arrived, and they would be considerable.

And yet he could not wish his friends the loss of what they'd found. He understood why Brenna would cleave to Vali and risk the wrath of the jarl. She had come to Åke as a slave and sworn fealty as a condition of gaining her freedom. A bond of loyalty made on such a condition of course had its limits.

Leif's own oath had been made unconditionally. He had grown up in the Geitland hall. His father had been a close advisor to Åke, and upon his death in battle, the jarl had taken Leif under his arm. His life had been entwined with Åke's as if they shared blood. It had been the jarl who had arranged his marriage to Toril, and he had been the first visitor upon the births of all their children.

There had never been a question of his allegiance, and though he did not agree with every choice Åke made, though he had observed the man he loved as a father become brittle and petty as his power grew and his age increased, Leif could not imagine what could possibly happen that might cause him to turn his back.

If such a cause existed, it would definitely not be rooted in personal interest.

While his fellows talked and laughed around him as they returned from this routine patrol along the boundary between Toomas's lands and theirs, Leif watched the sun move in blue sky and felt melancholy. He liked it here in Estland. Never before had he known a life like this one, one of quiet and peace. Even as they prepared for a very likely battle when the warm sun settled down to stay, the air in the castle was peaceful.

And Olga. Over these months, Leif had grown deeply fond of that small, marvelous woman. Built like a wee woodland creature, yet with a steady, strong heart. Most days, she sat on the edge of his mind, a constant presence. And at night, when he was alone in his cavernous, quiet stone rooms, in a soft bed that had taken him months to learn to be comfortable in—then his mind's image of her took over his body, too.

He knew she would be receptive if he went to her in that way. He saw it often in her captivating dark eyes, the desire to be closer. He felt it when he forgot himself and touched her—the way her body moved toward him, as if drawn by his mere touch. What he would give to have her, and he had only to go to her…

But he would not. Olga had become impatient and cross with him of late, taking to avoiding him when she could, and he thought he understood why. But he would not take her. He was sworn to Åke, and so he would be leaving Estland when the ships returned. Even were he inclined to ask to be released, or at least to ask to be allowed to settle here and be his agent in Estland, he knew that losing the God's-Eye would be trial enough for his jarl. So Leif would not ask him to let him stay.

Vali had asked him if he'd thought about asking Olga to return to Geitland with him, and of course he had. But his world was of war, and she was a woman of peace. It was apparent whenever he was near her, even in their aspects. Her delicate, graceful, small body, her sweet, open face, her slim, pale, long-fingered hands—and his broad bulk, his scarred body, the gnarled stones that were his hands. There was no safe place for her in their unforgiving world. So Leif would not ask her to join him.

And he would not take her and then abandon her. Men had brutalized her; he would not be listed among them.

He would honor his word, and he would do what was right.

~oOo~

As they came within sight of the castle, Vali, riding at Leif's side, made a sound that was part sigh and part groan.

"Trouble, my friend?" Leif asked.

Vali offered a rueful laugh. "No. No trouble. I'm only thinking of Brenna and wondering which wife will greet me when we return."

"Ah. Her mood is changeable of late, yes. It is a part of the making of a child." Watching Vali negotiate his wife's pregnancy, and advising him as one who had experienced many, abraded an old wound in Leif's chest, but the pain was not wholly unwelcome. The memories had a sweet taste as well as bitter.

"So you say. I seem to vex her most when I try most not to—and she discards reason on a whim. She would have ridden her horse to the village today! With her belly so round! When I made to keep her from that mistake, I would swear she would have cut me down had her sword been in her hand."

Leif had watched Vali send off his wife this morning and knew that her ride to the village, seated on the sledge between Tord and Sigvalde, who were running supplies, had been the result of a tense negotiation between a pregnant woman at her wits' end and a protective husband and father at his.

"It cannot be much longer now, and then she will be awash in love for the babe and for you."

Vali grinned. "I hold such hope dear. Olga told her at least two more months. I will be lucky if my head is still on my shoulders by then."

There was good chance that the ships would have returned by then. Vali would indeed be lucky to keep his head on his shoulders, but Leif doubted that Brenna would be the one to swing the sword.

He sighed and watched the castle grow nearer. Danger lurked just beyond them. Danger and loss.

~oOo~

It had lurked closer than he'd known—than any of them had known.

When they had reached the castle, old Orm had told them that the sledge hadn't returned. It should have been back before they—long before they.

The sledge, and the village, had been attacked. By soldiers of Prince Ivan, whom they had discounted as too weak to be a threat to them. The village, all the livestock, and the men who had been working there—all lost. Sigvalde and Tord were lost.

Leif sat in the somber castle hall and stared at the fire while in a room above him Olga worked to save Brenna and her babe, and Vali, who would not leave his wife's side, watched his family leaving him.

He and Toril had, together, buried four of their children, three of them when they were still swaddled, and one of those while her life cord had still dangled from her small belly. Alone, he had buried a daughter, and now their son Einar. He had also buried Toril and the child that had been inside her.

Until Einar, only Toril and that seventh child, a son, had been lost to violence.

While Leif sat in the hall, among likewise silent friends, and waited to know if Olga would save Brenna and her babe, his mind retold him the story of finding his own wife attacked.

He had been fighting in the center of Geitland, fending off attacking raiders, and he had not known of his loss until later, when he'd secured the jarl and had seen Brenna, then a slave, save Åke's children and Hilde, his wife.

The fighting had been brisk and heavy around the hall. He and Toril had had a small house toward the edge of town, far enough from the hall that Leif had not thought them at risk.

He had been wrong. And he had come home to blood and gore and foul death.

On this night, with Brenna's bloody body so fresh in his mind, his memory wanted to braid the two images together—of Brenna lying in the bloody snow, and of Toril at the fire pit, her hands still over her open belly as if she'd tried to save their child as it had fallen from her.

The blood had still been fresh and warm, the insides of their bodies still glistening. Had he been only moments faster, he might have saved them.

A blast of thunder rocked the castle walls, and Leif looked around reflexively. The others in the hall looked about as well, surprised and curious. Thunder in winter, even late winter, was unusual. Thor was announcing his presence.

Perhaps he had come to save the child.

Another pound of Thor's hammer. And another.

"Thor is angry tonight," Orm muttered nearby. "Foul deeds and sad news."

"Yes."

Before Leif could say more, a door crashed above them, and he stood. In moments, Vali rushed into the hall and immediately through it, toward the front of the castle.

In his arms he carried a small, bloodied bundle.

"It is over, then," Orm sighed. "But what of Brenna?"

Leif didn't answer; his attention was on his friend, who had just run out into the night, leaving behind a violent wake of stormy snow. Thor had brought winter back with him.

He followed Vali out to the castle grounds. Others followed as well, but he paid them no mind.

His friend stood in the middle of the grounds, holding the naked, impossibly small body of his child high above his head, while snow fell in thick white sheets and thunder and lightning crackled around them.

"HE IS THORVALDR," Vali shouted into the angry sky. "AND HE IS YOURS. YOU HAVE TAKEN HIM ALREADY. WHAT MORE WOULD YOU HAVE OF ME? WHAT GREATER SACRIFICE WOULD YOU HAVE THAN MY CHILD? WOULD YOU TAKE MY LOVE AS WELL? BETTER YOU TAKE MY HEART FROM MY CHEST!"

His own chest aching in grief for his friend's loss and remembered grief for his own, Leif put his hand on Vali's back. Vali whirled, his braid flying, and glared furious pain into Leif's face.

"Vali, my good friend. My brother. You tempt the gods."

"I care not! Let them do what they will!"

But he would care. Time would blunt the edge of this loss, leave a bruising ache where slicing pain now dwelt, and Vali had much more left to lose. This was not the time to call Thor down as if Vali could face the god and win. "Your woman yet lives. You mean to give up before she has?"

Vali stood and stared, gasping in each breath as a growl. Snow coated his hair, his brows, his beard, but he made no notice.

Leif held out his hands. "Let me take your son. I will see to it that he is treated with care until you are ready to say goodbye." He was unhappily practiced in such a farewell.

Vali yanked the child from his reach. "Brenna will want him."

Toril had wanted their tiny daughter, their first loss. She'd held her for hours, until the body had gone cold and stiff, and he'd had to pry their child forcibly from his wife's arms. Toril had gone briefly mad, screaming and beating at him with her small fists. The thought of Brenna in that state chilled him.

"No. It will cause her more pain, when she struggles already with so much. Of this I know. She awaited a child she could nourish. And she is in no state now to say goodbye. Your attention should be with her."

Leif lifted his hands again and held them steady in the whipping snow. This time, his face warped with sorrow, Vali set his son in them. He bent and picked up the linens from the snow at his feet, and he covered the body.

Then he walked away, and Leif cradled the lifeless bundle to his chest.

~oOo~

For a long time, Leif sat before the fire in the hall, holding the body of the child in his arms. He had offered to take him, to spare Vali this pain, but now, he could not seem to act.

So he sat and held the dead child, and old memories carved themselves afresh into his mind. The storm thundered and shrieked beyond the walls.

"Leif."

Surprised to hear Olga's voice, he looked up and saw her standing just at the farthest reach of the fire's glow. He also saw that they were alone in the room. He'd sat there longer even than he'd thought.

It was rare for the hall to be empty at any time in night or day; the castle was full of raiders and villagers sheltering from the winter. But the heavy happenings of this night must have driven everyone to a quieter corner.

"How is Brenna?"

"Weak. She had lost much blood before bringing the babe. Her chest is broken."

"Her heart, too, I imagine."

"Not yet. That will come if she wakes."

"If?"

Olga sighed. "She bleeds inside, where I can't help her. Only her own will can save her now. And Vali's, perhaps. He will not be parted from her." She tipped her head toward him. "You have the child."

"Yes. I promised Vali I would look after him."

"Come." She stepped forward. "We will make a place of rest for him until his father is ready."

He stood and followed her to the kitchen. As he waited near the banked fireplace, she pulled a basket from a hook in the wall and set it on the long, scarred table. From a chest, she gathered clean linens and padded the basket with them. She filled a bowl of water from the barrel and brought it to the table.

Then she came to him and held out her hands. She wanted the babe.

Once his little body was in her arms, she nestled him close and removed the bloodied cloths. Leif watched as she carried him to the table and washed him, then swaddled him in fresh linens as if he could be given comfort in the snug binding.

She laid him in the basket and brushed her fingers over his slender brow.

Then she turned to Leif and pointed toward the ceiling. "That bundle of herbs there, and that one. Will you bring them?"

He lifted his head to see what she had pointed out, then took down two aromatic bundles of dried plants, one of plain, pale greens and the other of purple flowers atop slender stems. He brought them to her.

She pulled some pieces from the bundles and wove them together.

"Do they mean something?" he asked, his voice low. Reverence and respect was due this happening.

Olga stroked a finger along the pale green leaves, like shaggy grass. "This cleanses the aura and protects the spirit."

"And the flower?"

"It is known as heart's ease. To lift the weight of sadness." She settled the little braid of herbs inside the swaddle, over Thorvaldr's chest.

"How can he feel sadness?"

"They are not for him, but for those he leaves behind."

The thought of Vali and Brenna's loss, the potent, personal knowledge of it, racked Leif's own heart, and he sighed and leaned on his hands on the table next to the basket. Olga stepped to him and put her hand over his.

"You know this loss—you have had one like it."

"Yes," was his only answer. The full depth of his knowing was too much to share in this moment.

With a squeeze of his fingers, she let go and lifted the basket. Again, Leif followed her. She carried the babe into the room off the hall where they took their leisure. In that room was a table carved with strange markings. After months of wondering, they had decided that the marks made a likeness of Estland itself.

Olga set the basket in the middle of that table, and it became the babe's bier.

They stood together and looked down at the sweet, perfect face of a tiny child at rest.

"I know this loss, too," Olga said, after a long silence. "I had a boy. I lost him in this way—my husband beat me while I carried him, and my son came too soon. Since then, it seems I can have no more."

Leif turned and studied her delicate profile. She had endured so much violence, and yet she kept her peace. He couldn't understand how. "I'm sorry."

"It is the way of things. And now that man who beat me and killed my child is dead. The world keeps its balance."

She left the room and went into the hall. Leif followed her to the fireplace and again stood at her side. He couldn't seem to take his leave of her. He should—he wanted more than he could have, tonight he wanted it desperately, and he knew he should make space between him and his want.

She turned and faced him then, looking up at him with her soulful, beautiful eyes, and Leif's resolve teetered. He was lonely. He felt desolate in his heart on this sad night, and what he wanted most in the world was to pull this good woman into his arms and hold her close. He wanted to feel her, to fill her, to be joined with her and feel complete and alive.

As if she'd read his thoughts, a small, tender smile turned up the corners of her pretty mouth, and she lifted her hand to his face and stroked his beard. Her touch shot through him like lightning, and he grabbed her wrist. What was between them had not changed. They couldn't be truly together, and he wouldn't simply use her.

"Olga, no. There is no future for me here. I won't take you when I can't make you mine."

She jerked her hand free of his hold. "Men! Always you speak of taking. What of giving?"

Her burst of temper had shocked him. "What do you mean?"

Rather than answer, she picked up one of his hands in both of hers. She turned his palm up and traced her fingers over the hard skin. That simple touch made his belly clench and swelled his sex to fullness.

She bent her head and pressed to lips to the center of his palm, and Leif was nearly undone.

"Olga," he groaned.

"No man has ever cared what I want. They have only taken what they want. Even you never think of what I want."

That was untrue and unfair. Hurt, he moved to pull his hand back, but she resisted, and he let her keep it. She turned her eyes up and searched his face, her brow furrowed. "It is true, Leif. You make choices for me, like any other man. Different choices, but they are yours, not mine. You think you are saving me from something—from disappointment or sadness, or loneliness, perhaps. But no one can be saved from these things. They are part of living. I am lonely now."

She let go of his hand and came even closer, laying her palms flat on his chest. He could feel the heat of her body, and he couldn't resist resting his hands on her waist. Holding her. The span of her body at that point was so narrow that his fingers and thumbs nearly touched.

"You say you won't take me and leave me. This is my meaning: you speak always of taking and never of giving. But all that men have taken, they have never taken *me*. That is something that can be given only, never taken."

Her fingers slid into his tunic, where the fabric was split at the neckline, leaving a space of his chest bare. She seemed to give intent consideration to her fingertips playing through the hair there, and Leif closed his eyes and steeled his body against the urge to tremble under her touch.

She spoke again, her voice low, almost distracted. "No man has ever asked me what I want. *You've* never asked me. Never have I had a chance before to want. Now I do. I want to give myself to you. I want you to give yourself to me. For the first time since I was a girl too young to know the way of things, I want to know this giving."

When she paused, her fingers and her words both, Leif opened his eyes and met hers searching his face. "Do you care?" she asked.

"I care. Gods, yes, I care. But, Olga, soon I will sail from here and from you. I cannot stay." In his mind, it always came back to that, and he had no better rebuttal. "I cannot."

"Have you never thought that I might leave?

He had. Often. But she was so small, so delicate. "My home—it's a harsh place. Only the strong thrive."

"You think my home is such an easy place? That I am so weak?"

He knew her to be strong. On this very night, she had shown her strength. Enduring the life she'd had must have taken real fortitude. Yet he thought of her as fragile. Why? Because she was small and slight? Was the strength of her arms what mattered?

No. The strength of her heart and her will mattered. Her courage.

This world, her home, was nigh as harsh as his own. Only their little corner of it had, until this night, seemed different.

Leif's mind opened and became bright with the possibility. "You would leave with me?"

"I think," she said, her hands snaking up his chest and around his neck, as far as she could reach, "that if any would ask what I want, my answer would be that I want to be with you. Wherever you are."

His hands moved from her waist, smoothing over her back. Never before had he allowed himself to touch her in such a way, to feel her without resisting the impact of the touch. While they stared into each other's eyes, his hands traveled up to her shoulders, and then her head. He caught the fabric of her headscarf in his fingers and tugged. As it fell loose from her dark hair, it caught in the knotted braid at her nape and unwound it. Her heavy plait dropped over his hand.

He had never seen her hair unwound, and he felt a powerful need to see it now. To see all of her, to feel her.

This woman. She had been brutalized. Enslaved. Wrested from her family. And yet she carried no ill will. Calm surrounded her. Even when she had borne a rope around her neck, that had been true. She lived among men who had savaged her, who had killed many of her people, and she had made them her friends. Her serenity infused the people near her.

She gave Leif peace. She eased his heart.

Could he have her? Could he bring her to Geitland and begin a new life? Was that fair to her? Did it honor her in the way she deserved?

He didn't know. But he'd heard the words she'd said, the desire she'd expressed. The intent.

"Olga," he murmured, wrapping her braid around his hand. "I don't wish you to know more pain."

"Then do not hurt me," she whispered back and rose to her toes.

Leif bent to her and claimed her parted mouth with his.

5

Leif's mouth touched hers, just softly, and Olga sighed at the caress of his warm lips. He lifted away, a hairsbreadth, and then returned, covering her mouth so that she felt the wet of him. At the press of his tongue against her lips, she opened for him.

At that, hesitation disappeared between them. Leif groaned into her mouth, and his arms tightened around her. Olga wrapped her arms around his neck and grabbed fistfuls of his long hair. When she tugged, he made an animal noise, feral and needful, and then her feet left the floor. He'd stood straight and taken her with him so that she dangled against his body.

Men's mouths had been on her before, but never like this. Everything Leif did, he seemed to be asking her, with only touch, to follow. And she did. Their tongues slid together, their heads moved to and fro, and there was a rhythm that seemed to be known to them both, even this first time.

He groaned again, the sound trapped in her mouth, only for her, and swept an arm under her bottom, shifting her so that she was cradled in his arms. The brisk sensuality of the move shocked her, and she gasped.

The kiss broken, Leif opened his eyes. They were so blue, like the deepest part of the sea. And alight with desire for her.

"This is what you want?"

Olga nodded and pulled on his hair, wanting his mouth on hers again. "*Jah.* Giving, not taking."

"Yes." He kissed her again, lingering as he turned and headed toward the doorway that would take them to his room.

"No. My room," she corrected. "So that Vali can find me if I'm needed."

Leif stopped, and in his expression Olga saw second thoughts. Indeed, he said, "There has been so much loss tonight. Perhaps it's not—"

"Hush," she interrupted, knowing the concern he meant to voice. "Now is the time. This place needs good to heal. What is between us is good. You feel that, yes?"

"Yes. I do."

"Then now is the time."

They searched each other's eyes for a moment. Olga sought for more conflict in his, but at last she found none. He was with her.

He turned and crossed the hall, carrying her to her room.

~oOo~

"You deserve a grander room," Leif said as she set the bar across her door.

She liked her cozy space—much smaller than the suites of rooms Leif, Vali, and Brenna and the other raiders had, but more luxurious than any home she'd had before, even including her husband's officer's quarters. And because she was not far from the kitchen, her room was generally warmer than the more elegant chambers above. The stone walls drew and held the heat of the cooking fires.

Among the villagers, Olga's room was better than most. Many others bedded in larger quarters meant for nobles, but slept many to a room. This small nook was hers alone.

"I like this one, and I deserve no more than I need."

Before she could turn around, Leif was behind her, his tall, broad body like a wall against her back. He kissed her shoulder, and she felt his fingers move lightly over her hip, then the soft tug as he picked up her braid and untied the strip of cloth that bound the end.

With a slow, gentle touch, he unwound the simple plait, all the way to her head, and then combed his strong fingers through her long tresses, scratching lightly at her scalp with each stroke. Olga sighed and leaned her forehead on the door, giving herself up to the feeling of sultry indolence that came with his caress.

"Your hair is magnificent." His voice was so low he might have been speaking to himself.

Olga had often noted the raiders' seeming fascination with hair and with grooming in general. Although they reveled in the wash of blood and gore during battle, at times of peace, and in preparation for war, they took great care of their appearance.

They cleaned their clothes and their armor regularly and carefully. They washed often—more than the habit of her people—and they cleaned their teeth. And, men and women alike, they fussed over their hair. They kept many different styles, and they combed and brushed and trimmed and braided and beaded the hair on their heads and, for the men, on their faces. Nearly every single man had a full beard. Some were more impressive than others, but few men chose a smooth face.

Their braids were often works of art. Vali, who kept his head shorn on the sides but the hair on the top and back nearly as long as hers, wove his hair from scalp to ends, twisting two braids around each other to hang like a rope down the length of his back. Brenna kept a simple twist in peaceful days, but Olga had seen her dressed for war, and on those days, she had made an elaborate pattern of tight braids.

Leif wore his hair plain—long and straight. Olga had never seen it any other way. But, except when it had been covered in blood, it was always clean and smooth and gleaming.

She thought it funny that a man from a world where hair appeared to mean so much would marvel at her unremarkable dark waves. But there he stood, twisting the strands through his fingers, bringing them to his face to rub them over his cheek.

He gathered the thick hank of it in his hand and set it over her shoulder, then smoothed his hands down her arms and untied the apron at her waist. She stood with her eyes closed, her head still on the door, sensing in the movement of his body that he had tossed her apron away. His hands came around her waist then, and he loosened the woven belt over her skirt. When he tossed that away, too, her skirt, which wrapped around her body and had been held to her by the apron and belt, fell to her feet.

Wearing only her long, embroidered blouse and her woolen leggings and little leather shoes, Olga felt anxious. No one had undressed her before, not completely, and not in this lingering, favoring way. When Leif's hands came back to her, resting on her shoulders, his thumbs began to knead the muscles at the base of her neck, and she trembled.

He felt the quiver and paused. "This is what you want?" he asked again, his mouth at her ear.

She turned and put her back to the door. Leif loomed over her, blocking her sight of everything but him. "Yes. I want this. You."

He cupped her face in his rough hand. "*Sa oled mulle...kallis...väga.*"

Olga covered his hand with hers and smiled. "You are as dear to me, as well."

With an answering smile, Leif took a step back and unfastened his belt. He tossed it aside with the same lack of concern with which he'd discarded her clothes, then pulled his blue woolen tunic, stained with blood from the tragedies of the night, up over his head. His hair settled over bare, broad shoulders, rounded with muscle.

Olga had seen Leif's bare chest a few times before, when he trained with the other men in the hall, but she had kept her distance, knowing that he wouldn't join with her, and seeing no reason to torture herself more.

Now he stood mere inches from her, a golden mountain. She smoothed her hands over the firm expanse, learning the feel of his skin, lightly furred with darker curls and broken by scattered scars. So many scars. Never before, not even when blood had dripped from his beard, had she so clearly understood the violence of his life.

And yet he was beautiful. "*Sa oled ilus,*" she breathed, not realizing that she'd spoken in her own language.

A laugh lightened his voice when he replied, "Not so beautiful as you."

She drew a finger over the wend of a long scar above his left nipple. A grave injury had made such a scar, and so near his heart. How many times had he nearly died?

"May I see you, too?" he asked, bringing her away from that dark thought.

She had never been fully bare with a man before. Not even in the raiders' pen; Leif had taken her from it before she had been so abused as the others, and she had kept most of her clothes. Her husband had never been interested in any part of her but that between her legs, and he had never taken the time to expose anything else.

Shyness came over her. But she wanted this. She had made it happen. So she untied the ribbon at her neck and pulled her blouse loose so that it fell from her shoulders.

Leif pushed her hair back and then hooked his fingers into her blouse, helping it on its path down her body. He crouched before her and took her leggings down, too. Then he lifted a foot and untied her shoe, and her other. And then she was only herself, unadorned.

Crouching at her feet, he looked up. Olga bent her head and watched his eyes travel up her body until they met hers. He smiled. "You are a treasure."

When he stood, he pulled his boots off and shed his breeches, and they were naked together.

Her eyes and hands explored him, and he stood still and let them. Over the ridged muscles of his belly, the smooth planes of his hips, around to feel the swell of his bottom, then down over the massed muscles of his thighs. That darker, reddish-gold hair covered his legs, too, and guided her to a thicker thatch of it at his sex, which stood stiff between them. Thick and long and smooth.

She had seen many of these, but they had either been the soft worms of ailing men in need of healing or the hard weapons of men meaning her harm. Only in this moment did she feel curiosity and desire, and another thing as well, something that stirred deeper in her chest and made her sigh.

"Will you put your hand on me?" Leif asked, his voice like stones rolling in his mouth.

Olga looked up into needful blue eyes. "You want that?"

"Yes. And to touch you. To touch each other."

She had always imagined that coupling between two people who cared even a little about each other could only have been different from what she'd known. All her life, she had seen women who sought out the attentions of men, and she understood that there was something different in the act for others. Here in the castle with these earthy raiders, village girls sometimes went with more than one man at a time, and giggled while they did.

Olga had been making quite a lot of a particular kind of tea lately, for the girls who went giggling.

She lifted Leif's hands and set them at her waist. Immediately, those wide, hard palms skimmed up her sides and in, over her ribs, until they covered her breasts. She gasped, and her back arched; the touch seemed to draw her body toward him. He brushed his thumbs over points grown sharply sensitive, and she moaned. Something low and deep in her belly fluttered, and the small muscles between her legs went tight, and then loosened completely.

"Touch me, Olga," he gritted, his head coming toward hers. "Touch me."

As his mouth covered hers and his tongue pushed between her teeth, she touched him, wrapping both of her hands around his shaft. It bobbed in her hold, and Leif groaned, a sound of savage pain.

Suddenly, nothing was the same. Between them, in her life, in her ken, all was new.

His hands left her breasts and curled around her sides. He picked her up, lifting her high while their tongues writhed together and she still held his sex. She let go as her feet left the floor, and he tore his mouth away.

"Put your legs around me."

She did as he'd asked her—or told her; that didn't matter now—folding her legs around his waist, and her arms around his neck as well. He held her close, and she could feel the rod of his sex on her bottom. This was no way that she had ever experienced coupling before, but with his heat against her folds, she could imagine it.

She very much could imagine it. So much that she squirmed against him, making them both grunt like beasts.

"I don't wish to cause you pain, Olga," he said in that low, roughened voice as he walked to her bed. "You are so small."

Always he told her how little she was. Until these strange large people had taken over her life, she had never thought herself remarkably small. Skinny, yes, but otherwise, only smallish. But seated as she was in his immense arms, against his broad chest, her thighs stretched around his middle, she indeed felt tiny.

And now, understanding his meaning, she felt a thread of trepidation weave into her desire. What she'd held in her hands would fill her, would go deeper inside than she had room to take. She knew the pain of that, and it could never become pleasure.

She found his eyes and let him see her dawning fear. But he smiled. "If you want this, I know a way. But you must lead us."

"I...I don't know how."

"I will show you." He sat on the side of her bed. Olga realized then that her bed, like her body, was too small for him. If he stretched out, his feet and calves would dangle off the end.

With her still wrapped around him, he turned and leaned his back against the headstead. Her legs were trapped between his back and the bed, but he lifted her hips, and she drew them back until she was kneeling, straddled over his hips.

Before he set her back down, she thought she understood what he wanted her to do. "Like this?" she asked.

"Like this. You choose when to stop."

He moved a hand between them, between her legs, and brushed gentle fingertips over her folds, then between, his path smooth and silky and wet. Such a tender touch was unfamiliar to her, and she flinched and whimpered—and felt her body wet him even more.

"Ah," he breathed. "You are ready. So soft. You want this."

Not a question this time. A statement. And correct. Olga nodded. "*Jah. Jah.*"

He took hold of himself and, with the hand that still grasped her hip, urged her to settle onto him.

She did, moving slowly, not for fear, but for the desire to feel him, all of him, come into her. Both of his hands grasped her hips again, his fingers pressing deeply into her flesh, but he let her move and didn't force her to take him in more quickly than she wished.

Her legs were not yet settled on his when she felt the tip of him press against her limit. Then she opened her eyes. He was staring at her, his eyes on fire. She leaned forward, trembling when her slight movement shifted him inside her, and kissed him.

For long breathless moments, time stopped, and all there was in the world was the tangle of their tongues together and the fullness of his body in hers. She didn't move on him, and he didn't make her. She knotted the golden silk of his hair in her fingers and kissed him, tipping her head to and fro so that his beard would brush again and again over her cheeks and mouth, making her skin tingle and grow hot.

Then the ache of need inside her grew too sharp, and she couldn't be still. She didn't think about it; she simply moved in the way her body clearly wanted, making his sex touch her in the way she needed. They kissed, and she moved, and their breaths got louder and louder, until her thighs began to burn with tension and Leif's breath was nothing but bestial groans that filled her mouth.

And oh, what was happening inside her. She knew the feel of a man in her sheath, and yet she did not. There was no punishing pressure, no pain, no shame. There was only building, burgeoning pleasure, her body heating, her urge changing again and again, shifting from pleasure to desire to need to something without definition.

It wasn't only the slide of their sex together. His tongue in her mouth, his beard on her face, the harsh rasp of his breath, of her breath, the bind of his hair around her fingers, the ache of his fingers pressing into her skin—all was part of a greater whole, one she could no longer contain or even comprehend.

Just when her need became so great that she lost control over the flex of her hips and the pace of her breaths, Leif tore his mouth from hers with an otherworldly growl, and he pushed her back, taking control for the first time, but not of their rhythm, except for the way his movement had interrupted it. Instead, leaving her to her desperate, syncopated flexing, he bent down and caught her right nipple in his mouth, sucking deeply, ravenously.

She arched back so hard at the explosion of pleasure that she sat down on his legs, taking him almost fully into her, deeper than she had thought she could. And then she needed more than she knew how to meet. The flex of her hips on his thighs wasn't enough. The grasp of his hands wasn't enough.

Not even his beautiful mouth, his glorious beard, on her breast was enough. She didn't know what she needed.

But he did. She knew that Leif knew. "Take me!" she gasped.

At her words, he left her breast, and Olga whimpered with loss. "Olga?" His voice spoke all the strained need she felt.

"Take me. Please. Please. I need—I don't know. Take me. Us. Take us." Words wouldn't come except in bursts.

But he understood her. He gathered her into his arms and rolled them over. Now she was on her back, in a position she knew well, but the face above her, looking down on her with care, sheltering her in the drape of his hair—that was new and wonderful.

He kissed her and began to move. His practiced, attentive rhythm began slowly, but she didn't want slow, and when she writhed under him and drew her nails up his back, he sped up.

This was what she'd needed, this pressure of his body, this chance to feel and give up thinking. To give up. To give over. To give. To choose it.

He broke free of their kiss again and looked into her eyes, and what she saw in his was the end and beginning of her life.

Her release broke over her like fire and ice together, making her body tense and release again and again in a series of flailing spasms, and when his mouth covered hers again and muffled her, she realized that she had been nearly screaming.

His body went rigid while hers yet spasmed, and then he dropped his head to the bed next to hers. They panted in each other's ears until their breath, keeping time together, settled.

This was nothing like what had been done to her before. It was barely even the same physical act. This was what the girls who went giggling, and the men who chased them, were always after. She understood now.

More than that, she understood what drew Brenna and Vali so tightly together. Not merely a coupling. A bonding.

Leif pulled out of her, moving slowly, his eyes on hers, and then rolled to her side. "Are you well?" he asked.

Feeling full and sore, but a good, satisfying, happy kind of sore, a life-changing kind of sore, she rolled to face him and drew her fingers through his beard. "I am very well. You?"

"*Sa oled mulle kõige olulisem.*" He kissed the tip of her nose.

Olga snuggled against his chest, tucking her head under his chin. He was the most important thing to her, too.

~oOo~

The next day, Olga stood at the window in Brenna's room. Brenna slept, buried in furs, her pallid face stark against the bearskin under her chin.

Her chest rose and fell fitfully, and the sounds of her breath grated. Olga worried. Her friend still bled from the birth, and from the damage done to her by her fall, and by the earth only knew what else. She bled more than between her legs, in places Olga could not reach to staunch. Though she dripped as much healing brew as she could into Brenna's slack, dry mouth, if mother did not follow child into the earth, Olga doubted it would be for any help she'd been able to give.

Thorvaldr was not going into the earth, however—the cold was too deep, and the earth too hard, to take him. Instead, Leif and a few others had made a small funeral pyre in the woods just outside the castle walls, and Vali had carried his son, still in the basket Olga had nested him in, out to send him to the next world the raiders so valued.

She had opened the shutters, letting in the cold for just this moment, because from this room, she could see the little pyre. Vali had chosen the spot because their chamber looked down on the small glade where he, and Leif, and most of the other raiders, and a few of the villagers, now stood, circling the pyre with still, bowed heads.

Olga watched as Vali set his son atop the peaked wood. When he took a step back, Orm, the oldest of the raiders, spoke; Olga could hear his speech but not the words themselves. Leif then came forward with a torch, but Vali stopped him with a hand on his arm and took the torch from him. He set his son's pyre afire himself.

When Olga finally closed the shutters, worried that the room had grown too cold for Brenna's healing, Vali and Leif yet stood, now alone, watching dwindling flames.

Thorvaldr was gone.

~oOo~

Not long after, Vali came into the room. With his great shoulders curled as if under a heavy burden and his expression slack, his eyes drawn, he was the embodiment of sorrow.

Olga had turned Brenna to her side so that she could massage her back—gently, taking care not to cause greater hurt to what was likely broken inside—and urge the blood up from her lungs. Though she groaned in her sleep, her breathing seemed steadier on her side, and Olga left her like that as she went to Vali and set her hand on his arm.

He smelled strongly of smoke. Without acknowledging her nearness or her touch, he asked, "Why won't she wake?"

She remembered when he'd last asked her that question, when Brenna had swooned and fallen from her horse. Then, she'd had happy news to give him as a reason: his seed taking root inside her.

Now, the babe that had grown from that seed had wafted into the air as smoke and spirit, and Brenna lay weak and pale as ash.

"Her sleep helps her heal, Vali. It is good she not wake until she is strong enough to bear her loss."

"Our loss."

Olga didn't argue. He couldn't understand how much greater Brenna's loss was than his own. She simply squeezed the hard heft of his forearm, and when he moved past her and sat at his wife's bedside, she gathered up the old wound dressings and left him and his beloved alone.

~oOo~

When Olga came down the back stairs late that evening, after settling Brenna for the night, Leif emerged from the shadows and met her at the foot of the narrow stone steps. He wrapped his hand around her upper arm and pulled her close.

"I have missed you today."

Except when Vali asked for solitude, Olga spent almost all the day with Brenna. She didn't want her friend to wake alone, and when Vali was there, her presence seemed to give him comfort, too. But at night, when he was ready to strip and take to the bed at Brenna's side, Olga left them.

She was tired and sad, but Leif's touch made a charge in her blood, and she felt it rise and color her cheeks. "I think she might be healing. Her breath makes a softer sound tonight."

He stepped forward, pushing her gently to the wall. "That is good. The loss of her as well—it would be too great."

For more than Vali, that would be true. The two lovers had unified the castle in some way, like a great story they all shared.

When Leif bent his head toward hers, Olga put her hands on his chest and pushed. "Leif, I think…"

A frown drew over his brow. "You are sorry about what we've done?"

She had left him sleeping in her bed before dawn that morning, folded up so that he fit. His arm had been heavy over her, and his body warm behind her, and she had scooted from the bed, careful not to wake him.

Never had she been so sorry to leave her rest.

"No. Never. What we've done is special to me, and I hope there is more. But I think…perhaps this is not the time to make it known, the change between us."

"You said the castle needed something good."

"The energy, yes. We brought health into this home, and that is good for more than you and me. But the sorrow must make its way. When the grieving is done, that will be the time to share our news."

They were alone in the stairwell, and, with a quick check to be sure of it, he bent his head and pressed his lips to her throat. Olga moaned almost silently and put her hand on his head.

"I would come to you in private, then. In the quiet hours," he murmured, his breath and beard tickling her skin.

"*Jah. Oh, jah.*"

He stepped back with a smile and lifted her hand to his lips. "Do not bar your door tonight."

Then he turned and left her, and Olga stood on the step, shaking.

6

Vali roared and swept a tense arm across the table, sending cups and candles flying to clatter on the stone floor of the hall. He leapt from his chair, overturning it so that it, too, crashed to the floor.

"I am weary of this talk! I want to ride south! Ivan must pay!"

They had not expected an attack from Prince Ivan in the south. His holding was poor and weak, and the raiders were the stronger force. They'd focused their energies to the north, and Prince Toomas, who controlled a rich holding and a well-appointed army, and had a history of incursions against Vladimir, but even so, they hadn't expected trouble in the winter. Buried deep in snow, snug in the castle, they'd seen the season itself as the most pressing concern. Though they'd maintained patrols in the north to every extent they could, they'd expected—they still expected—Toomas to march his army on them when the weather would better accommodate the movement of a large force.

They'd all but forgotten Ivan, who had sent a small band of soldiers on foot, creeping into their land like bandits and wreaking havoc.

Now the village was destroyed, almost all of their livestock killed, and they'd lost several good men, villagers and raiders alike.

For Vali, though, this was much more personal. His wife—awake now but suffering badly—had been harmed and his child lost. Leif had real concern that his friend would ride out alone if he didn't get the result he wanted from this planning meeting.

But his idea was folly.

Leif stood, too, more calmly, at the other end of the table. "You will have no vengeance if we lose, Vali. None of us will. We have lost enough already—if we lose more, we will lose all. The small band you speak of, sneaking into Ivan's keep, might only be quashed and provoke him to ally with Toomas. And then we've lost our best fighters and are left to face united foes. If that happens before the ships arrive, we will be overrun. The snow is deep again. They cannot move on us in force any more than we can move on them. Better we wait for the true thaw and face Ivan head on, before he allies with Toomas."

Vali roared again, this time slamming his fists on the table before him. "I would act! I would not stand here while he breathes and my son does not!"

"This matter is greater than your own loss, Vali. You and Leif are our leaders here, and you must think of the whole of us." Orm had spoken, sitting near Vali. His voice had been low and measured, but Vali turned on him as if he'd shouted.

For a tense moment, there was no sound in the room but the breathing of the men, and Astrid, who had sat around the long table to discuss plans for retaliation.

Leif hated the table, on which his son's head had been perched, resting on a golden tray, when the raiders had first come into the castle. Not once had he sat at this table, or even passed it, without seeing that sight behind his eyes. He would happily have hacked it into pieces and burned it, except that it was the only table in the castle long enough to seat everyone who would be party to their discussions like this—the castle's own version of a thing.

No one else seemed to think of the table as anything other than a convenient assemblage of lumber. So Leif set aside his personal pain and sat here often, leading meetings, for the good of the group. Vali needed to find that strength in himself as well.

But he would not find it now, it seemed. With a last, baleful glare at Orm and at Leif, Vali turned, kicked his upended chair, and stormed from the room, toward the stairs that would take him up to Brenna.

~oOo~

Thanks to Brenna herself, reason finally prevailed, and Vali was calmed. The day after his display of temper in the hall, he'd come to Leif with an idea Brenna had shared with him: to enlist the aid of Ivan's subjects, who would make them sufficient number to crush Ivan with little fight. They would face the prince head on, drawing his attention and that of his army toward the front, and they would beset him on all other sides with his own people, from positions he thought he held secure.

Olga had been born on Ivan's land, and her family—a father and two younger brothers—were Ivan's subjects still. She had told Leif, one night in her room, as she'd lain naked on his chest, that she had been brought to Vladimir as part of a truce agreement. Not as a slave, precisely, but subject to royal whim nonetheless. Ivan had sent her in a parcel of people to Vladimir as workers in his village, sundering her from her family.

She had been mother to her younger brothers since shortly after the youngest's birth, when their mother had died of fever. In the years since she had been forced to leave them, she'd seen her brothers only a few times, and her father even fewer.

Vladimir had given her as a gift to one of his officers. It was that man who had most abused her and who had killed her child and her chance to have any other children.

Leif felt some need to see Ivan pay, as well.

Olga had known how a messenger might make his way into Ivan's sole village and seek the assistance of the people there against their prince. That messenger had come back with good news: the village was eager to stand up with the raiders; the story of the raiders' defeat of Vladimir and their community with his people had reached their ears. They'd reported back that they were ready and able to fight.

Leif and Vali and the others had made a plan. A good one, Leif thought. One that, if all went well, would allow Olga to be reunited with her family.

When Vali had brought the idea down from his talk with Brenna, with the thought that, should they win, they could bring the people and resources of both holdings together, Leif had immediately seen the chance to give Olga her family.

It wasn't until hours later, lying with her as she slept, that he understood that doing so would be the end of them. He knew she wouldn't leave her homeland if her family were with her again.

He hadn't mentioned the chance to Olga, because he didn't want to bring her hopes up too soon. Upon recognizing his own looming loss, Leif decided to say nothing to her at all, not until and unless her family returned with them after the battle. What little time he had with her like this, he wanted every bit of it.

And now they were on their way to fight.

Their plan had not included the still-healing Brenna God's-Eye, yet Vali had just helped her off her golden horse, and she had limped off into the woods, looking pale and damp, as they'd stopped to rest their horses and themselves before they crossed into Ivan's territory.

In the days between their forming a plan and implementing it, summer had finally begun to push winter away. A true thaw, Leif hoped it would be the last thaw, had finally come, and most of the high snowpack was gone. With the sun and warm air, Brenna had rejoined the world as well.

She was not ready to fight. How could she be? Barely more than two weeks had passed since she'd been hurt. Yet Leif understood why she had insisted, and, seeing the straight set of her shoulders as she walked from their stopping place, he knew that she would be strong in battle. Perhaps she would not be so strong as her peak, but she would be brave and determined, and her legend would grow on this day. Even if they were vanquished, he thought that would be true.

And Vali and Leif would stay at her side and make room for her to have her revenge.

~oOo~

At the head of the forward group, with Brenna and Vali, Leif pulled his shield from his back and brought it forward. He left his sword sheathed. At his side, Brenna did the same. Vali, a berserker who fought with a different style from theirs, had stripped to his bare chest. He carried no shield and wore no armor, but wielded his axes and his body so deftly he had need of nothing else. In this battle particularly, his furious need for justice forged stronger armor around him than any smith could.

They had teams in place ready to attack the castle from all sides when the forward group engaged the soldiers, with the villagers coming over the back wall in droves.

The raiders approached, and the castle gates opened with a reluctant shriek. A unit of soldiers came through on foot, in perfect formation. At their head was a single mounted man—their leader, by the look of him.

He stopped, and the soldiers stopped behind him, all at once. In the Estlander tongue, he said, "I am Captain of the Guard. At the bidding of Prince Ivan, I ask why you have come to our door. You are strangers to him and not welcome here. If you seek parley, elect an agent, and we will escort him in to make arrangements."

Nearly fluent in the language of this country now, Leif understood every irrelevant word. They did not seek parley. They sought the utter destruction of Ivan and every man who stood between him and them. Leif made the gesture with his hand that they had agreed upon, and from behind him, Knut hurled his spear. It whizzed between Leif and Brenna and hit true, impaling the Captain of the Guard through his throat.

The raiders jumped from their mounts and sent them running to safety, then met the charging soldiers head on. Leif bellowed and swung his sword, slashing the neck of the first solder he met. He threw that body to the side and blocked an attack with his shield.

Their intent was to drive the soldiers back into the castle, to hem them in as the other groups came over the walls. Though the raiders in the single forward group were outmanned by the soldiers, the balance would shift dramatically once all of the fighters were engaged. So they made no shield wall. Instead, they ran full-bore into the soldiers, pushing them back with their heavy shields and blades.

Leif kept a sense of Brenna as he fought, and of Vali, too. He had promised that he would not leave the weakened shieldmaiden unprotected. Without a specific plan to do so, he and Vali moved in tandem, keeping Brenna between them, jumping between her and soldiers' blades, shielding her from the more exposed edges of the fight.

Leif knew Brenna's fighting style; he had trained her and fought beside her for years now. She preferred the edges of a scrum, a place that allowed her to move her body freely. But she was not her full self, and the edge put her at a distance from aid. So, working instinctively with her husband, he kept her close, in the midst.

Even in the cacophony of battle, he did not miss her growl of frustration.

Seeing a soldier charge straight for her, Leif shouted and dived before her. He took the point of the blade in his chest and felt it sink between his ribs, but the Estland blades were narrower and lighter than their own, and Leif drove his down and broke the soldier's in twain. He grunted as the impact drove the point even deeper and shifted it upward, but waited until he had opened the soldier's belly, his sword slashing through the cracked links of battered mail armor, before he knocked the broken blade from his own chest.

There was no pain, and there wouldn't be, not in the thick of the fight. His arms were not weakened, nor his heart. So Leif fought on, unimpeded by his injury. When he saw Brenna and Vali argue in the middle of the fray—and then Brenna save Vali from a blow—Leif eased his vigilance over the shieldmaiden. They were doing her more harm than good, and she too, was suffused with the righteous power of battle. She was not weak. Not now.

So Leif turned and fought on.

The smell and splash of blood set afire the lust for it in his belly, and he felt a greater strength swell his muscles. This was what he was born for; this was what he knew. Perhaps his head was cooler and his heart warmer than his jarl or many of his clansmen, but he loved the fight no less for that. The sight of his blade breaking a blow aimed at him, the sight of it cutting through the body of a soldier who meant him ill, the spray and gush of an enemy's blood over his face and hands, his chest—all of these fed his ravening soul.

Here on the field of battle, Leif found the balance Olga talked so much about, the correction in his life against the many losses he had suffered. Here was his power over a fickle fate. Here he made the choice to live or die, to kill or be killed, to be victor or vanquished.

He would live, and not be vanquished. So he bellowed his warrior's shout and fought on.

~oOo~

Leif surveyed the scene of their victory.

Prince Ivan had hidden in the bowels of his paltry castle, but now his blood soaked the straw in the middle of the grounds. All of the soldiers were dead as well.

They had lost eleven of their own villagers and two raiders. The toll among Ivan's villagers, less trained and prepared, was greater, but Leif did not yet know exactly how many had been lost.

Around him, people sorted through the dead and wounded, and Leif tried to make a count of the bodies of the villagers. He saw two young men, both with dark hair, crouched beside the body of a man with iron grey hair. The broken shaft of an arrow rose from the dead man's chest. He had fallen early, then; their archers had taken out Ivan's in the first rush. He must have been one of the first villagers over the wall. Brave, then, and a leader in the village.

He went to the young men—boys, really, beardless and skinny. And short. The older of the two stood and pulled the younger up and behind him as Leif advanced. Two sets of dark brown eyes looked up at him, one set wary and the other simply stunned.

"I mean you no harm. Are you Anton?" he asked the older boy, who didn't answer, but seemed surprised that Leif knew their tongue. He tried again. "I am friend to Olga, and I seek her family."

The younger fought his brother's grip and came forward. "Olga? Is she here?"

Leif thought he had his answer. The body at his feet, then, was likely their father. Olga's father. His heart grew heavy. Crouching before the smaller of these small boys, he said, "You are Kalju?"

The boy nodded. "Is Olga here?"

"She is not. She is safe away, but I would bring you to her." He turned his attention to Anton. "I am Leif, her friend."

Anton gave him a reluctant nod, still suspicious, then gestured to the body. "Our father."

"I am sorry. I would bring him with us, and you may be with your sister to send him on in your fashion."

"No. This is his home. He should go into the earth among the sacred trees he knew."

Leif did not have their trust and couldn't argue such a point, so he nodded and prepared to do what he could to help them bury their father.

Again, he wondered what the future held for Olga. And for him.

~oOo~

Leif paid little mind to his wound until they had returned to their castle and he had retired to his room, well into the night. There, he pulled off his boots and stripped to his breeches, setting aside his damaged leather chestpiece and wincing as his tunic, which had become stuck to the wound, pulled free, taking the first of the healing with it.

His chest and side were red with dried blood, but the wound itself was not so bad. It was the length of his first finger, and split wide enough for him to see the meat of his muscle, but the bleeding had, until he'd torn his tunic away, stopped.

The gash crossed through an old scar that had been a far more serious hurt, one which might well have ended his life. At the time of that wounding, he had been seeking Valhalla with more reckless vigor than usual. And yet he lived.

He went to his washbowl and soaked a linen cloth. He would have liked a bath, but the trouble for one seemed too great. So he made do with the bowl and the cloth. As he wiped the dried blood from his skin, he thought of the scene when they'd come into the castle grounds. Before he could get to Olga, Brenna had presented her brothers to her. She had gathered them up, sobbing.

Never before had he seen Olga cry.

He had gone back to his work: caring for his horse, ensuring that weapons and gear were tended to. Olga had made her brothers comfortable and sent her women to tasks in the castle, then gotten to her business of healing the wounded. He had not seen much of her since.

His wound was seeping fresh blood again, so, once he was clean enough, he folded a linen and pressed it over his heart, then sat down in his chair by the fire.

In the time since he and Olga had first coupled, he'd spent only one night in this room. It was much more comfortable than hers, with a bed he could stretch his legs in, but it felt lonely and cold now, even with the fire well fed.

The door behind him opened, though there had been no knock. Leif turned and looked around the chair. Olga closed the door and came toward him. The hour was late, and she was dressed only in her sleeping gown and a woolen shawl. Her lovely hair was loose, the waves cascading over her elfin body.

She was beautiful. Always so beautiful.

He stood. She had never come to him here, this way. They had agreed to keep the privacy of her small chamber, tucked away near the kitchen. Several raiders had their rooms along this corridor, and she would likely be seen, if she hadn't already been.

"Olga."

As he'd stood, he'd dropped his hand from his chest, and now she frowned at the wound. "You're hurt." She came and laid her hand on him, her fingers pressing lightly just beneath the cut.

He resisted the impulse to wince at the discomfort of her examining fingers on his damaged flesh. "Not so much."

"It should be treated. I will fetch some healing paste."

She turned, but he caught her arm—so lithe and frail-seeming in his clumsy hand—and pulled her around again. She was here, and he didn't want her away from him. He wouldn't have her for much longer.

"No. I'm well enough."

"Leif..."

"You're here, and I want you to stay."

She smiled then and relented. "Let me bind it, then, at the least."

At his nod of concession, she pushed him to sit again and then went to a chest and brought linens to his chair.

As she folded and looped and wrapped, making a pad over the wound and crossing linens over his chest to hold it, she asked, "Why did you not come to me tonight?"

"I thought you would be with your brothers. They are well?"

"*Jah*. Sleeping. They were exhausted, but unhurt. Thank you for bringing them to me."

Not all of her family had come to her. "I'm sorry about your father."

She paused and met his eyes. The quiet contentment that had brimmed in them receded a bit, and sadness filled the space. "As am I. But I know he was happier to leave in this way than he would have been to simply fade. He was lonely without my mother." Leif sighed, and Olga's brow wrinkled in concern. "You do have pain."

He understood then that Olga had not thought about their future. She was caught in the happiness of having her brothers with her, of Leif and her friends returning victorious, and not even the death of her father much dampened that bliss.

It hadn't yet occurred to her that her brothers would change her intent to leave her home and go with him, that they two would be separated from each other, likely forever.

Or perhaps they wouldn't. Her brothers could join them, Leif realized. He would do what he could to bring them back to Geitland, too. They were small and skinny, young men of full age who looked like boys, but he had learned well not to underestimate the strength of the Estland spirit. Kalju was Einar's age. They might not make raiders, but they could learn craft or trade. Or he could give them farmland to work. If they would agree, he would bring them all.

Åke would allow it, he was sure; he had never asked the jarl for personal consideration before. A case could be made that he was due a favor or two.

Leif's heart lightened. As Olga finished her ministrations, he caught her hand and pressed her knuckles to his lips. "No. No pain. Only need."

Taking his meaning, she cast a cocked brow at his bandaged chest. "Too much effort will make you bleed again."

He grinned. "Then it would seem the effort must be yours."

The firelight danced in her eyes as she closed her fingers around his and stepped back, urging him to stand. He did, dwarfing her. There was no physical force she could have exerted that could have moved him if he resisted her at all, but he willingly followed her pull and let her lead him to the bed.

At the side of the bed, she dropped his hand and took hold of the tie of his breeches, pulling the lacings loose and pushing the leather from his hips. She crouched at his feet, and he stepped out of the legs and kicked the breeches away.

They had undressed each other before, but this was the first time she had taken complete control and he had remained passive. Leif found the vision of her, at his feet but in control, achingly enticing.

She trailed her long, lithe fingers over his bruised legs. Fighting as he had today, he'd taken several shield bashes to his hips, and he'd driven his own shield into his thigh to block a blow that he'd nearly seen too late.

"These don't pain you?" she asked as her fingertips made the dark-red skin prickle and twitch.

"An ache I know well. Not of consequence." The greater ache was in his sex. He throbbed before her.

She looked up. "There is so much strength in you."

"And in you. Olga—come up."

Instead, she smiled and took hold of him. He groaned at the touch of her soft—they were soft; how could they be so soft when she worked so hard, had been through so much?—hands, and his hips rocked forward as her curled palms slid up and down his length.

Then she kissed his tip. She had never done so before, and he had never asked. He treated her with care always, letting her tell him what she wanted, what she was comfortable with. He'd never asked for details about what had been done to her, by her husband or any other man, and he didn't feel he needed to. He had seen enough in his life to know, as Olga so often said, the way of things.

When she sucked lightly at his end, sensation sliced through him as if on the point of a blade. He jerked and groaned her name, and this time she stood. Leif mourned the loss as she left his sex and pressed her hands on his belly. At that urging, he took a step back and, finding the bed against his legs, he sat.

She pushed her body between his legs and bent her head to kiss him, her hands taking firm hold of his face, her fingers curling into his beard and pulling lightly. Her hair fell all around them, curtaining them in darkness, and filling the intimate space inside with her scent.

He hooked his hands around her thighs and returned her kiss, letting her small but limber tongue lead their dance. His heart pounded, making his ears ring and his wound ache.

The scent of her, the taste of her, the feel of her.

Oh, how he loved her.

He had loved his wife. Not when they were wedded, but Åke had made the match well, and they might have fallen in love anyway, given the chance. Married before they knew much of each other, just after they'd both been considered of age, they grew quickly to fondness. Love caught in that tinder, and Leif had been a happy young man indeed by the time Toril was round with their first child.

His love with Toril had been a quiet thing at first, a friendship above all else. They had learned to be married, and to be grown, together, and a powerful bond formed in that place. She had been a strong woman of their people. A good wife, a good mother, a good helpmeet. Then they'd begun to lose their children, and his love for his wife, and hers for him, had become something else. The losses turned her, weakened her, and their love had then been made of her needing him and him attempting to be what she needed. He'd turned his own grief inward to make strength in himself to see Toril through hers.

And he'd learned that guilt was a constant companion to grief.

Now, he wasn't sure he knew how to grieve any other way than alone.

The love that had grown in him for Olga was different. She looked nothing like Toril; his wife had been tall and fair, like the greater share of their people. Like Leif himself. Still, at first knowing, Olga had not seemed not greatly different: a quiet woman, strong in her way, who understood her role.

But at the heart, they were profoundly different. Loss and grief, trial and tribulation, seemed to make Olga stronger, not weaker, like iron forged in fire. Her spine didn't break under a heavy burden; it bent and learned to carry the weight. This slip of a woman, her back so narrow he could almost span it with a single spread hand, held inside her the fortitude of a band of fierce raiders.

His love for her held him with that kind of strength. He wanted to take her home to Geitland, to bring her brothers along—her brothers who were of an age to be his children—and make a family. He wanted that with a consuming urgency.

He groaned into her mouth, and she laughed lightly and pulled away. With her eyes on his, she pushed on his shoulders, and he did her bidding and lay back, shifting to stretch out on his bed.

Still wearing her sleeping gown, Olga crawled onto the bed and over him, settling her knees at his hips. This was a position they knew well. He was too big for her body; she could not take him completely in, and they had found ways to be and move that allowed them to be lost in each other without her being hurt.

She liked to be on top, in control, at first, and she had found that if she rested on his thighs, his depth was no greater than she could enjoy. And he had found that the downward pull and pressure on him in this way added a new dimension to his own enjoyment.

Often, at the end of things, she wanted him to take over. Leif liked this as well. It was difficult to be passive while Olga found her pleasure. The sight of her seeking it would well undo a less patient man.

There was something different in the sight of her atop him now, however. Something in her eyes. Staring down at him, she loosened the ribbon at the neck of her gown and pulled the filmy linen over her head, baring her wonderful body to his gaze. Thin as she was, she had a womanly shape, with hips that swelled gracefully from a slender waist, and small, round breasts with tiny dark dots for nipples. The mound of her sex was covered with dark wisps of silk curls, and the rest of her body was nearly hairless.

She bore the scars of past hurts and pains, but those, too, made her beautiful, made her strength shine from her moon-pale skin.

What Leif loved best about her shape, though, were her collarbones, those perfect, elegant arches across the top of her chest. From shoulder to shoulder they showed, and he often, when they were alone like this, drew his finger over their graceful shape.

He did so now, and Olga smiled down at him, a mysterious smirk. She rose up and took hold of him, making him steady so that she could sheath his sex inside hers.

She was silky-wet, and he groaned as her beautiful body accepted him, her most sensitive flesh sliding over his. He shut his eyes so that he could focus on only that—the perfect heat of her most intimate embrace.

"Open your eyes, Leif."

Smiling, he did as he was bid. Then she shocked him utterly. As her hips began to flex on him, picking up their beat, she brought her hands to her chest and cupped her breasts. She had never touched herself before, not that he had seen, and now, as she smiled down at him, the corner of her mouth turned up in a wry curl, her own fingers played with those little peaks.

Of their own volition, his hands left her thighs, wanting to join hers, to feel her hands moving on her own body, but she shook her head.

"The effort is mine, tonight, *jah?*" she said.

Leif heard a hint of strain in her words and knew that she was exciting herself. Gods. The sight of her, the knowledge of what she was making herself feel, how she was using her hands and his sex to give herself pleasure, how she knew that what she was doing gave him great pleasure, too—Leif struggled to control his body's desperate race to completion. He was nearly ill with desire, with the need to move with her, to fulfill them both, but his every flex and writhe, she met with resistance. She wanted him to give over to her.

So he lay and watched her, and he suffered a swirling bath of exquisite sensation.

He was woozy by the time the change in her happened, when she left behind intent and seduction and focused entirely inward, on her own driving need for release. He loved this moment, when her eyes and mind lost focus and her body gained it, when every part of her moved toward the same goal.

Her eyes clamped shut, her brow drawing down. Her teeth came down on the pillow of her bottom lip. Her hands dropped from her breasts and latched onto his forearms. Her breath became loud and erratic, and her hips picked up a new rhythm, faster and less practiced.

Seizing his moment, as violent need racked his own body, Leif sat up and swept his arms around her. His sex heaved inside her, and they both gasped. Olga's eyes flew open, and Leif locked them with his. "Stay with me," he said, hearing the grit of painful need in his voice. "Look at me. Olga, heed me. *Ma armastan sind. Armastan sind kogu südamest.*"

She went still in his hold, and Leif could have wept—he was so close. She was so close. But it had been his words that had stilled her.

He hoped he'd said them right. He'd meant to use her own language to tell her, for the first time, that he loved her, and he knew those words. But the second sentence, that he loved her with his whole heart—in the extremity of his need, he could only hope he hadn't missed a word or a sound and said something terrible instead.

Then she smiled and fed her fingers into his hair—the touch pulled a little; traces of dried blood yet lingered from the battle earlier in the day. In his life, this was the way of things—battle and blood, love and sex, life and death mingled together in equal measure.

"Ja ma armastan sind. Ma ei suuda sinuta elada."

He didn't think that was literally true, that she couldn't live without him. She was too strong to break under any pressure. But he believed the sentiment behind those words, and he believed that she loved him as he loved her. And he believed that they would be together, she and her brothers would be with him. They would come with him and make a family in Geitland.

His heart would know ease, and so would hers. He would see to it that her life was one of comfort and peace.

Staring into each other's eyes, they picked up their rhythm and found completion together.

7

They were no longer boys, her brothers.

Anton, with sixteen years, was a full head taller than Olga, at least. His shoulders had grown square and strong, and he had a light dust of dark hair under his nose. Even Kalju was taller than she, though only just, and his jaw had begun to sharpen and his nose widen, changing his face from that of a child.

Olga had been saddened to learn of their father's death, but he had died in the fight, and she knew that would have given him a satisfaction unfamiliar to him since their mother had gone into the earth. The grief she held in her heart was softened by that knowledge. Her brothers had been right to put him in earth he'd known, in his home. A wretched home it was, yes, but the only he'd ever had.

There was still much of the boy in Kalju. He goggled at everything he saw, in the castle and beyond it. The big raiders, with their braided hair and beards, the massive swords and shields everywhere, the stony grey opulence of this castle, so different from and greater than anything they'd known before, the ampleness of the food and drink, of warmth and good cheer—Olga's youngest brother was impressed by it all.

Anton, however, had grown hard as he'd grown tall. He was quiet around the raiders, suspicious, and at every turn, he pulled Kalju back from his eagerness. Olga thought Anton felt suspicion even toward her. She had found him glaring at her while she spoke or laughed with her friends, and his greatest suspicion seemed focused on Leif above all the others.

The years since they had been together as a family had made a great distance between her and Anton. He was much changed, and she didn't know him as she once had. She supposed she was changed as well. It was the way of things: the tides of life shifted sands, smoothed some edges and made others.

But Kalju was still Kalju, despite the squaring of his jaw. Olga believed that Anton held the credit for that. He had protected their little brother, left him his innocence.

His own innocence, however, seemed long gone. The impish boy he'd been was no more.

She had asked Leif to keep their relationship private yet longer, until Anton could be made comfortable with the changes in his life.

When she'd asked, they had been walking together beyond the castle walls, along a path dusted in the fresh green of the first days of summer. He had looked up toward the blue sky of the western horizon, where the sea lay, and sighed, but he had agreed.

She knew the weight of that sigh. His ships were coming soon. Now that the weather had broken, those ships would arrive at any time, and she was meant to go with him when they sailed away again. She wanted that, a life with him, wherever it was, more than she had ever wanted anything in her life. She loved her golden giant with all her heart and spirit.

But she could not leave her brothers behind.

Leif didn't want her to. He wanted to bring them back to his homeland as well, to make a family together.

Anton would never go, not as he felt now. Olga could not go without her brothers. They had lost father and mother. Their older brother had been lost to them out in the great world. But Anton and Kalju had been returned to her, and she to them; she would never leave them again.

She had to make Anton see, to make him trust.

~oOo~

Anton stood in the doorway, watching the men training in the hall. Olga came up behind him and touched his arm. He jumped and turned.

"Why not join them? Your friends learn to fight now, too."

Weeks had passed since the taking of Ivan's lands. At the raiders' suggestion, the surviving villagers from both holdings had agreed to come together and rebuild here, doubling the size of the inland village. Some of the raiders had elected to stay on as settlers—even Brenna and Vali, though that was not widely known. Vali had begun to build their house without much fuss or attention, as if he were simply erecting another building in the town.

Olga knew that Leif was deeply troubled by their friends' decision, though he was not surprised. He most certainly would not consider staying himself.

His ships hadn't yet arrived, and that was a good thing, in Olga's estimation. Anton was still wary of the raiders and of Leif. Even as his friends from his home were here, in this castle, training for war with lifelong warriors, Anton stood on the edge, watching.

In answer to her question, Anton shook his head. "They bring war here. Death and blood. I want no part."

"Death and blood is part of all life, and war was here before the raiders. You look for cause to keep yourself apart, when everyone else comes together. Why?"

"Their ways are not our ways. They are changing us." He waved angrily at the hall. "Our women wear breeches now. And wield swords!"

That had shocked her at first, as well, but by now she had grown used to warrior women. Anton was right; the raiders had changed them. "A woman who can fight is one a man need not protect. And breeches are just coverings in a different shape. The changes are for the better, brother. We are healthier, better fed, happier. We are stronger. I was there when they came from the sea, and I thought them monsters, too. They did monstrous things. But they are men and women, like any other. Some are worse than others, some are better than most. They didn't simply wrest our home from us. They made a home with us. If we're changing, so are they."

Her brother scoffed and turned from the door. "There is something more they want. Anyone with power wants more. There is a game at play, and we are simply the pieces to be moved. You will see."

Olga had six years more than Anton, and she had done much of his raising, but he spoke to her now as if he were a learned man and she a simpleminded girl. Her irritation stifled her speech, and before she could think of a likely retort, he had turned and stalked off. She watched him go, angry and offended, then turned back to the doorway.

Leif stood in the hall, not far off, golden and gleaming, his bare chest damp and heaving from his training exertions. He faced her, and his expression told her that she needn't wonder how much of her exchange with her brother he had heard.

His deep blue eyes were sad. He had heard enough.

~oOo~

"Which house will be ours?" Kalju asked a few days later, when they were all in the village, the men and strong boys constructing houses and stables and the women preparing the midday meal. Olga's youngest brother had come for fresh water skins to bring to thirsty builders.

Olga sank a skin into the water barrel, focusing on the simple task as if it took her undivided attention. She didn't know how to answer Kalju's question. She didn't want a house here, not without Leif. Thus one had not been started. But the new village was half finished. They had made a peace with Toomas, and they had been able to work freely on remaking what winter and battle had destroyed.

If Anton had been invested in these changes, it would have been he who'd wondered about their house, and long before.

But he had elected to make himself useful by hunting in the woods. Solitary work. He wasn't interested in a house, or a village, that the raiders had helped build.

"Vali works on it now."

Olga turned at Brenna's voice and saw her friend smiling at Kalju. Brenna's gaze shifted to Olga, and she gave a slight, conspiratorial cock of her head. Aside from Leif, only Brenna knew that Olga hoped—no, planned, *meant*—to sail with Leif and bring her brothers, too. Only Brenna knew that the plan now hinged on Anton. It was a plan Olga meant to keep secret until she could be sure that Anton was ready to agree. He was too suspicious to hear it yet.

Olga didn't think even Vali knew. Leif and Brenna both had seemed to keep that confidence tight.

And Brenna and Vali had not spoken widely of their plan to stay here and settle. That Vali was building Olga's house rather than his and Brenna's own—longhouse though it was—made a story that served many purposes.

But they were running out of time. As Olga wiped sweat from her brow on this warm, sunny day, she knew their time could be counted in days. Soon, she would have to talk to Anton, whether he had warmed to the raiders or not.

Could she really watch Leif sail away from her if her brother would not leave?

She had left them once. She had not chosen it, but she had left, when they had most needed her. She couldn't choose to do so now.

Kalju turned and gaped at the big house the big man was building. "But it's so big."

Brenna nodded. "Olga's work is important. She makes people well. She needs a big space."

Her words had been broken as she'd spoken in a tongue she still struggled with, but she'd done well, and Olga was proud of her.

"Why don't you help him?" she added, smiling as she said it, and Olga smiled, too. Vali didn't much like people helping him unless he'd asked for it directly. He would grumble, but he'd find something for the boy to do.

Kalju hooked the skins over his shoulder and trotted off to be a help. Brenna stood at Olga's side and watched him go. "The ships are tardy already, Olga. You should speak to them."

"*Jah*, I should. I must. But I know already what Anton will say, and it will break my heart."

"He is a man grown. Kalju also. In our world and in yours, they might both have been wedded by now. Can you not go without them?"

Brenna had chosen to leave her family. Olga had been taken from hers. Her friend could not understand how that had been, to know she was needed, to know she was wanted, to know where she belonged, and to have no choice to make it right. Now she had a choice. She couldn't abandon them again. Not even if they had all been old and grey.

"I cannot."

She felt Brenna's hand squeeze hers. "Leif will understand."

Olga knew he would. She would break his heart as she broke her own, but he would understand and love her still. That was the kind of love, the kind of life, she would give up when she watched him sail away.

And it would be her choice. As sailing would be his.

Oh, how she wished he would stay.

~oOo~

She opened her door that night, and Leif stood waiting, his posture straight and centered in the doorway. He had stopped knocking weeks before, and yet tonight he waited for her to bid him enter. When she smiled and stepped back, making way for him, he stood still.

"I saw you speaking in earnest with your brother tonight. It didn't seem a happy talk."

It had not been. "Come in, Leif. Sit with me."

For another moment, he didn't move, and his eyes remained locked with hers. Then he blinked and stepped in. He glanced at her bed, and Olga thought that he would sit there, but he turned from it suddenly and sat on her single chair, near her little fireplace, which held no fire; her room had no need of its heat now.

His choice left Olga only two seating options: the bed or the floor at his feet. She chose the floor.

"You aren't coming with me." Leif stared at the fireplace as if there were flames to see dancing there.

Olga's talk with Anton had been difficult at best. She had explained what was between her and Leif, and that he wanted the three of them to sail with him to his home. She'd explained that it would be a new start, that Leif was important in his world, and that they would not struggle.

Anton had called her a fool. What little deference he'd still had for her as his older sister and replacement mother had left his eyes and his attitude as she'd tried to talk. He'd seen a silly woman hoodwinked by a handsome, powerful man.

That much, she had no need to share with Leif. "Anton has no wish to ride the sea to a strange place. Estland is his home. If I had more time—"

Leif dismissed those words with a brusque wave of his hand. "The summer grows warm. Our ships could arrive at any moment."

"I know. It is why I spoke to him today. But it was too soon. These weeks have not been enough to warm him to your people."

"The ships will bring settlers. My people will be here, even when I am not."

"But here is a world he knows. An earth he has farmed. Woods he has hunted."

He sighed and slumped against the back of the chair. "The truth of it is that there is no time that would persuade him. I see it in his eyes. I will never have his trust."

"You are likely right. I hoped. I hoped with all my heart, but he will not leave here." She set her hand on his thigh.

Sitting forward, he picked up her hand and held it close. "Then let him stay. Come with me, Olga. He is a man. Kalju is a man as well. They are old enough to make their way on their own."

"You brought them back to me. Would you so quickly take me from them again?"

"I would take you all with me, if that was your choice. All of you should make your own choice. I would have you choose me."

"You could stay. You could choose me and stay." She pulled her hand, but he wouldn't let it go.

"I do not have the choice."

"Why not? Brenna and Vali have chosen."

He dropped her hand and stood abruptly. When he walked toward the door, Olga thought he meant to leave. But he stopped and stared at the bare stone wall for a moment swollen with tension. At last, he said, "It's *because* of Brenna and Vali's choices that I cannot stay."

She had expected nothing at all like that for a reason. "I don't understand."

"In our world, they are both legends. Stories are told about them."

"I have heard this before."

He turned back to her. "Yes. Brenna is known as the God's-Eye. She is thought to be..." he hesitated as if he searched for the right word.

They were speaking in the blended language that had become the habit of all who'd resided in the castle over the winter. He had two languages from which to choose a word.

"Otherworldly," Olga supplied, in his tongue. "Because of her strange eye."

"Yes."

These giants and their gods. Leif had tried to explain it to her, but it all seemed absurdly complicated. "Here there is no other world. There is only this one, and Brenna's eye is only unusual."

"I know. Our world is not like yours. What I mean to tell you, however, is that Brenna is believed to be more than human, and she is sworn to my jarl."

Olga knew this. "Åke."

"Yes. He believes her to be his gift from our greatest god."

"Odin." Leif had told her the story of Odin's eye, and thus of Brenna's. He knew that she knew this, so Olga listened to his words and searched for the heart of his story now.

"Yes. Vali is sworn to another jarl. He is a powerful warrior and a legend, too. Åke sees him as a threat. And now, Vali has married his renowned shieldmaiden. When my jarl learns of that—and more, that they plan to settle here—he will be outraged. He might well see it as an act of war. I have cause to believe that the alliance that brought us all here under the colors of two jarls was broken while the ships were away. I already worry that blood will be shed when Åke learns that Brenna has married an enemy and that she means to stay."

"Vali is no enemy."

"Not to me. He is my good friend, and I have grown to love him as a brother here. He is a good man. But he is enemy to Åke if he is sworn to another who is not Åke's ally. Åke will reel from the news that Brenna has bound herself to Vali. If I were to seek to leave him as well, even as his agent here, as I am now…" Leif stopped and then began again, his voice thick with regret. "He does not suffer disappointments. He would kill all I hold dear and take from me my reason to stay. He would kill you. He might well do it in front of me."

Still sitting on the floor, Olga stared up at him, her jaw slack with shock. "You are loyal to such a man as this? You have cut down two princes here who were no worse."

"You would have me kill him?"

Olga didn't answer with words. She let her eyes say yes. If this jarl was so petty and cruel, then his power tilted the world from its balance.

But Leif shook his head. "He has not always been as he is now. He has always been hard, but he was reasonable and took good counsel. Power has changed him, and age as well. But he has been like a father to me, and he has loved me as one of his own sons. I swore an oath to a better man, but I swore. On that oath, I gave him my life and my sword. I did not swear on any conditions. I simply swore. My word is the most valuable thing I have."

That made no sense to her. An oath sworn to a bad man was a bad oath. How could that be anything but true? "So valuable you would leave me behind to keep it. Even to a man such as your jarl."

He came back and crouched at her side. "I would not leave you. Gods, I would not. Olga, please. My love, come with me."

All this talk had changed nothing. She could not understand his fealty, and he could not understand why she wouldn't leave her grown brothers.

No—that was wrong. She thought they both understood. Leif was loyal and self-sacrificing. As was she. Their love was doomed.

She brushed her hand through his soft, thick hair. "I love you. But I cannot leave any more than you can stay."

He dropped his head. "I know."

"What are we to do?"

Looking up at her, his eyes dark with sorrow, he smiled and caught her chin in his fingers. "We take the time we have left, and we love each other."

It was all they could do. Her chest ached with the coming loss, but she found a smile as well. "I will never be sorry that we have known this love."

"Nor I."

He stood and helped her to her feet. Then he picked her up and carried her to bed.

PART TWO
FIRE

8

Two days later—a mere two days—the raiders from the castle rode to the coast to meet Åke and his ships.

Only Åke. The ships had arrived under his flag alone.

Already bonds that had formed among those who had stayed behind, bonds forged in joy and friendship as well as hardship and battle, shook as those who had been sworn to Snorri wondered what had befallen their jarl that he had not made the journey. They cast suspicious eyes on Åke's people, and men who had laughed together the night before now rested their hands on their weapons when they spoke.

Vali, leader of Snorri's men, had spent these hours since the ships had been sighted exhorting them all to remember that they were friends and to leap to no judgments.

But Leif thought of Calder's evasions in their last talks the summer before, his hints of a bigger plan, and he felt sure that Snorri was dead. If that was true, if Åke had moved to claim a holding far to the north of his own, and this holding across the sea as well, then his plans were indeed bigger. The large holdings of two jarls sat between Snorri's northern lands and Åke's in the south. If he had hemmed them in, then he had great plans. Epic plans.

Kingly plans.

As they approached the jarl's camp, Brenna and Vali in the lead with him as always, what Leif saw was a raiding camp. He saw no signs of settlers. It would seem from this arrival that Åke had no intent to settle in Estland.

That made no sense. Why had they stayed at all, then?

There was so much he didn't know. His choice to stay and hold the castle had pushed him from Åke's inner circle. He had to get back in. Only from the inside could he hope to prevent disaster.

They dismounted at the head of the camp, and Åke and his eldest sons, Calder and Eivind, came to greet them.

Dressed in his finest leather and furs, a jeweled medallion on his chest, the jarl spread his arms wide and came to Leif.

"Leif Olavsson! It is good to see you! I have missed you as I might have missed a son of my own blood."

Leif embraced his jarl as the father figure he'd once been to him, and he felt real warmth and affection returned. When Åke stepped back, clutching Leif's shoulders, Leif made a respectful bow of his head.

"Jarl Åke. The winter was long. We're glad to have you safely here."

The jarl smiled and patted his shoulder briskly, then turned to Brenna. "And Brenna God's-Eye. My own great shieldmaiden. The ships carried home to us more stories of your exploits for the sagas. And you look very well. Odin's presence has been strong with you this winter, I see."

Åke touched her face then, and Leif saw Vali shift into battle-readiness. The difference was subtle, an overall tension in the man's broad shoulders, and a frown on his brow, but Leif had spent the greater part of a year in close company with the Storm-Wolf, and he knew his body's language. And more, he was especially alert for trouble in this event.

Brenna, on the other hand, took no offense at her jarl's affectionate touch. She nodded and acknowledged him as she knew to do.

When Åke turned to Vali, Leif paid close heed. Still in his mien of readiness, Vali looked down on the shorter jarl.

"Vali Storm-Wolf. You are famed as well, and I am glad to see that your story continues." Leif could hear insincerity in Åke's tone—or perhaps he was seeing trouble everywhere, even where it was not.

Vali barely tipped his head. "Thank you, Jarl Åke, it does. I would know how fares my jarl, Snorri."

And there it was. The trouble Leif knew was coming would arrive in Åke's answer; he was sure of it.

Åke had not appreciated being called out so directly, and in the middle of the greeting. But he kept his noble bearing. "Snorri is drinking with the gods in Valhalla. I am sorry, friend."

There was a long silence. Åke and Vali stared at each other. Brenna and Leif stared at them. Leif turned and met the eyes of his friend, Calder, and saw more cool remove than friendship.

So much had changed while he was here.

The jarl invited Brenna to his tent for a talk. When Vali stepped forward as well, Leif set his hand on his sword.

He heard his friends proclaim their marriage. He saw the surprise, and then the ice, in his jarl's eyes at the news. He saw Calder take note of his sword hand and find his own sword as well.

Leif's mind spun as it never had before. He needed to see, to understand. Would blood be shed right here? If so, at least they were away from the innocent villagers. At least Olga would be safe.

But Åke smiled. "Then good tidings are in order, and we shall drink to the lasting goodwill of the gods. And I welcome the great Storm-Wolf into my clan."

Vali didn't protest the jarl's assumption that he would swear to him, and Leif felt a slight relief. As his two friends followed after the jarl, he let his hand fall from his sword. He had not been called to join them, which was unusual. Just as he worried that he was being cut out, though, Åke stopped and turned back. "Come, Leif. We seek your wisdom as well."

His heart and belly churning with concern and confusion, Leif followed. At least he was still on the inside, where he might best see trouble—and might best dispel it.

~oOo~

"I see longhouses here." Åke sat astride the mount he had chosen and surveyed the rebuilding village.

They had broken camp at dawn the next morning and returned to the castle. Once he had made a cursory pass through the castle, Åke had declared that he wanted to see the village. They had seen the burned ruins of the coastal village already. Though there were plans in place to rebuild that as well, in smaller scale and better protected, everyone's first focus on been on the inland village and the farmland.

Leif and Knut had escorted Åke and his sons, and now they all stood in the center of the town. It smelled strongly of fresh wood and tilled earth. A good, calm scent. But Leif knew no calm.

"Yes," he answered. "The Estlanders prefer small huts, but we build for settlers, too, homes made in the way of home."

Åke pulled on his long, white beard. "I hear that the Storm-Wolf builds here."

Knut shot a glance in Leif's direction. There had been talk, but Brenna and Vali had not confirmed their decision widely. There was no reason Knut should know, but Leif couldn't decide whether that quick glance had been one of surprise or concern. He sought a thing to say.

"We all build. Helping any who seek the help. This is a place of good people, Åke. We made for you large holding and a strong settlement."

One the jarl had yet shown little sign of wanting.

These hours back in Åke's presence, after so many months away, had made in Leif a new understanding. All his life, he'd known a complicated and powerful man, harsh and cold in many ways but warm and open in others. A man who had shown him love and favor. He knew Åke's ways to be severe, and he had seen the years change him, but Leif had known the man he'd loved, even as the warmth in him had dwindled.

He hadn't been blind to Åke's changing. He had simply honored his oath and remembered the man who had been, and he had borne in his own heart the consequences of his continuing loyalty to a man he agreed with less and less.

Brenna, too, was loyal to Åke—was trying to be even now—but Leif thought her loyalty came from a different place. She had offered herself to the jarl as a slave, and he had taken her on as such. When she had saved his wife and young children from the raiders who had killed Leif's wife and unborn son, Åke had repaid that great debt by freeing her and handing her a sword and shield of her own. He had made her swear her fealty, holding her in thrall in another way.

But he had given her a home when she'd had none, and he had been honorable when he was indebted. Her fealty rested in that. Leif knew her better than most others, and he thought that she reconciled her loyalty with the man Åke had become by simply not seeing that there was any way to be jarl but his way. She closed her storied eyes to his failings and saw the man she wanted to see.

Leif had no such luxury. He saw Åke as he was. Now, with the clearer eyes of distance, he saw him truly.

And he was ashamed.

But it was not a matter of simply turning his back. The consequences to any action any of them took now would be profound. Vali was not willing to see beyond what he saw was right. He had taken a wife, and he had decided to settle here, knowing fully the danger in those choices, and he cared not, because he disdained Åke. Leif had tried again and again to talk with him about what they would face. But always he'd simply shrugged and said what would come would come.

What was coming was ruin. It was down to Leif, then, to be the one to turn the ship from the rocks. To try, at least.

Now Åke cast a searching look at him, and Leif returned it steadily.

"Do you build a longhouse, too, my friend?" Calder asked, his tone artificially light.

This was the moment when he settled his place inside Åke's circle or locked himself out of it. "I help. As I say, we all help. But if you ask if I mean to stay, I do not. My home is Geitland."

Åke smiled warmly and, with a nod, turned his mount back toward the castle.

~oOo~

Shortly after their return, Leif sought out Olga. He caught her coming down the back stairs and dragged her along the dark service corridor, not stopping until he had turned into the nook that sheltered her own door and had pushed her in and barred them inside.

"Leif! What of this?"

Rather than answer, he kissed her. He grabbed her arms and pulled her hard to his chest, and he slammed his mouth over hers and kissed her fiercely. Desperately. He tried to put every bit of feeling he had for her into that kiss. He tried to put years of love into that kiss.

When she overcame her shock and confusion and kissed him back, he released her arms and picked her up, holding her to him with her feet dangling against his legs. She threw her arms around him, and they fed each other's souls in that kiss that would have to last them the rest of their lives.

Because it would be their last.

Olga finally pulled back, flushed and gasping, but Leif didn't set her down. He couldn't. Her fingers were in his hair, her lips on his cheek, above the line of his beard, and he couldn't give up the feel of her.

"Something's wrong," she whispered.

Everything was wrong, but he did not yet quite understand how it would fall apart. "This is the last of us, my love. You must stay away from me as long as Åke is here, and I will leave with him. He is suspicious of everything here, and he did not come to settle. I don't know his intentions, but they are not what they should be. I am a danger to you now. All the raiders are. I would that you would go to the village."

She pushed back and looked him in the eyes. "You know that I can't. I must manage the castle. Now, with so many new people, there is much to do—and if all of us who work here ran, would that not make your terrible jarl more dangerous?"

Leif had only thought of Olga. "I don't want you near Åke or any of the men who came today."

"Your clansmen."

Yes, his clansmen. He couldn't claim her as his own, and his clansmen were rough with women subordinate to them. In their world, the people who served them were slaves. It had taken weeks to curb the ways of the raiders who'd stayed last summer. And now Åke and Calder were here, in charge. They would ignore the coarse whims of their men.

Leif had already spoken with the raiders who had called this castle home, and they would do what they could to deflect that kind of trouble. But they were outnumbered—by many times.

"Send as many away as you can, then, and Olga, please—stay back from Åke and his sons, and from me especially."

Her beautiful, bottomless dark eyes studied him before she nodded. "I will try. This is goodbye for us?"

"It is. *Ma armastan sind.*"

Her eyes brimmed, but the tears didn't fall. "And I love you. *Igavesti.*"

"Yes. Forever," he nodded. And then he kissed her again. A kiss to last a lifetime.

~oOo~

Åke sat down, and from his seat on Calder's other side, Leif could feel the jarl's anger, like a wave of heat rolling down the table.

Brenna had just announced her intention to stay in Estland with Vali. No—she had been smarter than that. She had asked to be allowed to stay. She had not turned her back on their jarl; she had not broken her oath.

That he had granted her wish almost without resistance told Leif more than he had learned since the ships had landed. He had held out a slim hope before, but now he didn't believe at all that Åke would actually allow her to stay. Agreeing so quickly to her request had simply made him time. There was something in play.

When Åke turned an angry eye on him, who had only hours before deflected and evaded a question about Vali and Brenna's plans, Leif felt sure that Åke meant the two legends to die, and soon.

Leif had to prevent that. At any cost. Not only because Vali and Brenna were his friends, but because they were greater than themselves. The loss of them would be a blow to their people, a shock to their faith.

And because Åke had to be stopped. Leif had been sorting through the questions and inconsistencies he'd accumulated, and he thought he understood why there were no settlers. Åke had no intention of moving into Estland. He never had. The raid that had brought them here the year before had not even been about plunder.

Åke and Calder had allied with Snorri for last summer's raid so that Snorri's Úlfheðinn berserker, Vali Storm-Wolf, and many of his strongest warriors, would not be at his back when Åke turned on him. He had gambled wisely that Vali would stay behind when Calder tried to claim the land in his father's name alone.

But he had not expected Leif and Brenna to stay behind as well.

Even without them, he had vanquished Snorri. And he'd arrived here, geared for battle, not to settle a claim but to trounce the last of Snorri's men. Leif was sure of it.

An alliance made with such malice aforethought—that was not the act of a complicated but valiant man. It was the act of a coward. Deceit and lies, petty jealousies and cold cruelty: these made up the jarl—the man—Åke had become.

Leif owed him nothing. The man he had sworn his life and sword to was gone.

But that knowledge gave him no ease. It changed nothing. Here Åke was, in their castle, with shiploads of loyal raiders, warriors who had not had this time to know another, better way. Leif's people were hopelessly outnumbered. There was no possible victory for them. Not here.

He couldn't talk to Vali. His friend's personal hostility toward Åke was too great. He would seek to fight headlong, and that would only get them killed all the faster—and likely take innocents with them.

No. They had a peace with Toomas. If Leif could get Åke to sail again quickly, the village would be safe. Olga and her brothers would be safe.

He had to find a way to keep Vali and Brenna alive as well.

~oOo~

After the meal, Åke and his sons moved to chairs near the fire, clustered as if for privacy. Uninvited, Leif sat where he was and left his mind to its work of solving the many puzzles this night had set forth.

Then Calder dropped his hand on Leif's shoulder. "Come and sit with us, brother. We would drink more of this sweet Estland mead with you and know how you yourself fared this winter. You have been missed."

Leif smiled up at his friend. Still his friend. A lifetime at each other's sides. Countless small oaths made and secrets kept, in the way of boys. Calder had been shaped by his father, but he was not his father. He would know reason. He would see beyond the betrayal Åke perceived.

But Calder had been party to these machinations. Perhaps his father had shaped him more than Leif had thought.

Taking his cup, Leif stood and followed his oldest friend to the cluster of heavy chairs where Åke and Eivind sat.

Before he was settled into the chair that was left, the jarl said, his voice low, "She dies. Tonight."

"Who?" Leif knew, but he asked nonetheless.

"The whore who calls herself Odin's own. The God's-Eye."

Brenna had never called herself any such thing. She loathed the name that had been forced upon her.

"And that smug bastard, too. I care not how it's done. I want it done tonight. We'll leave his naked body on the wall when we leave and lash hers to the prow of my ship. When they're dead, we'll take any who'll swear to me and kill the rest. We leave before the dawn."

Leif's heart hammered against his ribs. His mind worked furiously, and he picked a simple, neutral observation to give him time to think. "The ships need to be provisioned anew before we sail."

"Viger is seeing to that as we speak," Calder answered, and Leif realized that he hadn't seen his clansman in quite some time. Then Calder smirked and punched Leif's arm affectionately. "Unless you mean that dark little wench that had your eye last summer. I see her roaming around here. Would you bring her as your pet? Or have you had you fill of her? I might have a poke before we go, if you're done with her. Little bit of a thing like that, I imagine she's tight, unless you've torn her wide by now."

Calder knew well Leif's tendencies with women and had often japed at him for it. Perhaps because he'd been untried before he was wed, Leif had never been one to rut at the least urge. Since Toril's death, he had favored a few women, but those few, he had favored particularly and treated gently. Otherwise, he had dealt with his needs with his own hand.

So his friend's laughing remark now, so crude, had the dark ring of hostility.

For a moment, all of Leif's will went to his hands and forced them not to become fists. He would kill Calder with those hands, in full sight of his father and brother, if he made a move toward Olga. Whatever that meant for the future.

But Åke slammed his fist on the arm of his chair. "There is no time for rutting. I want justice, and I want to be quit of this place. We already have anything that was ever of value here. Calder—you take the whore. Leif—you end her wolf."

As he made to stand, Leif threw out his hand to block him. "Hold!"

The jarl and his sons gave Leif their full, suspicious attention.

Thinking fast, trying to keep his mind ahead of his words, he said, "What does killing her do? It makes her a martyr. Unless you kill her in combat, or by the judgment of a thing, the stories will say that a coward ended the God's-Eye. And such a dark death might call Odin's attention as well."

Åke's eyes narrowed, but he let Leif continue. "Why not instead make her your thrall again? Enslave her. Show that her oath to you cannot be broken."

Until those words were in the air, Leif would not have believed he could have made such a suggestion. With that one sentence, he knew that he had lost his friends. Brenna would despise him. Vali would kill him with the same fire he himself had just felt toward Calder. They would see only the betrayal on the surface and not the good intent underneath. But he was trying to save their lives, and the lives of their whole family here.

That was what they had made together in this place: a family. And Leif was losing it. Another family. Another love.

At least this time, he was giving it up so that he might save it.

"Bring her home in bonds. It's a good idea, Father," Eivind said. "That is a lasting justice. A victory. She is Odin's gift to you. I believe the Allfather would see justice in such a correction."

Åke pulled on his beard, and then he turned to Leif and smiled. "You are my son like any other, Leif Olavsson. Your father was my good friend and advisor, and I am glad to have you at my side now. I have missed you." He held out his arm, and Leif clasped it.

Leif was sick. Sick at heart, sick to his stomach. But he could see no other way.

Before Åke let him go, he said, "Make it so. Calder, take her alive. Leif, the Storm-Wolf dies. And we shall see who will yet stand against me."

He rose and left, gold chains jingling. Olga was right; he was no better than Vladimir or Ivan.

Leif looked across the hall, where Vali sat at the table, alone. Their eyes met, just briefly, before Leif had to look away.

Gods, what he was about to be part of.

~oOo~

A short time later, he put out the torches in a side corridor off the top of the east staircase and waited in the shadows for Vali to come up to the room he shared with Brenna.

Brenna, Leif knew, was not in that room. Calder had already subdued her and put her out of the way. He now sported a bruised cheek, but he had overtaken her, while she was in her sleeping shift, caught unawares. Coward's work indeed.

What Leif planned was little better. When Vali came up the stairs, Leif stepped forward.

Surprised, Vali asked, "Is there trouble?" and reached for an axe that was not hanging from his hip.

"Yes, my friend. There is." Leif swung his own axe, poll side forward, and hit Vali on the side of the head. He'd hit hard and true, and his friend crumpled to the floor, his great size and heavy weight nearly shaking the castle itself.

Months before, it had taken four strong men to carry this one man up stairs like these, on the opposite side of the castle. Leif had been one of them. Now, alone, in the dark, he grabbed his sleeping friend's arms and pulled him down the corridor. He had to find a place to shelter him so that he would live through this night.

Blood flowed freely from the wound Leif had made in Vali's head. He hoped he had not killed him after all.

~oOo~

It was he who started the bloodbath, albeit unintentionally.

He managed to get Vali down the back stairs and to the stable in the cover of the dark, while Åke spoke in the hall, making his claims and conditions. He bound his friend and left him in a far stall, hopefully out of danger.

But coming out of the stable, he was surprised by Knut, one of Åke's own men.

Unsure where Knut would stand on this matter, but sure that he was a threat to him in any case, Leif drew his sword. Knut blinked, equally surprised, and drew his own.

"Åke means to tear this all down, Leif. All we've built. We must stand against him."

Knut was yet a friend, then. Vali would need as many as could be saved. And Leif saw his true chance to save Vali—and possibly also Knut, if he were careful.

Making his voice carry over the grounds, he said, "Like you, I am sworn to Åke. He is my jarl, and I have no other allegiance. The Storm-Wolf is dead. You can join him, or you can be true to your oath and live." He swung his sword.

Knut blocked him, his expression shifting to hostile intent. Leif was the stronger warrior and the better swordsman, but he traded blows and blocks, drawing out the fight, making a show of it. From their side, the unearthly shriek of Astrid's battle cry resounded in the night, and Leif swept his eyes in that direction to see her coming right at him, her shield up and her axe raised. She was blocked by Oluf, who ran at her and took her down. Leif saw the axe fly from her hand as she landed in the dirt.

Then everywhere around him was fighting.

~oOo~

It didn't last long. All of Snorri's men resisted Åke, as well as most of the village men who had been at the feast. Some of Åke's warriors, Astrid and Knut among them, resisted, too. But not many. Not nearly enough to tip the scales.

Tried though he had to keep friends whole, the instinct for self-preservation had taken over in the thick of the battle, and he had killed three who had been Snorri's men. He might also have killed Knut, though he had left him breathing at the time. Astrid was down as well. And Orm, with his face split open, lying near the castle door. And so many more. All who had resisted Åke, dead or assumed as such.

Leif thought Orm had moved. He hoped so.

The ground was littered with bodies. The stench of bloodied earth filled the air. And it was yet full dark.

"Where is the body of Vali Storm-Wolf?" Åke asked at Leif's side. "I should like to piss on it, as I did his beloved jarl."

Too tired and disheartened to put on a show, Leif sighed and tried to think of the right answer to this next problem.

"I saw him," called someone from behind them. "He was cleaved clear in twain! Over there!"

Åke and Leif both turned toward the sound, but no one stood forward, and Leif hadn't recognized the voice. He didn't know if it was someone who meant to distract Åke, or who simply wanted to have his hand in the story that would be told.

In any case, that call was a help to him.

Just then Calder came out with Brenna over his shoulder. She was bound, gagged, and blindfolded, wearing only her thin sleeping gown. Calder dropped her to the ground near Leif's feet, and she grunted.

Calder stalked to his father. "She wakes. Already she tries to fight."

"Then put her down again. I don't want her awake until we are at sea," Åke barked at his son, and Calder came back and kicked her in the head. After that, she was quiet and still.

Åke scanned the benighted grounds. "Burn it!"

Yet more Leif had to think quickly to save. Fatigue screamed in his skull. "Jarl. A fire will draw the villagers here."

"So? You think farmers are a threat to us?"

"No. But they will slow us, and we're ready to be off. Why not leave the bodies to rot?"

He hated the proud grin on Åke's face. "Yes. We will leave the bodies. And we will leave this puny place and return to make our destiny."

As they mounted, Leif looked around the grounds. So many bodies. People he cared about. People who had trusted him.

He hoped that some had survived, but had enough to be of any real help to Vali? That was the only hope, the reason he had done this rather than take his stand here, side by side with Vali and Brenna: to keep the people he most cared about alive. To make a chance to fight another day, when there was a hope to win. To see beyond this one moment to the day when Åke would meet justice.

He had not seen Olga since he had glimpsed her across the hall, just after the feast. He would never see her again. He didn't even know if she had lived or died.

Gods, what if he had made a terrible mistake? What if he had given up everything and gained nothing?

~oOo~

The sun had risen on a clear, bright, summer morning when the ships left the coast of Estland. The wind was brisk and friendly, and the air had the kind of glassy chill that came on a summer morning at the sea. That chill would deepen as they moved to the open sea, even if they held good weather for all the voyage.

Leif stood near the stern and watched the land drift away toward the horizon.

He had struggled as hard as he knew how to save his friends, but all he'd left behind was blood and betrayal. He didn't know if Vali or Olga or anyone were still alive in the castle. Brenna lay behind him, bound and beaten, and left to the elements.

If he had simply sunk his blade into Åke's soft belly, at least the jarl would also be dead.

He had failed.

He turned from the last view of the land of his love, his true home, and focused on Brenna. All he could do now was all he could for her.

They were both warriors, so they would fight on. He would keep her alive. And he would keep hope alive in them both that Vali still lived as well.

9

"Will he live? We need him."

Olga paused in her stitching of Vali's scalp and looked over her shoulder and up at Orm. "The blow was hard, and the swelling is great. But there's no break in his skull, and that is good. I cannot say if he'll live, but it seems killing this giant of a man is nigh impossible."

Orm made a stunted chuckle and rearranged the clumsy bandage over his face. His own wound was serious, too, and under that awkward wrapping, nearly half his face flapped loosely, but the old man wouldn't take any care until Vali had been found. When he was found alive, he became the entire castle's priority.

Vali was, by a notable margin, the tallest of any man in the castle—any man Olga had ever seen. Even among the generally tall raiders, few neared his own height. Leif was among the few who did. Such a sharp blow, straight across the side of Vali's head—Olga had tended many wounds in her days as a healer, wounds of violence as well as of accident. She had learned the ways they were made. She thought someone nearly as tall as Vali himself had made this wound.

Leif. In her heart, she knew it was Leif who had tried to kill Vali.

With her own eyes, she had seen him fighting her friends—his own friends. She had seen him spill onto the castle grounds the entrails of Toke, who was a young man not much older than Anton, and whom she had seen Leif laughing with many a time in the hall.

Bodies were piled up against the walls outside. The earth was yet soft with blood. Nearly all the raiders were dead or gone. Only seven remained—assuming that she could heal all those who still drew breath, because not a single one of them had gone unscathed.

Not even she. Not unscathed at all. While a battle raged in the night outside, some of the new raiders ran through the castle, ransacking the rooms, taking what was of value. Olga had done as Leif had bid and sent away as many as she could of the women who worked the castle. But for those who stayed, the night became a raid like any other, and the raiders behaved as they would.

It was the way of things.

Olga, who had run from the sight of Leif slashing his way through their friends, had been caught in the kitchen and shoved against the stone face of the fireplace. As before, she could hear the cries of the other women, but this time, she didn't call out and offer comfort. The large hand driving her head into the rough stone as she was taken had made it impossible to speak.

Now her mouth was swollen and split, her body was abused yet again, and her heart was broken.

When the raider was called away and had left her, she'd found a place to hide until there was quiet in the castle. When she came out, the silence was of death. Bodies lay everywhere. The stench of blood and gore and waste hung heavy in the air.

As those few who could move began to do so, the story filled in among them. They found Vali, bound and insensible in the stable. Brenna was gone, taken by the terrible jarl and his terrible men.

And Leif had been among those terrible men.

Anton was right. She was a silly woman who'd been hoodwinked by a handsome, powerful man.

Caught in a cloud of love, Olga had forgotten the way of things, but she remembered now. And she would not forget again.

Finishing her stitching, she cut the dark thread. "He is the most gravely wounded of those who live. Call in some of the strongest from the village and have them take him up to his own bed. When he wakes, it should be as gentle a waking as we can make it."

Work on the village had paused as many men and women returned to the aid of those who had been assailed. The men took on the dark work of carrying bodies of friends to the sacred woods, and piling the bodies of enemies for disposal. The women helped Olga, or they packed up what goods and gear were left. They meant to abandon the castle as soon as the wounded were well enough to travel.

She stood and gave Orm a steady look. "And then I will put your face back together."

Her heart was broken, but her spirit was not. She would not mourn a loss that had never been what she'd thought it was. She had given freely of herself for the first time, and Leif had crumpled up the gift in his fist, but she would not be crushed.

Not even a golden giant could take her from herself.

~oOo~

Vali's fury and grief upon waking was her undoing, however.

In the face of his desperate rage, the horror in his still-unfocused eyes as he tried to make his injured head understand all that had happened, all that was lost, and that Leif had been the chief agent of their destruction, Olga's spirit collapsed.

When the huge bear of a man, that indomitable, indestructible legend, fell to his knees, bellowing his wife's name, Olga felt in his howls the vicious depth of her own grief. She knelt at his side and tried to embrace him, to comfort him, to share in his feeling, but he shoved her away.

Their grief was their own, then.

~oOo~

The world kept its balance.

In all things, the world would ever keep its balance.

It was the way of things.

It was the way of things.

It was the way of things.

Olga sat up in the night, alone in a narrow bed, in the village hut she now shared with her brothers, and she said those words over and over like a litany. An incantation to ward the dark away.

There were no incantations in her world, no ghosts or ghouls, no gods or giants. There was no magic. There was power. Power in the elements themselves: earth, air, water, fire. To know their power and their influence, to respect their pull and sway, was to know the world in its fullness, to see the balance in all things and to know that when the world tipped too much one way, there would be a tipping in the opposite way. Always a sway, but always a balance. A world in motion.

Day and night. Sun and moon. Summer and winter. Sowing and reaping. Life and death. All of it bound by the tangible, tactile, present world. Earth, air, water, fire.

There was spirit, too, but it was not an otherworldly thing. It was will and soul; it was the thing that drove the mind and the heart. It was the thing that could only be given.

Olga had a talent for healing not simply because her ken was great for the properties of plants. The strength of her healing came in her elemental understanding of their world. She saw the balance. She knew the way of things. The knowing opened her mind and steadied her hand. Made her calm—a powerful calm that moved through her, into her medicines, into her touch.

To know the way of things was to know the way.

Olga had known shock in her life. She had known horror and sorrow. She had known pain. But she had never known fear. Fear came from not knowing the way, not seeing the balance, and Olga knew. She saw. So she had not feared.

Until now.

Now, Olga feared everything with an intensity far beyond her ken. She feared the dark. Sleep and its dreams. The uncertainty of the future. The truth of the past. She feared what she didn't know, and what she did.

She could not find the balance. She had lost her way. She had lost herself.

~oOo~

Kalju came into the hut and held out a large bunch of mouse-ear. "For you. To make your healing tea. There's a large bed of it on the far side of the field."

She smiled and took the bundle from him. "Thank you."

"You look tired, sister," Kalju said as he washed his hands in the bowl.

She was tired. She was weary. A week had passed since she had lost her way. The world was finding its balance again, but she was not.

The villagers were back at work building, and planting a small crop at this end of the sowing time. The few raiders who were left had come to the village as well.

They had no ship that could sail the sea, so they were settling.

All but Vali. Determined to get to Brenna, he had stayed at the castle, alone, and was building a seaworthy vessel with his own hands. He seemed to have gone mad with need—the need to save Brenna, the need for vengeance, the need for action.

She set a bowl of hearty stew on the table with a hunk of fresh bread, and she smiled as her young brother sat. "Not so tired, *kullake*. Was Anton behind you?" She picked up another bowl and prepared to fill it.

Kalju grinned and pointed toward the window. "I don't think he'll join us this meal. Anna was in the circle."

"Anna?" The girl was a great help to her and was learning the healing arts. Olga had not known that Anton had paid her any notice, however.

She went to the window and looked out on the circle. There were some buildings still being constructed, and some spaces yet to be built, but the village was already becoming a town.

And there her brother stood, at the well, leaning close to sweet Anna in a way that made Olga's heart ache. She now knew what it was to have a man pay that kind of tender attention.

Her brother was courting. Well, he was well old enough to take a wife. To start a family of his own.

It was the way of things. Life moved forward. The world found its balance.

But she did not.

Olga stood at the window and watched life move forward for her brother. Anton smiled at something Anna said and then stepped back. With a shy tip of her head, the girl turned and headed toward her parents' hut. Anton watched her walk away.

He was halfway to the hut he shared with Olga and Kalju when Harald, once a raider and now a settler, rode hard into town from the north, his horse lathered and foaming—he'd ridden long at that pace. He had been out with Astrid and Dan, riding a patrol.

"Soldiers!" he shouted, riding through the town. "They ride for us! Gather what weapons you can! We fight or we die!"

Anton turned and started in the direction Anna had taken, then stopped and ran for his sister and brother instead.

~oOo~

Some of the people in the new town had shields and swords and axes; they had trained with the raiders over the long, hard winter, and their smith had forged them tools for their new skills, as he'd forged the weapons of Vladimir's soldiers in the world before.

Olga and her brothers had no such weapons. After the raid on Ivan's castle and the death of their father, Anton had wanted no more part in war-making. But he ran into the hut now and grabbed the pitchfork off the wall and threw it at Kalju, and he took the scythe down for himself.

He pushed Olga back. "Stay hidden!" he shouted, then turned to Kalju. "Protect her!"

Without waiting to gain agreement from either of them, Anton ran out, just as the thunder of many horses' hooves began to fill the air and shake the ground.

Olga picked up her knife from where it had lain on her worktable. She would not stay hidden. Women who hid themselves ended up turned over a table or shoved into stone or earth. They were taken. It was the way of things.

She would never be taken again.

She would kill anyone who tried, or she would kill herself. One meant the same to her as the other now. But she would not be taken. Never again.

Kalju stared at her with eyes wide and wild with fear. The pitchfork shook in his hands. But when she tried to take it from him, to take over and protect the boy, he stilled his muscles and stiffened his spine, and he pushed her back.

"I won't let you be hurt, sister." His voice barely shook.

~oOo~

The soldier who would kill Kalju came through the door with a flaming torch in one hand and a sword in the other. Olga's little brother shoved his pitchfork forward with a high-pitched warrior's shout, and the tines went through the looped mail of the soldier's armor but got caught before much damage had been done. The soldier knocked the fork away, knocking Kalju back as well. He fell into her worktable, upending a basket of dried grasses Olga had planned to bundle as that night's work.

With a malevolent grin, the soldier dropped the torch onto Kalju's chest. The dried plants and his light linen summer tunic went up like the ripest kindling, and her brother began to scream.

Olga held back her own scream and ran forward, leaping onto the soldier's back. She buried her little knife in the nape of his neck, pushing upward, into the meat under his skull. He flailed for a few short seconds, then dropped to his knees, and then his face.

Her brother's screams nearly overwhelmed the sounds of battle and death that rang in the air around them. Olga lunged for the water bucket and dumped it over him. He screamed louder as the flames died and steam rose over his body. He screamed and screamed, and Olga saw the blackening skin melt and slide over his face and neck.

There was no healing for him. There was no herb to take this pain away.

There was only one thing.

She knelt at his side and sank her blade into his chest.

~oOo~

When Kalju was gone, Olga set her knife aside and stood. She picked up the sword of the dead soldier and went out into the battle.

There was no thought in her head as to what she would do out there. Her thoughts were consumed by young Kalju, who had known no mother but her. Her mind whirled with the sight of him burning, the feel of the knife sinking into his heart, the smell of his cooking flesh that filled her nose. There was no room for any other thought.

She picked up the sword and walked through the door as if called to do so by a force beyond herself. She walked out and through the town in what might have been a straight line, only barely aware of the fighting going on around her, and of the smell of fire and smoke. The overwhelming smell of fire and smoke and burning meat. The whole town crackled and waved with fire.

"Olga!" Anton shouted in her face, and she came back to the moment. His face was covered with blood. He still had his scythe, and he had picked up a shield as well, one of the thick, round wooden shields the raiders carried. "What are you doing? Where's Kalju?"

Words failed her, so she shook her head. Grief made a wave across her last brother's face, and then he threw the scythe away and yanked the sword from her hand, shoving her hard from him as he did so. She landed on the ground and scrambled back to her feet just as a soldier charged in and swung.

Anton was insufficiently trained, but he blocked the blow with the shield and then swung the sword. The scythe had been a better weapon for him. The soldier brought his sword up under the attack, and the sword Anton wielded flew away with such force that it made a loop in the air. Next, his raider's shield went flying, this in Olga's direction. It landed within her reach, and she grabbed for it, meaning to get it back to her brother somehow.

Before she could, Anton fell, his throat gaping and his lifeblood gushing.

Then the soldier turned on her. With the shield still in her hand, she screamed and threw it up, and the sword bashed against the wood so hard her whole body, all the way to her teeth, shook.

He swung again, and she managed to block him again. And again. Her arms sang and screamed from the force of the blows.

On the next blow, she blocked again, but this time, the shield broke right in twain.

He swung again, and Olga knew she would die in that moment. She didn't care. She was glad, in fact. She would go into the earth, and this hard life would be over, and she was glad.

But then the soldier's sword fell to the ground, along with half his arm, and Vali was there.

She should have been dead. She wanted to be dead.

He shouted something at her, but she didn't understand him. She understood nothing.

~oOo~

Of all the raiders, and all the villagers from Vladimir's and Ivan's lands both, only twelve people remained alive: five raiders and seven villagers, eight men and four women. Vali had gotten those few safely back to the castle.

Then he had brokered a truce with Toomas, one that ceded all the land to the last prince and allowed the twelve of them to sail away. In a fishing boat modified with a strange sail. Over the open sea.

Vali had brought Olga back to understanding with the promise that Leif would pay for what he'd done.

She now understood one thing clearly, and one thing only: hatred. There was nothing left to her but that.

So she sat in the rickety boat with the few people left known to her in the world, and she watched the only world she'd ever known recede into the horizon. She would go to the place where Leif would meet his justice, or she would die on the way. There was nothing else.

The world kept its balance.

10

"She's strong, Jarl. A bitter bitch is what she is. I could soften her up, though, if you'd let me—"

When Åke flicked his hand, Igul, the fat sloven who did the jarl's darkest bidding, closed his mouth and let his sentence go unfinished.

"You'll not touch her. She is the God's-Eye, and she is mine to do with as I please. But you say she is not tamed."

"No, Jarl. She kicked out this morning, and tried to spit at me with her dry tongue."

Leif sent a sidelong glance to Calder. They had spoken this morning, and Leif had tried to convince the jarl's eldest son, Leif's own old friend, that Åke tempted the gods with his treatment of Brenna. He needed Calder to speak for her, because Åke was growing suspicious of Leif and his reservations. Thus far, he still had Calder's ear, but he was losing the jarl's.

He hadn't considered the consequences for himself if he lost favor completely. They would be dire, but that truth didn't change what he had to do.

They'd been back on Geitland soil for days, and Brenna was chained to the ground in a grimy hovel at the edge of the town. Her health and strength had deteriorated badly. Åke waited for her to break—to beg for food and water, for herbs to curb her fever, for anything, but to beg.

She never would, no matter what the jarl did, and Leif knew it well. She hadn't died already in Igul's brutal care because Leif himself had been sneaking her bits of bread and water, meat as he could get it, and herbs to make her well. More well. Slightly less ill.

He had Brenna's trust again, and it had been not so hard to win it back. When he told her that Vali still lived—he hadn't suggested any doubt on the matter; doubt would not give her strength—and that he'd done what he had to save them, she had simply believed him. Perhaps it was her desperate need of a friend, chained as she was and starving, or perhaps it was their years of familiarity and goodwill, but she had taken him at his word, and he felt her trust as a great boon.

Now he balanced on the edge of a blade, trying to stay in Åke's good graces and so have power to protect her and know where their opportunity might come to deliver justice unto the jarl, and trying to keep her alive and as strong as he could. But every time Leif spoke on the matter of Brenna now, Åke stared long at him, and Leif could feel in that questioning gaze the erosion of the jarl's trust.

It would do Brenna no good if Leif ended up chained beside her, or if his head turned up impaled on a pike.

He needed to convince her to yield. Not to beg, and not to give up. To yield in deed and not in spirit. To make time for them to wait for Vali's return—or to find their own moment—and destroy Åke for all the destruction he'd wrought.

Now Åke said, to no one in particular and everyone in general—his sons Calder, Eivind, and Ulv; Leif; Viger; and Igul—"Then she must desire more attention from her jarl." To Igul, he said, "Clean her up and bring her here. We'll see how strong she is."

~oOo~

In will, Brenna God's-Eye was strong as ever she had been. She stood before the jarl, in a dingy, rough-spun shift, her body and hair carelessly washed, leaving soft swipes of mud and grim over her skin, her matted hair a damp clump. She was shackled at the wrists and neck, and Igul held a chain from her neck like a leash.

Åke sat in a grand chair covered in furs, a chair that Olga would have called a throne.

But Brenna's back was straight as a spear. Her head was high, as if she had no care for the vicious shackle tearing at her flesh below it. Her eyes were fiery sharp. She had a habit in battle of staring with her eyes somehow widened in the center and tightened at their outside points. The effect made it seem as though she were focusing her strange right eye particularly on her target. Her warrior face. Leif had seen men falter at that look before she had as much as lifted her sword.

She turned it now on Jarl Åke.

"I abjure you," she snarled, spitting each word like a weapon itself.

Åke had been behaving as a long-suffering jarl who only wanted to put unpleasantness behind them. He had offered to ease Brenna's hardships by making her his thrall again. Enslaving her anew in exchange for a fresh oath of fealty.

It was that so-called mercy that Brenna had spat back at him.

Åke gave up the pretense of kindness and surged forward in his chair. "What power do you have to abjure me? I am your jarl!"

"No, you are not," the brave shieldmaiden replied. She might have been standing before them with her sword and shield at the ready, there was so much confident strength in those words, even as they came from a throat gone too long with too little to wet it.

The room crackled with tension, until Åke sat back with a sigh and relaxed his posture again. "You will break, Brenna God's-Eye. And I will watch it happen. You know where to take her." The last sentence, he'd spoken to Igul, who stepped forward, rattling the chain by which Brenna was tethered.

Åke meant her to go to the dark room, where he perpetrated torture and torment on people he'd deemed unworthy to be judged at the thing. Shocked, Leif stood. "Jarl Åke."

Every eye in the hall turned to him. The jarl's narrowed dangerously. "You have something more to say, Leif?"

In that room, Brenna would be broken. No one could withstand the agonies arrayed there. He had to save her from that. He took a breath and, through sheer will, kept his voice steady. "She is the God's-Eye. Do you not invite the gods' displeasure to do her harm?"

This was a refrain Leif had sung often since he'd returned to the jarl's company, and he knew its power was weakening, but he had no stronger course that might hold sway. Calder was still moved by such an argument, and his father still gave it heed. Fear of the gods was a powerful deterrent.

Åke turned back to Brenna before he answered. With his eyes on the shieldmaiden, he said. "So you say. Yet the gods gave her to me, and she abandoned her oath. She lay with my enemy and wed him. The gods agree that such disloyalty must be punished."

Fear of the gods had lost its power, then. Leif had lost his best argument for Brenna's safety. And, he knew, he had lost the jarl's favor as well.

Åke nodded at Igul. "Take her and prepare her. I think the rods will do. Let us see the limit of the God's-Eye's strength."

The rods. Leif's stomach rolled at the thought of what the jarl might want done with those.

As Igul yanked Brenna away, Leif managed to meet her eyes for a scant moment. Before her face settled into its stoicism, he saw a flash of fear.

~oOo~

Åke called Leif to join him and his sons and witness the God's-Eye's undoing. Leif knew the jarl meant it as a punishment, and it would indeed be one, but Leif would have asked to go in any event. He had failed in his efforts to save Brenna. He would not spare himself the full knowledge of the consequences of his failure.

She was stripped and bound prone to the large oaken table in the center of the dark room, a table that had gone dark and soft soaking in the blood of others bound to it.

Igul had stoked the fire, and iron rods stuck out from it like bristles. Leif's heart knew more weight than it could carry, but he settled his eyes on Brenna's bare back, bruised and dirty, and sickly thin. He would not look away.

Åke went to the table and bent down near Brenna's face. She stared at him, stoic and defiant even now.

"You will break, Brenna God's-Eye. You will beg for my mercy."

Brenna simply stared.

"Leif," Åke said as he stood back, and at that, Brenna flinched, making her bonds clank and clatter.

Leif flinched as well. Åke wanted him to torture her. This he would not, could not, do. There was no way to allay the pain Åke's chosen torment would cause her. He could not make it easier by being the one to wield the rods, and he could not be the one to cause the kind of pain she faced.

He would fight before he caused her any more hurt than he already had.

In this dark room with Leif and Brenna stood Åke, Calder, Eivind, Ulv, Viger, and Igul. Ulv, the youngest of Åke's grown sons, was gentler than his father and older brothers, and he seemed pale and ill at the prospect of what was about to happen, but Leif did not think he could count on Ulv to turn on his father now. Perhaps he would be slow to fight, but he would not turn—and if his father were attacked, he would not be so slow to fight at all.

Brenna was chained and naked. Even were she willing—and he knew well she would be willing—she was not able.

Everyone was without sword or axe or shield, but the room was full of weapons. Leif could kill Åke first, and that at least would be accomplished. Then he would have to fight five men, four of whom were young and strong trained warriors. He could, at best, hope to kill two, maybe three before he was killed himself. And then Brenna would be left to the whim of the survivors.

Prepared to fight, Leif first tried talk. "Åke, no."

The jarl showed tired contempt in his eyes. "You would deny me?"

Choosing his words carefully, Leif replied, "I would ask you, as one who loves you as a son loves a father, please do not ask this of me. I have chosen you and renewed my oath, but it was you who made the God's-Eye my friend."

Åke stared long and hard, and Leif returned the look, scanning his image of the room in his mind's eye and choosing the weapon he would grab and shove into the soft meat of the old man's bearded chin.

Then the jarl sighed and gave Leif something that might have been meant to be a smile. "Viger, then. Would you deny me as well?"

"No, Jarl. I serve your will."

Relieved of that burden, Leif focused on the other. He made himself watch as red-hot iron rods were laid across Brenna's fair back, and left to rest there until the glow had faded. One after another, until her back was a ladder of long chasms from her shoulders to below her waist.

She twitched and flinched, and every muscle in her body flexed to complete tension, but she never screamed. She seemed to swoon as the last rod, the fifth rod, rested on her skin, but she never screamed.

Åke had not broken her. But he would kill her if she wouldn't bend.

"Enough!" Åke barked, and Viger, looking ill and sad, lifted the final rod. "Take her back to her pen."

The jarl turned and stormed from the room. His sons and Leif silently followed him out.

~oOo~

Leif convinced Brenna to bend. He convinced her to yield and take on the yoke of the thrall once more.

It was that or see her be killed as Åke continually tried and failed to break her.

Åke had promised to be gentle with her, to heal her and feed her and bring her back into his hall to serve him as she first had. But that had been before the rods.

Instead, he left her in her dark prison, chained all the night, and in the day he put her to the lowest women's work there was. Åke had the shackle around her neck closed at the forge. She wore it always, even as she worked.

At Leif's urging, Calder had convinced his father to allow her salve to heal her burns, and a straw mat to lie on.

And that had been the frayed end of Leif's influence. Since, he had been set aside. Not pushed out, but not brought close, either.

No longer family.

But he stayed as close as he could, and he searched the hall for any who might also see Åke as he was. There were stirrings of concern, among freemen and thralls alike; many were unsettled the see the God's-Eye brought so low, and some worried that Odin would be displeased and bring that down on Geitland and all loyal to Åke.

But others saw Brenna's abasement as a testament to Åke's power and his favor with the gods.

He had long been a powerful jarl, and before that he was a great warrior. He had led, and then sent, countless successful and storied raids. He welcomed shieldmaidens into his ranks as equals in a number like few other jarls, and all of his warriors had grown rich in their fealty to him.

Åke had been a great man once. But no longer. Now, he was only powerful. Yet that power was persuasive.

As the days passed, became weeks, and Vali did not come, as Brenna's wounds began to heal under her shackle, Leif began to lose his last shred of hope that Åke would be unseated.

~oOo~

Settled in his victory over Snorri and his triumph over the God's-Eye, and with his seer portending a prosperous future, Åke sent his raiders out, with Calder, Eivind, and even Ulv sailing.

He kept Leif back, making an ostentatiously halfhearted statement that he needed his trusted advisor with him. It was a punishment, Leif knew; and Åke knew he knew. The whole hall knew.

But Leif was glad. He didn't see how he could've left Geitland and Brenna, and even if he had, he doubted he would have returned home from a raid this time. He had lost his lifelong friends.

Of all the losses he had suffered, it was the least.

~oOo~

What a beautiful sight was the look in Åke's eyes, on his whole face, when his doom sailed in from the north. Leif would never forget it.

Viger, who had been injured in a drunken squabble the night before the raiders set sail and had stayed back as well, ran into the hall a few days later, shouting that three longships sailed into Geitland, ships teeming with warriors and bearing the colors of Jarl Snorri Thorsson, and that Vali Storm-Wolf himself stood at the prow of the center ship.

Leif was in the hall. Åke didn't trust him enough to keep him close, but didn't trust him enough to let him go far, either. So he was there to see the recognition in the jarl's eyes that he could not win a battle with the Storm-Wolf. He had sent all his best warriors out to raid, to fill his coffers for the war he planned nearer to home, where he meant to oust Jarl Ivar and Jarl Finn as well and make himself king.

He recovered quickly and ordered what men he had left out to meet the ships, and then he flew from his chair and at Leif. When the old man grabbed him by his tunic, Leif didn't resist. He simply met his eyes. It was not time yet to reveal his true allegiance. There was Brenna to think about.

Brenna God's-Eye, the great shieldmaiden, favored of the Allfather, slaving in the stables.

"You said he was dead! You said you killed him! You swore to me!"

"I did not swear, Jarl. I thought I killed him. I was mistaken." And all thanks to the gods for that.

Åke drew his dagger from its sheath on his hip. It was an ornamental piece, encrusted in jewels. An affect more than a weapon, but its point was sharp. He set it against Leif's chest, over a heart already covered in scars. "I treated you like a son. I loved you like a son. But you are a traitor. An oathbreaker."

"No, Åke. I am not."

Viger came back into the hall, the limp that had kept him from the raid barely noticeable now. "Vali calls you out, Jarl. He challenges you to single combat."

Leif had not expected that. He'd expected his hotheaded friend to leap from the ship and charge up, axes swinging.

He saw his chance. To turn everything around. To bring Vali and Brenna back together. To give them their vengeance on

Åke. To save Geitland from his depraved ambition. And, perhaps, to redeem himself in the eyes of his true friends.

"I will fight for you, Åke. Let me prove to you my loyalty."

Åke stepped back. "You will bring me the head of the wolf?"

"You will never again have cause to doubt my fealty, Jarl Åke Ivarsson."

"Make it so, Leif Olavsson, son of my friend. Son of my heart."

Leif nodded, gathered his sword from the wall near the door, and went out to face Vali, his true friend, in single combat. Viger came with him, carrying Leif's shield.

Vali had brought with him an army; his men were arrayed across the pier and the shore around it, all the way back into the sea. At the top of the berm stood Åke's men: half the number, at best. Leif walked through them, toward his friend, who stood at the cross of the piers, bare-chested and unshielded, as always, his great axes in his hands.

"Vali Storm-Wolf," he called. "Jarl Åke accepts your challenge and sends me, Leif Olavsson, as his champion."

If Vali were surprised at that, he didn't show it. "I will gladly kill you, Leif, for the hurts and betrayals you have made against me and mine. But I will see Åke on my axe this day, whether he stands like a man in combat, or dies a coward's death instead."

Åke had become a coward; he could face no greater death, no matter what. Leif smiled. "I understand. I would offer another plan."

He spun and swung his sword, opening Viger's throat. The cut was swift and clean, and Viger simply stood there, looking shocked, holding Leif's shield, while blood washed down his chest.

Before he finally fell, before Åke's men around him had understood the turn of events, Leif turned back to Vali. "I am your friend, Vali. Always have I been."

He couldn't wait to see if his friend were persuaded; when Viger fell, Åke's men shook off their surprise, and they turned their weapons on Leif.

As he fought for his life, a shadow fell over him. Vali was at his side.

~oOo~

The men and women Leif fought that day were not Åke's best raiders. They were the old, the young, and the lame—the weary, the untested, and the impaired. They had been known to him all his life, or all of theirs. They were his friends, his clansmen. He had trained them, or been trained by them. He had supped and drunk with them. Laughed with them. Observed the rituals with them. They were the citizens of Geitland, his home, and he had no wish to lay waste here.

There were few among them he had any wish to kill.

But they were loyal to Åke, and he was no longer. He was their enemy; therefore, they were his. He stayed on the defensive, making every effort not to attack, but he cut them down when they came at him.

Old Egill whooped a battle cry and charged at Leif, his ancient axe high, and his long-used voice cracked and weak. Leif knocked the axe easily away and sank his sword into the elder's chest.

Egill had been old in Leif's father's time. But he had been a powerful warrior in days long past. It was told that he, in his hale peak, had killed eleven men at once, using only his bare hands and his teeth.

Leif caught him and held him in his arms while the battle—it was no battle, truly, but a massacre instead—boiled around them. He laid the old man on the ground and pulled his blade free. Then he crouched low and bent to Egill's ear.

"You have achieved Valhalla, great old one. Good travels to you."

Egill smiled. Blood oozed, and then poured, from his toothless mouth, and he closed his eyes.

Leif doubted he would see Valhalla should he die in this bloodbath. Vali's much greater, stronger force had come up over the berm and overrun a town defended by those not strong enough to raid. There was no valor to be found for him here, he knew.

But neither was there a choice. Åke had to fall, as did anyone who might prevent it. There was valor, there was righteousness, in bringing Åke down. That, he also knew.

When Leif stood, Vali was watching him. The Storm-Wolf's eyes held neither love nor affection for him, but he gave Leif a single nod and charged on toward the hall, where cowered the jarl.

Åke had been defeated before Vali's boots had hit land.

~oOo~

Two days later, Leif stood again on the pier and watched as Vali and Brenna and a score or so of Vali's men sailed away in a small karve, leaving his great ships moored where they were.

Jarl Vali Storm-Wolf, lord now over the lands that had been Snorri Thorsson's.

And Jarl Leif Olavsson, who claimed Åke's lands.

The rituals and sacrifices had been observed to ask the gods to favor this new world.

Åke was dead, on Vali's axe. Brenna was freed and restored to herself and her husband. They had had their revenge. Most of Vali's men had stayed behind, volunteering to wait in preparation for the return of the raiders, when Åke's sons would learn of the change in their family's circumstance, and the new Jarl Leif would fight his first battle.

Vali had not stayed. He wanted Brenna far away from this place, and Leif agreed. She had suffered enough. She needed to heal and grow strong again.

Leif had shown Åke his true fealty. He and Vali were allies, and he was Vali's true friend.

But Vali was not his.

He blamed Leif for Brenna's abasement and injury. He blamed him for every horror she'd withstood, every new scar on her body. He blamed him for the deaths of their friends and the loss of their homes in Estland. He blamed him, and he did not trust him. He swore he would never trust him again.

But Brenna trusted him, and she held great sway over her husband. Leif held out a hope that Vali would see that he had done the best he could, that all he had done had been in the interest of his love for them. That his wife would make him see, and that someday they would again be friends.

Because Olga was in Karlsa, Vali's home. She had survived, and she had sailed west with Vali and the others. She was only two days' sail away from him. If Vali could be made a friend again, perhaps she could be as well. She was alive, and she was close.

Perhaps he had not lost her after all.

11

Olga fed another log into the pit and held her hands over the blossoming flame. Karlsa was well north of her homeland, and even what they called summer here was cold to her, especially now, at its end.

At Vali's behest, she had taken a smallish hut near the center of town, what had been Sven's home and workplace. The healer she'd helped in that long-ago time when the raiders had come, when Leif and Vali and Brenna had overrun her world, had been killed at sea, on the voyage home.

All of Vali's friends from the raid had been killed at sea. The dark man Leif had treated like a good friend, whom she knew to be his jarl's eldest son, had ordered his men to kill them all.

It was men like these Leif had chosen over his true friends. Over her. And she was alone in the world because of his choice.

Not quite alone. Jakob stirred and sat up, looking sweetly disoriented as he woke. His chestnut mop showed the restless night he'd had; chunks of hair stood nearly straight on his head. He shivered and buried his arms under his fur.

"Good morning, *kullake*. There will be porridge soon, and warm milk."

The boy grunted and rubbed his eyes.

Jakob had fourteen years—the same as Kalju. Without making a plan to do so, Olga had taken him into her care. If she was replacing her brothers with him, she hadn't meant to, precisely. But the lost boy had filled part of an aching emptiness inside her.

It was only Olga and Jakob, and Jaan, Hans, and Georg, who had survived the horrors that the last year had brought to their people. Anna and Eha had died during their long, hard voyage to this strange place. All the others had died by the raiders' hands or in the bloodshed after their abandonment.

Jaan was away now, fighting Vali's vengeance and their own, and the others were left among fair-haired giants who didn't know what to make of them.

There had been fighting again immediately after they had finally, finally set their feet on the ground, when Vali and the others, weak though they were, had exhorted the people here to rise up against their leaders. Olga didn't understand much; she had been ill and weak and lost in the world—she still was all those things—but Åke had taken Karlsa during the time Vali had been away, and he had left a band of men in charge. They had not treated the people here well.

And then Vali had learned that none of his friends from the raid had come home.

While his cheeks were still carved with hunger, Vali had stormed the hall here, his clansmen at his back. Olga had yanked Jakob back from joining them, and she had hidden with him under a cart. He was young and ill, and he had almost drowned on the voyage. She could not lose another boy to this madness.

She had had enough of war and blood and loss. Enough.

With the people of Karlsa in charge of their home again, their little band of refugees had taken a moment to be healed. They had been fed and warmed and rested. The people here treated Vali like a hero and a savior. Like a god. And his friends, even the strange ones from across the sea, were havened in that esteem.

Then they had planned their attack on Geitland, and Vali and most of the strong men and women in town had sailed away.

With Vali gone, Olga noticed more cautious looks among the Karlsa people, especially since Vali had announced that she was a healer and set her up in Sven's old house before he'd left. She could see in their eyes that they thought her a witch. She had heard them use the word *völva*, and she had learned that it meant something like it.

But there were no witches in her world—not in the way these people meant it. There was no seeing beyond what could be seen when one looked closely, no knowing beyond that which one could know when one opened all of one's senses.

No one had yet come to her for healing, even though there was no other healer or midwife in the town. It was perhaps early yet to despair, but despair sat always on the doorstep of Olga's heart now, and she feared that she might be wholly dependent on Vali for all the rest of her days.

Jakob rose and shuffled to the table, and Olga ladled a bowl of barley porridge and set it before him. As he shoveled spoons of it into his mouth, she combed her fingers through his wild, dark hair. Curly, like Anton's. And like Mihkel, another brother she'd lost.

"You slept badly," she observed as she filled a bowl for herself and sat across the rough table.

He paused with the spoon caught between the bowl and his mouth, and he met her eyes. "Did I bother you?"

"No. I didn't sleep, either. The night is...difficult."

He nodded. "The sounds are wrong. And too many."

"Yes." Karlsa was much bigger than their little village, and even with most of the men away, people kept later hours.

Long past deep dark, people yet moved around. Olga supposed that had to do with the how much of night there was. The hours of daylight seemed already to be dwindling quickly, and Orm had told her that in the deep midwinter, almost the full day would be spent with no greater light than twilight—and that in midsummer the opposite was true, and the sun barely set.

In her world, the winter nights and summer days were long, also, but not such as this. Everything about this world was different. This was not the balance that Olga knew.

It was that lack of balance more than the night sounds that kept Olga awake. It was fear that left her curled under furs in a strange house in a strange town. It was the abject loss of all she knew. It was the image behind her closed eyes of her own knife in her brother's melting chest, of Anton's blood gushing at her feet as she fought to save herself for no other reason than instinct. It was the remembered feeling of the fireplace stones abrading her face as the raider took her, a taking so very much worse than any other like it she'd experienced, because it would not have happened if she had not been betrayed and abandoned.

It was the knowing that she had given herself, and all the love she had, to a man who had used her, who had tricked her, who had connived to have her give herself to him and then left her to abasement and loss.

What Leif had done was the worst abuse she had ever suffered. It had emptied her, and it had broken her.

That was what kept her awake all the night.

~oOo~

"Here." Nodding to Rikke to take the bowl of mess away, Olga held out a cup to Brenna. "Try this."

Brenna pushed it away. "I cannot."

"You must keep nourishment, daughter." Brenna's mother, Dagmar, took the cup from Olga and sat on the edge of the bed, holding the cup up to Brenna's lips. Brenna turned from it like a petulant child.

The great shieldmaiden was always a difficult patient—too stoic and silent when her pain was truly terrible, and sulky when it was only unpleasant.

"I will simply heave it into the bowl again!" Looking past her mother, she sent pleading eyes to Olga. "This is so much harder than the first time."

That was true. Many days, her sickness with this child had her too weak to stand. Olga sat on the bed, too, and set her hand on Brenna's foot, with the furs between them. "It will be better soon, I promise. Remember that before it passed in weeks, and you say that you were seeded weeks ago."

Dagmar nodded. "Oili said it would be a hard carrying, but a strong daughter grows inside you."

Brenna and Vali had returned to Karlsa victorious, but without most of their fleet. They had arrived in a smaller ship, and Brenna's mother had been with them. Most of the warriors who had left Karlsa to fight Åke had stayed behind after their victory, to aid Leif in another coming battle.

There was more fighting to be done, but Vali had put Geitland at his back and brought Brenna home. And more that Olga didn't understand: Brenna had forgiven Leif. Vali had not, but they were allies again. And both men were jarls. Vali had come home as lord of this place, and the people here rejoiced.

Olga thought of the princes of her world and the jarl she'd known of this one, and she couldn't say that she was pleased to find her friend so elevated. There was something in such power that twisted men into monsters.

That Leif lived and was a jarl as well, that he was friend to Brenna and no enemy to Vali, confounded her. He was certainly an enemy to her. She would kill him happily, sneak up to his bed in the middle of the night and slide a blade into his chest, through the scars and into his black heart.

Brenna had come to Karlsa emaciated and badly scarred—and sure she was pregnant, even though she and Vali had been reunited barely more than a week, because a seer had told her so. Olga had been deeply skeptical that, after such horrible trauma as Brenna had clearly experienced, she could have been seeded, and know it, in so short a time. Not by Vali, at any rate.

But she had assured Olga that no one had violated her in that way. And she had, indeed, soon shown the signs of a babe growing. The seer had seen true.

Olga wasn't quite sure what to make of that. The seer had also been correct, so far, about the difficulty of the carrying, but Olga couldn't say whether that was true because it was true or because Brenna had expected it to be so.

At any rate, it was very difficult to keep food in her. Olga had tried every concoction she knew. Some of the growing things in Karlsa were familiar to her and others not. No one here had the full knowledge of a healer, so she had relied on the few who could and would give her some insights, and she had tested others on herself—and made herself ill a few times in the process.

Since Vali and Brenna's return to Karlsa, Olga and Jakob had found the way easier for them. They were true good friends to the beloved jarl and his storied wife, and, again, they found protection and respect under his aegis. She was gaining custom among the people, and Jakob had found apprentice work with a shipbuilder.

Olga had found something to settle her broken spirit, too, with her friends home. Taking care of Brenna—and of Vali, who was deeply anxious for his wife and struggling not to overwhelm her with his care—had given her a thing to focus on. Something she could do. Something to make right and well.

It didn't heal her, but it eased her, and that was enough. She had survived again and again when nearly all others had not, and when she wished she had not. She had survived the torture and servitude of her marriage. She had survived the pillaging of the coastal village. She had survived the raiders' camp. The betrayal of the castle. The burning of the inland village and the deaths of her brothers. The sea voyage in the fishing boat.

She lost and lost and lost, and she lived on. She had finally lost herself, and yet she lived on.

If the earth was not yet ready for her, then at least she had her friends to care for and fill her days. At least she could feel the ease of their love and know that there was yet balance in the world for some.

Brenna took a tremulous sip of the tea Olga had brewed for her. She pulled back, a light frown creasing her brow. "It's hot but tastes...cold. Like the tea you made before, when my son made me ill."

Olga smiled. "Yes. It's not the same mint as home, but it's close, and I found a good winter berry—still young, but ripe. And alfalfa. The mint and berry will soothe, and the alfalfa will nourish. Go slowly, but it should stay."

Brenna smiled and took another, more confident sip. "It's good. Thank you."

This, at least, Olga still had: The power to make others well. A boy to care for. Friends who sought her comfort.

She survived because she was yet needed, and that was enough. It let sleep dance over her mind at night, in the interludes between despair and ill dreams.

~oOo~

Later, she left Brenna resting and went out to the hall, where Vali was seated in a massive, fur-covered chair like a throne, listening to people air their concerns, pleas, and grievances. She sat along the side of the room, beyond the notice of the others, and watched.

He seemed lonely, sitting alone, an empty chair at his side, where Brenna would have sat if she hadn't swooned earlier. Nearby, but not quite with him, stood Orm, the only of his friends still in Karlsa. The few other friends he had left—Bjarke, Harald, and Astrid, who was not of Karlsa—had stayed behind in Geitland to assist Leif. All other of his friends had been killed.

His friends among Olga's last people, Hans and Georg, had stayed in Geitland, too. Jaan was here, but he was young and not of these people and so did not offer advice to Vali. Only friendship and loyalty. He was elsewhere, but Olga knew he wouldn't be far.

Vali sat before his clansmen and women and seemed alone and unhappy.

Olga was glad to see it. She thought that if he were too comfortable on that fur-covered throne, he would cease to be the man she knew. The man she trusted. And she had little trust left in her.

There was an interesting fairness in the way he did things, a fairness that his people appeared to expect. He didn't make pronouncements. Instead, he offered his opinion—often glancing at Orm before he did so, and not infrequently glancing at the curtain through which his wife lay in their private quarters—and the people before him agreed, or spoke another opinion. And then there was discussion before a thing was decided.

This was not the way of things in Olga's world, where princes had made dicta and the people had bowed under their weight.

If she had never heard of Åke, perhaps she might have been moved by this balance. But she had heard of Åke. She had suffered because of him, and she knew that power in this world was no different from power anywhere. It twisted and warped and wrung the good away.

The taste of Olga's thoughts was now always bitter and cold.

~oOo~

When the business was done, the people in the hall didn't leave. They simply made themselves comfortable, and slave women brought food and drink. Vali left his lonely throne and came directly to Olga. She hadn't realized that he had noticed her.

"How fares she?"

"She is better. She had some rich tea and kept it, and now she's sleeping. This time of sickness will pass, Vali. As it did before."

He sat at her side, and Olga could stop craning her neck to see the giant's face. Worry creased it deeply. "What if what happened...what if she's yet hurt inside? What if this babe hurts her?"

That was a possibility. The early birth of their son and the trauma that had brought it on might have made scars where

Olga couldn't see. But she didn't need to say that to Vali; he already knew, as did Brenna. She smiled and laid her hand over his. "Your seer said there would be many children, and that this one would be strong. Put your faith in that, and in Brenna's own great strength."

He smiled and gave her a grateful nod.

It didn't matter what Olga believed. Vali and Brenna believed in gods and in otherworldly knowing, and that faith gave them ease now.

Not until her own spirit had been broken had Olga begun to understand the power of such belief. For her, there was only the one world, and it had gone end over end. She could not be eased by promises. She had no faith to hold her while her world spun out of balance.

A slave girl came with a jug and cups, and Vali nodded. She filled a cup and handed it to him, then offered one to Olga. When Olga smiled and shook her head, the girl dipped her own head in a shy bow and receded from them, out of Vali's notice as soon as he had taken his cup.

Olga watched her go, feeling sad—and disappointed, too. She had thought her friend, who had freed her and had made Prince Vladimir's subjects his equals, better than to keep slaves, and it grated at her whenever she saw him or Brenna think so little of those they kept in bondage.

Vali took a draught from the horn cup and then cocked his head at Olga, his long braid swinging over his shoulder. "You frown, my friend."

"Brenna was a slave. She bears the scars of shackles. Why do you keep others enslaved?"

Now he frowned. "It is different for Holmfrid than it was for Brenna."

"You know her name."

"Of course I know her name. She serves me."

"How is it different for her? Brenna served, too."

Olga could see that she was causing Vali irritation, and she could see him struggle and succeed to master it. He answered calmly. "Holmfrid was born into her life."

"We are all born into our life."

Now his irritation showed, and his voice honed to a sharp edge. "And hers is the life of a slave. Her father and mother are slaves. Their parents were slaves. Those who are slaves here are born into it, or they have been vanquished in battle. That is, as you say, the way of things."

Vanquished in battle or dragged from their plundered homes. To Vali's people, there seemed to be no difference. Olga shook her head. "There is no way of things. There are only people—being good, or being bad."

If her refutation of her own way of thinking surprised him, he didn't make it known. "And I am bad because I do things as they have always been done?"

"You are not good because of it." It was a baldly bold statement to make to a powerful man, but Olga was speaking to her friend, not to the Jarl of Karlsa.

He raised his eyebrows in surprise at her frankness, however, and then he frowned more deeply than before. "Those in thrall here are not ill-treated. That was the case in Snorri's time, and it will be in mine. Their work is no more taxing than any other's. They have food and comfort, family and friends."

"But they don't choose. They are not free."

"And were you? Whatever you were called, were you free, under a prince who took all you made as toll and let you starve?"

"I was free when I was in the castle. With you and Brenna and—" she stopped before she uttered that other name, and she dropped her head.

He set his cupped his hand over her cheek and lifted her head so that their eyes met again. His expression had softened. "And you are now. Always will you be." With a sigh that had the lilt of indulgence, he added, "It is not so easy a thing to free so many people. Slaves have value to their masters, in silver and gold. And I am no prince, who simply decides and decrees. But I will speak with Brenna and Orm. Perhaps there is a way to change our ways."

Vali kissed her cheek and stood. Taking his leave with a nod, he headed through the woven curtain and back to his wife.

Olga thought that perhaps the Jarl of Karlsa might resist the warp of power after all.

12

Astrid moved her attacker and sat back, smiling smugly. Leif leaned on his elbows and studied the board. She had left a path open for his king to advance toward safety, and she wouldn't have done so without a plan.

"Usch!" Astrid grumbled. "Every move you quibble at all day."

That was a gross exaggeration. He took minutes, not hours, to move. But Astrid rarely paused between the end of his move and the end of her own.

Leif looked up at his opponent and smirked. "Hnefatafl is a game of strategy, my friend. It is not a race."

She rolled her eyes. "You play like a jarl, not a warrior."

Still studying the board, he ignored that gibe and discovered the likely intent of her next move. It was a good one, well obscured, but he blocked it with one of his lesser pieces, capturing one of her men and creating another line of defense for his king in the process. Before he lifted his hand away from the board, he glanced up and saw her scowling at it.

"Jarls are jarls because they win," he chuckled.

"You are not so close to victory yet," she rejoined and captured a piece he had exposed. She had blocked his king on three sides, and she leaned in with a brash smirk. "Too much thinking makes you slow."

Before he could respond, Harald and Bjarke came into the hall. They had been out riding along the coast, looking for signs that Calder and the raiding ships had returned.

Weeks had passed since Vali and Brenna had left Geitland. The summer had ended, and the ships were not yet back. Last summer, a late raid had meant dark schemes from Åke and his eldest son, but Leif had heard no such plans for this raid—though it was true he had not been in the inner circle as it had been planned.

Still, any stratagems in play were moot now, with Åke dead, and if they did not return soon, the weather would become too treacherous to sail at all—and they could not know what awaited them upon their arrival home.

Leif had Vali's two hundred warriors still in Geitland, waiting to break the last of Åke's men. The sides would likely be well matched, but Leif had used these weeks to prepare for a battle Calder would not see coming. They were well fortified and well armed, well rested and well trained. They were prepared for a pitched battle, but Leif did not expect one.

He had also used these weeks to smooth the worries of the Geitland people about the death of Åke and his own transition to the role of jarl. He was well liked and respected among his people, but he had also turned on their jarl, and many of their own had been killed in that fighting.

It was his fortune that Åke had bestowed most of his favor on his warriors and had had little regard for common freemen. Those most loyal to the dead jarl were off raiding; it had not been much for Leif to show the common people that he would give them heed Åke had not.

Convincing those who had been in Estland with him, who had been left behind, left for dead—that had been the greater challenge.

Astrid, his own clanswoman, had spat at his feet when she'd first seen him after Vali's force had overtaken Åke's, even though Leif had fought with them. Harald and Bjarke were Vali's clansmen, and they would happily have seen Leif killed.

They were all three his chief advisors now. Harald and Bjarke would, he knew, be leaving for Karlsa with the rest of Vali's warriors as soon as Calder had been defeated, but in the matter of that coming battle, Leif had brought them to his inner circle. He and Astrid knew Calder well. Harald and Bjarke still had vengeance to deal. As did Astrid, who had been left for dead in Estland because she had stood up to Åke and fought to protect her friends.

Leif had won them by bringing them close. Or, more apt, he was winning them.

Astrid had spat at his feet again when he'd first asked if she would sit and speak with him. Feeling he deserved her scorn, even if his intent had been good, he'd not been offended—or dissuaded. With the specter looming of a fight with Calder and his brothers, she had seen the need to be part of the planning, and she'd begrudgingly agreed to listen and to speak. The same reasoning had brought Harald and Bjarke into his hall, though they both remained quick to argue with him, often for the sole sake of the argument.

He thought it good to have advisors who didn't quite trust him. If he gained their agreement, then he knew his plan was good. People who feared a leader could not be counted on to give good advice. It was a truth that Åke had forgotten. Leif meant to remember it always.

Harald and Bjarke came to the table where Leif and Astrid had been playing their game, and the slave girl Vifrid emerged from the shadows with mead for all. While she poured, Leif raised his eyebrows at Bjarke, the senior of the two, urging him to speak.

"There is word of the ships approaching. These still winds do them no service, but even at the oar, tomorrow or the next day will have them ashore."

"At last!" Astrid huffed. "My axe grows dull with waiting."

Bjarke grinned. "Then whet it, shieldmaiden. You will spill the blood of the traitors soon."

Leif saw his move on the board and swept his king free, ending the game. Astrid made a sound of angry surprise, and Harald and Bjarke laughed.

"Patience and forethought, my friend," Leif said, setting his king on the table before him. "There is victory in wisdom."

With another angry grunt, Astrid swung her arm and knocked the pieces to the floor.

~oOo~

When Calder's ships approached, Leif stood just back from the pier, with Astrid, Bjarke, and Harald behind him. Arrayed to either side were more than two hundred warriors, archers at the front line. Behind the archers, several rows of warriors held shield and blade at the ready.

At the moment that the ships were close enough that those ashore could discern the figure of Calder standing at the prow of the lead vessel, when they were too close to change course and flee, Astrid began to beat her axe against her shield. The others picked up her tempo, and within the space of a few heartbeats, the air trembled with the thunder of looming war.

Leif called, "ARCHERS!" and his bowmen raised their weapons.

"NOCK!" he shouted, and each archer pulled an arrow from his quiver and set it.

Leif believed he saw Calder's expression change, saw his surprise, his shock, as he comprehended the implications of the vista before him. He turned and shouted a command.

"DRAW!" Leif yelled. Under the thunder of the beaten shields, the creak of dozens of gut-strung bows pulled back at once resounded. Knowing their targets, they all aimed.

"LOOSE!"

Dozens of arrows released into the sky, following the same great arc, and landing in the ships, well before most of the raiders aboard had hidden themselves under the shelter of their shields. Leif heard the screams and splashes of men felled by that rain of death.

"ALL HOLD!" Leif called, and the archers waited, their hands at their quivers.

Two of the ships shifted toward the open shore, away from the piers, and men began to jump into the water before they could run on the bottom. Around him, Leif could feel the tense anticipation of his warriors, but he didn't release them.

Calder stayed at the prow of his ship, and Leif kept most of his focus on that one man. For that, he saw Calder's archers stand in his ship and draw while the others were still swimming and slogging to the shore.

"SHIELDS UP!" he called, and the drumming went silent. An oaken ceiling blotted the sun just before arrows pelted down.

In the following silence, Leif shouted "ARCHERS AT WILL! WARRIORS CHARGE!" The day exploded in riotous noise as his warriors whooped and rushed toward the shore, and

Calder's splashed up. Archers from earth and water sent arrows into the air.

And still Calder stood in his ship. By now he was close enough that Leif could see his old friend staring at him.

Too late, he heard the light shriek of an arrow, and then the sun disappeared as a shield nearly flew before his head. The arrow struck wood, and at his side, Astrid muttered, "Are you entranced? You keep me from the fight."

"Go. But see to it that Åke's sons survive. And I want Calder myself."

The shieldmaiden gave him a skeptical look, but she agreed with a tip of her head and charged down the berm, her warrior's cry cutting through the chaos.

Leif walked forward, using his sword and shield only to block the few blows that came his way. He would let his warriors have the kills; he wanted only one. The fight was lopsided, and as he stepped onto the pier, he wondered if this feeling he had, of sad dissatisfaction, were anything like what Calder had felt as he'd carried out his father's command to sack the castle. To raid their own people, their friends and their clansmen.

"Leif," Calder called down as his ship settled at the pier, the only of the three to do so. Still aboard with him were archers and rowers, but neither of his brothers. They must have each taken command of a vessel.

"Calder." He sheathed his sword; Calder had not yet drawn his, and the pier was a short distance from the fighting, so he wasn't in immediate danger. His shield he kept at the ready, a guard against the few archers still aboard with Calder.

But then Calder gestured with his hand, a sign of release, and the rest of the men in the ship jumped out and into the fray.

He came down from the prow. "My father?"

Leif looked back at the piked skull at the end of the pier. Brenna had wanted Åke's head on a pike to greet Calder on his return. But the raiders had been weeks away, and animals and the elements had had their way in the meanwhile. Scant shreds of flesh were left on the bone.

"If he was worthy of Valhalla, he is there," he said, turning back to Åke's son.

"You think he was not?"

"I think it is for the gods to judge."

"His death?"

Leif shook his head. "Craven. Shielding himself behind a shackled slave."

Calder's mouth twisted into an ugly shadow of a grin. "You mean the God's-Eye. Hardly a mere slave. Was it you?"

"No. It was Vali Storm-Wolf."

A cocked eyebrow. "You told my father you killed him."

"I lied."

Calder grabbed a shield from the wale of the ship and leapt onto the pier, and the two men faced each other, no greater distance between them than the joined lengths of their swords, had they been drawn.

"Lies and sneak attacks. Not like you, my friend." With a nod past Leif's shoulder, to the battle behind him, Calder said, "Yet your ambush has been successful."

Rather than take his eyes from Calder and look, Leif merely nodded. He could tell by the sound alone that the fight was coming to its end already, and such a fast conclusion could mean one thing only.

"Do you yield?" he asked, and Calder laughed and drew his sword. Leif drew his as well.

"Never. I will kill you for a traitor and display *your* head at the pier for all to see, and then I will reclaim all that my father fought so hard to gain."

He lunged, and Leif swung his sword to block the attack. The meeting of their blades rang out in the quieting day. They both swung free, the metal glinting as it arced through the sky, and then Calder charged again straightaway, coming in from the side and forcing Leif to turn into the block.

Leif saw his opponent's strategy then: they were on the narrow pier, and Calder had just forced him sidelong, rendering his shield too unwieldy to be effective and making it difficult to take more than one stride directly forward or back without coming to the edge and overbalancing into the water. If he fell, the fight wouldn't be over, but it would give Calder the distinct advantage, as Leif would be forced to charge up onto the shore—just as Calder's men had done.

When Calder came in with the blow meant to overbalance him, Leif ducked low and moved into it, under it, throwing up his shield just as Calder's arm was at the midpoint of its path.

His shield bashed his former friend's hand. He heard bones crack, and Calder's sword flew free and splashed into the water.

Leif spun and stood, now at the end of the pier, with the steady shore at his back. The men who had been fighting and were now victorious, seeing Leif and Calder and recognizing their clash as single combat between two well-matched warriors, formed a loose ring; Leif felt more than saw it.

Favoring his dominant hand, Calder threw his shield away and pulled his axe from its ring.

Leif dropped his shield as well. His fight for Geitland had been lopsided on both occasions, but this battle between two men who had loved each other as brothers all their lives would not be.

"COME!" Calder roared and brandished his axe.

Leif shook his head. This was his seat now. He was no raider, no usurper. He would not attack on his own soil.

"I am Jarl of Geitland. This seat is mine to defend. If you would yield and swear to me, I would gladly accept your fealty, Calder Åkesson." Without taking his eyes from Calder, he raised his voice and added, "The same is true for any who landed here today sworn to Åke Ivarsson. Yield and swear your oath, and live. Keep loyal to the defeated coward whose skull rests on that pike, and die."

What came from Calder then was an almost womanly scream, as it came from a throat twisted with rage. His axe was high over his head, and Leif moved to block it high with his sword, but Calder changed his arc at the last moment, and the block missed. As Leif spun, the axe sliced across his chest, and he promptly felt the warm flow of blood down his skin, under his boiled leather chestpiece.

The cut was deep but not immediately mortal; Leif knew it at once, even as he faltered from the force of the blow. He spun just in time to block Calder's next attack, and sword and axe locked together. Caught in a bitterly intimate embrace, the men stared at each other.

"I loved you," Calder gritted as he tried to push the axe into Leif's throat.

"And I you."

Leif knew the rush of blood down his chest was enough to be a danger to him very soon. He called up all of his strength at once and shoved Calder back. Calder barely stumbled, but in that brief breath of time, Leif caught his sword in both hands and swung. He felt his chest gape open between the press of his arms.

Calder's head went flying from his shoulders, and in the moments that his body remained upright without it, a bright fountain of blood surged into the air and rained onto Leif and the already sodden earth.

"NO!" came a shout from the crowd, and Leif turned to the sound. Eivind, now Åke's eldest surviving son, had been driven to his knees, and Astrid had her axe against the side of his throat. Furious grief masked his face.

Exhausted, badly wounded, and awash in his friend's blood, Leif walked up the berm and stood before another friend. The warriors around them made way.

"Swear to me, Eivind Åkesson. I bear you no ill will. I know you saw your father clearly, and you know the way of things"—his erratic heart stuttered as Olga's words came from his mouth. "What I did was for the good of our home. Swear to me, and I will bring you into my hall as an advisor."

"My mother? My brothers and sisters?" Eivind's mother, whom he shared with Calder and Ulv, was dead. But he had been small when Åke took Hilde to wife and had called her mother as long as he could speak. As had Ulv.

"She lives. She and Turid and the children. We provisioned them and sent them away to make their lives. Swear fealty to me, and go out to find them."

Eivind spat in his face.

Without wiping the spittle away, he met Astrid's eyes and nodded. With one blow, silently but for the sing of her axe, she took his head.

Even wearier now, Leif then turned to Ulv, who was already staring directly at him, his eyes wide, but his head steady, showing no other sign of fear. The youngest of Åke's grown sons, Ulv didn't yet have twenty years, and he had never been an enthusiastic raider. He was quiet and gentle, and a disappointment to his father. But he was no coward.

Before Leif could ask him to swear, Ulv said, "You didn't kill them? Mother and the children? And Turid?" Turid was also Åke's wife, taken when Hilde gave him only daughters. She was near Ulv's own age.

"It is as the jarl says," Astrid answered. "They live." She looked—she was—highly displeased with that fact. It had always been Åke's way to kill anyone connected to his enemies, irrespective of age or sex. He'd called it a guard against the future. Astrid agreed.

Leif smiled. "A friend told me that if we kill everyone who might someday be an enemy, we will have no one left to be our friend. I think that is good wisdom. So no, we did not kill two women and their small children."

Ulv struggled in Bjarke's hold. Leif nodded, and Bjarke released him. Immediately, Ulv stood and raised the arm around which was wrapped the thickly plaited gold of his arm ring.

"On my arm ring, my life, my sword, and my honor, before the gods, I swear my undying allegiance to you, Leif Olavsson, Jarl of Geitland."

Leif glanced at Bjarke. "His sword?"

After a moment's hesitation, Bjarke produced Ulv's sword and handed it to Leif, still coated with the blood of those Ulv had killed or wounded in this battle. He handed it back to its owner. Around them, Leif's men and women stirred suspiciously, but Ulv only wiped the blade on his breeches and sheathed it.

"I am glad to have your sword at my back, Ulv."

Ulv bowed his head.

"Come," Leif called to all as he set his hand on Ulv's shoulder. "Let us honor the dead of this battle."

He took a step forward, toward his friends and clansmen—and that was the last thing he knew.

~oOo~

"You take many more wounds to the chest and you'll not need leathers. The scars will be too thick for a blade to cut through." Without the slightest hint of gentleness, Birte, Geitland's healer, slapped her paste over the wide track of sewing across Leif's chest. "You'd think the gods are trying to get to your heart, as many times as men have carved at it."

He grunted as she laid a linen over the paste and pressed down. "And yet it still beats."

"Hmpf. You should keep your shield up. I saw what you did. You had him, and you threw your shield down. Stupid men with their stupid ideas about honor. The victory was yours before he opened your chest, but you had to make a fair fight. You might *both* have died of your honor. What good is a dead jarl?"

He tapped his chest lightly, above the edge of the linen. "Thump, thump, Birte. Not dead yet."

Astrid stepped into the room but stopped when she saw that Leif lay naked on his bed. Birte had washed him as well as changed his dressing. "Are you finished?" the shieldmaiden asked.

The healer finished wrapping Leif's chest and then pulled a fur over his legs. As she collected her materials, she said, "He needs rest. He thinks he's strong again, but see the pallor of his skin. Don't tax him, daughter." She turned on her patient. "And you! You stay in bed. I will be back in the afternoon."

Astrid nodded to her mother as Birte left Leif's quarters. Then she came and scowled down at the bed. Leif knew the look to be her version of concern.

Leif smiled. "I am well."

She scoffed. "You are white as the snow. You are not well."

No, he was not. His chest felt like fire, and he could barely keep his head steady. Calder's axe had cut deep, scoring bone, and he had lost a great quantity of blood. "Then I will rest until I am."

She crossed her arms in a display of impatience. "Those of Karlsa are eager to return to their home."

He had been insensible more than a day, the blood loss making his memories of that time like dimly remembered dreams. Two days had passed since then, and he was only now able to sit upright and hold a coherent conversation. "Then they should be off. But I would see our friends before they go." He would be sorry to see Bjarke and Harald leave; he had only just won their trust back. He assumed that Hans and Georg would go north as well; they were of Estland, and the only others of their people were in Karlsa. Jaan. Jakob. And Olga.

Olga. She was so close, but it mattered not.

"Do you not wish to travel there as well? Olga is there. And you should bring the news of this victory to Vali yourself. It would go far to rebuild his trust."

He could not go to Karlsa. His friends had told him about the aftermath of Åke's sacking of the castle—in which Leif had played a principal role. He had believed Olga and her family, her people, safe because a peace had been in place with Prince Toomas.

If he'd had even a bit more time to think, he would have seen the folly in that belief. *Of course* Toomas, a warlike prince in any event, would have leapt at the opportunity to overrun lands defended by such a depleted force. Taking that holding meant full control of the entire western half of Estland and more. Soon, Toomas would be able to crown himself king of all Estland.

Now, because of what Åke had done, what Leif had helped him do, Olga's brothers and virtually all of her people were dead, and her home was burned.

Had she been standing in the room with them, yet she would have been too far from him to reach. No, he couldn't go to Karlsa. He couldn't hurt her again, and he knew the mere sight of him would hurt her.

He cared to share none of that with the glowering shieldmaiden standing over him. He sighed, holding back a grunt of pain at the stretch in his chest. "As you have noted, I'm not yet well, and they are eager. They should sail and bring the story of this battle with them. I'll see my friends in the north later, when Geitland and I are both recovered from our trials."

Astrid cocked her disapproving blonde eyebrow at him and then left him to his several pains and discomforts—most of them settled in and around his heart.

13

"Crush two blossoms—only two!—and mix it into the dough." Olga handed a small bundle of dried flowers to a thin young woman with wide, wary eyes. "It will calm him as it fills his belly." As the woman tucked the herbs into her hangerock, Olga added, "Go to Vali, Elfa. He would not let this stand."

She reached out to touch the woman's bruised cheek, but Elfa pulled her head away. "I cannot. It would humiliate him and cause him trouble in trade. He is not a bad man. Only quickly out of temper."

Olga sighed and nodded toward the now-hidden bundle. She understood all too well, though she disagreed that the man in question was not bad. "That will settle him." She looked Elfa in the eyes. "More than two blossoms can be dangerous. Six would be very dangerous."

Elfa dropped her eyes. "Thank you, Olga. I will bring payment when he is next away."

"Well enough, *kullake*. Well enough."

When Elfa left, Olga closed the door against the harsh winter wind and turned back to her worktable, where she was preparing the ingredients for a new batch of traveler's tea. She shooed a chicken from the table and found a new egg in her bowl of dried mustard greens.

Her house, bigger than ever she'd had before but smaller than many in Karlsa, was packed to the rafters after months of living here in the north. Under Vali's high regard, she'd taken

Sven's place as the town healer. In her homeland, she'd been paid, when she had been paid, mainly in meals and supplies. Here, where people were more prosperous, she was paid in goods and, rarely, in bits of actual silver.

She had a small purse full of hacksilver. She didn't understand its use or its value, but she had it, and it apparently made her fortunate.

On several occasions, she had been paid in animals. She had four chickens and three small goatlings. Payment for setting the smith's son's leg had been made in the form of a small pen to keep the animals during the day, but in the way of these people, the animals spent their nights in the house. It was crowded.

"Did you tell Elfa how to kill Ole?"

She had. Never before had she done such a thing, but now she had no qualms at all.

Without turning to the sound of her apprentice's young voice, Olga answered, "I told her how much would be dangerous to use."

"But why? It is known that Ole beats her. Now she knows how to kill him quietly."

Frida came and stood at her side. The girl had celebrated her thirteenth year a few weeks before and already she was showing signs of being an accomplished healer. She had been working under Sven, her uncle, before the fateful raid. Her mother, Sven's sister, had been deeply suspicious of the foreigner who'd been given Sven's house, and it had taken some many weeks before she had allowed Frida even to speak to Olga.

But now, Olga had an apprentice and a sweet young girl to look after. She was glad, because Jakob had moved to the shipbuilder's house as his training had advanced, and she'd had a spell of black loneliness in her solitude. Frida had five younger siblings, so her mother had not been so averse to letting her move into the healer's house, once she decided that Olga wouldn't corrupt her away from the gods.

That was the hardest part about becoming a member of this community. These people believed fervently, aggressively in their hard-drinking, hard-fighting, jealous, vengeful, self-indulgent gods. They believed that they lived high above them—that they *lived*, that they breathed and bled—and yet somehow cared about the people here, and intervened on their behalf, or on another's. They killed animals, bathing in their blood, as sacrifices to these flawed gods. And she had heard of rituals in which they killed people as well—their own most beloved, even.

She didn't believe in these things, and it was known that she did not. It made her a curiosity and a project. People were always asking her questions or telling her stories. It made her different, but no one seemed hostile for that reason. She thought that if she worshipped a different god, perhaps they would not be so amiable in their curiosity. But because she worshipped nothing and respected everything, she was seen as merely ignorant. And teachable.

Olga had come to understand the idea of godly reverence. Sometimes, she thought she might like to believe that there was someone else, or a whole race of someone elses, who might have a hand in her life, who might be placated or angered and thus provide a reason or a purpose for the way of things.

But she did not believe. The only hands in her life, or any life, were human hands. She didn't even believe in the balance any longer. One must make one's way, no matter how the sea surged.

She set the pestle in the mortar and turned to Frida. "I told her because it's knowledge she needs. Whether she needs it to be sure to keep the amount safe or for another purpose is not for us to say. It is up to Elfa to decide the course of her life."

"And of Ole's."

Olga smoothed her hand over the girl's flowing red hair. In Karlsa, people gave a kind of reverential space, a bit of fear, to those with red hair, even their own clanspeople. She had heard it said here that those with the sunset in their locks had been touched by magic.

"You are wise beyond your years, young Frida, but there is more to healing than salves and teas and stitches. A healer's calling is to give ease to those in need. What I gave Elfa today is control, in a life that has none. There is ease in that. Whatever she chooses, it will be her choice. And Ole has made his course, as well. His choices brought Elfa to us."

The girl searched Olga's eyes. Then she nodded, and the women returned to their work.

~oOo~

Olga opened the window and let the sunshine in. The air was still brittle with the cold of winter, but the sun was shining for the first time in ages, and she stood in the cold fresh air and closed her eyes, enjoying the light of the sun, though it came without much warmth.

Still, it was the sun, and the winters here were much without it. At her feet, the hens collected in the sunbeam she'd let in and fussed irascibly. They, too, had grown weary of being cooped up in the dark. She opened the door and shooed them into her little yard, where she would plant her herbs once the ground grew soft enough to take a hoe.

Jakob walked up with a warm smile. The boy, now fifteen, had grown broad and strong in the service of the shipbuilder, and a new growth of beard scattered over his cheek and chin. Though he lived with Amund, Jakob came to visit often.

She tipped her head now to accept his kiss on her cheek. Before he did or said anything else in the way of a greeting, Jakob asked, "Might I speak with you?"

"There is trouble?"

"No." He smiled. "Not trouble. But news, and questions."

She pulled him inside and closed the door. "Sit. Talk."

They sat together at the table, and Jakob fidgeted with the sewing she had left there. Before he could undo her work, she huffed and took it from him. "What news, Jakob?"

"I…I would like to…to wed Frida."

Surprise wasn't among the emotions Olga felt. Since Frida had come to live with her, she and Jakob had developed a friendship. Though Olga had seen no evidence of more than that, she needn't tax her mind to believe two handsome young people, coming into their age and already friends, would want more.

"Does Frida know this?" She smiled when Jakob blushed dark.

"Of course. I have spoken to Amund as well, and he would have her with us. But I want your good wish, too."

Olga slid her hand under his wrist and lifted his arm. He now wore a metal band, gold and silver twisted together. Vali had given it to him at the last thing, marking Jakob's manhood and his welcome into the community. Jakob had then sworn on this 'arm ring' his loyalty and love for Vali.

"This makes you a man, yes? You need only Vali's good wish, and Frida's. Mine is of no importance."

He seemed hurt by her response and pulled his arm free. "It's important to me. Do you withhold it?"

"Frida is young, Jakob, and not yet finished with her training."

"She has had her blood."

Olga lifted her eyebrows at that. She, of course, knew that, but it surprised her that Jakob was so much in the girl's intimate confidence that he knew it, too. "Have you and she...?"

Jakob's brow compressed in a dramatic grimace. "That is not for you." Then he blushed again and added, "But no."

Putting her hand over his, she gave it a warm squeeze. "You are a fine, strong young man with a good head and a clear future. If it pleases you and Frida both to be wed, then you have my good wish. I will miss her very much, but in this life you grab the good there is and hold it as long as you may."

Jakob grinned and sat back, relieved. "She will still be your apprentice, if you'll have her. Amund has no need of her to work for him, and he sees value in her healing. When we are wed, she will live with me, but come to you every day, if you wish. She would want it."

"You and she have discussed much."

"Yes. I want her to be happy."

Her heart aching with sorrow and pleasure both, Olga stood and embraced the young man who had come to mean so much to her. "Then she shall be."

~oOo~

On an early summer day, with a warm breeze frolicking through the town, traders from afar moored in Karlsa.

Olga and Frida had stood in the yard and watched as the men stood armed and ready, while the strange ship approached. Olga's body had been rigid with memory of the last time strangers had approached the shore of her home, and she had clutched the hilt of the knife she wore on her belt. Frida had only the little clips she wore on hers, but she was not so worried. She had lived in Karlsa all her life, and in Karlsa, danger from the sea always had come in ships like their own. She had expected this strange vessel to be what it was: a traveling market.

Once the ship had moored, Vali, Orm, and Bjarke had gone out to meet the leader. Now, the heart of the town bustled with life and color, and Olga had never seen such wondrous wares in all her life.

And the men on the ship! She had never seen their like before, with skin of so many different earthen colors, from the dark dusk of mud after hard rain to burnished bronze and gold. Only a scant few were the pale of stone or moon that she knew like her own.

Almost all were black-haired and heavily bearded, and many wore beads and jewels and gold. Many were short, by Karlsa standards, but the leader and his second were tall and burly.

None was so big and broad as Vali, however, and Olga saw them often stare sidelong at the giant jarl, as if they didn't quite trust him to be peaceable.

So many different kinds of men could only have hailed from many different kinds of places. Olga thought of her brother, Mihkel, and his life spent adventuring. The few times he'd made it home, he had come by land—no such wondrous vessels as this had ever landed on Vladimir's desolate shores—but he had been darker and rougher than the young man who'd struck out in the middle of the night those years before. His stories had been always about the people and places and things he'd seen and never about the things he'd done.

But he had taught her the raiders' tongue. He had met people like these before, and often enough to know their words. He must have been on a ship like this.

She stared hard at every trader, hoping against hope to see her brother's eyes look back at her. But she did not.

Brenna hooked her arm through Olga's. "Do you think your brother might still live?"

Not realizing that she had been so transparent in her search, Olga felt her cheeks warm a bit. "I don't know. It has been years, and I have long thought him lost. But I've never seen a ship like this. I had a small hope that perhaps the path of my life might bring me to him." She frowned at her friend. "You should be resting."

Brenna's time was nearing. She had yet weeks to go, but the babe rested very high and pressed always on her lungs and stomach, and she again had trouble keeping her food and drink. She was thin and wan, with dark circles under her eyes, and her lovely golden hair had gone dull. The carrying of this child had been difficult from the first, and these months had taken their toll. Olga thought it would not be long before Brenna would be unable to leave her bed.

But now her friend smiled and gave their linked arms a tug. "The traders are here. Such beautiful things unlike we have. I cannot miss this." She canted her head to the side. "And Vali watches like an eagle, so if I need help, I have it." Olga followed Brenna's gaze and saw Vali, standing with Orm and Bjarke and the ship's leader, and paying no heed at all to the men. His eyes were on them, and he smiled at his wife and nodded at Olga.

Thus granted permission, the two women walked among the chests and barrels of strange items for trade. Olga picked up a bolt of unusual fabric, a brilliant purplish pink like rosebay, in an intensity no dye she'd ever made or seen could approach. The fabric shimmered and felt like—like *air* in her hands.

She dropped Brenna's arm and lifted the fabric to her face. It was cool and soft, like a whisper.

"You like, pretty wee lady?" said the nearby trader, a thick and alien lilt to his words and a smile that glinted with gold. "From far, very far. Very special to make pretty ladies more pretty."

"What—what is it?" she asked.

"It's called silk," Brenna answered. "Vali says that worms weave it. I think that is a story from this very far place." She gave the trader an icy glare. "How much?"

"Five gold pieces for bolt," the trader answered, the seduction gone from his voice. Now he was all business.

Brenna laughed. "You can wipe your arse with it, then."

As Olga gaped at her friend's sudden hostility, Brenna pulled her along.

"Wait!" the trader called. "You no understand the way of this. Tell me price. Then we talk."

Her warrior's glare in full effect, Brenna waddled around to face the trader again. "I understand. You insult me with such a high first price."

The trader made a wounded face. "Very good silk. And the color…unlike any other, yes?"

Olga almost nodded. She had never seen its like, and it was so beautiful it almost hurt to look on it. And the way it had felt!

But she refrained, knowing well enough about marketing to understand what Brenna was doing.

"Two pieces of gold," Brenna finally countered.

"Too little! Four. I must have four. I flee bandits to bring fine silk to you."

"Three. And the yellow as well."

Acting as if Brenna had demanded his firstborn in trade, the man slapped his hand to his chest. And then he nodded. "Never do I make a trade bad like this before."

Brenna pulled gold from her purse and handed it to the trader, then waved behind them, and Rikke, a servant from the hall, ran up and took the bolts. Vali and Brenna had freed the slaves under their personal control, but the jarl hadn't required anyone else to do so, and he wasn't inclined to make such an edict. He had brought the question up at a thing, to a cool reception, and the matter had mostly been dropped.

But at least her friends no longer claimed dominion over other human beings. Olga could take some ease from that.

"Take the silk to Olga's, please," Brenna instructed her servant, who turned and did just that.

"What?" Olga asked, shocked. "No, Brenna, it is too much."

Her friend waved the protest away and hooked arms again. "When we took over in Geitland and I wore Hilde's things because I had nothing of my own, I learned I don't like silk. But the light in your eyes when you touched it to your face is one I haven't seen for many months. Any little piece of happiness you can find, you more than deserve."

In the first months that they had been in Karlsa, Brenna had tried to plead Leif's defense. She had kept at it with dogged determination until the winter solstice. On an endless night, when the sun had never truly risen, Olga, worn to a nub by her friend's stubbornness and depressed by the relentless bleak of the winter, had finally broken down. Sobbing like she had never before in her life, she had told Brenna everything. What had happened to her during the sacking of the castle. The sea of bodies everywhere afterward. Their terror in thinking Vali lost, too. Vali's wild madness. How Anton had died. And how Kalju had died.

With a full understanding of Olga's unhappiness and her hatred of Leif, Brenna had not again mentioned his name in Olga's presence, for which she was deeply grateful.

"Perhaps you can make something for Frida to have when she is wedded." Brenna smirked and added in a low mutter, "Or when she is bedded."

Olga laughed. "You are bawdy with this child, Brenna. And thank you. Very much."

Brenna shrugged. "I don't feel well enough to act on it, so I suppose it comes out my mouth instead. And you're welcome, my friend."

"Summer is here. It won't be many more weeks now."

~oOo~

Brenna gave birth at the summer solstice, on an endless day of midnight sun. The birthing was as hard as the carrying had been; the babe was large, and Brenna had grown weak. Until Olga had made a small cut and widened the birth channel, she had not been so sure that all would be well.

But finally, as Brenna screamed and fell back exhausted, Olga caught a bundle in her arms—the little girl that Brenna had been so sure she was having, as it had been foretold.

She wiped the babe's nose and mouth, and she immediately let loose a lusty wail. Then Dagmar leaned over, pulling something from the small leather pouch she wore always around her neck—a tiny vial of red liquid.

Olga lifted her eyes to Dagmar, who smiled. "An unguent from home. To draw the gods' attention to her." She dabbed a bit on her thumb and then swiped a small circle over the bawling child's forehead.

Used by now to the ways of these gods, Olga only smiled and lifted the babe up so that Vali could see. "She is strong and well."

His creased face smoothed into a great grin. He kissed his wife's sweat-soaked forehead and came down to where Olga held the child. Bending low, he looped the life cord around his hand, lifted it to his mouth, and bit it, separating mother and child.

She had been both healer and midwife among her people, but here in Karlsa, where Sven had been their healer, they had had a midwife as well. It was the normal case in this world. But the town's midwife had been killed by Åke's men when they took over, so Olga had helped several children into the world here since she'd arrived. This biting of the cord seemed one of the many small rituals of these people—so earthy, yet so godly.

Vali took his daughter, eschewing the linens Olga held, and cradled her to his chest. "I will protect you all my days, little one, with my axe, my heart, and my life. You will grow strong and fierce like your mother and live a great life. And I will be with you all the way."

"Vali," Brenna's voice was soft but strong. "Please. Please." She had never had the chance to hold their firstborn, a wee son. He had been born and died while she had been near death herself.

Without taking his eyes from the little face in his arms, Vali turned and carried their daughter to her mother. Brenna opened her shift and bared her breasts, and Vali laid the child there.

Brenna's arms went round her daughter. The child turned toward the promise of nourishment. Vali sat on the bed with his family, his vast back blocking Olga's view of that private, lovely moment.

Her heart felt swollen with the feeling of glad sorrow that was the closest thing to happiness Olga knew any longer how to feel. She took no happiness in her own life, though she sometimes felt some warm pleasure. And the happiness she felt for those she loved came always with loss. A dark, bottomless loss. Of all the things she could never have. All the things that had been taken away.

Or given away and then destroyed.

~oOo~

They named their daughter, born on a day of endless sun, Solveig, which meant something like 'the way of the sun.' She even had a tiny birthmark on her shoulder, a little kiss the color of Olga's favorite silk shift, that made the shape of a bright summer sun.

Her personality was just as luminous. Olga had never had the pleasure of loving a child of her own, but she had known and cared for many, and never before had she known such a young one to have a demeanor so easy. The babe rarely cried. She smiled early and laughed less than a month after her birth. The entire hall was in love with the pretty, happy little girl. Even Brenna's many wild, enormous cats doted on the child, allowing her to tangle her chubby little fists in their bushy fur.

Vali was completely besotted. On several occasions, Olga had come into the hall to find that massive, ferocious warrior on his hands and knees, hovering over the babe, making ridiculous noises and faces, drawing gales of tiny giggles. Solveig's favorite thing to suck on was his braid, and he had held meetings with her in his arms while she noisily sucked and chewed.

And Brenna. From the first time she had been pregnant, with her son, Olga had seen the signs in her friend that she would be a natural mother. As hard-shelled as she seemed to be, as often as she scowled, inside was a soft, warm heart, one that took in stray animals and people and brought them close. She had mourned her son desperately, and now she poured a doubled portion of love into her daughter's heart from her own.

Olga loved them all fiercely and treasured the close bond she had with them. She held Solveig and could almost feel that she was her own. But she was not, and under that fierce love and happiness for her friends was always that bitter loss.

It kept her awake at night, alone in her house with her chickens and goats.

She sat in the hall one day as another summer waned. Solveig had two months and was a fat, fair, beautiful little girl. Olga held her, bouncing her lightly on her knees and quietly singing an old tune her mother had sung to her in the world before. Vali and Brenna sat in their fur-covered chairs at the end of the hall and heard the petitions and concerns of their people.

They had not raided this summer. Vali had wanted to stay close to Brenna, and after the struggles of the previous year, he thought it good to take the year to rebuild. Olga hadn't concerned herself with much about that business, but she'd heard enough around the town to know that some had not been happy with a full season of idleness. Now, at the end of a season without plunder, people had complaints. Vali heard and addressed them all.

Bjarke ran in through the open hall doors. "Vali! A ship approaches." Everyone turned in his direction. Olga, seated at the side, brought Solveig close, feeling the need to protect her.

Vali and Brenna both stood. "Friend or foe?" Vali asked.

"It bears the colors of Jarl Leif Olavsson."

"Friend, then!" Brenna's voice rang out happily. "He comes at last!"

Leif was friend to Brenna and ally to Vali and Karlsa, but he was foe to Olga. She waved Rikke over and handed the babe to her. Without seeking the attention of her friends, she left the hall.

She had no wish to see the Jarl of Geitland. Ever again.

14

No one met him on his way, so Leif walked the full distance of the pier alone. Vali stood at the end, with Bjarke and Orm on either side, and Jaan, Hans, and Georg arrayed at the front as well. Vali's hand rested on the head of his axe, hanging at his hip.

Time and distance had not warmed his friend's heart, then.

No sign of Brenna and her babe. Or of Olga.

When Vali did not speak in greeting, Leif waited until he came close enough that he would not need to raise his voice and said, "Vali Storm-Wolf. I come as a friend and an ally. Am I welcome here?"

Vali took an awkward sidestep, and then Brenna was pushing past him, babe in arms. "Enough of this posturing. Of course you're welcome here, Leif!" She stopped just before him, smiling brightly, and there was an uncomfortable moment when Leif didn't know whether to embrace his friend, with her husband's scowl at her shoulder. Brenna herself wasn't usually easy with physical affection, but when last he'd seen her, she had hugged him hard.

The tension broke when the babe in her arms squealed and reached out and tried to grab at Leif's chestpiece.

"This is your daughter?" He cupped his hand around her soft, fair head. Such a lovely young miss, with deep, keen blue eyes.

"Yes. Solveig. She likes shiny things." Brenna patted his chest, too, and her smile curved into a smirk. "Jarldom has made you extravagant, it seems."

His new leathers were deep russet brown, and hundreds of small metal rings had been embedded into the chestpiece, something like the armor the princes' men had all worn, but not linked together. The metalwork in the center formed a shape with five points, bound in a circle, which Olga had told him described the balance that was so important in her view of the world.

"Astrid's idea. She says I lead too much with my heart and should protect it better."

"She's wise, then." Brenna cocked her head, though, and her eyes narrowed slightly. "Are you and she close?"

Leif laid his hand over Brenna's, still on his chest. "Astrid is my good friend and gives me wise counsel. But my heart is elsewhere."

A shadow of dark emotion moved over Brenna's face, but before Leif could ask after Olga, Vali stepped up and pulled his wife back. "Leif. As an ally, you are welcome in Karlsa. You and your crew should come to the hall. We will fill you with food and drink, and you can tell us why you come now, after so long."

He took his daughter from her mother's arms, turned, and stalked up toward the great hall.

Leif stood where he was and sighed. "I had hoped."

"He is not so cold toward you as he seems. But he took your distance as an act of guilt. Why did you not come last year, after you bested Calder? You said you would."

"I was wounded." He left it at that. A true enough answer for several reasons. Again, he searched the crowd that had amassed, as one always did, at the arrival of a ship. Olga was not among the curious onlookers.

"We heard. I didn't realize it was so serious to keep you away for a year." Brenna's arm snaked around his waist. "I'm glad you're here now. You have been missed."

He squeezed her shoulders. "It is good to see you, my friend."

~oOo~

His other friends were glad of his arrival, too, and it took some time before he and the small crew he'd sailed with arrived in the hall. Vali sat in his seat with Solveig in his arms. The babe had the end of her father's braid in her mouth. He glowered at Leif until Brenna went up and sat next to him. She leaned in and whispered, and Vali scowled more deeply, then smoothed it from his face and smiled down at his daughter.

The hall was quickly full, and food and drink were already making their way to the tables. Leif allowed himself to be drawn into discussion with Bjarke and the others, who were full of questions and news of their own.

Leif answered their questions to the extent that he could. There were things he wanted to discuss with Vali and Brenna, too; this visit was not solely for friendship. But he would wait until he had a moment of quiet with them. It was not yet news for all.

After a while, Brenna came down and leaned over his shoulder. "I'm going to feed her. Come with me and talk."

Surprised, Leif shot a glance toward Vali, whose attention was homed on them. "Will your husband not mind that?"

"What you and I have been through together—watching me nurse is no great thing. He will abide it. I would do it in the hall, but she settles at it better in quiet."

Leif doubted that, but he could tell from the look Vali was sending in their direction, and the one Brenna was returning, that her husband knew what she intended. With a nod to his friends, Leif refilled his cup and stood.

She led him into the private quarters. This hall was not so elaborate as the hall in Geitland, and Vali and Brenna's private quarters looked little more sumptuous than that of any other prosperous freeman.

He felt uncomfortable back here, alone with Brenna while she unfastened a brooch from her hangerock and pulled the neck of her gown loose. Their people didn't cling much to personal privacy, and he had seen many women with babes at the breast. It was no unusual thing. Part of life. But he worried it would be different with Brenna.

When his wife had nursed, he had always found it…compelling. Sensual. He felt close to Brenna—in a different way, true, and more fatherly than anything, but he loved her. He very much did not want his affection for her to get bound up with sensual feeling, so he busied himself exploring the space until Solveig was settled at her meal.

Turning, he saw that Brenna had covered herself and the babe with a linen, and he relaxed.

"You look happy, Brenna."

"I am. It's a strange thing, to be happy after so long. I feel jealous of it, like someone might take it from me at any time."

"You have been tested again and again. Perhaps this happiness is the gods' gift to you."

She rolled her unusual eyes. "I very much hope not. Gifts from the gods always have their price, do they not?" She gazed down at her daughter. "She is well, Leif."

He knew she didn't mean Solveig. "Is she happy?"

Brenna shook her head. "No. I think sometimes she is content, but there is always a dimness in her eyes. It wearies me that the people I love are so at odds. I love precious few, and you are my family. I would have wounds healed."

"As would I. Brenna, I…" he didn't know what to say. He had tried hard not to speak of Olga during their time in Estland, to keep their love private. Astrid had laughed at him and told him that everyone had known—but she hadn't known how close they had truly been. Now, he didn't know what Brenna knew, so he didn't know what he could say to her. Though he had known the shieldmaiden many years, now, here, he felt like the interloper. He *was* the interloper.

"You love her," Brenna said as if she were filling in the sentence he'd left incomplete.

He wasn't sure if that was what he'd meant to say, but it was true. "Yes. With all my heart, I do. I hurt her, though, I know."

"I doubt you know how much."

"I know that her brothers were killed. I don't know how she will ever forgive me for that. And she doesn't seem to want me to try. If she's here, in Karlsa, she is not seeking me out."

Brenna stared at him for a long time. She shifted the babe to her other breast, mindless of her exposure, before she spoke again. Leif realized with relief that his response to Brenna nursing was not like it had been with his wife.

"I think you should go to her. She won't want you there, she will probably be furious to be faced with you, but the last time she saw you...you were letting Toke's guts out on the ground."

Leif dropped his head as his own memory of that horror surged up. Toke had been good-natured and eager, a good and loyal young man. But in the chaos of that night, Leif had been fighting for his life like any of them. It had been kill or be killed, and he had had to survive to save Brenna and Vali.

"You killed our friends, Leif."

Her words, said gently, without malice or anger, were like claws.

"You know why."

"I do. Because I heard it from your own mouth. You need to make her listen. I don't know if she can forgive you, or will even soften, but I do know that every day, she hardens that much more. She is a shadow of who she was. At the least, she needs a new last memory of you."

"Don't meddle, shieldmaiden. Olga knows her mind." Vali came into the room and stood between Leif and Brenna, blocking Leif's view.

"Usch! Stop. You are being absurd," Brenna snapped, and Leif saw her hand slap at Vali's leg. "Sit. Speak like the grown men and friends you are."

Vali sat, and Leif saw that Brenna was fully dressed again, and Solveig rested on her shoulder.

With a wave toward Brenna, his hand at the level of her neck, which bore a choker of darkened, uneven skin, Vali sneered, "You see her scars? And this?" He drew his finger over the long scar on the side of his head. "A man Brenna calls my friend made them."

"Vali. Please." Now Brenna's voice was softer. "Please." But the hostile light in her husband's eyes didn't fade.

Leif had spent a long year wallowing in his guilt and his loneliness. That time had given him understanding and perspective. "You would both be dead had I not acted as I did. Now, you are jarl, and you have this beautiful daughter with your shieldmaiden. Åke and Calder are both dead. All of this happened because I acted to save you. Are your scars not worth your future?"

"You say you saved us. And yet only you sit here unscathed."

With a laugh roughened with his own bitter losses, Leif stood and unlaced his chestpiece. "I bear scars, you may take heart in that. They ache still. But only this one can be seen. He dropped his leather to the floor and pulled his light linen tunic over his head.

Brenna gasped, but Leif wasn't looking at her. He was watching Vali, and he was heartened by the flare in the stubborn jarl's eyes. The scar that crossed his chest was thick and wide, puckered and angry. "Made by Calder's axe. They say it scored the bone and showed my heart beating in my chest."

He thought that last part was likely an embellishment for the stories, he couldn't see how he'd have lived if his heart had truly been exposed, but the wound had been dire and the scar severe.

"And yet you killed Calder," Brenna said, her voice low.

"Yes. After this, I had one swing left in me, and I made the most of it. I loved him, but I killed him. Because it was right." He faced Vali again. "I am your *friend*, Vali. I am sorry for what you've suffered, but I did save you, and at no small cost to myself. I, too, have lost much. I *sacrificed*. For you."

When Vali didn't respond, Leif yanked his tunic back on and snatched his leather from the floor. As he tugged the lacing tight, he said, "I am your ally always, and your friend, but I will not press the point again. I have news I would like to share with you, when tempers are cooler and the hall is quieter. Tomorrow, perhaps. I won't stay longer than I have need and am welcome, so we will sail again the day after. Is there a place I might put my head to sleep?"

Brenna opened her mouth to speak, but Vali stood. "Holmfrid will show you to a house nearby. It's small, but warm and well-appointed."

"Thank you." He turned and left.

~oOo~

Leif was angry. He lay alone in this borrowed bed and stewed in real rage. In the time since everything had fallen into chaos, he had known many emotions, but anger had not been among them. Now it was almost all he felt.

He wanted to bash Vali's scowling face until it turned inside out. The Storm-Wolf had glared at him as if he thought Leif meant to take his wife and child, as if Åke's vengeful spirit had possessed him and put everything Vali had at risk again.

And there the Jarl of Karlsa sat, beloved of his people, at home with his wife and child. He had likely returned to Karlsa a hero. He would have died in Estland had it not been for Leif. They all would have.

Leif had had to scrape for every bit of respect he had earned as a jarl. He had turned on his own jarl, and he'd had to prove his worth and his honor again and again. And he was alone. He had given up the deepest love he'd ever known.

Yet Vali would not forgive him.

Enough, then. Enough of begging forgiveness. Enough of attempting to prove his friendship. Enough of it all. If Vali would so easily throw away a friend such as he, then he was not worthy of the gift.

The only person to whom he still owed atonement would not even bear his presence on the same soil.

Leif tossed the fur back and stood. The fire pit glowed dimly red with the embers of a dying fire, but he needed no more light. He had grown used to the dark; he seemed always to be living under shadow. Even home, where Geitland was strong and prosperous and they had just completed a successful season of raids, his chest felt full of black void. The ache of his wound still vexed him somewhat, but it wasn't that. It was so much deeper.

He was without love, without children, without brothers. Those for whom he felt most deeply were far away, in space and in spirit. The friendships he had left were not enough to fill the emptiness.

A dog howled, and Leif went to the door of the borrowed house and opened it. The night was bright with a full moon, but nothing but, somewhere, that howling hound stirred.

Somewhere in this town, Olga lay sleeping. He had been in Karlsa for hours, but he had yet to catch even a glimpse of her. She did not want to see him.

But Brenna was right. He could not allow Toke's unfortunate death to be her last memory of him. He had to speak with her, if only to let her revile him. He had to tell her he loved her. That he had loved her truly and that he always would.

It was deep in the night. Even were she to want to see him, now would not be the time.

He went back inside and put on a light woolen tunic against the cool of a night pressing against a new winter. He pulled on his boots. And he went out into the moonlight to see if he could find her house.

~oOo~

Not far from the hall, he found a house with a little garden in the yard, and an empty animal pen. On the door hung a braid of dried herbs. Certain he had found what he'd sought, he pounded on the door.

It swung open within seconds, and Olga stood there, the dim light of a candle glowing behind her. She was dressed. She had not been sleeping after all.

She wore the clothes of the women of his people now: a pale hangerock and an underdress. Her dark hair was woven into braids. She was more beautiful than even he remembered, so beautiful it stole his breath.

And for the first time in more than a year, she was close enough to touch.

The cool shine of the moon met the warm glow of the candle and made her seem unreal, like a specter in the night. But he could see her eyes, large and dark and round with surprise.

"Olga." His voice came with no more force than a lost breath. His chest, his heart, pained him too much to push sound from it. "Olga."

"No," she gasped and pushed the door closed.

Without thinking, Leif threw his hand up and barred her from getting to the latch. "Please. Olga, please."

She pushed, and he pushed back, harder, and she released the door and stepped quickly backward, almost running. He stepped into her house and closed the door.

The room was dim, with only that one candle and a guttering fire to brighten it. Leif could just see that she was standing at a long table against the wall. He gave her that distance and didn't move.

"I'm sorry to come to you so late, but I couldn't stay away any longer. Olga, I've missed you so."

"I don't want you here." He heard the fear and fury in her words. "I don't want you here."

Her fear of him was tearing him apart. "I won't stay, then. I needed to see you and know you were well. I need to tell you that I love you. I need to beg your forgiveness. I would never mean to harm you. You are precious to me."

With a sudden move and a metallic scrape, Olga charged at him and stopped just before him. She held a small knife; it glinted red in the glow of the fire. "I will bury this in your heart before I listen to another of your lies." Her voice shook, but she lifted the knife in both her small hands and held it up before her face, at the level of his heart.

The sad anger that had beset Leif and kept him sleepless surged again, and before he'd made a choice to do it, he had closed her hands in both of his. They both held that sharp little knife now. Leif pulled and brought it to his chest.

Shocked, Olga resisted, but her strength had never been in her body, and Leif barely struggled to overpower her.

"Stop," she gasped, but he ignored her.

He pulled, forcing the blade to his chest, then through his tunic. When the point pierced his skin, when Olga was whimpering with her frantic resistance, he stopped, but he didn't back the blade off or release her hands.

"We might as well push it all the way in, my love. There is nothing inside me now but hollow space. My heart died when I lost you."

He pushed, and the blade entered his chest, and he felt the dull pain of it. There was no wash or leak of blood; the scars there were too thick, and the metal had not yet gone through them.

Now Olga was fighting him hard, flailing her body around the hands he held firmly, trying to free herself from him and this thing he was doing. He pushed again, until he finally felt the warm ooze of blood.

"STOP! STOP! *PALUN! EI! EI! EI!*" She was loud enough that Leif thought it likely someone would soon come to her aid.

And then she collapsed. Her knees gave out, and she dropped to the ground, the pressure of her suddenly-slack body jerking the knife in his chest and at last doing real damage, causing real pain. Leif released her, and she finished her fall, curling into a sobbing heap on the floor.

He yanked the blade from his chest and tossed it to the far side of the room.

15

Trapped in the vortex of agony that was her memory of the day the village had been overrun and her brothers had died, Olga was lost to the present around her. She coiled her body as tightly as she could, her arms over her head and her hands pulling at her braids.

She could feel her blade pushing into Kalju's thin chest, sliding past his ribs, piercing his heart. She could feel it now because she had felt it then. The air seemed as hot and acrid now as it had then, when fire turned her young brother's skin to black tallow. She could taste on the back of her throat the stench of fire and blood and cooked flesh that had hung over the village like a fog. She could see Anton's blood flowing from his open throat like water from the mouth of a stream.

"Olga." With the deep rumble of that voice she'd once loved, that she yet loved, she felt the heavy, warm press of Leif's hand on her shoulder. "I ache with your pain. Please forgive me."

She had been prepared for a late visitor on this night. The smith's wife was great with child and had shown signs earlier in the day that her time was nigh. So when the heavy beat of a fist came to her door so late, it had not been in her mind that she would open it and find her golden giant there, filling the space.

The first reaction of her heart upon seeing his handsome face was not the hatred that she had expected. Instead she'd felt the flutter and throb of love that she'd always felt in his presence, and that powerful thrill of a happiness now unknown to her had made the black hate, when it came fast on the heels of the love, hurt all the more.

All the day, she had stayed in her house with her shutters closed, seeing only those who'd come to her, hoping that she might somehow avoid Leif's presence. As the day had gone on and he hadn't sought her out, and as the bustle of the town ignored her, she'd come to believe that she would achieve her aim and be left alone.

Yet he was here, he had caught her unawares, and he had forced her to stab him. Now, she was snared in a nightmare of memory and confusion in her heart and her mind, and all she knew was that the warm weight of his touch, the gentle love she felt in it, was like to tear her into shreds.

She screamed and knocked him away, then scrambled backward as far as she could get, only stopping when her back hit the little table at her bedside and rattled the dark lantern atop it.

The goats bleated crankily in their pen in the corner, and the hens fluffed their feathers in protest of the noise.

It was darker here; the only candle she'd had lit sat on the table at the front of the house, and all her shutters were closed. When Leif followed her, all she could really see was a mountain of shadow coming toward her. She might almost have believed that she were dreaming, caught in the jaws of one of the terrors that fed on her sleep, but the mountain crouched before and said her name again.

Then he said, in the mother tongue she so rarely heard any longer, "*Ma armastan sind. Ma igasten sind. Palun, Olga. Sa oled mu päike, tähed, kuu.* My sun, stars, and moon, and my earth and air as well. My life and breath. Olga, please. I love you. I miss you. Talk with me. Whatever I must do to make things right between us, I will do it."

"The man with the scar through his left eye." She was surprised that her voice was steady, as much as that she had spoken at all and had found that, of all things, to say.

She couldn't make out Leif's face, but she heard the uncertainty in his tone. "Who?"

"Your jarl's man. A scar in his scalp that crosses through his left eye and into his cheek."

"Geir. I don't understand. He died in the fighting when Vali came to Geitland."

Now that she had begun to speak, Olga found a calm focus. She wanted him to know everything he had done, everything he had allowed, every way that he had abandoned her. Why she could never forgive him.

"Good. While you were betraying us all, helping your jarl destroy people who thought you a friend, *Geir* was in the kitchen. With me."

Leif sat down hard, and the floor shook. "What did he do?"

The shocked menace in his low voice didn't move her at all. She rolled onto her knees and leaned close so she could snarl the answer right in his face. "He did what men like him, like *you*, always do. You storm and slash and pillage and destroy. You take. You rape."

"Olga." His naked pain lanced through her name, but she didn't care. Her anger was in full flower now, and she was *glad* he'd sought her out, forced this on her. She wanted him to know *everything*. She slammed her hands to his chest, and he grunted.

"When we few who were left tried to rebuild a home, Toomas beset us and destroyed it all."

"I know. I know Anton and Kalju died. I have no words to express my regret, my love." He reached for her again, but she swatted him away again.

"*Ei!* Do not call me that! Do you know how they died? Anton fought like a warrior, even though he wanted nothing of war. A soldier slashed his throat open, right in front of me."

"Gods," Leif muttered.

"And Kalju! Another soldier set him afire. His skin oozed and crackled. He was in such pain, more pain than I had ken to ease. *I* killed him. I sank my own knife into my brother's chest because I had no other way to save him. I killed him. I killed him! I killed him! I KILLED HIM!"

She was screaming, and at some point she had started lashing out, hitting his head and chest. He sat there and let her, until she grabbed hold of his tunic—it was wet; why was it wet?—and hung there, on her knees, her back bowing, her head nearly in his lap. "I killed him. His skin melted like wax, and he couldn't even scream for the pain, and I killed him."

When his arms went around her, she needed them. She let him gather her up and set her in his lap. So long since she had felt his touch, had taken ease from his love. Their time together had been brief, but her life had been materially changed by it. *She* had been changed—by his love, and by the loss of it.

So long since she had felt safe. She craved even this corruption of what they'd had, even this double-edged blade of love and hate.

When he spoke, his voice shook with emotion, with pain and regret, and Olga was, this time, moved. "I am more sorry than I have words. I cannot give any of that back to you. I would atone, but I don't know how. I can only swear that what I did was not a betrayal. Always you have had my love, always my good faith. If I had not acted as I did, if I had done what Vali thinks I should have, and we had fought Åke in Estland, we would all of us be dead—those who died *and* those who lived. I did what I did to save you."

"No. You did not," she sighed, allowing her head to rest on his shoulder, too tired and despondent to fight any longer.

He turned his head, and she knew he was staring down at her, though the room was yet too dark to see him, even so close. "I swear to you, Olga. I did."

And this was perhaps the greatest pain of all, the wound that remained raw and festering and would not allow the other wounds to heal. "No. You did it to save Vali and Brenna. You gave no thought to what might happen to me. You had already left me. You left me before your jarl dismounted on the castle grounds."

The long stretch of silence that followed her words told Olga that she was right. She had been far from his thoughts on that horrible night.

"No," he finally whispered. "Olga, I have never left you. Not in spirit. I thought you would be safe."

All she could do was sigh. After months and months, more than a year, of anger and heartbreak growing roots in her soul and choking her spirit, Olga found that the twisted growth had died. Now, she felt no hate or fury. Only fatigue.

And love, she felt love. But it was a different sort. She didn't understand it, but its power came from a new place and shone not nearly as brightly as it had before.

"Tell me you love me, Leif." He had told her, but she needed to hear it again, now, even if she had no understanding of its worth.

She felt his surprise in the quick tension of his arms. "I do. You are dearer to me than anything, anyone else. I love you with my whole heart."

"The heart you said is dead?"

"Olga. Please. What can I do?"

There was nothing that could repair the damage that had been done between them, nothing that could assuage her losses or restore her balance. But there was something that she needed in this particular moment. One thing that she craved, that could, for a time, give her respite from the darkness.

"Take me."

If he had been surprised when she'd asked him to tell her he loved her, he was shocked now. His body went rigid, unyielding as stone. "Olga?"

She sat up in his arms and grabbed handfuls of his hair. Holding his head thusly, she stared into eyes she could barely see but knew better than any other, better than her own. "Take me. All we had before was crushed under the weight of what you did. All I ever had that was mine and good was you, and all that remains is dust. I need something more of you, or what's left of me will die. Take me. *Take me*. Please."

She kissed him. When he flinched back, she tightened her fists and pulled, holding him to her. A moment hung suspended between them—their mouths joined but neither of them moving. It wasn't enough, it wasn't nearly enough, but it was so much more than she had felt in so long that Olga thought her heart would break her chest with its violent beating.

And then Leif gave in.

His arms clamped around her like iron bands, and his hands dug into her hair, tearing at her braids as his mouth opened wide and his tongue plunged past her lips and teeth. The force of him was something Olga hadn't known before, and she was glad. This was new.

She pulled savagely at his hair and bit down on the fullness of his bottom lip. He made a wild, animal sound in his chest and yanked her head back by her braid. She could almost see him, see the jeweled blue glint of his eyes; dawn must have been nigh.

His chest heaved against hers. She wanted these clothes away, wanted to feel the warmth of his skin on hers, wanted to feel warm and safe, even if it were only an illusion, a dream to break apart in the rays of the dawn.

Clutching at his tunic, she tried to pull it up, to pull it free, but he knocked her hands away, his hands hitting hers so hard they stung, and yanked instead at the brooches that closed the straps on her hangerock.

In an effort to seem less strange to her new people, she had taken the custom of their dress, and once she'd grown used to it, she'd found it preferable to the garb of her homeland. More convenient to this place, though plainer. She had taken to showing some of the women the styles of decorative stitching that her mother had taught her long ago.

As for the hair, she had always worn hers in a braid, so it had not been so much to change the style.

Leif tossed the brooches away, and Olga heard them clatter across the floorboards. Then he tore at the side lacings until the hangerock was a loose puddle at her waist and only the linen underdress separated her from his touch. Rather than pull it, too, loose, Leif grabbed her head in his big hands and slammed his mouth over hers again.

He had yet to ask her if this was what she wanted. She hoped he would not.

This was not a pale shadow of what they'd had before, which had been gentle and peaceful, which had been innocent. This was dark and bitter, full of all that had happened. This was not a giving; Olga had nothing left to give, and perhaps that was true for Leif as well. On both their parts, this was a taking.

And yet, in its ferocity, their love still pulsed, deep and steady.

As his mouth ravaged hers, and she returned the punishment, Olga plunged her hands between them and pulled the lacing of his breeches loose. She could feel his sex, forged iron under her hands, and as soon as he was free of his leather, she shifted and hiked her skirts up. She clutched him hard in her hand and dropped down onto him, impaling herself so fast and deep that Leif tore his mouth from hers, threw back his head, and roared.

She had taken him too deeply. It hurt her, felt almost as if he were piercing her, but she didn't care. She wanted it to hurt. She wanted this pain to cleanse the other from her mind and heart and spirit. She wanted to feel him inside her for days, for weeks if that were possible. For the rest of her life.

Flexing on him as hard as she could, Olga bit down on her own lip and sought the pain. Every rough bounce brought a groan from Leif that sounded like she had taken his guts in her clenched fist, and she was glad of that, too. She wanted him to hurt like she did. She wanted him to remember this, to feel it, forever.

He brought his head forward and jerked the neckline of her underdress over her shoulder, baring her breast. Then his arms clamped around her again and he pushed her backward until she was arched over the vise of his hold. Still, she rocked and bounced with as much power as she could call up, and when he dropped his bearded mouth on her breast and sucked hard, she tangled her hands in his hair again and pulled until she could feel the strands popping free. He made that animal noise again and sucked harder.

Olga was violently dizzy; the swirl of emotion and sensation, this driving compulsion for the pain that was bound up in her still-consuming love and need of him, the man she had thought him to be, was more than her unstable world could withstand. Her heart skittered in her chest like a snared rabbit. Her stomach spun and flopped. And through it all, all around her, was the scent and touch and sound and taste of Leif. Her love.

Suddenly, the pain she needed became something else. She still ached viciously, but now she could feel pleasure rise up and coil around it—not the pleasure in the pain, that twisted need that had come upon her, but the pleasure she had known with him before. She felt the molten warmth soak her joints and make her loose. She felt her body open for him, seeking more, wanting everything.

The room swam around her, and Olga could no longer be sure that anything that was happening was truly happening. In the dark room, all of this could have been smoke and ash.

Leif's hands gentled and smoothed down her back until he gripped her bottom in his palms. In that hold, he took control of her brutal rhythm, changed it to something no less intense but without that bruising pain she had sought. He left her breast and claimed her mouth again, and this kiss bore only the passion of need. The fire of the pain was gone.

The thing that had clutched at her, made her want them to hurt each other like this, was gone. It was just them. She was in Leif's arms, twined around him. And for one short moment, a heartbeat only, she felt warm and safe, home in his embrace.

Her release came over her, wave after wave of it, until she thought she would truly drown. She broke free of his kiss and hooked her arms around his neck, burying her face against his neck. The silk of his hair stroked her cheeks. And still he moved her on him, his hands yanking her to and fro, to and fro, until he threw himself—and her with him—backward and his hips came up off the floor. He groaned and groaned, one long, anguished sound that barely left his throat but rumbled sharply against her chest.

Then he went slack, and they lay on the floor, next to her bed, in her still-dark house, tangled together and panting like hounds.

"*Unistan sinust nii päeval kui ööl*," Leif gasped as his arms came up to cradle her to his chest. "*Ma armastan sind. Ma armastan sind. Igavesti.*"

Too tired to think of anything, still dizzy and breathless, Olga left his beautiful words in the air and closed her eyes.

16

"Olga?"

Her weight had settled fully on him, and her body had become soft and yielding. Leif might have worried, if the position he'd found himself in hadn't been so comfortable and familiar. She had fallen asleep on his chest, while they were still joined, while he had not yet gone soft. They'd slept like this often in Estland—she snuggled on his chest, his arms around her—though normally he had been propped against the stead of her small bed.

Perhaps the rough floor of her Karlsa house was even less inviting a place to sleep, but he was with Olga, he had her in his arms, and he would have lain on spikes and called it perfect.

He didn't understand what had just happened between them. He didn't know if he'd been forgiven, if she was with him, if anything had, in fact, truly changed. What they'd done was different from what they'd had before; it was angry and painful, and she had been so unlike herself that Leif felt unmoored.

It had hurt her, what they'd done. He'd seen it, and he'd seen her want it, seen her—felt her—move to *make* it hurt, and he didn't understand. She'd found pleasure, too, he knew that. He could still feel the memory of her throbbing sheath.

He didn't understand, and he knew some worry because of it.

But he was lying with Olga in his arms. Their bodies were joined, the scent of their coupling hung in the air around them, and she slept quietly on his chest. They could not have been more close, in physical space at least, and it was more than Leif had hoped to have again in his life.

For now, in this waning dark, it was enough. He turned his head, burying his nose in the tousled braids of her hair, and kissed her temple. Then he closed his eyes.

~oOo~

"Oh! Olga? Oh!"

Leif woke at the young voice before Olga did. The room had brightened with the day, and sun pushed through the edges of the shutters. A wide bolt of light lay over the floor. He craned his neck to look behind him and saw a small pair of boots and the hem of a hangerock. Further investigation showed that the voice belonged to a pretty young woman with hair like fire.

"Hello," he said, and Olga stirred at his voice.

The girl blinked. "You are Jarl Leif." She dropped her head in deference, which Leif found absurd, considering the circumstances of the moment.

Olga tensed in his arms and sat up with a gasp. She was exposed, her gowns rumpled at her waist, and she noticed it at the same moment that he did and crossed her arms over her chest.

"Frida!" she snapped.

"Forgive me. I...I'll...forgive me." The girl backed to the open front door and left.

Leif turned back and looked up at Olga. He smiled, but she wasn't looking at his face. She stared instead at his chest.

"You bleed."

He had forgotten about the way this encounter had begun. Now, remembering, he knew an ache in his chest, sharper and more physical than the one that always resided there. It was nothing important, though, and he doubted he still bled. But he lifted his head to regard his chest and saw the stain of blood on his tunic. When he turned back to Olga, he saw the dried smears over her bare chest and shoulder, too.

"It's of no consequence."

She didn't like that, and he saw the hard sheen of offense in her eyes. Abruptly, she yanked her underdress back over her shoulders and cast her eyes about for the brooches to her hangerock. Leif lay still and watched her until she pushed off from him and stood.

He had softened and fallen from her body while they'd slept, but he'd hardened again since waking, with the natural thickness that came in the morning, and with the press of her bare mound on him. Even in this awkward moment, his body could not resist her any more than his heart could.

As she affixed her brooches, she glanced down at his ready member and then looked away. "I will check your wound."

He stuffed himself into his breeches and tied his lacing before he sat up. "It needs no care. Olga…"

"I will check your wound," she said again. "Come sit."

He stood and went to the stool she'd indicated, but he remained standing, towering over her. When she finally looked up at his face, he lifted his hand to brush loose strands of hair from her eyes, but she flinched away from his touch.

No, then. What had happened between them in the dark hours had not been a true unity.

"Sit. Remove your tunic."

He obeyed. As he laid the tunic across his lap, he asked, "Will you not speak with me?"

Perhaps she had not heard him. She was staring at his chest, but her attention was not on the fresh, relatively small wound over the many others. She reached out and traced the wide scar that sliced him from side to side, and not until her fingertips met the clotted blood of a newly-forming scab did her eyes shift to his.

"How many times have you almost died?" she whispered.

"A few. But I've known no pain from scars such as these as great as the pain I've known since I lost you." He grabbed her hands and held them to his chest. "Olga, I love you. I want you to come to Geitland with me. Sit at my side as my wife. Marry me."

Their eyes locked, and Leif tried to read love or hope or some kind of encouragement in her dark depths. All he saw was turmoil.

She pulled her hands free and went to a table against the front wall of the room. When she came back, she had a bowl of water and a clean linen, and he sat back and let her tend to the wound they had made.

In silence, she washed his chest and examined the cut. She cleaned it and daubed a creamy green paste, then laid a clean strip of linen over that.

When she turned away, Leif grabbed her hand. "Olga. Will you not answer me? Have I lost your love entirely?"

She peered into his face, and he knew that at last, at least, she would answer—and that he wouldn't like it.

"I love you. I gave you all the love I had to give, and it is yours forever. But the trust I gave you with it is destroyed, and I have no more left of that. I am glad you came to me in the night. I'm not sorry for what we did, but now we are at our end."

It was nothing he hadn't believed already, but to hear the words aloud, from her lips, was like that blade of hers striking its target.

But Leif was angry, too, as he'd been with Vali. He had not broken faith with anyone he loved. He had made mistakes, yes, and he'd not seen far enough to predict the many dark consequences of that last night in Estland, but only he had been acting to control the damage Åke would have done.

"I don't know how to make you see that I didn't betray you. You say I left you before Åke arrived, but *that is not true*. I could not stay, and you could not leave. We decided that *together*, and it broke my heart. I was tortured by the loss of you, but what I ended between us purposefully that night was only a better goodbye than the one we knew was coming. I needed to keep you distant from him, and that meant staying away myself. You never left my thoughts. I told you all this then."

"Yes, you did. And yet I was left to the whims of savage men."

The thought of Geir assailing her had Leif wishing the man still lived so that he could kill him in his own way. But if she'd complied with his wish, she wouldn't have been in Geir's path. "I would avenge you if I could. I would cut off every part of him that touched you and feed it to the swine. But I wanted you to leave the castle. You chose not to."

Anger flashed in her eyes. "The village was no more safe. My brothers died in the village. Hundreds died there."

"That was my only error, and my regret for it is deep. I should have seen that Toomas would break the peace, but I had no time to think through every chance." He squeezed her hands. "I am sorry that your brothers were lost. I'm sorry for your pain. I truly thought the village would be safe. But Olga, I have not betrayed your trust in me. If it is destroyed, it's your anger that ruined it."

That was the truth of it. She would not forgive him. She didn't love him enough to offer him that.

She shook her head. "It is no matter. It is dead. I will not go with you. I will not marry you."

He dropped his head with the weight of his regret. "And yet you say you still love me."

"As much as ever I have. I would that I did not, but I have no choice in the matter."

That answer did little to offer ease. Leif sighed and let her hand go. As he had with Vali, he understood that he'd reached the end of his atonement, the end of his power to change a heart and mind. Now, the option he had left was only to leave her to her own choice and accept the consequence. "Then the unhappiness we both feel henceforth *is* your choice." He stood and pulled his tunic on. "I will love you as long as my soul lives. That is my vow to you. But I'll not vex you further."

He bent low, and she tipped her head as if expecting his kiss. Instead, he rested his forehead on hers. "*Ma armastan sind,*" he whispered.

He wanted the last time he could tell her he loved her to be in her own words.

~oOo~

Later that morning, Leif sat in the hall with Vali, Brenna, Orm, Bjarke, Harald, and Jaan. Until this meeting, Leif had not comprehended how fully he'd been exiled from the family he'd been part of in Estland. Of the few who had survived since that time, only Astrid was with him in Geitland. Only they two and Brenna had been sworn to Åke. The others had been Snorri's men or Estlanders, and they were all here in Karlsa. They made up Vali's inner circle.

He had known this in his mind, of course, but until this moment, a guest in Karlsa, shunned by Olga, sitting in Vali's hall as the outsider, he'd not felt it so keenly.

They all regarded him as an outsider, and even those who had fought with him against Calder and his raiders had picked up Vali's skepticism.

But he was done with defending himself, done with apologies. Karlsa and Geitland were allies, and that would have to do until and unless Vali let the past go—or broke the alliance.

And then they would be enemies.

Now, he unrolled a piece of thin, pale hide until it took up the middle of the table. Vali and the others all leaned in.

"This is like the table in Estland," Brenna noted.

"Yes. When Calder and the ships returned, they came very late—winter was nigh. Ulv told that they had gone south, meaning to raid there, but a storm took them and turned them west. They thought they were lost. But they struck land. It was settled, but by people who had never seen raiders before. Unprotected. With a stone building filled with gold and jewels, nearly so much as Prince Vladimir's bounty, and no blade in sight to guard it. They found this among the plunder, but they didn't know what it was. Ulv kept it because he thought it pretty." He smoothed his hand over the lines and shapes on the hide. "But Astrid and I knew. You know."

Orm crossed his arms. "What good is this if we don't know the place? The table in Estland showed us the place we were. This...thing shows us a place we don't know."

"Ulv has been there. He knows the way."

"Ulv," Vali grumbled. "Son of Åke. Are we to trust him? You should have killed him."

"It was you, Vali, who told me that we do ourselves no good if we kill everyone who *might* be an enemy." Leif turned to Brenna. "You know Ulv, Brenna. He swore to me while his brothers' bodies lay at my feet. He has been true to that vow since."

Brenna nodded. "I know him, yes. He was a disappointment to his father and, so, not much tutored by him in his ways. If Leif is satisfied that his oath is true, then I believe it, too."

Vali studied his wife, and the table was quiet while he did so, until Leif broke the silence.

"Vali." When he had the jarl's attention, he pointed to a square with crossed lines atop it, in the center of a cluster of plain squares, just on the edge of the hide. "Ulv says that he believes this is where the gold and jewels were." With a sweep of his hand over the map, he added, "Look."

Everyone at the table leaned in. When they saw what he was showing them, they looked up, grinning.

There were two score boxes with crosses on them, strewn over the hide.

Vali leaned back and smoothed his hand over his beard. "You raided this summer, yes?"

"Yes. Good raids in the south."

"You didn't take Ulv to this magical place where gold lies about in heaps?"

Deciding to ignore the bite in Vali's tone, Leif answered, "It's too far for a small raid. Calder was cast off course to find it, and he almost lost two ships. We need skeids to make a true raid at such a distance, and my ships, like yours, are snekkjas. We need new ships and the men to sail them. We are allies, yes?"

Vali nodded. Brenna answered, "Of course we are."

"Good. Then let's ally and raid in the next summer."

Bjarke cut in. "You assume that men will go so far from home. These are waters we don't know."

"Water is water," Harald said. "Traders come here from far in all directions and seem to make their way. It cannot be so very treacherous. And we didn't raid this year. Men will be eager to wet their blades in blood and carry gold home to their families."

"Men and women," Brenna corrected, her voice low but clear.

"Of course," Harald agreed, blushing.

"But not you, shieldmaiden," Vali said, and Leif knew that he had his raid. If Vali was already thinking about what Brenna could or could not do, then he had made his decision.

Brenna sighed. "I know. I will stay home with our daughter and keep your jarldom in order, and you will go and plunder."

Vali kissed his wife's hand and turned to Leif. "I will bring it to the people here, and we will all decide together, but I think the answer will be yes, we will build great ships and explore the world with you in the summer."

~oOo~

That night, after the last meal, Leif sat in the hall drinking with seemingly everyone in Karlsa. Almost everyone—Olga, of course, was absent. He expected nothing else. His chest was a cold hollow, but he was accustomed to that emptiness. He worked to keep his attention on things he had some control over, lest his mind crawl into the dark loneliness and stay there.

There had been great enthusiasm for the idea of a new raid in a new place and the work their preparations would bring. The shipbuilder was especially pleased, as was Jakob, his apprentice. Leif noticed that Jakob treated the flame-haired girl who'd come on him and Olga that morning—he couldn't recall her name—with a possessive gentleness. He wondered if they were mated.

He hadn't had a chance to ask him, because Jakob did not seem inclined to be friendly.

While the revelry was in its fullness, Leif felt a hand on his shoulder, and he turned toward Vali, who had come up at his side.

"Might we speak in quiet?"

Leif nodded, but he wondered whether he was walking toward an ambush. Brenna had retired with Solveig not long before. Perhaps Vali had been waiting until his wife wasn't paying attention to finally exact his revenge.

He followed Vali out into a night that again had the crisp chill foretelling of winter rolling toward them. Vali went around the corner of the hall, and Leif's senses heightened further, but he relaxed when Vali simply sat on a stack of crates near the back and gestured to another. Leif sat, too. Another bright moon shone over them.

"Brenna wants us to come to terms. But I don't know how we do that. Every time I see her back, I think of you standing there, watching it happen, *letting* it happen, and I want to reach down your throat and tear out your heart."

Maybe Vali meant him violence after all—but Leif didn't think so. The words had not been said angrily.

"I know. Vali, I am out of words. I know of no more ways to apologize, and no other way to explain. If we are not friends, then I will accept it. I will not beg your forgiveness again."

Vali nodded. "Have you seen Olga?"

He hadn't expected the sudden change of topic, so Leif took a breath before he answered. "I have. She is not my friend, either."

"I'm sorry for that."

"Are you?"

"Yes. For her. I think I understand her in this."

"Do you?"

"Perhaps. We are the ones who were left behind, and we nearly drowned in fire and blood, and then in the sea as well. We knew only that Åke had taken Brenna and destroyed us, and that you had helped him, and in that knowledge, we watched the little we had left fall into ruin. We struggled across an angry sea seeking vengeance against you as much as any other. Brenna says I don't understand, and she's right. But she doesn't understand, either. And neither do you. I would let it go if I could, Leif. I remember our friendship and miss it. I remember that you took care of my son while I sat with Brenna. I remember that you counseled me that Åke was a threat to her, and I thought he was no match for me. If I had taken him more seriously, perhaps we might have been better prepared for what he did. I see my own fault, too. I remember that you were my good friend."

Vali paused and looked out toward the dark water beyond the shore. "But I look at Brenna and see her neck, and her back, and each of the other scars she suffered in those weeks, and I cannot remember how to be your friend."

Why they'd had to come out into the night to say things that had already been said, Leif did not know. He regretted making this trip; apart from the plans for raiding, all he'd done was tear open wounds that had at least scarred over. He could have sent Astrid to negotiate for the raid. He was heartbroken and exhausted, and he just wanted to go home.

"Well enough, then. Alliances don't require friendship."

Vali seemed truly disheartened. There was a small comfort in that, Leif supposed.

"I do believe that you didn't betray us purposefully. I believe that you acted with good intent. But I do not understand how you thought it was right. I cannot forgive what you let happen."

"And I cannot explain any better than I already have. I will not." Leif stood. "So I will sail in the morning and we will make our preparations, and come the summer, we will raid together. We need have no other contact."

~oOo~

As his ship left the pier the next morning, Leif stood and scanned the crowd. He had said his goodbyes to the few friends he had here, and Brenna had given him a hard hug.

But he wanted at least to see Olga in the crowd, to catch a last glimpse of those wide, dark eyes.

She wasn't there.

Just as he had given up and was ready to turn and settle in the ship, he caught sight of her, standing far apart from the crowd, alone near a house at the edge of a bluff, most of her dark hair loose and whipping in the wind like a flag. He raised his hand to her. She didn't return the gesture.

After a lonely moment, he dropped his hand, but he couldn't make himself turn away, not as long as he could see her. She stayed, too, at the edge of the bluff, and they faced each other until the horizon came up and took her away.

PART THREE
AIR

17

Olga had been wrong to think that coupling again with Leif would clear the darkness from her spirit. Being with him again had cleared the anger and the hate, but without those potent guardians, all that was left was love and loss.

She had fallen into an abyss of shadowy despondency after his ship had disappeared from view, and when that had at last abated, she was left feeling tired and ill. Her body was made of aches.

More than two months later, as Karlsa prepared for jul, their celebration of the winter solstice, Olga would rather have spent all her days abed. If it hadn't been for Frida's smiling face appearing every day to begin their work, perhaps she would have.

This time of year was much more difficult for Olga to bear here in Karlsa than it had been in her homeland. Here, there was a long stretch of days with no sun at all and only the barest lightening of the sky at the height of midday. The darkness weighed on her as if the sky were made of lead.

As the solstice approached, and the sun abandoned them completely, Olga's mood sank more and more deeply into despair, and the toll on her body was heavy. Things inside her seemed to be shutting down. She had grown ill enough that she struggled to keep food down, and the work of making her most common healing aids—her salve for healing wounds, traveler's tea for digestive difficulties, and trader's vinegar for ailments of the breath—had begun to repulse her. Of late, she had simply sat and supervised Frida, whose skill had advanced to the degree that she needed little in the way of instruction.

Frida had been the center of gossip in the town lately, as she was many months married and still had a flat belly. Olga knew the reason: Frida made Jakob spill his seed on their bed. She was not ready, she asserted, to be a mother yet. She wanted to complete her training first.

Gossip or not, Olga was proud. Frida was a young woman who knew her mind.

On the day of the solstice, the first day of jul, the town began a celebration that would last days. That morning—an irrelevant notion in a world of night—Olga crawled from her bed, dressed in the near dark of her smoldering fire, and slumped to the hall, where Brenna had asked her to join the women to break their fast together and deck the hall for the festivities at the midday. She felt weary and nauseated, and the bright glow of hundreds of candles and a roaring fire and the happy chatter of women already at work nearly sent her hurrying back to the safe solitude of her house.

But Dagmar, Brenna's mother, saw her and came over straightaway. She hooked her arm around Olga's waist. "Come. We have warm food and good cheer today. Today is the beginning of new hope."

It had been much the same in Olga's world, though they'd had no gods demanding the death of living creatures for no purpose but their deaths. The winter solstice marked the bleakest, darkest day of the year, thus it marked the beginning of brighter days. Each day until the summer solstice would be a bit brighter than the one before. The sowing would return. New life would rise up. Dark became light. Death became life. Ice became fire. Balance.

~oOo~

Struggling against her inner sorrow, she'd had no appetite for the morning meal, and she'd sat quietly and listened to the happy chatter around her, taking her chance to play with little Solveig, who had half a year now. She remained a happy and sweet-natured child, much in demand by all the women. She sat on many laps, babbling and grabbing at all she could reach.

Brenna's favorite cat, a queen named Lofn, after some goddess or another, stayed near the babe all day. She was enormous, her back as high as Olga's knees, and her long, thick fur was the color of a morning fog. Seeming to have taken Solveig on as her personal charge, the cat sat near the babe and watched the people around them with regal green eyes. When Solveig yanked on a fluffy ear or clutched a fat handful of fur, Lofn simply turned and licked her until she let go.

Olga found her attention drawn especially to Lofn on this day. That cat seemed to have what she herself had lost: the ability to live in the world as it was.

But she was learning how to pretend. So she helped festoon the hall with fragrant pine boughs and, when she began to feel a bit better, she went out and helped hang bundles of food, and ribbons, and little carved wooden figures on the massive pines on either side of the great hall entrance. The people of Karlsa believed that spirits lived in the trees, but the deep cold and dark chased them away. The gifts were meant to entice them to come home and bring the warm with them.

To Olga, the trees hung with little packages and figures were pretty, and that was enough to warm her heart a little.

At midday, two men pulled an enormous boar into the meeting place before the hall, and Vali stepped into the circle of his people. The height of the day was nearly as dark as the deepest of the night, and the ring of torches was lit.

He held a sword high and spoke over the squealing boar. "Sunna is birthed by Sól after she is swallowed by the wolf. She shall ride, as the wolf dies, the old paths of her mother. We offer this boar to help her on her way."

Olga didn't know what most of it meant, but he had said the same words the year before. He bent and drew his sword across the boar's throat. A bowl on the ground caught much of the blood. But Olga turned away. The sight of the blood made her woozy, and the death of the boar swelled her throat with pity.

~oOo~

Much of the jul celebration, like much of every celebration among her new people, consisted of consuming great quantities of mead. They toasted the gods again and again, and before the feast was over, men and women were beginning to keel over in drunken heaps. Those still celebrating didn't take much notice; they went on with their toasting and singing and drinking and shouting, and Olga would have sneaked away to the quiet of her house if she hadn't been sitting with Jakob and Frida, who would have fussed if she'd left.

Jakob had gotten well drunken himself, and he was singing along with everyone else, despite knowing only a few of the words. As one high-spirited song ended with a shout, his voice broke, and he began to cough. At first, it was just a quick bark, as if he'd inhaled something he oughtn't have, but then it built on itself until he was doubled over and tears streamed from his eyes. Frida and Olga helped him to sit, and Frida filled his cup with mead and urged him to take a drink and wash away what vexed him.

At last the coughing ceased, and he worked a smile onto his flushed face. "I'm well," he gasped, his voice as rough as a husk of bark. "I'm well."

Olga smiled back and brushed his dark curls from his forehead. He was hot—but not the muggy heat of exertion. The dry heat of illness. She caught Frida's eyes. "You're not. You're ill. Let us get you home to bed."

He began to shake that idea away, but Frida slapped his shoulder. "Don't be stupid, Jaki. If you're ill, then you take care and get well quickly." She set her hand on her husband's forehead as Olga had done. "You are too hot. We go now."

Another attack struck him as he bent to stand, and by the time it was over, he went meekly from the hall with them.

As Olga reached in to close the door, another song ended, and in that moment of quiet, she realized that there was a secondary chorus going on in the hall.

Many people were coughing.

~oOo~

"I believe it is borne on the breath. That is the most dangerous of all illness, because it is so difficult to keep it contained. The vinegar isn't working. I am trying to come up with something new, but it is winter, and I have only the herbs I'd dried."

Olga was overcome with fatigue, and she rested her head in her hands on her table, at Vali's side. He sat there with Brenna. They'd come to her for understanding about what had happened to their town.

Four days after the solstice, more than fifty people now lay on pallets on the floor of the great hall, in varying degrees of critically ill. Six had already died.

Karlsa had a plague.

And Jakob and Frida were both among the sick. Bjarke as well. Thus far, Olga had remained well—or as well as she'd been before the sickness had taken over the town. She and Dagmar and some of the servant girls from the hall were tending to the ill.

But what Olga was seeing, she'd never seen before. The pace of the disease's progress, the way it overtook the chest and the head and stole the breath and senses from its victims, it was beyond her ken and her skill.

Vali turned to Brenna. "You and Solveig must stay far from the hall. As far as you can. Go to Åsa."

"The seer? Vali, no!"

He cupped his hand around her face. "She is farthest but still close enough for me to know you're safe. This isn't like when you were a girl, and you know that. You must go where you and our daughter will be away from this illness."

"And you?" There was a strident note in Brenna's voice.

"I am jarl. You know I must stay."

Brenna didn't protest further, though Olga saw torment in her eyes. She was nursing their daughter; she could not allow herself to be ill, so she could be of no help, and Vali was right—he could not abandon his people. He was a better jarl, and a better man, than that. If he took ill, he would die with them, but he would not leave them.

When Vali and Brenna were ready to leave, Olga stood to see them out. The room seemed to shake, and then she sat down again, hard enough to rock her chair. Vali crouched immediately at her side and put his huge hand on her face.

"You're cool. That is good. But you feel ill?"

She took his hand away, setting it in her lap and holding it there. Brenna was at her other side, looking down with stern worry. "I'm not ill. Only tired. I don't sleep much." She looked up at Brenna. "You know that. But I'm not ill. The sickness is in the breath." She took a deep, clear breath and smiled. "It does not have me."

Brenna's eyes went to her husband. "Vali, go to my mother and collect Solveig. I'll be along."

Vali looked from one woman to the next, then nodded and stood. "Do not tarry." He kissed Olga's cheek, and his wife's mouth, and he left.

When he was gone, Brenna turned to Olga. "When Leif was here, did he bed you?"

Olga blinked, surprised by the question, but not by its directness. Brenna was nothing if not direct. As she tried to decide how much to tell her friend, understanding dawned about why she had asked.

"Brenna, no. I cannot be. I…I cannot bear children. You know that." Over the course of their friendship, they had spoken often and deeply about their lives. No one knew Olga as well as Brenna did.

"And you are sure this is true?"

"I've never been seeded again since my son. Years ago. Yes, I am sure. This—how I feel—is only sadness and weariness coupled with work and worry for the ill. I will rest before I return to the hall, and I will be well."

Her friend's expression softened into compassion, and she set her hand on Olga's shoulder and squeezed softly. "But Leif fathered many children with his wife. Seven children. Perhaps his seed is more powerful than most."

"We were together in Estland from the time of Ivan's attack until just before…the end, and I was not seeded. I am barren." The topic chewed on Olga's heart, and she wanted it over.

But Brenna persevered. "Have you had your blood since he was here?"

She hadn't, but nothing inside her had been working well since winter had fallen. The thought was both beautifully tempting and crushingly painful, but it was impossible. "I am not. My womb is dead. Nothing can grow there. I am a healer and a midwife, and I know my ken."

Brenna took her hand from Olga's shoulder. She bent forward and pressed on Olga's belly. "Then air must make you fat, my friend. Because you don't eat and yet your belly grows. You need to come to the seer's with me. Karlsa is too dangerous for you, as well."

Olga pushed Brenna's hand away and left hers in its place. Her belly had swollen a little, but she could name several causes vastly more likely than a seed sprouting in a womb that had died long before.

"No. You are wrong, and I am needed here."

The two women stared long at each other until Brenna nodded. "Very well. If you are sure."

"I am."

~oOo~

Frida and Jakob lay next to each other on the hall floor. Olga knelt between them, dripping a new concoction between Jakob's slack, bluish lips. More than a week had passed since the solstice. The dead now numbered nearly thirty, and the ill almost one hundred. But Jakob, one of the first ill, held on.

His end was coming, though, and soon, Olga knew. His skin had taken on the flat grey hue that told of sluggish blood, and his eyes, which hadn't opened in days, had sunk into the caves of their sockets.

His coughing had eased, but not for any good reason. He had lost the strength to cough. Now, when a fit overtook him, he simply strangled weakly until someone could reach him and turn him to pound on his back.

Frida was rallying a little and thus struggling more noticeably. She wheezed at his side, and her eyes and nose leaked corruption. In some of the worst cases, the seepage fused the eyes shut. When Olga had given Jakob all she could of the new brew, she turned and pulled Frida to a seated position and cradled her head on her shoulder. She wiped her face clean.

The girl's fever still raged, but in the past ten days, Olga had seen that those with the worst fevers often seemed to rally, as if the heat burned the pestilence away. On first noticing as much, she had thought to let the fever take hold—and then had promptly lost four young people to the fever itself. She could not make sense of the ways of this plague.

One in three of those stricken had regained or were regaining their health, Frida among them. Nearly one in three, so far, had died—some more quickly than Olga could treat, and others lingering like Jakob. The others were in the throes of the illness, and she could not say their fate. And every day, new sufferers staggered, crawled, or were carried into the great hall. The sickness was tearing through the town like a band of raiders.

Orm and Bjarke. Rikke and Elfa, who had nursed the others. They all had pallets in the hall now. Hans was among those taken quickly. Whatever this was, it fed on the weak, the strong, the young, the old. Four children in swaddling were gone.

Olga, Dagmar, and Holmfrid had remained well despite spending their days amongst the ill. Vali, Jaan, and Georg had remained well despite carrying the dead to the earth.

Vali and some of the strongest men standing had dug deep into the frozen ground to make a grave in the woods for all the dead. And now they were preparing a ritual of blood sacrifice to seek their gods' aid. Olga left them to their beliefs and tried to understand the disease.

"He's leaving me," Frida gasped.

"Hush, *kullake*, hush."

The young wife shook her head. "I can feel him going. I should have let him seed me."

Olga closed her eyes. Since Brenna had brought up the idea the week before, it would not leave her mind. She was barren, she knew, and the thought that she might be with child was nothing more than a new torment to add to her vast collection of them. "If you had a child inside you, it would also be ill."

Frida suffered a jag of rheumy coughing, and Olga held her and rubbed her back. "But I'm not leaving. I can feel that, too. My body is pushing the pestilence away." She was quiet, staring at the still form of her young husband. "His is not. And I will have nothing of him."

"Shhh. Shhh." Olga stroked the girl's hair and could make no words for the sorrow in her heart. "Shhh."

~oOo~

Jakob died that night, while Olga had gone to her house to make a new batch of the brew that at least seemed to offer ease in the chest. When she returned, Frida was lying at Jakob's side, holding his cold hand, her head on his stiff chest.

Vali came in and carried the boy's body out himself, and Olga followed. Frida, still rallying, had tried to stand and go with them, but she hadn't the strength. So Vali and Olga, and Jaan and Georg, stood at the side of the grave, into which Jakob's body was laid with two others who had also died on the same day.

She had lost another brother. Another boy like a son.

"When I pulled him from the sea," Vali sighed, "I had the help of the gods. I thought he was meant for great things."

Olga took his hand and squeezed it. "He had love, and he made a new home. You saved him for that."

Jaan leaned close to Olga's ear. "Can you say our words?"

She closed her eyes. When tears came, she let them fall unhindered, and they made cold tracks down her cheeks.

In the language of their homeland, in a voice broken by grief and rusty in her own tongue, she said, "We send you into the earth, our friend and brother, our son, so that you may begin the path anew. We put your name into the air, Jakob, and cry our tears onto your body, so that you may be prepared for the next turn of the wheel. May the sun warm you and the earth hold you while the world rolls forward. May your spirit now be free."

~oOo~

Two days later, Frida's fever broke, and her chest began to clear. She was listless and pale, but Olga understood that to be mourning as much as illness and knew that she would, if she chose, regain her health. She had only fourteen years and was already a widow, but her spirit was strong.

When, later in the day, Olga saw her sitting up, speaking gently with the old woman lying at her side, she knew it with certainty. Frida would be well.

The pace of the newly ill was becoming stable, with no more than two or three coming to the hall each day for the past few days. The pace of the dying was increasing, however, as more of the lingering ill lost their battle.

Vali had sacrificed a great steer in search of their gods' aid to lift the pall of illness from the town. Olga thought of the horse he'd sacrificed before they'd left her home. Brenna's horse, a lovely golden mare.

Their voyage had been arduous, but the tossing seas had brought them here, to Vali's home, where an army had been waiting to aid him in his quest to save Brenna and avenge them all.

Perhaps there were gods in the skies and the sea. Perhaps the blood of that steer would appease them in some way and gain the people of Karlsa some relief from this pestilence.

Olga set a cooling cloth over the eyes of a feverish child. She stood and bent to pick up her water bowl, and she felt something inside her, a flutter in her belly. Straightening quickly, she laid her hand over the spot. As Brenna had pointed out, and as she herself had, of course, known, her belly swelled slightly, where always before it had been a flat plane. Always before except once, for a few precious months. And now something inside was moving.

Could Brenna be right? Could she be with child? She should know. It was her job to know.

She thought of her aches and illness for the past few months. She had believed them to be signs of her despondency, and they could well have been. But she had missed her blood three times as well. And her belly grew. And now that flutter of movement. It could have been a spasm, nothing more than a twitch in her vitals. Any of these could be signs of other ailments of body and spirit. But all of them together?

Yet years of barrenness said it was impossible.

What would she have told a woman who came to her like this?

She would have said that when the signs are strong, the truth is clear.

She was with child. Leif's child. She had thought it impossible, she had been blind to the signs, had denied them, and now she was well along.

Leif's child. Her child. A child.

What would that mean for the future?

It didn't matter. She was with child, and for the first time in many, many months, Olga cared about the future.

She was surrounded by deadly illness. Though she had not taken ill, she couldn't risk that she might yet. She prepared to tell Dagmar that she would have to leave the hall. These weeks tending to the afflicted had trained the others well in their care. She would stay close, in her house, and make the brew, and be available for counsel, but she could no longer be in the hall herself.

Before she could find a moment alone with Brenna's mother, Olga felt another flutter, this one in her throat. She tried to clear it.

Then she couldn't stop coughing.

18

Leif rested the longsword on his fingers. "The balance is good." With a flex of his hand, he tossed the heavy blade up and caught it by the grip. "I don't like the weave on the hilt, however. Too soft."

The smith nodded and took the blade from him. "You would prefer it unwrapped and polished?"

Leif nodded.

"As I thought. Young Dag"—he indicated his apprentice—"thought the jarl's new sword should be fantastical. He wove the grip and even hoped to carve the fuller. But I told him that was not your way."

Smiling at the boy, Leif said, "The weave is good work. An elaborate blade is well and good for rituals and ceremonies, boy. But a jarl should carry a blade like those of his clansmen. It is a tool. The most important tool a man will ever have, but a tool. When I forget that, I won't be worthy of wielding it."

The boy blushed. "Forgive me, Jarl Leif."

With a sharp pat on the boy's back and a nod to the smith, Leif left the smithy and continued on his way to the shipbuilder's.

The celebrations of jul had ended, and the town had recovered from the days of revelry. They were still in deep winter, but here on the Geitland shore, the snows weren't so deep and the water moved freely. Each day brought them more sun. There was work to be done to prepare for the great raids of the coming summer.

The plans for this raid kept his mind engaged and his body active, and that was a good thing. In the quiet dark of the night, alone in his quarters, loneliness ate him raw. He could feel himself becoming bitter, the guilt he'd felt for the consequences of his actions festering into resentment because he had not been forgiven, would not be understood, by those he loved best, and he knew that if he let those dark feelings get their claws into him, he would become someone he did not wish to be.

Astrid believed he should find a wife. He needed living heirs, she insisted, and he needed companionship, and if Olga did not want him, then he should find someone who did.

Luckily, she had not been offering herself in the role. Leif cared for Astrid; especially since he had become leader of Geitland and she his right hand, he admired her very much and preferred her company to any other in town. But she was sour-tempered and quick to fight, with words, fists, or weapons, and he thought that any man she might mate with would need a great deal of fortitude and perseverance.

Leif had no intention of marrying again. Although he had married once without love and been fortunate to have grown into it, now he was already in love and knew he couldn't love anyone else. He would have Olga or no one, and she didn't want him. Besides, Olga could not have given him more children, so there had been no more heirs in his future in any case. If he was still jarl when he died, the people of Geitland could fight out the question of who would take his seat.

The shipbuilder's house was the largest of any building in the town save the great hall itself. Inside, Grimulv and his five apprentices were hard at work finishing the first of two skeids they would sail to the west. North in Karlsa, Leif expected that Vali's men were building two similar vessels.

Two great fire pits kept the large space warm while the workers climbed over and into the nearly-completed hull of the massive new ship. Off to one side, Grimulv's wife and several other townswomen were at work on the sail, striped in Leif's colors: black and white. He had chosen them for the simplicity of their contrast. The darkest color and the lightest.

Grimulv's wife had sighed at him when he'd chosen the colors in his early days as jarl; apparently black was among the most difficult dyes. But he had been resolved on the point. The result of the women's efforts was, on close inspection, more of a deep grey, but the sea would have its way eventually, anyway, so Leif was satisfied.

"How goes it?" Leif asked when the shipbuilder had climbed down from the ship.

Grimulv ruffled his hand over his head. "We won't be sure it's seaworthy until it sits on the sea, but I see no problem yet. We will be ready to begin the next in a fortnight, perhaps." Since Grimulv was of a melancholic nature and tended to be subdued about his ability to meet other people's demands, his assertion that there had been no problem yet was high confidence on his part.

"That is good. On your schedule, yes?"

"Yes. Come." He started off toward a table, where a heavy sailcloth was draped over an odd shape. "I work on this at night." He pulled the drape free to expose a large, intricately-carved dragon bust. "I have a plan for the other as well. You didn't ask, but ships as great as these should have a great beast on the prow."

Leif traced his hand over the carving. The dragon was rendered roaring, its head cast high, its great teeth bared. "It's magnificent. Thank you, friend."

Grimulv merely nodded and pulled the sailcloth back over the figurehead, forcing Leif to move his hand.

~oOo~

When he came out of the shipbuilder's house, Astrid stood there with her arms crossed. "What do you think?"

Leif grinned. "We will have magnificent ships to sail to this new place. What news with you?" He turned toward the hall, and Astrid fell in step at his side.

"There is a rider in the hall, seeking to speak directly to you. He bears a message."

"A rider?" Though travel was far slower over land, it was the safest path in the winter. Icy winds that gusted from the north played havoc on the water, and in the north, the sea itself froze, well out from the shore. "From where?"

"He would not say. He will speak only to you anything regarding his message. But he came into town from the north."

Karlsa was far to the north and through two other jarldoms. A journey over land, even by relay, would take nearly a fortnight, and more if the weather were bad. Only a crucially important message would come so far in winter. It was more likely to be from Finn or Ivar, the nearer jarls. Even if it had come from Karlsa, it would likely be Vali, with some need or trouble regarding their plans for the summer. It would not be Olga. She would have no desire, or understanding, to send him a message this way.

But Leif's heart began to thump with worry nonetheless. He picked up his pace, moving so quickly toward the hall that Astrid was forced to trot to keep up.

Once there, he saw the rider immediately, sitting near the fire, still in his furs, with a cup of mead and a heaping plate of hot food. When Leif strode toward him, the man stood and bowed his head. "Jarl Leif."

"You have a message?"

"Yes. I am Erik, of Dofrar. I carry a message from Vali, Jarl of Karlsa."

A strange blend of relief and disappointment surged through Leif's veins. He had been correct. Olga would not convey any message to him, certainly not in this way. Instead, the message likely meant trouble for the raid. Unable to help himself, he sighed. "What is it?"

"Only five words. They are exactly the words conveyed to me by the rider before me. The message is this: 'Come now. She needs you.'"

~oOo~

He left that very day. It nearly crazed him to ride; he was a man of the sea, and riding long distances took far too long. But he had no choice. The sea would be too treacherous for a journey so far north, and they would have faced a strong headwind all the way. By mount, he could ride alone—or, at Astrid's insistence, with a single companion—and find shelter should a storm come up.

Ulv rode with him, and they pushed hard every day, changing their horses often and sleeping and supping rarely. And still, it was a full fortnight before they made it to Karlsa. Almost a month since Vali had sent the message.

The message had been maddeningly vague. All relayed messages, by necessity, were; they had to move through many mouths and ears before they arrived at their intended audience, and so they had to be short, lest they be misremembered. All the ears and mouths heard the information themselves as well, so a sensitive message could not be too specific. But for many days of the journey, Leif's mind gnawed at the question of Olga's need, one so great that Vali himself had intervened to bring Leif to her.

Then they began to hear word of Karlsa, and his worry grew until he thought it might crush him.

As they'd traveled farther north, a story had developed about the state of Vali's people. By the time they were moving through Jarl Ivar's holding, adjoining Vali's, those they encountered had cautioned them strongly to turn back.

Karlsa had been stricken with a great plague. Every person had a different accounting of the numbers of the ill and the dead, each one growing more extreme, and everyone had a different story about the illness itself. By the time they saw the town of Karlsa ahead, Leif and Ulv had been half-expecting the dead themselves to walk, and none other.

Olga was their healer. Vali's message was that she needed Leif immediately. It could mean only one thing. She had been stricken.

And nearly a month had passed since the message had been sent. Leif spent the last days of the journey preparing himself for the likelihood that he was too late.

Not far from the town proper, they came upon a large open grave and two snowy mounds next to it that Leif knew were others just like it that had been filled with bodies and covered.

Was Olga already in one of these holes? Leif's heart sank heavily at the thought.

Ulv pulled up his mount. "Leif. If we cross into town, we might not leave it."

That was a truth. Even if they didn't take ill themselves, they could bring the sickness with them when they left. They would have to stay until it lifted. Leif turned to his friend. "You are right. You should turn back. Return to the house where we took our last meal. They'll keep you for the night, and you can return to Halsgrof and ask Jarl Ivar to provide you with lodging."

Ulv considered him for a few moments, then shook his head. "No. I'm with you. I only wanted the import of what we do said aloud."

Åke had been disappointed in Ulv, his quiet, thoughtful son, but in truth, he was the best among the former jarl's heirs. Leif nodded, and they nudged their horses to continue this last stretch of their long journey.

Vali rode up just before they entered the town. He looked haggard—not ill, but exhausted and full of sorrow. He cast a surprised eye in Ulv's direction and then turned to Leif.

"I'm glad you came." He didn't come near enough to touch.

Relieved that Vali hadn't stood on the niceties, Leif asked the only question in his head. "Is she…" He couldn't say the word.

"She is gravely ill, but she yet lives. Before I take you to her, we must talk. There is much you need to know."

He had not ridden so hard and long to have another accusatory talk with Vali. "No. After I see her, we'll talk."

Vali smiled without humor. "I am not making a request. Come with me, or I will not allow you to see her at all. Where we're going is free of pestilence."

Without saying more, Vali turned his black steed and led them into the woods.

They rode until Karlsa was again out of sight, and Leif thought he would go mad. Every muscle in his body was clenched, and he had one clear intention upon arriving wherever they were going: he was going to punch Vali in the face.

Which he did as soon as they'd dismounted before a small hut. He hit the man so hard that Vali fell into the snow, and then Leif stood ready to defend himself from retaliation. At his side, Ulv put his hand around the grip of his sword.

But Vali only stood and wiped the blood from his mouth. "Perhaps I deserved that. But you won't get a second. Go. Brenna and Solveig await inside."

Surprised by Vali's reaction to his punch and by the words he'd said, Leif cocked his head. "Are you not going in?"

"I handle the dead every day. I will not risk my wife and child."

Brenna and Solveig were just on the other side of the door they stood before. "How long?

Pain flashed across Vali's features. "I haven't touched either of them in more than a month."

Again, Vali and Brenna had been separated by events beyond themselves. Leif sighed, wondering whether the gods truly favored the God's-Eye and the Storm-Wolf after all.

The door opened then, and Brenna was there with Solveig in her arms. The babe saw her father and leaned forward, arms outstretched, and cried "BA! BA!"

"Hello, my sun." Vali grimaced with pain and stepped back, making greater distance, and he and his family stood, in sight of each other but out of reach. The longing between them was so powerful the air seemed to crackle. When her father wouldn't come to her, Solveig began to cry, and Vali reacted as if he'd taken another physical blow.

Brenna turned and handed her daughter off to someone inside, then turned back.

"You are well?" Brenna asked her husband.

"I am." He gestured toward Leif and Ulv. "I bring you the guest we hoped for. May we speak out here?"

Brenna nodded and came to Leif with her arms up. Vali backed away even farther as she left the hut.

Leif hugged her long and hard. "I'm glad to see you are well," he whispered into her hair.

She stepped back and smiled up at him. "Vali would hobble me before he'd let me near the town—or him. I'm not fighting him. I want Solveig safe." Turning to gesture at the woman in the hut with the crying babe, she added, "This is Åsa." Leif and the seer nodded at each other.

"We have all the mothers with babes at the breast, and the very young children, moved away from the contagion, and the women who are with child, too…those who didn't fall early, before we understood." Vali's expression changed as he spoke, and Leif couldn't read it.

"You sent for me long ago. I came immediately, but it's been weeks. Has she been so ill so long?"

Brenna answered and took Leif's hand. "No. She wasn't ill when we sent the message. She fell to it just more than a week ago."

"I don't understand. The message said she needed me." He looked into Brenna's eyes and was shocked to see them well with tears. "What? What is wrong?"

It was Vali who answered. "She carries your child, my friend. We sent for you for that reason."

Leif heard Vali call him friend, and if he had uttered any other sentence imaginable, perhaps Leif would have cared more about that signal that his friend was finally thawing toward him. But the sentence that preceded it had Leif's mind staggered. "I don't...she can't...how can this be?" More questions unfolded and spun through his head. "If she is with child, why isn't she with the others, away from the illness?"

"She didn't know for a long time," Brenna said. "When I challenged her, she denied it. She didn't believe it possible, and she wouldn't stop helping the ill. I thought she was wrong, and I worried. So I told Vali, and we agreed we should send for you. She doesn't know we did."

Leif understood only one thing. "I need to see her. You have the sick in the hall?"

Vali nodded and stepped to his horse. "Yes, but Olga is in her house. I'll take you to her."

"I know where her house is."

"And yet, I will take you to her."

Arguing only slowed him down, and Leif felt as though his head might burst, so full of worry was it. So he nodded his agreement.

Before Leif could get to his horse, Brenna was on him again, embracing him. "This is the last time I'll be able to be close with you until the sickness passes. Once you go into town, Vali won't let you be here."

The implications finally landed hard on Leif's shoulders, and he turned to Ulv. "Now, we part. Stay here. If you wish to stay close, then be here. If you wish to return home, I give you leave. But you have no cause to take the risk of the contagion. You know no one here."

Ulv huffed as if he were offended. "I know you. You are my jarl, and I am here to be at your back. I go where you go. I might be of use in the town."

Vali regarded Åke's son seriously. "Or you might take ill and die eight hundred miles from home."

"Mayhap. I know my duty. And my loyalty. I am not my father, Vali Storm-Wolf."

"It would seem you are not." Vali gave Leif a significant look, and Leif, understanding it, nodded. "Very well, then. I am sure you can be of use."

~oOo~

On the ride into town, Vali told Leif and Ulv that in the weeks that the plague had gripped them, they had lost more than two hundred souls, and nearly that many were yet ill. Half the town's population had been brought low, or brought down, by this plague.

But the past week had brought only ten newly ill, and Vali called that great progress. He thought perhaps they were reaching the end of their trial—the beginning of its end, at the least. At the rate that the plague had taken the ill thus far, he yet expected to bury another few score more bodies.

Jakob and Hans were both dead. Bjarke and Orm had fallen. Bjarke was well again, but Orm remained ill, caught in a murky place of gravely poor, but no longer worsening, health. Several of the ill were in that place. Vali described it as leaning on the doorway to the next world.

Vali, Jaan, Georg, and Harald all appeared immune. When Leif pointed that out, Vali offered him a tired, humorless chuckle. "I would have said that about Olga not long ago. Until everyone is well, I won't guess at the whims of this disease. She couldn't understand it, either. It is like nothing she's ever seen."

"How is she, Vali? In truth."

Vali pulled up his horse and turned to face Leif. "She is poorly. She has been insensible for days now."

"And the babe?" Leif's heart gained an extra beat at the question and its thought.

"I don't know. Beyond my ken. But Brenna's mother, Dagmar, and Olga's apprentice, Frida, are in charge of the healing now. And they are worried."

Leif nudged his horse into a gallop and left Vali and Ulv to catch up. He knew where Olga was.

~oOo~

He frightened young Frida when he stormed into the house, but she recognized him right away, and her expression shifted from shock to something much softer. Relief, perhaps. Without a word, she tipped her head to the back room, through the open doorway, where Olga's bed was. Leif wasted no time. He heard Vali step into the house behind him, but Vali, at that moment, was irrelevant.

The goats and chickens were gone, and the room was deadly quiet but for the strident rasp of labored breathing. She lay on the bed, under furs, her long hair that he loved so much loose and flowing over the bed. She was propped high on a mound of more furs, and her head lolled to the side.

Her skin was red—bright red, nearly glowing in the candlelight—and her eyes seemed crusted shut. She breathed that rattling, wheezing rasp from her open mouth. The movement of her chest was so erratic and shallow that Leif couldn't believe air was moving into her body.

She was dying. Anyone who looked could see it.

Looking, he could also see quite clearly, even under the furs, the small but obvious mound of her belly. Their child inside her ill and failing body. The love of his life and his eighth child on the brink of death. Leif wondered what it was he had done to earn such contempt from the gods.

He went to her and crouched at the side of the bed. Digging under the furs, he found her hot, dry hand and closed it in his own. "Olga. I am here, and I am not leaving. I will not go from you again, ever. *Ma armastan sind.*"

He leaned over and kissed her, long and gently, on the mouth.

19

Olga swam through a fog made of molten iron, and she was drowning. It coursed through and around her, filled her lungs, her brain, and her blood, and she knew nothing but its heat. Any other sensation or impression came at her from a long distance, muffled and distorted by the warp of the searing heat and burning pain.

Sometimes, she would catch a glimpse of something—a touch or a sound or a taste—and she would want to hold onto it, but it was gone before she even understood what it had been. Sometimes, she would think she understood—the sound of a voice she loved, or the press of lips on hers—but they were things that couldn't be real, and she let them go.

What wouldn't go was heat and pain.

~oOo~

Olga woke to darkness, a relentless black, and her first thought—the first one she was able to keep hold of in what felt like a very long time—was that she had been wrong, and there was a level of wakefulness after death. She believed that the spirit left with the body, that the body went into the earth to become a part of the circle again, renewed and changed, and that the spirit evanesced. But that first thought, that she had died and woken into a black abyss, frightened her more than she had ever felt fear before.

Then she felt a pull on her eyelids and realized that her eyes were closed and would not be easily opened. At that, she had her first fully coherent thought: the plague. She had fallen ill. The sickness swelled and gummed the chest, eyes, and nose.

Her chest felt both swollen full and crushed flat, and every breath came in like the air was full of metal shards. But she was awake and alive, and she thought that meant that she had survived the illness—or would, at least.

Finding her hands, she brought them to her face—an effort that seemed far beyond her capability—and rubbed until she could open her eyes.

The room, her room, was dim, but not deep dark. Light shone through the closed shutters, enough to tell her that it was day.

She was alone—no, she wasn't. From the foreroom, she heard low voices and the familiar sounds of a meal being had. When she opened her mouth and tried to speak, nothing would come. Barely even a breath could come.

As soon as she gave up, she began to cough, and she had never known physical pain so intense. She tried to roll to her side, to curl up and find some kind of comfort, but her strength was not sufficient even for movement such as that. She could only lie where she was and let the cough have her.

Then the people of the foreroom were with her, and Olga was too shocked to feel pain. Hunching through the low doorway was a golden giant. Her golden giant. Leif.

He met her eyes and smiled broadly, even as his brow was furrowed with worry. "Olga!" he said and sat at the side of the bed. Without hesitating, as if it were a move he knew well, he pulled her gently forward until she leaned against his chest, and he patted her back. She felt the press of his lips on her head.

When the fit finally eased, she remained resting there, framed within his arms, and his patting changed to a sweeping caress, long ovals up and down her back. After a few moments of quiet, he murmured, "Are you with me?"

Olga was in strident pain, and she was exhausted and confused. She wasn't sure what he was asking her—if she was still awake? Or if she was with him in a greater sense? In any case, it didn't matter. Right now, she was so relieved that he was with her that she would have wept, had she had the strength. Whatever he meant by his question, there was one answer.

She nodded.

Leif's embrace tightened tenderly, and he laid her back on the bed. He brushed her hair back and smiled down at her. "I have no words to say how glad I am to see your beautiful eyes again."

"You're here," she tried to say, but all she could do was shape her lips to the words. No sound left her throat.

He seemed to understand her nonetheless. "I am here. I'm not leaving you. Not ever again. I love you." He moved one hand and rested it on her belly. "I love you both."

Olga thought that a very strange thing to say, but the fog was filling her head again, and she shut her eyes.

~oOo~

When she next woke, it was night. The hot, crushing pain still filled her, but it did not seem so much to consume her, and her mind felt more her own. She remembered her last waking as if it had been a dream, but she could make sense of it. Leif was here.

At that thought, she cast her eyes around the dim room. It was dark, but she could make out the shapes of her sparse furniture and see the soft moonlight through the shutters.

And the large, still form lying on the floor at the side of her bed. Leif was *here*.

She moved her hand from under the furs and let it drop off the bed until she could tangle her fingers in his hair. He flinched instantly at her touch—he could not have been deeply asleep—and sat up.

The room was too dark to see him clearly, but what light there was showed his silhouette and a pale gleam at his eyes. She smiled and tried to say his name, but no sound would come forth.

He moved, and she felt his hand on her forehead. "You are cool. Thank the gods. Olga, are you with me?"

Recalling that he'd asked her the same question before, she still wasn't sure what he meant—and it still didn't matter. She nodded.

Leif came up from the floor and sat at her side, facing her. He leaned to her little table and poured water into a cup. As he helped her drink, he asked. "How do you feel?"

She couldn't answer, so after the pleasure of the cool water had ended, she tried to make a shrug, but that hurt.

"Forgive me. I'm relieved to have you awake and getting well. You were very ill, Olga."

She nodded; she knew. As her mind cleared and hooked its hands around reality, many things she knew emerged from the fog—and many things she wondered. But she had no way to seek answers to her wondering.

After a moment of quiet, Leif laid his hand on her belly—and something else she had known before broke free of the fog. She was with child. She had been, at least. Her hands went to her belly, too, and Leif moved his to make room for her. She was relieved to find the slight roundness still there.

He covered her hand with his own. "Do you know if the child is well? Can you tell?"

She remembered having felt a few flutters just as she had taken ill. She had no understanding of how long ago that had been. In this moment, she lay quietly for a few heartbeats and tried to feel. All she felt was the thick pain in her chest and the sharp pain behind her eyes and in her throat. She shook her head.

So many questions had begun to fill her head. She didn't know if her child still lived inside her, or if he was well. She didn't know how or why Leif was here, or how he knew about the child—though she guessed that both of those answers would have to do with Vali and Brenna. She didn't know what it meant for her, for them, that Leif was here with her. She didn't know what it changed about all that was between them.

She didn't know why she was in her own house rather than the hall, where all the sick had been. She didn't know how many were yet ill, how many had died, whether the end of this struggle was nigh. She didn't know if Vali and Brenna or any of her other friends still lived, if they were well. She didn't know, she couldn't ask, and she was already exhausted again from trying to sort through her thoughts.

All she knew was that she would live, and that Leif was here, holding her hand.

~oOo~

Dagmar held up the silk sleeping shift, the vibrant color of rosebay, that Olga had made for herself in a time that seemed long ago. She shook her head.

Ignoring her completely, Dagmar pulled the silk over Olga's head and held it up until she slid her arms through. "He has barely left your side, you know. And today is the first time since he arrived that he has stepped out of reach of the front door."

A week had passed since Olga had first come back to her senses. She was not well yet, but every day brought improvement. Yet her voice remained elusive. The breath she needed to make sound was still too much to spend.

Today, for the first time, Dagmar had helped her wash fully. Not in a bath, but with warm water and a sponge, all over her body. When she had been shy to disrobe before Leif, Dagmar had shooed him away.

Once bare, she had stared long at her belly. It was larger than it had been. Not much, but enough for her to see the difference.

And she could feel the babe move. He, or she, was still alive inside her, and every day he, or she, moved more noticeably.

Leif had been with her when she had first felt stirrings again. Through pantomime, she had managed to tell him what she could feel.

He had kissed her belly and then laid his head on it and wet it with tears.

Olga felt confused by her lack of inner conflict concerning Leif. He had betrayed her, he had caused her horror and pain, and she had lost everything because he had broken her trust. She had sent him away because she knew she could never trust him again, and she had spent months despondent and alone.

And now none of that seemed to matter. It should have mattered, and each day, Olga told herself that it would matter again, when her mind was clearer, when she was stronger, more well. Every day she felt clearer and stronger, and yet every day it mattered not.

She loved him, that had never been in doubt, but she wasn't sure if she trusted him. How could she? The past was unchanged. Her loss was unchanged. His treachery—unchanged.

Perhaps it was only the babe, their child, pulling his, or her, parents together.

Dagmar took the washbowl and linen away, and Olga heard her moving about in the foreroom. The aroma of a kettle of skause on the fire began to waft into the air. Olga's belly rumbled—and then fluttered. She smiled and set her hand over the spot. She could not yet feel her child moving against her hand, but inside, the feeling was unmistakable.

When Dagmar came back, she picked up Olga's comb—an elaborately carved piece that had been a gift from Jakob—and pulled a stool close so she could work the comb through Olga's tangled mass of hair.

"Frida will come to check on you shortly, and tonight she might make a visit of it. There are only eighteen ill yet in the hall, and most of them are recovering. No new ill for three days. She is going to sleep the whole night tonight in her bed. Though I suppose that her bed won't be hers for much longer. She was in Amund's house as Jakob's wife. She will have to find a new place to live." Dagmar gave Olga an unnecessarily meaningful look. Olga didn't need prompting; she would be happy to have Frida living with her again.

She patted her chest lightly and then pointed down at the floor. "She should come here," she barely whispered.

Dagmar smiled. "I think that would be well, for Frida to be in the healer's house. She has great skill, that young one. You've taught her well."

Olga thought that the plague had taught Frida more than she ever could have about healing the sick—and the limits of human ken to do so.

The front door opened, and Leif filled the space. He looked through the foreroom and the doorway to the back and seemed slack-jawed, staring at Olga. "Don't bind it. Please," he said as he closed the door and came close. He meant her hair, she knew.

Dagmar dropped her hands from Olga's hair and stood. "I will check again on the skause. Frida will be hungry, I expect, when she comes today."

Leif stepped fully into the room to make space for Dagmar to pass. Then, when they were more or less alone, he came and crouched at her side. "You look well—and beautiful."

Her cheeks warming with something other than fever, Olga smiled.

Leif brushed his fingers over her shoulder, and her eyes closed at the dance of sensation under his touch. "This is lovely. And unusual. It suits you."

She blushed more deeply. "Silk," she whispered. "Traders."

Leif nodded. Well, of course he would know about traders and silk, even though both had been a marvel to her. She felt silly. But his fingers had continued their exploration of her decadent shift, and Olga was too captivated by his touch to remain abashed. His fingertips brushed down her arm and back up, over the curve of her shoulder—and then left the silk and brushed over her bare skin, tracing her collarbones, as he had so often done before. His brow was furrowed over blue eyes that flashed with heat.

Overwhelmed with feelings, she caught his hand in both of hers. He met her eyes, and she saw guilt there, but not the tormented regret she had seen when he'd last visited Karlsa. This was a needful kind of guilt, which said he wanted more.

"Forgive me," he said, his voice low and husky. "I don't mean to press you. I know you are not yet well. I'm only happy to have you happy to have me here. I have missed you, my love. Are you with me?"

Still unsure how she could be so sure, she nodded.

He smiled and leaned close, pulling his hand free of hers so that he could slide all his long fingers into her hair as he held her head. He kissed her, gently, barely brushing his lips over hers. When his tongue slid tenderly between her lips, Olga thought she would swoon.

It didn't matter. The past didn't matter. She was alive. Leif was here. She was with child—a chance she'd thought never to have again. The only man she had ever loved was holding her close, kissing her, saying he loved her. They would be bound always by the child inside her. The past didn't matter. He was with her. She was with him.

But did she trust him? Would she come to regret it if she did?

She didn't know.

And she thought that would matter. If not now, then someday.

~oOo~

"Should you not return to Geitland? You are jarl."

Olga's voice was yet weak and rough, but she could finally make herself heard, as long as she had no need to speak loudly. Another week had passed, and the plague, after two months, had at last released Karlsa from its poisonous clutches. Olga was among the those who remained still weak, but there was no one left who was truly ill.

The full count of the dead was three hundred and ninety-seven. Karlsa had lost nearly one-half of its population.

At her question, Leif, who had been stoking the fire against the cold of a storm outside, turned to her, his eyebrows lifted in surprise. "The jarldom is in Astrid's capable hands for now. I told you I would not leave you again. Until you are able to travel with me, I go nowhere."

Her contentment with his presence continued to vex her. She tried and tried to find the limit of her renewed ease with him, but she could not. She even brought forth horrific memories of the last days in her homeland, but her rage at Leif did not come with them. The sorrow and pain were there, but not the blame. It would return, it had to return, and she would be caught unawares when it did, unless she remained vigilant now.

But it was difficult. He was here, taking care of her, loving her—openly, for the first time—and now Brenna and Solveig were back, the hollowed-out town was beginning to move toward recovery, and Leif and Vali seemed to have made their peace. She felt happy, at ease. And she shouldn't have.

Now that she had her voice, however, she could push the limits harder.

"You assume that I will go with you. But Karlsa is my home now."

Leif stepped away from the fire and came back to sit beside her at the table. "You carry my child. I love you. You know my wish—I would have us wed."

"Does my wish not matter? Again?"

Leif frowned and looked away. "Of course it does. It always has. We will have a child. You don't wish to raise him together?"

She did. Very much. "I don't wish the child to be the reason we wed."

He turned back and locked eyes with her. "You know it's not my reason. Is there no other reason for you?"

There were many reasons, a host of them. But one reason held her back. "I am afraid."

When she dropped her eyes, he caught her chin on his hand and lifted until she looked at him again. "Of what?"

"That it will be a mistake to trust you again."

He pulled his hand back so quickly that her head bobbled a little. They sat there, quietly, and Olga wondered if she was wrong to push him. Or would she be wrong to trust him?

Did it matter? No, right now, it didn't. What she felt in this moment, as he stared at his clenched fists on the table, was contrition. She wanted to slip under his arm, into his embrace, and tell him that she loved him, that of course she would wed him, that they would live in Geitland and raise their child, that they would be happy.

Would the past ever matter again? She wished she could say no. But she wasn't sure.

Finally, Leif broke the silence. He stared at his fists as he spoke. "I will always be sorry for your pain in Estland. Knowing what happened after I left—it will haunt me all my days. But the time of my atonement is over, Olga. I have said that I did not break faith—not with you, or Vali, or any of my friends in Estland. I broke my oath to Åke, and for that I'm not sorry. It was right. I did what I did trying to do what was right. I made mistakes, yes. I didn't see far enough. Others would have made different choices."

He turned his head and looked her straight in the eye. "But I did not break faith. Not with you. I have explained myself many times and will not do so again. You will have to believe me—or not. That choice is yours. But you are right: we should not be wed because of the babe. We should be wed because we love and trust each other, and we want to live the rest of our lives side by side. That is what I want. If it is not what you want, then so be it. So if you wish me to return to Geitland without you, I shall."

He lifted her hand from her lap and brought it to his lips. "For now, I need a moment to clear my head. I won't be far."

Taking his heavy fur from a peg in the wall, he opened the door and walked into the storm.

For the first time since she had woken from her sick slumber, Olga was alone.

20

Leif walked through the storm to the great hall, which had finally been returned to its primary use as a meeting place for the town. The last of the ill, all recovering, had been sent to their own homes a few days before. The plague had run its course.

Leif and Ulv had been in Karlsa nigh on a month, and neither had taken ill. He'd spent nearly two weeks at Olga's bedside before she had ever woken enough to know he was with her, and he'd spent two weeks helping her come back to her life. They'd been close in these two weeks, as they had been before. He knew it was true. He could feel her pleasure in his company, her reliance on his steady strength. He could see it. She loved him as ever she had.

And on the day that her voice had returned to her enough for conversation, she'd tried to drag them back to the dark place they'd been when he'd last come north.

No. Although he'd just told her that he would leave Karlsa without her if she so chose, he had no intention of doing so. He loved her, and she loved him—he was certain of it. She carried his child. *His child.* They were a family, whether she wished it to be true or not, and he would not be separated from either of them. No.

As he stalked through the buffeting wind and deepening snow, his thoughts as angry and churning as the storm around him, Leif told himself that he would bind her and carry her south as his prisoner if she would come no other way.

Entering the hall, he pulled the door closed with the force of his mood, and the wind pushed as well. The ensuing slam shook the walls and rattled the swords and shields hung there. Everyone in the building stopped and stared, and Leif simply glared back.

Vali sat at the head table with Bjarke, Orm, Jaan, and Ulv, and Leif knew he should go there and see if they discussed anything of import. But he didn't want to speak yet again about the western raid that, considering the devastation Karlsa had just experienced, would no longer be happening in a few months. He was not in the mood, and he'd left Olga alone. She was nearly well, but he didn't think she'd been left alone until now, so he would go back as soon as he was calm. Talking with the men would not calm him.

Instead, he scanned the room. Brenna and another woman Leif didn't know were sitting on the floor playing with Solveig and another child of about the same age. He went there. Brenna and her daughter had only been back in town for two days.

He crouched at the edge of the fur the children played on, and Solveig crawled to him at once. She put her pudgy hands on his knee and worked her way to her feet, smiling brightly and showing her first few teeth. She was a friendly, trusting little girl.

"Hello, pretty," Leif said and caught a pale curl between his fingers. Solveig worked her way closer, between his legs, until she could reach up and take hold of his hair. She pulled, and he made a silly sound, as if her pull had made it. She giggled and pulled again, and he repeated the noise. When she let go to clap in glee, she sat back on her bottom and giggled at that, too.

No, he would not be leaving Karlsa without his woman and child. Whatever he had to do to make it happen, Olga was going south with him.

"You're upset. Is Olga well?"

At Brenna's observation and question, Leif realized that he had wandered off into his thoughts. He focused and smiled at her. "She grows stronger each day. I'm not upset."

His friend made a face and a noise that quite clearly conveyed her utter disbelief. She had a talent for that—saying what she thought with her face rather than words.

So he relented a little, though he was unwilling to be detailed while the woman he didn't know was near. "She and I have things to talk about."

"She loves you."

"Would that were enough."

"It will be. I know it will be. She is going to be a mother."

"You think that makes her love me more?"

"I know it makes different things important. It changes everything. And you know that, too. Only give her time. She is still healing and adjusting."

Motherhood had certainly changed Brenna. They had known each other many years, and until the last few, she'd been a taciturn, solitary, suspicious young woman, both ostracized and revered for her difference. Leif didn't think she would have called him her friend until these latest years, despite all the time they'd known each other and fought together. He'd even trained her in the ways of war. But she had been close to no one.

Until Vali. Now, she had love and family and friends, and she had changed much.

When he'd met Olga, she'd been warm and quick to forgive, despite the many hardships and pains of her life. Though her body was slight, her spirit had been indomitable, bending with the storms life threw into her path but never breaking. It was her love for him that had changed her, made her suspicious and unforgiving, made her spirit brittle. He wanted to repair that damage.

Trussing her up like a boar and dragging her back to Geitland was probably not the answer, then.

But he was not leaving without her. Absolutely not.

"I need to speak with your husband." He kissed Solveig's flaxen head and squeezed her mother's shoulder, then stood and sought out Vali.

~oOo~

Vali led Leif back to the private quarters he shared with his wife and child. Now that the plague was over, the hall had been cleaned and was back to its rightful purpose—and people who had been ill, or simply consumed with fear and worry and grief, congregated together in their smaller number. The hall was crowded and loud, and privacy was at a particular premium.

Two servant girls who'd been working looms at the side of the room left at a wave of Vali's hand.

"If you wanted to speak politics or planning, we could have done so with the others. This is personal, then?" Vali asked as he indicated a stool for Leif and took one of his own.

Leif faced his friend straight on. "Are we friends enough again that I might seek counsel?"

"The tables have turned indeed if you seek counsel from me." Vali smirked and leaned back against a table, the picture of affectionate smugness.

Leif could only return a rueful grin. They had made their peace in these weeks Leif had been in Karlsa. One night shortly after he'd arrived, while Olga was still insensible and near death, Vali had come to her house. He'd sat with her for a while, and then he'd sat with Leif in the foreroom at the fire. They'd said very little, but Vali had put his hand on Leif's shoulder, and he'd kept it there, squeezing fiercely, as Leif had sagged forward, dropped his face into his hands, and wept.

And they were friends again. But they had not yet spoken in depth about the trouble between them or why it had been settled.

Vali continued, "As for our friendship, yes, we are true friends again. The time of this pestilence has made me think long about what I value and what I judge. Since I found Brenna in Geitland, I've believed that you meant to help. Now I've found understanding as well, and I've realized trust is not trust if it hasn't been tested. I was wrong to hold you at odds."

Leif took a deep breath of weary relief. "I would that Olga could see that."

"She does not? I thought you were well together. She seems at ease with you again."

"She doesn't trust me. She won't come to Geitland with me. She carries my child, Vali. I will not leave her behind. Never again. She must go with me. This is the counsel I seek."

Vali stood and went to a table where a pitcher and several cups were arrayed. He poured mead for them both and came back. After they drank, he said, "She suffered badly in Estland."

"I know," Leif sighed. "And I cannot unmake what happened. All I have are words, and I have no words left to say."

"Perhaps she simply needs time."

"This is what your wife says as well. I will give her the time she needs, but you know that my lingering in Karlsa has a cost. I trust Astrid with my life, but the longer I am away, the weaker my hold on Geitland grows. I would not have her face a challenge in my stead, and I would prefer not to face one on my return. It is bad enough that I will return with news that we won't be making our great raid in the summer."

"Would that we could," Vali muttered. "Karlsa is crippled, Leif. We've lost half our people and could not man a raid of such scale even if we had finished the ships. But we need the plunder. Two summers without any good raid will weaken us even more."

They had talked often and long about Vali's concerns for his people. Leif had come up with a plan. Since it seemed Vali would not be able to focus on Olga until they spoke again about Karlsa, Leif shared his idea with him now, rather than in the hall with the others.

"Send the men you can to me in the summer. We will raid again to the south and test the skeids we've made in Geitland, and we will split the spoils. We will have our great raid the next year."

Vali sat forward, interested. "That would be good help. Thank you. And you will raid? With Olga's time upon her?"

"No. I have been too much away this year as it is. Astrid will lead the raid, and I will stay and lead Geitland and see my child born. But first, I need Olga to be my wife and come home with me—which is why I am seeking your counsel. You have changed your feeling. What can I do to make Olga do the same? To see that I am and have always been in good faith?"

"You know the answer. You cannot *make* her see, Leif. You can only wait until she sees. I also know Olga well. Perhaps I now know her better than you do." Leif bristled at that but did not interrupt; it hurt but was true. "She has been changed by events, and perhaps hardened, but she is Olga. She loves you. You and she are bound forever by the child she carries. She will see."

Leif shook his head, dissatisfied. She had turned him away once, despite the love she felt. If she turned him away again, with his child growing inside her…

No. He would give up Geitland before he gave up his family. He would wait until she could see.

~oOo~

When he returned to Olga's house that afternoon, she was no longer sitting at the table. He found her lying curled on her bed, facing the wall. Worried that she had taken a bad turn, he hurried to her and crouched at the bedside. He hadn't been away long, but if she'd needed him during that time, if he had abandoned her after all…he sighed.

"Olga? Do you feel ill?" He put his hand on her head. She turned, moving her head and then her body, and he saw that she had been crying—or on the verge of it. "What is it, my love?"

She picked up his hand and pressed her cheek into it. In the husky tone of her still-weak voice, she murmured, "I…I'm afraid."

Resisting the need to react in frustration, Leif answered only, "I know."

"I don't wish you to go."

He brushed back from her face the strands of hair she'd loosened from her simple braid. "What do you wish, Olga?"

"I don't wish you to go."

A deep, slow breath gave him a moment to compose himself. It would be untrue to say that he felt no anger in this situation, that there wasn't something in him that wanted to shake her and shout at her and *force* her to see what was true.

Frustration coursed through him; perhaps he had not been calm enough to return to her after all. But clearly, he'd been away too long as it was.

"I went only to the hall. I told you, I will not leave Karlsa without you. Even if you will not have me, I will not leave. I will love and protect you and our child all my remaining days."

"But you lead Geitland. You must return."

"If you will not come with me to my home, then it is my home no longer."

She curled forward, to his chest, and Leif sat on her bed and shifted her onto his lap so he could hold her well.

~oOo~

Ulv was eager to begin the journey back to Geitland. They had traveled weeks to get to Karlsa and now had been in the town for a full month and nearly half of another. The plague had cleared, and it was safe for them to be among people beyond the borders of the town again.

Moreover, in the past few days, winter's grip had begun to loosen as well. The sun was brighter and lingered longer. Snow and ice thinned.

Olga was fully recovered, but she remained guarded. She would not come with him.

Leif and Vali stood with the young man on the pier. They all three studied the gentle undulation of a calm sea, the sun sparkling over its pale grey surface.

The time was coming when Leif would have to send Ulv home with word that the seat of the jarl was vacant.

Vali was nearly as unhappy about that decision as Leif himself was. Karlsa needed to lean on the strong shoulder of its southern brother while it recovered, and Leif's choice to stay with Olga would put that support in jeopardy. The wrong victor in a fight for the seat in Geitland could well put Karlsa at even greater risk.

The two men had discussed all this in great depth, but Vali hadn't tried to change Leif's mind. He understood, but he was deeply worried. Leif worried, too, but he would not again make a choice that put another above Olga. She'd been right that Brenna and Vali had been his first concern in Estland; they would not come first now, even if that meant the further suffering of an entire town—a town which included Olga as well.

He felt that conflict keenly, but his vow not to leave without her was one he held more sacred than any other.

"If you wait another few days, a week," Vali offered, "the sea will welcome a ship. You will make Geitland in days rather than weeks and be ahead of your plan."

"We have no ship," Ulv grumbled. "And we must be off."

"We have the karve you offered us, Leif, when we last sailed from Geitland. When we are sure the tidewater will not slush, we can float it and send you back with the men to row it. Those men can remain with you for the summer. As we discussed."

Ulv turned and regarded both jarls. "Discussed?"

Ulv didn't know that Leif might not be returning to Geitland, and Leif was not yet ready to tell him so. In any case, the karve, which Leif had forgotten about, bought him time, and if that time was not sufficient, perhaps Ulv returning with a score or so of Karlsa raiders would bolster Astrid's claim to the seat Leif will have given up. "We will bring raiders from Karlsa with us on southern raids this year. Their share of the plunder will help them bring Karlsa back so that we can have our western raid next summer."

Ulv was quiet, scanning the sea.

Leif was yet jarl, and he had tired of the conversation. "You stayed when I gave you leave to go, Ulv. Now you stay until I do so again." He did not often assert such authority, but his tolerance for the censure of a twenty-year-old pup had ebbed.

The younger man's expression shifted from surprise to resistance to discomfiture within the space of a heartbeat or two. "As you wish. You are my jarl."

Yes, he was. For now.

~oOo~

Frida was with Olga again, and Leif no longer stayed in the house. He now slept in the great hall, but he would need to take up a house elsewhere in town soon, if he were staying permanently in Karlsa. He wasn't ready to make that commitment to such a decision yet. He still held out hope. Dwindling hope.

Despite no longer staying with her, Leif visited Olga every day. He helped where he could, and they spoke comfortably with each other. He'd stopped pushing her on the point of her trust of him. She would, or she would not, and if he didn't know by the time he could no longer put off Ulv, then he would give up his seat. The decision had been made. Only the timing remained a question.

After taking his leave of Vali and Ulv at the pier, Leif walked to Olga's house. She and Frida were at work, sitting together at the table, preparing the ingredients for some kind of concoction.

When he came in, Olga gave him a sharp, suspicious look and sent Frida from the house. Shocked, Leif simply stood there while Frida scurried off. The girl gave him a sidelong glance, also suspicious, as she passed him at the door.

"What is wrong?" he asked when they were alone.

"I saw you at the pier with Vali and the other."

"Ulv."

Her terse nod indicated that she didn't care who he was. "You are leaving."

"What?"

"You were planning your return to Geitland. *Jah?*"

The anger that simmered low at the base of his mind flared to a flame, and Leif stepped to the table and swept the makings Olga had been working on off to the floor. She leapt up from her seat and stepped back, dark eyes huge with shock.

"No, I am not leaving. I have told you again and again that I will not leave you. If you will not come with me to Geitland, then I will give Geitland up and remain here. I mean to do this whether you will have me or not. *I love you*! What's more, *you carry my child*! You think always of your own losses. What of mine? I have buried seven children! Do you think I would turn my back on this one?"

Overcome with months of building anger, Leif slammed his fists on the table, then was still, leaning over, his knuckles digging into the scarred wood, his breath heavy, his hair swinging at the sides of his face. "I will not leave without you. I have sacrificed again and again for those I love. And I will sacrifice now. If you don't want me, so be it. But you will not raise my child without me. I will stand between you both and more suffering. At any cost to me."

He looked up into her stunned, beautiful face, flush with health again at last, and now with emotion as well. "*I am not leaving without you.*"

He left her house without giving her the slightest chance to respond.

~oOo~

Leif had every intention of sitting against the wall in the hall and drinking mead until the cup fell from his hand. He stormed from Olga's house and started immediately on that plan, doing all he could not to think. Too much rage had flooded his mind for thinking to be anything but destructive.

The people in the hall cast their eyes sidelong at him but did not disturb him. The serving girl who filled his cup did so as quickly as she could. His body must have been showing exactly the state of his heart and soul.

So he drank faster.

He was staring into the amber liquid of only his third cup when a pale red hangerock came into the corner of his sight. He looked up into Frida's pretty, nervous face.

When he only stared up at her, she made a nervous little cough—not illness, just a gesture—and said, "She sends for you."

He laughed bitterly. "I am otherwise occupied." He'd told Olga he wouldn't leave Karlsa without her. Well, here he sat in Karlsa, and he was not inclined to be summoned.

Frida dipped her head and turned away. After two steps, though, she turned back. "I think you should come." She didn't tarry to see if he would answer.

~oOo~

He followed so soon after Frida left that she had not even made it back to Olga's house yet. When she went in and turned to close the door, he was only strides behind her. She smiled and stepped back out, walking away without a word.

Leif went in through the still-open door. Olga stood near the fire. She had changed her clothes and wore a hangerock he hadn't seen before, one with delicate stitching across the top, like the stitching that had been common among the women's clothes in Estland.

And she had taken her hair from its braid. It flowed over her shoulders and to her waist in long, lovely waves. He couldn't help but stare.

Remembering why he was back in this room, he blinked and said, "You sent for me."

"Forgive me."

He blinked again. "What?"

"Forgive me." She came toward him, carefully, as if she feared he might bite. "You have asked me for forgiveness many times. Now I ask you. Please forgive me."

Reaching him, she laid her hands on his chest. He realized that he had not donned his fur before he'd left the hall.

He was confused and wary, and he picked her hands up and held them away. "I don't understand."

She let her head fall forward and didn't look at him as she next spoke. "You spoke the truth earlier. I have not thought of what you lost. I was trapped in my own sorrow and blamed you, and I never tried to see more than what I already saw. I am sorry."

Leif let go of her hands and held her face instead. Relieved that he hadn't had more time with the mead, he turned her head up so that he could see into her eyes. "What are you saying?"

She blushed, the pink rising prettily in her cheeks. "You are right. I love you. Very much." Her hands went to her belly. "We have a child coming. I know what I want, but I have been too afraid to embrace it. I have lost my way, and I have not tried to find it. But a new life comes into the world soon, a new chance for us both, and our child will need a guide. I need to find my way again. I see now that I will not find it without you."

"Olga, say it plainly. Please."

She swallowed hard before she spoke again. "I love you, and I have been wrong. If you will have me, I will wed you and go with you to Geitland as your wife. We will raise our child as a family."

Relief and love drew his cheeks wide in a grin, but he had one more question: "Do you trust me?"

She brought her hands up and cupped them around his face. "Trust is a choice. I see that now. Yes. I trust you. I choose it. I choose you."

Leif could scarcely believe his ears. Months and months and months he had been snared in a trap of futile need and poisonous regret, and she seemed now to have freed him. I hadn't been easy, it had been anything but easy, and yet now that it was here—what he wanted, all he wanted—he struggled to believe the truth of it. "Olga, I…"

Before he could find the words to complete his thought, she asked, "Will you forgive me?"

Words continuing to fail him, Leif pulled her into his arms and answered her with a kiss.

21

They were to have two weddings: one in Karlsa, within days of Olga agreeing to be married, and another in Geitland, where they would make their sacrifices to their gods and Leif would give her a sword. She remembered the fuss about swords when Vali and Brenna had been married.

Here in Karlsa, where dwelt the last few of her own people, they would have the binding ritual that was her heritage. None of the men had known the words, but Vali had offered to learn them from Olga, and he would say them over her and Leif. Leif had bound Vali and Brenna, so it seemed only right that Vali would bind them.

Leif was eager to return to his home, and Olga had made him wait so long already that she hardly felt that she could delay him further. She was leaving yet another home, this one still full of people she cared about, but she'd finally come to understand that her true home, her future, was with Leif. She was with child, a miracle of the earth or a gift bestowed by Leif's gods, she knew not which, but she was grateful. She was blessed. That child would know the love of a good father, and she would know the love of a good man.

She trusted him again because she had taken her will and her spirit into her hands and decided to turn away from fear and pain. Always before in her life she had known to let go of what could not be controlled and to take hold of what could. She had forgotten that and let life's storms knock her loose of her moorings, and as she'd cast about, lost, she had dragged others along with her.

It had taken Leif's steadfast resolve to release all else important to him and cleave to her, and his angry accusation that she had thought of nothing but herself, for Olga to see that fuller truth. In her pain, she'd turned inward and seen nothing but the inside of her own darkening soul.

When she had seen that much, as she'd stood and stared at the door Leif had slammed behind him in his anger and haste to be quit of her, she'd pulled her courage up from its dusty, disused corner of her heart and agreed to marry, choosing to trust him before her fear had truly abated.

Now, mere days later, the first day of true thaw, she stood and let Frida comb her hair while Dagmar fussed with her dress and Brenna sat with Solveig on her lap and watched, amused.

She was wearing her hair loose because Leif liked it best that way, but she felt as though she would be going out half-dressed, with no braid or any fixing. The gown she wore was simple; there had been little time for anything else, and her belly had grown enough that only something loose would truly do. It was yet too cold, to her, for anything filmy or delicate, so she wore a plain, pale blue woolen shift with long, wide sleeves and colorful stitching—she had stitched it herself in the few days she'd had to do so—across the bodice. The neckline—speaking of half-dressed—dipped lower than she had anticipated; her breasts had filled out, too. Dagmar was fretting with a lace at the back that would draw the shift snug across her chest, leaving the fabric to flow down, over her belly to the ground.

In her world, a bride and her party would have all dressed in white, a color of unity and balance, but in this world, there was no especial meaning to the color of a bride's dress. Olga, of this world now, had chosen the blue simply for the calm it gave her to look on it.

"I will freeze," she complained. They would be married at the shore, and while winter had passed, its back could still be seen on the path.

"I think you will not." Brenna smiled and seemed to exchange a look with her mother. Since Dagmar was behind Olga, she couldn't see what that was about.

"There," chirped Frida as she arranged Olga's hair over her shoulders. "You need one thing, and you'll be perfect."

A sharp knock at the door interrupted the women, and Vali opened it slightly and peeked in. Olga smiled at his uncharacteristic shyness.

"Do I disturb?"

"No," Brenna said and stood, shifting her daughter to her hip. "You come at the perfect time. Olga fears she will be too cold to wed our friend."

Vali stepped fully in, and Olga saw that he had a fur draped over his arms. A fur of a color so pale it was nearly pure white. Olga knew of only one animal in this world who might bear a fur like it, and it was a rare thing indeed. A white wolf.

He walked right to her, and the women stepped back as if they'd practiced. Only she, it seemed, was surprised by Vali's presence or the thing in his arms. He stopped directly before her; Olga had to crane her neck to see his face smiling down at her.

Taking the fur in his hands, he swept it around her and laid it over her shoulders. "You are a friend of my heart, Olga, and I will miss you every day. You and I have been through much together. You wed a good man. I think Brenna is right that he is a great man, and he will protect you and your child and love you true. But I put the pelt of a great white wolf over your shoulders to remind you that you always have the loving protection of the Storm-Wolf as well." Finished with his beautiful speech, he kissed her forehead and stepped back.

Olga wondered if Vali knew the great significance of a white wolf in her world. A white wolf was thought to embody all elemental knowledge. It was the epitome of wisdom and understanding. Of balance. And now she was wrapped in it, protected by it.

She lifted the fur to her face and began to cry. When Vali pulled her into his arms, she wept freely all the tears she had.

~oOo~

They stood at the shore, surrounded by the whole town of Karlsa, such as it was now. Leif wore a rich blue woolen tunic and gleaming dark breeches. His hair flowed in the breeze. Frida had presented Olga with a wreath made of dried barley, and she wore it over her loose mane.

When Olga walked toward Leif and Vali, with Jaan and Georg behind her, his expression was serious. She had expected him to be smiling, and she knew a thrill of anxiety that something was wrong, but she pushed it away. As she came near, he held out his hand and, when she took it, gently pulled her close. Then he brought her fingers to his lips and kissed them, lingering so long, his eyes closed, that Olga knew all was well.

Vali cleared his throat, and Leif finally lifted his head and brought Olga's hand down.

"We come together," the Jarl of Karlsa began, "to see two people bound fast. Because Olga is far from the home that she once knew, and because Leif is far from his home as well, today is the beginning of their rituals. We stand in the presence of the gods today and welcome them to join us, but

Leif and Olga will give them their proper honor in Geitland, where their ritual will be completed."

At last Leif smiled, and Olga returned it, squeezing his hand. And Vali brought forth cords of braided white and golden silk and held them out in his two hands. He spoke the words she had told him.

"Air is breath, weightless and irresistible. Love does not hold back. Fire is heat, passion and light. Love delights in desire. Water is emotion, still and stormy. Love is deep with feeling. And earth is bounty, nourishment and nest. Love is home."

He lifted their joined hands. "Will you honor and respect each other, give trust and keep it?"

Leif stared hard into Olga's eyes. She stared back. The most important question between them was the first, and she knew that she would have to answer first. "I will."

Leif nodded. "And I."

Vali looped a cord around their hands. "And so the binding is made. Will you share each other's pain and seek to ease it?"

Together, they answered, "I will."

Vali looped another cord. "And so the binding is made. Will you…" He paused, and Olga glanced at him. She saw him struggle to remember the words, but just as she was about to mutter them at him, he smiled at her. "Will you share your burdens each with the other so that your spirits will grow strong together?"

"We will," Olga and Leif answered, smiling.

Another cord bound them. "And so the binding is made. Will you seek your happiness together and keep each other's hearts in joy and ease?"

"We will."

Vali tied all the cords together in an intricate kind of sailor's knot. "Leif and Olga, you are now bound together, life and spirit. May your love be as vast and eternal as the night sky and your faith in each other as steady as the earth on which we stand. Good tidings to you, my friends."

~oOo~

The celebration of their union was the first joyful event in Karlsa since the night of the winter solstice—a night that had augured long weeks of suffering and death. So the town cleaved to the day, feting Olga and Leif well into the deep dark hours.

Olga had been near death only a few weeks before, and by the time Leif and she were able to free themselves from the revels, sneaking out while no one noticed, she was weary in every bone and sinew.

But it was the night of their wedding, and they had not coupled since that strange, painful, powerful night that he'd come to her and they'd made the child inside her. She wanted to feel him again, this time with nothing but love. Open and true and eternal.

Warm glow seeped through the closed shutters of her house as they approached, and Olga sighed to herself, thinking that Frida was there. But when they went in, they found it empty. Frida, seemingly with the help of others, had stoked the fire to cheerful warmth, and dozens of candles—far more than she possessed—lit up every corner of both rooms. The goats and chickens, which a healthy neighbor had taken to tend while she was ill, and had returned only the week before, were gone again.

She and Leif were truly alone on their wedding night, and Olga no longer felt tired. She smiled up at her new husband and laughed when he wiggled his blonde brows at her.

"Would we hurt the babe?"

Normally, she would have laughed at such a question. Many men had asked, as if they thought their spear so impressive it could reach deep into a woman's womb and disturb a child growing there, and her answer was always the same. It could not—and she knew that Leif knew that. He was no novice father. However, they were not well matched in size, and his sex was well matched to him. They had always had to accommodate for that. He would not hurt the babe, but he could hurt her—he had hurt her—when she was not with child, and she thought, were they not careful, he could hurt her more now.

"Not the babe, no," she answered.

His brows drew down in a worried scowl. "Then we will only sleep. It is enough."

She took his hands and placed them around her waist. "No, it is not enough. I only ask that you be careful, as you always have been."

"Not always," he murmured, combing the fingers of one hand through her hair, all the way to its end. "I am sorry for that."

"We needn't speak of that. I sought it out, and I'm not sorry. But I'm glad we're in another place now."

He bent and kissed her lightly. "*Ma armastan sind.*"

"No." When his brows went up in surprise and he opened his mouth to protest, she put her hand, just her fingertips, over his lips. "Say it in your words. They are my words, too, now. I love you."

"Don't give up your words, Olga. You have lost enough. Keep hold of your heritage."

"I shall keep the things I hold dear. My way of seeing the world. My memories of those I love. But your world is my home now. No one in Geitland will know my words. Your words are my words."

"I fell in love with you as we shared our words with each other. Mine to you, and yours to me. I would hold that dear between us. We were bound today by your way, and I feel no less bound for that. We will be bound in my way soon. I like that thought—that two ways have brought us together and hold us fast. Please don't give up who you were when we met."

"I was your slave when we met."

His mouth curved into a wry grin. "Never have you been a slave, my love. Rope around your neck or not. You are like Brenna in that way. Your spirit is too strong to be broken."

She might have believed that once, but no longer. She had been broken. She had come to Karlsa in pieces. But when she shook her head and began to say so, Leif caught her and held her still.

"You have been lost. Not broken. You stand here as my wife, smiling up at me, offering your trust. That is proof that you are found and whole. And now, at long last, you are mine."

She pushed her hands up over his shoulders, and he lifted her so that she could wrap her arms around his neck. As he carried her to the back room and her bed, she feathered tiny kisses over his lips and beard.

He set her down and turned her, and she saw that the floor of this room had been covered and mounded in furs and woven wool. "What is this?"

"I think our friends who lit the fire and the candles took pity on me and made us a bed on the floor."

She considered her bed. It was longer than the bed she'd kept at the castle, but it was narrow, and the rope supports creaked oddly when Leif even sat on it. "Is your bed in Geitland larger?"

"Our bed. And yes. Much." He bent low and swept his arms around her, resting both large hands on her belly. At her ear, he rumbled, "Room for you and me and your belly."

Before she could play at offense, his hand skimmed down and began to gather up the skirt of her gown. His mouth was still at her ear, his beard brushing over sensitive flesh, and she could hear the change in his mood in the sudden roughness of his breath.

"Olga." Her name was a groan in his chest. "I need you."

He had brought her skirt up to the tops of her thighs, and he plunged one hand under and found her center. His fingers brushed over that tender, private place, and she jumped in his embrace and reached down to grab his hand. Quickly, he pulled away, but that wasn't what she wanted. She shoved his hand back where it had been and held it there, and he groaned harshly at her forwardness.

And then he gave her what she wanted. Fully clothed, Leif bent over her, sheltering her completely under his broad body. Olga bent forward as well, holding his hand between her legs; he played with her body, his fingers sliding through her dripping-wet folds and paying especial notice to the tiny nub where every point of sensation in her body converged into a tangle of ecstasy. His other arm crossed over her chest, and that hand hooked her shoulder, holding her in a powerful grip. His face was buried in her hair, his teeth at her neck, his breath roaring in her ear. She could feel the iron heft of him pressing against her hip and the slight, the involuntary flex of his hips as his hand rubbed and swirled and plucked until black sparks filled her head and she thought she would swoon. Grunting like an animal, she completed.

She knew, because she had cared for many women in her condition, that more than the belly changed when a child grew inside a woman's body. The woman's needs changed as well, and her sensations. Many women she'd known—including Brenna—had become wild with their men during their carrying.

The first time she'd carried a child, she'd never felt desire before and she was too much consumed by fear and watchfulness, subject to a cruel husband, to feel it then. This time, she'd spent much of it sad or ill or recovering, and she had not, until the past few weeks, felt anything like it. But since she'd been well enough to appreciate Leif's presence, she'd known the deep itch of intense physical desire.

Leif's hands on her now were nothing like she had felt before, even with him. It was as if the parts of her that made the most pleasure had grown somehow, though they felt no bigger. The sensation had doubled, even trebled, however, and even as she sagged into Leif's arms, her release over, she could not let his hand go. She wanted his touch. She wanted to feel him all over.

"I want to be bare," she gasped, and Leif made a noise like a laugh and a groan and a grunt all coiled into one.

"As do I, my wild wife. I want to feel your skin on mine. I want to taste you and bring you that pleasure every way I can." He stood and turned her. While she watched, he put his fingers into his mouth and licked them clean.

This was not how it had been with them before. As they undressed, their eyes on each other, plucking playfully with each other's garments, Olga wondered at the change. Was it just the babe, making her feel more? No, it was also Leif. And it was her, too.

They were fully open with each other. Unguarded. Unreserved. Giving freely. Seeing a future together.

They were mated. For life. And that was new.

As soon as he had tossed his breeches away, Leif grabbed her and brought her down to the furs with him, so quickly she squealed. And then his head was between her legs and his mouth was on her, his tongue traveling the same short path his fingers had. His arms hooked under her thighs and curled around her hips, and he palmed her belly in both hands as he tasted her fully.

Almost at once, another release was on her, and she reached down and grabbed his hair, twisting it around her fingers as she tried to hold him more firmly to her. He chuckled, and she felt the rumble of it on her flesh. She couldn't be still. Her hips rocked under him, her hands pulled and pushed at his hair and head, her feet dragged over the rolling muscles of his back, and still it wasn't enough. She began to shake her head to and fro, not because she meant to deny or stop him but because it was the only other movement left to her.

When the waves crashed over her, Leif didn't stop or ease up. He stayed where he was, even as the sensations became too much, even as her body demanded a moment of rest. He denied her that respite and continued his feast, and, just as she was desperate for him to stop, ecstasy grabbed her again, and this time, she screamed.

He brought her softly down, kissing lightly, gentling her with hands and mouth and voice and breath. Only when she was at ease and had her full breath did he pull back and then ease up to loom over her, holding his weight from her with his arms locked stiff.

His beard sparkled in the candlelight, and she knew that it was her body that had wet him. She rose up and kissed him, tasting and smelling herself on his lips and beard. When she lay back, he cocked his head at her and smiled in a way that said he was pleasantly surprised.

"It is different between us now."

"I feel it, too," she answered, having already had this conversation with herself. "We are mated. That is the difference. We are bound fast."

She reached between them and took hold of his sex. With a light pull that wrenched a grunt from him, she led him to the place they both wanted him to be.

This way, he was more careful than he had been with his hands and head between her legs. He pushed in slowly, his eyes locked with hers, watching her, and he stopped just at the point where he could go no farther. For a moment, he stayed there, still, and studied her face. It was more than studying—he was telling her something, sharing with her. Love. She felt it like heat on her skin and in her heart, his love for her.

Smiling, she raised her legs and hooked them around his waist. She tangled her hands in his hair again and pulled until, with a grunt, he came down to his elbows instead of his hands.

He kissed her as he pulled slowly out and pushed slowly back in. Their rhythm began, and Leif was gentle and controlled, watching her, bringing her, with each filling slide, closer to yet another inferno of pleasure. This time, though, with her release achieved so many times already, she focused on him, on his taste, his scent, her scent mingling with his. She focused on the feel of their mouths together and moved her own in ways she knew would make him grunt with need. She focused on the slide of his body—large, the skin roughened with hair and scars—on hers, small and smooth. She focused on the pulse of him inside her and squeezed around him to lift their mutual pleasure even higher.

So intent was she on making feelings for him and for her, she didn't notice how close they both were until he was moving swiftly, struggling to keep control, and she was moving against him, trying to make him deeper, bring him closer—the things she'd asked him to be careful of.

With a roar of frustrated defeat, he suddenly grabbed her and rolled, setting her atop him. This was a position she knew well, and she picked up their dance immediately. Panting and grunting, he cupped her belly in his hands again and held on as she rode him as if he were a steed on the way to war.

And then his hands went to her breasts. At the first graze of his rough thumbs over her swollen nipples, her body filled with heat like she'd walked into a fire, and she went tense as bliss consumed her. As she did, he released as well, his shout loud and agonized.

She fell forward, and he caught her, rolling at once to his side. He pulled out of her, going easy, and then tucked her wet, breathless, thoroughly sated body into the shelter of his body in its similar state.

Now, she truly was weary.

"I love you, Leif." Her words slurred a bit, as if she'd had too much mead.

He laughed quietly and kissed the top of her head. "And I you. Rest, wife."

Nuzzling her nose in the dark golden curls that lightly furred her man's chest, Olga heeded him and slept.

~oOo~

Only two days later, Olga stood on the pier, wrapped in her white wolf pelt, and stared at the boat Leif was already in. He was helping to load her belongings, such as they were, into the hull. Or whatever the large part of the boat was called. Ship. It was a ship. A small one, but much larger than the tiny fishing vessel they had limped to Karlsa in.

And that was the problem. Only once before in her life had she been on a boat, or a ship, and it had been an arduous, painful, desperate journey that had lasted an eternity. She had seen friends die, and nearly die, and they had all suffered badly in body and spirit. It had been the cap of a period of horrible suffering and death.

Now Leif wanted her to travel by boat—ship—again. It was a good vessel, he assured her, strong and steady, and they had a crew of strong men with them. Only two days, he said, three at the most, and they would be home. But she was leaving a home, yet another home, and at her back were the friends she'd made and grown to love.

She'd said her goodbyes. Frida would have her house and most of her healing supplies. No longer was the girl an apprentice. Now, at fourteen, she would be the healer of Karlsa, and she had been well trained by circumstance as much as any formal teaching from Olga, or Sven before her.

She'd bid a tearful farewell to Brenna and Solveig and Dagmar. Leaving them was leaving family; her heart ached to know how far away they would be. She was leaving home again. Oh, how she hoped the home she traveled to would be her last.

Jaan and Georg were sailing with them, eager for the coming raid.

And Vali had decided to raid, too. He was leaving his wife in charge of their recovering home in the hopes of bringing great treasure back to them all.

They were all in the ship, waiting for her. And Leif's friend, too. Ulv. All waiting.

She was terrified. The thought of the rocking of the sea under her, or the chance of a storm tossing them about like a leaf in a breeze, had her frozen in place, clutching her wolf pelt around her shoulders. And she had a babe to protect. How could she get into that thing? How could Leif think to have her travel that way?

Leif climbed out of the ship and stood before her on the pier. He cupped her face in his hands and smoothed her cheeks with his thumbs. "Olga, do you trust me?"

She did. Again, at last, she had faith in him. And here was a test of that, she knew.

Still afraid, she nodded.

He smiled and jumped into the boat again. Turning back to her, he raised his arms, and she leaned forward and let him lift her and swing her into the boat.

The *ship*, that was.

It was time to go home.

~oOo~

The voyage took two days, as Leif had promised—a bit less, even. Olga took two more to recover from her sick stomach. The seas had been excellent, according to the men, but they had traveled with a strong tailwind, and the pitch of the ship through the water, coupled with the anxiety with which she'd struggled, had kept her at the side of the ship, heaving, most of the way.

Leif had been attentive and concerned, rarely leaving her side, and she'd spent the time she wasn't leaning over the side lying with her head in his lap.

And then she'd lain in his giant bed regaining her strength and composure, attended to by strangers while Leif reclaimed leadership of his jarldom and caught up with what he'd missed.

Still, he never seemed to be farther from her than the next room. The hall here, while much larger and more luxurious than the one in Karlsa, was built in a similar fashion: long, wide and low, the greater portion of it given over to the hall itself, a meeting space for the entire large town, in toil and leisure both, and a place for Leif to do the work of the jarl. The kitchen was a behind the hall, connected by an enclosed passageway. The back portion of the hall was the jarl's quarters. Three rooms: a large space that was the sleeping, living, and private meeting space; an open nook filled with looms and other materials of woman's work; and a room for bathing and dressing.

In Karlsa, the jarl's quarters had been partitioned with only woven wool sheets, and only the bathing room had its own door. Here in Geitland, a door with an iron bar separated the jarl's space from the meeting hall.

That was as much of Geitland as she'd yet seen—the hall, her home, and the short walk to it from the ship—as she stood in the middle of the quarters she shared with her husband and let two serving girls help her with her wedding dress, the same one she'd worn a week before.

The girls were servants but not slaves. Leif had freed his slaves when he'd returned from his first visit to Karlsa. The rest of Geitland still held slaves, as it had been in Karlsa before the plague. After that, with the town so gutted, and so many in thrall dead, Vali had brought the matter to his people again, and Karlsa had freed those slaves who'd survived.

When she was dressed, with another wreath, this one of dried wheat, on her head, Vali came to collect her, and they walked through the hall. As in Karlsa, this wedding ritual would occur outdoors, this time in the woods at the edge of town. They walked the path together, and people of the town stopped and watched as they went.

Olga hadn't needed her wolf pelt today. Geitland was notably warmer than Karlsa; the snow had gone its way, and already new greens had begun to sprout from the earth. Yet she missed the warm weight of Vali's gift. She was disoriented and still anxious here in this new place, and every touch of what she knew and loved gave her strength. She was more glad than she could say that Vali had sailed with them and walked with her now.

Leif, too, wore the same clothes he'd worn when they'd been bound in Karlsa, and he wore the same serious expression he'd worn then, too. He took her hand and brought her close, hooking his arm over her shoulders, and she was glad the pelt was back in their quarters. She could feel the warmth and heft of his strong arm.

A holy woman presided over this ritual. A goat was sacrificed, and the holy woman flicked a rod dipped in its blood over Leif and Olga and the people gathered around them. Olga had now seen this oddity in a few weddings, so she was not surprised, but she did mourn her beautiful dress—and was glad again not to have the wolf pelt.

As in their first ritual, there were words and vows, these directed to the gods. After nearly two years in this world, Olga had begun to wonder about the gods here and found herself thinking about them as real, as beings paying attention, or not, but as living beings. She didn't know if she believed in all their exploits and their power, but living among people who very much did and who structured their lives around the desire to please such beings, she discovered that they had made their way into her thinking, become part of her knowing.

So she felt a pull when she said words asking for the goodwill of Freya and Thor. She hoped they were listening.

Then it was time for the fuss about swords. The contrast between their two rituals—hers gentle, about binding and sharing, and his martial, with blood and sword—was stark and dizzying for Olga. It spoke of the difference in their ways of knowing. Olga didn't understand this ritual well, but she did understand that it was extremely important to Leif and the reason they had done two separate rituals, so she waited solemnly while he took both of her hands in his.

"In our way," he began, his voice low but clear, "I would give you my father's sword, so that you and our children might keep safe behind its legacy and pass it on to our firstborn son when he became a man. But that sword was lost in Estland, when Einar was killed. Its legacy was not so strong as I hoped. I have no other ancestral sword to give you."

He released her hands and reached over his shoulder. Fisting the grip of the longsword he'd carried all the time she'd known him, he unsheathed it. The blade sang as it slipped from the scabbard and glinted in the sunlight as he brought it forward.

"The sword I offer is this. I have carried it as long as I have carried a blade, and I stand here before you because it has kept me well. I have defended my home, my people, and my honor with this blade. I have protected what I love with this blade. I have sacrificed with this blade. Like me, it is not without its failings and its scars, but every cut we have ever made was meant good and true. I have never named it, but in offering it to you, to keep safe our family and to hold as our child's legacy, I name it now: Sinnesfrid."

Sinnesfrid. Olga knew the word and what it meant: heart's ease.

Leif laid it on his two hands and held it out to her. Olga studied his face, his eyes, and ignored the sword he offered.

That blade—everything he'd said in his pretty speech was true. But he'd wielded that blade in Estland. It had been that blade she'd seen slice through Toke's belly and spill his insides onto the cold ground. That blade, and his axe, had hurt, had killed, people who'd trusted him.

She gazed deeply into his eyes, searching, and saw that he had not forgotten those hard truths, either. He claimed them in the sword's history, its legacy, and she found his meaning in the way he stared back at her. What had happened in Estland was part of his sacrifice. He had made difficult choices with that blade. He had done what was right at great cost. His commitment was unshakable.

That devotion was what he was offering her on his outstretched hands. That peace of mind. Heart's ease.

Sinnesfrid.

"Olga," he murmured, and she saw worry darken his eyes.

"It is a good name. And a good blade." She held out her hands, and he carefully laid the sword on them. It was heavy—far heavier than she'd expected—but he'd laid it so the balance on her hands was perfect.

"I...I'm sorry, but I don't have a sword to give you in return."

"But you do," Vali said. Standing near Leif, he grinned at Olga and, stretching his arm toward the gathered people, made a beckoning gesture with his hand. A young, fair-haired boy, about Kalju's age—though Kalju would have been older now—trotted up, carrying a sheathed sword.

"Young Dag here made you the blade you will carry now, yes?"

Leif nodded, one brow cocked high. "He did. That is not it."

"No," Vali chuckled. "This is something he made on his own. It seems he disagreed with a point you made to him that a jarl has no use for a very fine sword." Vali went to Olga and took Sinnesfrid from her. Then he waved the boy forward. "Come on, boy. Olga requires a sword."

The boy—Dag—came shyly toward her. When he wrapped his hand around the woven leather grip of the sheathed blade, though, a light of confidence shone from his eyes, and he smiled as he pulled the sword free. In the same way that Leif had handed her Sinnesfrid, Dag handed her this new one.

Olga didn't know much about swords, but this one was beautiful. The part above the grip and just below it was deep, gleaming black. A pattern had been carved into the dark wood. The leather of the grip was black as well, and woven in an elaborate design. The narrow valley down the center of the blade was also etched with shapes—the same shape that adorned the shields of his people. A flared cross. Small versions of it repeated down the length of the sword.

It was, it seemed, a very fine sword. She smiled at the boy and turned to Leif, offering it to him on her hands.

With a broad smile, Leif took it from her. He hefted it and balanced it on one of his hands, then on a single finger. "Excellent work, boy. It seems I was wrong to discourage you."

Dag blushed and dipped his head. He handed Leif the scabbard and then faded back into the small crowd.

The disruption over, the holy woman instructed them to exchange rings. Leif did so by placing Olga's ring on the point of his new sword, and he guided her to do the same with his ring.

Together, they held the sword, spoke their vows, and exchanged rings, and then the holy woman said, "Now you are wed."

The people around them cheered, and Leif pulled her to him, his new sword still his hand, and kissed her soundly.

Olga understood then that their rituals, in their vast difference, were perfect complements to each other. Gentle and fierce. Silk and iron. Protection of the heart and of the body.

Balance.

22

"This is beautiful." Olga let go of Leif's hand and walked to the bluff, closer to the edge than he liked. She was growing quite round and was not always steady, and if she plunged to her death on the rocks below, taking their child with her, he would simply follow her right over.

"Olga, take heed," he scolded lightly and took her hand again and tugged until she stepped back to a place he deemed safe.

Summer was upon them, still new but in full flower. The air hung thick with the scents of warm, wet earth and fresh green life. One of his wife's favorite pastimes was to walk in the woods and dig in the earth, but as the babe grew, she was no longer able to get down to the earth easily or comfortably. She still wanted to walk, however, and insisted it was good for her and their child. So walk they did, every day.

This was the first time he had taken her in this direction, onto the bluffs. The terrain was not as smooth in these woods, and the climb was steeper, and he would never have let her go on alone in her condition. But today he had a motive of his own for this short trek.

The view of sea and sky from this point went on forever, so far that the horizon seemed to curve. On a clear day like this, one might think that Asgard itself was on view. Olga looked out over all of that, a sweet smile rounding her cheeks.

Leif, on the other hand, was more interested in the view below. He looked down at the vista of his town, which was a hive of activity. The raiders were to depart soon. Both new skeids, glorious beasts of longships, were moored on the water. They'd had to rebuild the piers to accommodate the size of the new ships. Now they rested there, gleaming like gold in the warm sun, and Leif's heart burned with pride and with longing. He ached to sail, and it gnawed at him that he would not lead the skeids' first raid. Vali would, and Astrid, and he trusted them completely. But he had envisioned an inaugural raid side by side with Vali, sailing four of these beasts to a new land.

And yet he would not trade, for any amount of pride or treasure, the chance to be with Olga when she gave him their child.

The skeids would sail south this year. He had been south. He would raid west next year. He and Vali and their fleet of sleek beasts, conquering a new world.

"Your thoughts are far off today," Olga said. "Are you sorry to be staying in Geitland?"

She was always with him, wherever he was. Even in his head. He smiled and drew her close. "I was thinking that I will miss the new ships' first voyage, and it made me a bit melancholy. But I would be nowhere but with you when our child comes into the world. Nothing is more important." He laid his hand over her belly, and she laid both of her hands over his.

"I love you," she whispered, looking down at their child.

Leif held her close and kissed the crown of her head, lingering there to take in her scent and the soft caress of her hair. Standing on this bluff, looking down at his home, his people, their accomplishments and ambitions, Leif knew real peace.

He thought of the last prophesy the seer had given Åke: that Geitland was entering a time of great prosperity. Åke had interpreted it to mean that he would be prosperous, but he had been killed as a coward shortly after hearing it.

Leif knew that he was not Geitland. He was merely its shepherd. The power and promise of this land was in all of its people, and they should all prosper in rich times, just as they all struggled in lean times.

And if he ever forgot it, he would come up to this bluff and look down and see just how insignificant any one man was, and just how much many could accomplish together.

"Come." He stepped back and took his wife's hand. "There is much to be done before the raiders go."

~oOo~

Olga retired early the night that the ships left, while the hall was yet crowded with those who'd stayed behind, making many toasts to the safety and success of the raid. Leif stayed longer, until most of the hall was a nest of unconscious or nearly-so revelers. Then he went back to the private quarters.

He stripped and slid into bed beside his sleeping wife, who had burrowed deep into the furs. Pulling them back, he kissed her bare shoulder. She had stopped sleeping in a gown when her belly had gotten large enough that all clothes seemed to vex her. He couldn't say he minded her naked body beside his every night, but he often came to bed after she was asleep, and he thus often struggled alone with the need her nakedness made in him.

Just as he was finally settling in for rest, there was a thump at the door. Checking that Olga hadn't been disturbed, he stood and grabbed his shortsword, pulling it from its scabbard as he walked across the room.

It was Sigrid, a former shieldmaiden who now served as a hall guard because she was a widow with three young children. She paid no heed to his nakedness, and he hadn't expected her to.

"Trouble?"

She shook her head. "No longer. Odd knocked over a lantern outside the stable, but the fire was out before it could do more than burn his cart."

"Odd is well?"

With a laugh, Sigrid answered, "He yet sleeps, not four strides away. He's in for a nasty surprise in the morning, but he is well."

"Why didn't you raise an alarm?"

"No need. As I said, it didn't spread."

"Well enough. Thank you."

Sigrid gave him a sharp nod, and Leif closed the door. When he turned, Olga was sitting up in bed, holding the furs to her chest. Her hair flowed over one shoulder. She was a glorious vision, like a goddess. An angry goddess—she scowled at him, and there was a fire in her eyes far more dangerous than what had burned Odd's cart.

Thinking he should get sharp implements out of the way, he crossed the room and sheathed his shortsword before he asked, "Is there something wrong?"

"That was Sigrid."

"Yes. There was some small trouble. It's resolved."

"She's a woman."

"Yes, true."

Her scowl shifted dramatically and became incredulity so broad is was almost parody. "Leif, you are bare. Completely."

Surprised, he laughed. She was jealous? He laughed harder as the thought took hold—and that was a serious mistake. Olga threw the furs back and worked her way to the side of the bed. She was nearing her time, and moving from one position to another was difficult. She had also become cross and easily offended.

All of which he understood to be the toll of her carrying. But the thought that she would be jealous of anyone, let alone Sigrid—even now, he found it funny and had to bite his lip not to laugh again.

"Olga—Olga." He went to her and stopped her from leaving the bed. "It matters not. I didn't know if there was trouble, so I didn't take the time to dress. Sigrid didn't even notice." He picked up his soft sex and wiggled it at her. "And I didn't notice, either. You are all I want or need. Forever."

She was staring at his sex. "You don't notice me, either?"

"Usch," he muttered, trying again not to laugh. Now she was hurt because he *wasn't* hard? The things carrying a child did to a woman. It wasn't easy to keep up. "I notice you, my love. I always notice you. Perhaps I'm soft because there was a moment just now when this part of me might have been in some danger." He took her hand and curled it around him, and he began to swell at once. He groaned softly. "See? I notice you."

She smiled a little, though she tried to hide it, and wrapped her other hand around him, too, working him expertly until he was hard as rock and grunting with need. When she leaned forward, as much as she could, and licked him as if he were a sweet, his need became painful and immediate. He wanted to be sheathed inside her. Anything else, no matter how delightful, was a shadow of that joining.

Each time, though, as the babe grew, true joining had become more difficult. She could tolerate less penetration, and the babe between them made even her riding him sometimes challenging. He had ideas for new ways, but they were not ways Olga had ever been willing to consider. And he understood why. He knew her story, by now he knew all of it, and he understood her reticence. She had been taken forcibly many times from behind, and she feared the memories should he come into her that way.

But they were writing a new story now. Forging a new way. And never would she know pain and abasement like that again.

He put his hands in her hair and stopped her. "Olga. I want to try something."

She looked up at him, her eyes trusting but curious. "What?"

"Do you trust me? Trust me completely?"

He didn't miss the hard swallow before she said, "I do."

Offering her a reassuring smile, he slid his arms under her and turned her over and around so that she was kneeling on the bed with her back to him. He felt her body stiffen when she understood.

"Leif…"

"Shh." He came close and kissed her shoulder. "This is us. Things are different with us. I won't hurt you. Not in body or spirit. Trust me."

"I can't see you." Her voice shook, and with it so did his resolve. But he took a deep breath, leading her to do the same.

"You can feel me. You can hear me. I'm with you." Gently, slowly, he eased her to lean back on his chest. In that position, he smoothed his hands lightly over her arms and legs, over her belly, her sides, doing nothing more until he felt her relax.

Then he took her breasts in his hands, massaging and plumping, avoiding the spectacularly sensitive points of her nipples until he heard a tiny purr in her throat.

While he excited her nipples, he whispered at her ear, "You like when I hold you up like this and use my hand. What I mean to do is little different. This is us, my love. Only us."

Gods, he might die of his own need and of the heady power he felt in her trust. He was taking her, body and soul, to a place she had always shied from, and she was letting him.

That purr had become an undulating moan, rising in pitch each time his fingers closed on her nipples and pulled. When her breath began to stutter, he eased her forward, encouraging her to rest on her hands.

She was wet and already throbbing. Leif licked his hand to wet himself and ensure that his entrance was gentle. Then he eased—very slowly—into her. At first, she tensed, so hard she stopped his passage. He leaned over and rubbed her back and shoulders, her bottom and thighs, pressing kisses down her spine. "It's me, my love. Only me," he whispered, until she took a shaky breath and loosened for him.

When he finally was sheathed, more of him in this position than she could take in any other, he held still, gentling her, whispering sweet words to keep her with him and away from memory. He reached around and caressed her belly, then eased his fingers through the dark wisps over her mound. When he was ready to move—only gentle pulses, no long strokes—he caressed the nub of her greatest pleasure. For an eternal stretch of time, they remained like that. Olga was on her elbows and knees, the furs clutched in her fists, her head down. Leif stood at the side of the bed, his legs spread wide, curled over her back, rubbing lightly in her folds and rocking his hips ever so gently to move inside her.

It was Olga who changed their tempo. Leif had found a level place from which he could control his own need, and he was focused there, determined to be slow and gentle and to ease Olga to her enjoyment of this way.

But there came a point when slow and gentle clearly was not enough for her. Her hips began to rock back when he pulsed forward. Each time, she grunted, and the next would be a bit more vigorous, until she was rocking back hard, and Leif had to pay close attention lest she take him more deeply than she could stand and send this whole beautiful moment into disaster.

When she released, she wet his hand and clamped down around him with such force that she pulled his release from him before he was aware that he'd been so close. He dropped his head to her back and groaned, his body flinching with each spasm of her sheath.

As soon as he could form words, he asked, "Are you well?"

Her reply was slow in coming. Just as worry flowered in his belly, she muttered, "Thank you." Which was not precisely an answer to his question, but it served well enough.

Chuckling, he pulled slowly free of her, then lifted her into his arms. He climbed into bed and settled in with her cradled in that way. He spent the night holding his wife and his child as they all slept.

~oOo~

"Enough. Get OUT, Leif!" Birte shouted, shoving him back from his own bed. "NOW."

"I am not leaving!" To emphasize his point, he shoved right back past Birte and went to Olga and grabbed her hot, damp hand. "I'm with you, my love. I'm here. I'm not leaving you."

His wife turned her flushed face, dark hair plastered over it, and looked him in the eye. "Get out, Leif."

"What? No! I told you I would be here! I am here!" He turned to Birte. "You know I cannot leave. My place is here."

Before anyone could answer him, another pain took hold of her. While he clung to her hand, and she closed her hand around his fingers with ten times the strength he'd believed she had, Birte went to her other side, muttering at him all the way, and helped Olga to come up into a crouch. The midwife, Gyda, sat between Olga's legs, staring intently, her arms deep under Olga's gown.

He had expected yelling. Toril had screamed and screamed with every birth, but Olga had yet to make a sound while she was in the midst of the pain. Even when she spoke during the moments of relief, she only whispered. It made Leif worried.

All of it made Leif worried. This was his eighth child coming, and sooner than was thought. Olga was greatly round and very much ready—in mood, at least—to deliver, but it was still early in the season, and, knowing precisely when she had conceived, she had said it would be midsummer.

His eighth child, and he had none living. Yes, he was worried. He was consumed by fear.

The pain passed, and Birte laid Olga back and went to talk to Gyda. Again, Olga looked at him. "You have to go, Leif."

"I told you I would not leave you. I swore. I must be here." Olga's ways were not yet always his ways, but his place was with her. At her side.

She smiled and patted his hand. "I don't want you to leave Geitland. I want you to leave the room. You may even stay in the hall, as long as you keep a closed door between us. But I need you to leave."

"Why?" He heard the petulance in his voice, but he was hurt and...petulant. "You let Vali stay with Brenna."

She laughed lightly and then rearranged her features and made them serious. "Your worry fills this room. It makes me tired. Don't go far, but let me do this work. It is bloody and painful, and you are too anxious. I love you. Let me bring our child."

"Olga..."

She pushed him gently away, and then another pain came on her, and Leif let Birte push him even farther back. He kept going, backing to the door and then out of the room.

He closed the door and went no farther. Dropping to a crouch, he stayed at the side of the door and waited, with no plan to move until he was allowed back in that room.

However, being still was impossible. So he stood again after only a few moments and began to pace. It was midday, but the hall was nearly empty. Only two servants and the random livestock that had wandered in kept him company.

The silence beyond the door was killing him. Shouting would have been preferable to this strangling quiet that told him nothing. Stalking around the hall, picking up a retinue of chickens and a lamb, he tried to force peace into his mind and think. She had been having her pains all the day, since before sunrise. Since even before that—she had woken him before sunrise to tell him she needed Gyda, but she had already been having pains by then. Now they were not far apart. That meant the babe was coming soon.

He had been with her all through the day, until now, when the time was near. It infuriated him to be closed away from the birth of his own child. It was wrong.

Time passed, and Leif paced, and fear chewed and chewed at his heart until it was raw, and still nothing but silence on the other side of the door. Occasionally, he pressed his ear against the wood, but he heard nothing. How could that be? She was bringing a child from her body! Had she lost consciousness?

And then she screamed. Loud and long—and then abruptly stopped. He was across the hall, and he fairly leapt back to the door. As he yanked it open, the first sound he heard clearly in the room was the cry of a newborn babe.

Birte's face was the first he saw. She rolled her eyes at him and shook her head. "I would have called for you in a moment. You have a son. A fat, loud boy." She stepped out of his path, and there was Olga, pale and exhausted, drenched in sweat, but smiling hugely, letting thick streams of tears run down her face. In her arms was a beautiful, beautiful boy, naked, covered in slime, and bawling angrily.

Ignoring the other women in the room, his frustration and offense for being sent away forgotten, Leif went to his wife and sat on the bed at her side. He kissed her forehead and then cupped his hand over his new son's small, utterly bald head. At his touch, the boy's cries stopped, and he turned his scowling face toward Leif.

"He knows who you are," Olga whispered. The boy turned to her voice.

"And you. He knows his mother."

"I never thought to have this—to hold my own child and have him see me." She sobbed and cut it quickly off.

Leif leaned in, sheltering his son and his wife with his body, and wrapped his arms around them. Olga lost her battle and began to weep, and their son picked up his wailing as well, and Leif could not have been happier.

With a sharp pat on Leif's shoulder, Birte separated them. She took the babe from Olga, who was reluctant to let him go. But, knowing the rituals, Leif laid his hand on her arm and nodded.

"The life cord," Birte reminded him.

He turned and leaned over Olga's belly. Picking up the thick, stiff cord that still bound mother and child together, he bit down on it and severed that connection.

Birte washed the boy while Gyda washed Olga and removed her soiled shift and the linens from the birth. Leif stayed close, holding his wife's hand. Now that his anxiety was behind them all, no earthly force would move him.

When Birte returned their son to them, they saw that he was looking for his first meal. Her expression suffused with serene happiness, Olga, bare now, offered him a breast. He rooted around for a moment and then latched firmly on.

Leif's reaction to that sight was potent and immediate—so much so that he gripped his thigh and squeezed his eyes shut as he fought it off. When he had control of his base urges, he looked up and was face to face with Birte, giving him a disapproving and far-too-knowing frown.

Olga had seen him, too; when his eyes met hers again, she smiled, and he thought there was a sheen of sultry heat in that look. But then she turned her eyes back to their child.

"What shall we call him?"

Leif studied the boy in his love's arms. His perfect, bald head. His sturdy little arms and legs. That scowling, serious face. "Magni."

"Magni," Olga tried out. "Mighty one."

"Yes. He is mighty. Conceived where there was no hope and brought forth where hope thrives. All his doing before he took a breath."

"It is a good name."

23

"*Äiu, äiu, kussu, kussu,*" Olga crooned in a whisper, brushing her fingers over Magni's satiny head as he nursed. "*Maga, maga, maimukene!*"

Leif slept at their side, facing them. He had been long away that day, riding out into the countryside to speak with farmers and make arrangements for their yield to come into Geitland for trading. He had returned exhausted and distracted, and she didn't wish to wake him.

"*Tsuu, tsuu, suuremasse,*" she sang, seeking to keep her son calm. Already, only two weeks in the world, Magni was a serious little soul. He knew what he wanted, and he complained mightily when he didn't get it. He liked her to sing while he fed, and he didn't much care if his tired father would be disturbed by his mother's crooning—or his own screaming. "*Kasva, kasva karjatsesse, äti nänni pikkutesse.*" She kept her voice a whisper, but he opened his eyes and furrowed his brow when she paused.

"I like to hear you sing, too. It soothes me as it does him. You needn't whisper."

Leif had spoken with his eyes closed, so he didn't see her smile. She reached over and brushed her fingers across his mouth.

"I wanted you to sleep." She always tried to keep her voice in a singsong rhythm while Magni fed.

He opened his eyes and took hold of her fingers, pressing them to his lips for a kiss. "I feel far more renewed awake in your presence than asleep anywhere, even at your side. How was your day?"

"Long, without you. But good. We took a walk through the town." Since the rituals for Magni's naming the week before, they had stayed close to the hall. One of the townspeople observing had had a hard cough, and Olga had been badly frightened. Leif had had the sick person removed and sent Birte after him for care, but they had both been glad to keep Magni from the public for a while longer.

The cough had been a cough, nothing more. Even that man had not been truly sick. Once assured of the truth of that, Olga had wanted to be out in the sunshine with her son. He could not grow tall and mighty cooped up under a roof. Still, she had kept him swaddled in the sling she'd worn across her chest, and she had not allowed curious fingers to probe at him.

Now, Leif cocked a concerned eyebrow at her. "Alone?"

"Sigrid was with us. But we don't need a guard. You are beloved here, and your son and I bask in that light as well."

"I would have someone I trust with you always, when I cannot be. My talks did not go as well as I would like. Perhaps I am not so beloved outside the town itself."

Olga traced her finger over the long, wide scar that bisected his chest. Pale, ruched skin where no hair grew, thickening into a web of scars directly over his heart. "Do they not see the man you are?"

He smiled. "No one sees me as deeply as you do, my love. But they do see my failings. In my time as jarl, I have given too much of my attention to the town and to…other matters."

"To me, is what you mean."

"To my family." He bent down and kissed Magni's head. "Where my attention was most needed. But my holding ranges far more widely than this town, and I have neglected those who work the fields that feed us. Today, I was reminded. Forcefully."

"Forcefully?" She didn't like that word at all, but at that moment, Magni unlatched and began to protest the interruption of his meal. Olga hushed him and resituated herself so that she could offer him a full breast. Now, her back was to Leif, and he made a rumble in his chest as their son latched again.

Leif's arm came around her, and his hand settled on Magni's bottom. Olga felt his sex grow against the back of her thighs, and she smiled. He had never yet acted on the need he felt when she nursed, and she would not want him to, even were her body ready to accept him again, but she did enjoy feeling his desire. Feedings like this, in the dark hours of the night, the three of them wound together in their bed, were the happiest moments of her life—a life that had become filled with happy moments.

She thought of all she had been through and knew that it had all brought her here, to this life, this home, with a child of her own and a love deep and true. She thought of that, and she could remember that the world kept its balance.

But her worry at Leif's comment had only been interrupted, not abated. "Forcefully?" she asked again.

"Shhh." He kissed her head. "Do not fret. There was no violence. Only anger—anger I deserved. I will make some changes. It seems that I was more influenced by Åke's way of leading than I'd thought."

That old jarl's way of leading was cruel and irrational. She didn't believe Leif was like him at all. "What do you mean?"

"I had forgotten that the sun doesn't rise and set only in sight of this hall. I think I would like to ask for your help, my love."

She looked back over her shoulder at him. "How can I?" Her days as a healer were over. Geitland had Birte and Gyda, and she had Magni to devote her attention to—and to keep away from the sick. Since his birth, she seemed to have developed a strong fear of contagion.

"You are calm incarnate. You know how to speak among people at odds, even when you are at odds yourself. I think more than your skill with herbs, your power is there—in your ability to heal the spirit. I think you will grow to be the true beloved between us, in the eyes of our people. You *are* heart's ease."

"Perhaps once, I was that way."

"And again you are. Do you not see that you have healed your own spirit as well?"

"You did that. And him." She lifted Magni's hand from her breast.

"No, my love. You only let us in. You reclaimed your spirit and chose."

~oOo~

One evening not long after the solstice, when the sun was in its low place, approaching the twilight glow that was the fullest dark of a midsummer night, a large trading ship came close to the shore and dropped its anchor.

The hall had been in the quiet stage of the end of the day, when people retired to their own homes and beds. Magni had a rash on his bottom and had been unhappy and sleeping poorly, so Olga and Leif were in the hall, taking turns walking him around the room, which seemed to give him some ease.

A town guard came in and reported the news to Leif, who handed Magni to Olga. "Go back to our quarters."

"A trading ship is trouble?" she asked, worried. The trading ships coming to Karlsa had been exciting events—but it was true that Vali had been cautious in his greeting of them.

"It is until I know it's not." He took his sword and strapped it to his back, and he slid his axe into its ring on his belt. "Go back to the quarters with Vifrid and bar the door." He waved to the servant girl he'd named and pushed all three of them toward the private door.

Vifrid barred the door, and Olga paced with Magni, wondering if her newfound happiness were at its end so soon. She clutched her son to her chest, so tightly that he complained and struggled, but she would not let him go. Her heart pounded and made her feel ill.

Years and years seemed to pass in that way, until there was a light pounding at the door, and then Leif's wonderful voice came, muffled by the thick wood between them. "Olga. All is well."

Smiling, Vifrid unbarred the door, and Olga ran to Leif, more frightened, now that it had passed, than she had known.

He held her and their son in his strong arms. "I don't know this captain, but I know his second. They come for trade and not trouble. They will rest tonight at anchor and come to moor in the morning. I've sent Ulv and a few others out to bring word to the countryside. We will have a few days of excitement, I think. None will take it amiss if you would rather keep Magni away from it. But it could be a help to me if you were seen. Especially for our own farmers."

Olga had loved the trading ships in Karlsa—so mysterious and exotic, with so many new colors and flavors and tastes and smells. "I will leave Magni with Vifrid or one of the other girls, and I will be with you. I would like to see what they bring."

Leif smiled and lifted her chin. "More silks, perhaps. I like you in silk. And out of it."

~oOo~

Olga and Leif wandered together through the market that had arisen at the docks. She did not see the anger Leif had spoken of on the night a few weeks before, when he had met with the farmers and shepherds. On these days, while the traders were here and commerce boomed, goodwill floated in the air.

Their farmers hawked the season's first millings of grain and carts of vegetables to the traders, shepherds and the butcher worked together to offer fresh meats, the smith was hard at work repairing weapons and gear, and the leatherworker and carpenters were likewise flush with new projects. All of that was good for Geitland, and Olga did her part as wife of the jarl, making conversation and sharing in the festive feelings.

But none of that was her true interest. What she loved were the barrels and crates and vast bowls laid out by the traders, full of splendor and beauty the likes of which could not be found in their cold, earthy world.

Leif had brought a fat pouch full of coins in gleaming silver, gold, and bronze. He haggled with the silk trader, and the spice trader, and several other purveyors of wonders, and behind them, Gulla, one of their serving girls, labored under the weight of a large basket full of Olga's new bounty.

He stopped at a dark-skinned man who displayed no wares but was spectacularly adorned with jewels. When Leif beckoned with a subtle flick of his hand, the man produced a large silk pouch from his clothes and opened it so that it sat on his two hands like a blossoming flower.

The pouch was full of jewels, smooth and faceted, loose and in settings of precious metal. Olga peered in as Leif probed through the pouch. Everything he lifted to examine took Olga's breath away with its exotic perfection, but he discarded piece after piece, jewel after jewel. Finally, he pulled a gold chain from the pouch. Dangling from it was a vivid green jewel, elaborately faceted and shaped like a teardrop.

"You pick well, my lord," the trader approved. "That beauty from far, far away. Many travels it takes. It called *emerald* and very rare."

Leif held it up, and it caught the sunlight and sent it dancing between them. Olga couldn't help the delighted gasp that escaped her lips.

The trader's smile was oily with anticipation. "Great beauty like your lady need gem worthy. Twenty gold for such treasure."

Olga sighed. That was far, far too much for a pretty.

Leif turned back to the trader. "No gem could approach my wife's beauty. This is no more worthy than any other." He set the emerald back in the wide pouch and took her hand to turn away.

"No offer, my lord?"

With a subtle smile for Olga only, Leif answered. "Ten gold."

She nearly gasped again. So much yet!

The trader frowned. "So rare, my lord. Worth so much more than that."

"To another, perhaps." Again, Leif made to walk away.

"Twelve!"

Now, Leif smiled broadly at Olga and opened his own pouch. "Done."

He paid the trader and took the jewel. Immediately, he put it around her neck so that the emerald tear lay just at the swell of her breasts. Oh, it was beautiful. Olga lifted it so that the sun shone through it. How could something so marvelous be hers?

"It suits you," Leif said and kissed her.

While they lingered in that embrace, a man laughed nearby—the loud, ready laugh of someone who knew how to enjoy life.

She knew that laugh.

She heard it again, and she shoved back from Leif as hard as she could and whirled around in search of its source.

"Olga?" Leif's voice beside her was laced with confusion and concern. She waved him off and listened hard. She scanned the chaotic scene of the market.

The laugh had come from her left. With no heed for Leif, she hurried that direction, staring hard at the people she passed, especially the traders. She came to the gangway to the traders' ship and looked up.

Standing on that strange ship, one black boot on the wale, dressed in black breeches and a laced white shirt—garb much more plain than most of the men who had come from that ship—was the man whose laugh she knew so well.

Leif thundered up behind her. "Olga! What is wrong?!"

At her name, the man on the ship turned quickly and stared down the gangway, directly at her.

"Olya?"

Tears filled her eyes "Mika. Mika!"

As she stepped onto the gangway, Leif grabbed her arm. "Olga! Hold!"

She yanked away without thinking. "That is my brother! That is Mihkel!"

~oOo~

She couldn't stop touching him. Years it had been since she'd last seen him, and she'd long thought him dead. Lost to her. Yet here he sat, in the great hall, in her home, holding her child, his nephew, in his arms.

She patted his arm, his face, his leg. She leaned on him. It was as though he might wisp into a dream if she lost physical connection with him. Here, sitting at her older brother's side, Olga felt fully, unreservedly, that *her* world, her life, had finally regained its balance. Her past was no longer lost to her, and the future opened wide before her, and in the present, she had bounty beyond reckoning.

On the gangway, Mihkel had met her and lifted her from her feet, and they'd embraced until there was no breath between them. Since then, she had held on.

He was different from the way she'd remembered him. Older, of course, but older even than the years themselves. His brow was creased, and the corners of his eyes, too, and there was a hint of salt in his dark hair, which he kept shorter now than he ever had. He wore a short beard, and it, too, had salt sprinkles. His skin had a bronze sheen. All of it, she guessed, was from long hours on the sea, in the sun.

Leif had been quiet since their reunion on the gangway, but Olga assumed it was because his limited knowledge of her language had become stale with little use, and she was speaking with her brother in that tongue they shared. She, too, had become a little stale, as had Mihkel.

"You make a fine, strong child, sister. I am glad that you could after all." She had been newly widowed the last time she'd seen her brother. He knew about the loss of her first son and the reason for it.

"He is a marvel, yes. I am blessed."

Mihkel gave her a curious look, and Olga realized that she had used a word not of their language to convey a concept not of their ken. The idea of 'blessing' was of this world, not of the world they'd been born in. She could see in his look that he'd understood her; he'd only been surprised by her usage. "Do you have news of our brothers? Our father?"

She cast a glance at Leif. With him sitting right there, she did not know how she would tell them of the deaths. Even with Leif away, she wasn't sure how to say it so that Mihkel would not look on her husband as his enemy.

Leif interpreted her glance as discomfort with his presence. He stood. In his own language he said, "I will leave you to be reconnected." Coming around the table, he held his hands out for Magni. "I will put him to bed for a rest."

When Leif was away, and they were, more or less, in privacy in the hall, Mihkel turned to her with a smirk. "I think he liked me better last night, when I was only captain of a ship bringing wares for sale into his town."

Her husband was acting jealous, and she didn't understand it, but it was a question for later. "He is surprised only. As am

I." She clutched his shirt. "Still I cannot believe my own sight! How are you here? And captain of that great ship!"

Mihkel laughed. "Not so great. Good and sturdy. She is my second ship. The first was lost to pirates—who are not so different from the people of this place. Taking from others to make themselves rich. I am surprised to find you among them, Olya."

"I am happy. Leif is a good man, a good jarl. And a good husband and father. Our love is deep. This is where I belong. But the story that brought me here is long and twisty."

Her brother refilled his cup with mead. "And I have time. I want hear your story, and I will tell you mine. But first, I want news of the rest of us. Have you word of our family?"

Olga took a breath and prepared to tell her brother her story. Though she would hold back the worst parts, still she hoped that Leif was right about her skill at bringing those at odds together, and she would say all she needed to say in a way that would keep her husband and her long-lost brother from acrimony.

~oOo~

A while later, Vifrid came out to summon her for Magni's feeding. Mihkel, who'd grown quieter and quieter as she'd spoken, took his leave, with the explanation—or excuse—that he had work on his ship. Promising her that they would talk more, he embraced her and then left, and Olga went back to her son.

Leif sat holding Magni, bouncing him lightly on his shoulder while the boy fussed and yanked on his father's hair.

Olga loosened her shift and took her son. As she settled him to feed, she asked, "Are you angry?"

Leif's eyes flashed. "No. Of course I'm not angry. I'm happy that your brother has been returned to you. I saw great joy in you today, and I would never wish you less."

She heard something low in his tone, though. Something sad, or at least reserved. "Then what is it?"

He went to her and lifted the new emerald pendant in his fingers. "I would not have him come between us."

"How could he?"

"Does he know all that has happened since you were last together?"

Olga understood. She'd had the same fear as she'd talked with Mihkel. But she hadn't realized that Leif would see it, too. "He does. We talked at length about it. He is sad to know of the loss of our family. But Leif, my love, I do not blame you now, and I didn't give you blame in my telling. I held back what I could. I think he is disappointed in me, for becoming part of a world of raiders, but he is not angry with you."

At that, Leif smiled wryly. "He does not like us here?"

"I think he likes your coin very well. But he doesn't make much distinction between raiders and pirates."

"I suppose we are not so different, to a man with spoils to protect. I would say that traders are no different, then, either. We are all looking to take as much of what another holds as we can get."

Olga thought of the raiders ransacking the coastal village. Killing the young, old, and infirm as readily as the strong and able. Raping the women. Burning and looting and whooping through town with smiles on their faces. Leif had been among them, though he had not been like the others.

Those who were now her dearest friends, and her greatest love, had raided that little village and made her a slave. Those were her people now, and she was happy here. She had come to accept, but not to understand, the way of raiding. She had come to see more than the monsters with painted faces, and she knew that this world was full of all kinds of people, most of whom were farmers and craftsmen and merchants, like any other place.

But she had not forgotten the fear she'd felt as she'd cowered in a corner with young Johanna, or the horror of the pen they'd kept the women and girls in. She remembered what it was like to be raided, and as painful as the memory was, she wanted never to lose it.

She thought Leif was wrong in thinking that traders, who gained the agreement of the buyer, who offered something in exchange for coin, were anything like raiders or pirates—or princes, for that matter—who took what they wanted by force.

Now was not the time to say any such thing. So she smiled up at her husband and said what was most important. "I love you. We are one. I am glad to have my brother here for a while and know that he is well, but he is not my life. You are. We came into each other's lives in horror and have lived through even worse, and we are together. Mihkel cannot divide us. Nothing can."

24

After a few days, Mihkel's crew packed up what was left of their wares, and what they'd acquired from the people of Geitland, and prepared to set off for their next port. Leif stood on the pier, a few strides from the gangway, and gave Olga a moment of privacy to bid her brother farewell.

The two men had been guarded with each other, but civil enough. Leif certainly didn't begrudge Olga this happy chance to be reunited with the last surviving member of her blood family, and Mihkel was clearly devoted to his sister. Yet Mihkel's presence made him uncomfortable in ways he was still grappling to understand.

His evident contempt for Leif and his people was one of those ways, to be sure. Even before he had known their family connection, from the night of their first meeting, Leif had sensed Mihkel's distaste for mooring in Geitland. In that meeting, he had inferred that it had been the captain's second, Antonis, who had argued to come into this part of the world.

Perhaps it was that distaste that had so unsettled Leif when he'd learned who Mihkel was. He didn't want that feeling leaching into Olga's consciousness again. She was *his* now, and this was her world now, and she had become comfortable here. He didn't want her brother changing the way she saw her home.

Yes, he was jealous.

He also thought Mihkel a hypocrite. Olga had argued that traders were different from raiders and pirates because people gave their coin of their free will and were given something in exchange. But that was her naïveté—and her brother—shaping her sight. Leif knew what traders such as Mihkel and the men on his ship did to get their barrels full of spices and their chests full of jewels.

There was blood on her brother's hands, too. Leif didn't judge. It was, as Olga would once have said, the way of things: strength took from weakness; weakness died out. Strength prevailed and made the world stronger for it.

Mihkel was strong. And so was Leif.

He didn't judge, but neither would he be judged.

Leif watched brother and sister embrace, Olga clinging to her brother, and he wished the man away from his pier. Finally, Mihkel pushed her gently back, said something to which she nodded, kissed her forehead, and stepped away.

His ship was laded and crewed. It waited only for its captain. Mihkel stepped at last onto the gangway; then he turned and met Leif's eyes. Leif stared back, and for a moment, nothing changed. Two men speaking volumes without a word.

With a brisk nod to Leif, without another look at his sister, Mihkel turned and trotted up the gangway.

When the captain was aboard, Leif joined his wife and pulled her into his arms. She held him tightly, quietly, and they stood there until the ship was well away.

~oOo~

Two days later, Geitland had a visitor Leif was much happier to see. Brenna came over land, by cart, and was in the hall before anyone realized that the great God's-Eye had returned to the place of her abasement—and of her triumph.

Leif and Olga sat in their seats at the head of the hall, in the midst of their weekly hearing of people's complaints and requests. As Leif had predicted, his clanspeople warmed quickly to his wife, and he had noticed that they already turned first to her when they had particular kinds of problems or requests. From him, they wanted justice. From Olga, they wanted compassion. He thought it a good balance.

It made him grow hard to watch her counsel people in need. She yet always looked to him as she offered a solution, prepared to defer should he object, but he couldn't imagine a circumstance in which he might. He trusted her heart and her mind completely.

When she felt insufficiently knowledgeable to offer counsel, she directed the petition to him. And then, when they were alone, she would pepper him with questions so that she would understand.

Next year, when the great raid with Vali would finally happen, Leif would feel that he left the jarldom in very capable hands.

As Olga talked with a woman whose husband had strayed, there was a small commotion at the back of the hall. Leif turned his attention there and saw Brenna walking toward him, Solveig in her arms and two shieldmaidens he did not know at her back. As the crowd separated and made room for her to advance, he was surprised to see her in a hangerock. Brenna preferred more manly clothing, especially, he'd assume, for traveling.

Then she stood at the foot of the raised platform on which sat his chair and Olga's, and Leif saw why. She was with child. She set Solveig down at her side, and the little girl kept her feet.

Four months had passed since Vali had sailed with Leif and Olga away from Karlsa. The raiders had been gone nearly two of those and were due to return soon, if the raid had gone well and the weather was fair. Leif thought he understood Brenna's visit as eagerness to be reunited with her husband, though he was surprised she would have taken a long overland journey in her condition.

Olga leapt from her chair and into Brenna's arms, and the two women held each other in the tight embrace of sisterhood. Brenna was substantially taller than Leif's small wife, and she laid her cheek on Olga's head. Her eyes met Leif's and they both smiled.

He stepped down, too, and took his turn in Brenna's arms. "It is good to see you, my friend. We expect the ships any day now."

She leaned back and looked up at him. "Good. I have another need as well." She picked her daughter back up.

"Anything. Come, let's speak in private." He announced the end of the petitions and called for food and mead for the people, then took Brenna's hand and Olga's and led them both into the private quarters.

When they were seated and Olga had called Vifrid to take Solveig off with Magni and made sure Brenna also had food and drink and had been made comfortable, Leif asked, "What can we do?"

Brenna took a sip of goat's milk before she answered. "Karlsa is in a state. We lost so many of our strong workers in the plague, and the rest are gone on this raid. The raid is crucial, you know I know that, but meanwhile, we starve. There aren't enough people to work the fields and make a good yield, and our stores are dwindled to nothing. I can't imagine that even the raid will bring us enough to restore us. And even if it does, gold itself cannot fill our bellies."

Leif leaned in and took her hand. "What can we do?"

"If you might spare some store of grains and hardy foods, I would bring them home with me. And…I don't know if this is a fool's wish, but my chest, from my time with Åke, is still here, buried near my little hut in the woods. Unless in all this time it was found and stolen. It's gold and silver, and if it's there, I would offer it to you in payment for the food."

It was Vali who had killed Åke, so all of the old jarl's holdings had been rightfully his to claim—Geitland and Karlsa both. Karlsa was far north, a small holding isolated by distance and climate, with a small town as its seat. Geitland was a holding four times the size, with a thriving town that served as a substantial center of commerce.

Vali had not wanted a jarldom at all, but, on Brenna's urging, he had finally agreed to claim Karlsa, his home. He had offered Geitland—the richer claim by far—to Leif.

At Brenna's request and offer, Leif shook his head. "You will not. I don't know if the chest is still there, but if it is, you will take it home with you, on the cart with the grains and supplies we will give you. Always you have only to ask, Brenna. I have this jarldom because of you and Vali. It is I who owe you."

Relief glittered in her eyes. "Thank you. This might save us."

~oOo~

Brenna's tiny winter hut had not weathered her years away from it very well, but her chest was exactly where she'd buried it. Leif had taken her out with two strong youths to unearth it, and her mood lightened considerably upon finding it undisturbed. Years of her spoils from her raids as a shieldmaiden had accumulated. Leif thought that such a wealth would have to be real aid for her people.

She wanted to wait for Vali, but, not knowing precisely when the raiders would return, and with her people in need, she decided she could not. Olga fussed about her traveling again so long over land in her condition, but there were not enough men left even in Geitland who could manage a karve, and the distance between their towns was too much for a smaller vessel. The big skeids had taken nearly all of their men of the sea.

The day before she was set to travel again, while her cart was being loaded for a morning departure, Brenna was saved from that arduous journey when a watcher on the pier saw the skeids approaching, flying Geitland's black-and-white sails.

People from all over the town came to the pier to welcome the raiders back. Leif was flanked by Olga, carrying Magni in the sling, and Brenna, with Solveig on her hip.

Leif saw it when Vali realized that his wife and child were there. His friend leapt from the ship the moment it came along the pier, and he ran toward his wife and daughter—stopping short when he saw her state. He fell to his knees and kissed her belly before he'd even embraced her or Solveig. Then he stood and enfolded wife and daughter in his arms.

Leif kept his gaze on them for a moment, his heart warm, then turned and watched the men unloading the ships. Four men heaved an enormous chest onto the pier. There were new slaves, too—ten or so. He knew he'd hear from his wife about that.

And the bounty kept coming.

Astrid came up to him with a grin unlike Leif had ever seen on her face before. In her hands she hefted a shield that seemed to be made of pure gold.

Gold was a terrible choice for a shield—it was soft and heavy and would provide virtually no resistance at all to a blow—

and even the silliest warrior would know better than to carry one, so that shield could only have been ceremonial.

He embraced Astrid in hearty greeting, then cocked an eyebrow at her, asking for an explanation.

"We had to go deep into the country to find spoils worth taking, but when we did—a king paid us most of this in ransom to send us away."

"A king wealthy enough to make a useless shield in gold?"

"No longer is he so wealthy," Vali smirked at his side. "It was a good raid, my friend. There is little left to raid in the south, but we found what was left. And next year, we go west!"

~oOo~

With the raiders back, Brenna and Solveig could return with Vali and the other men and go by sea. Leif gifted them the karve that had more than once conveyed them back and forth between their towns.

The spoils from this raid, and the food stores Leif had given them, would go far to bringing Karlsa back to its strength. Leif hoped so. Vali needed to build his skeids if he wanted to be an equal partner the next year.

Vali took his wife and child and retired early from the hall, while the other returning raiders were still deep in their celebration. Leif took his friends' leaving as a cue, and pulled Olga back into their quarters as well.

Vifrid had care of Magni, who was already sleeping, in the new swinging cradle that Leif had made for him. Leif relieved her of her duty, and he and Olga undressed.

They both slept bare in the warm months. He had always slept bare, except on a raid, and Olga had taken to doing the same, at least on her top, since her carrying and their son's birth, so that she could nurse him easily in the night. Since her birth blood had stopped the week before, she'd been again coming to bed completely nude.

Her small body was beautiful. Her hips flared out a bit more since Magni, and her breasts were noticeably heavier, filled with nourishment for their son. Her belly was not so flat as it had been before, and there were a few reddish lines at each side. To Leif, she was now even more lovely than she had been.

And her hair flowed down her back, covering her bottom, like a dark, silken cape.

Leif appreciated the nearness of her bare skin each night, but it had been a struggle, especially in these days since her blood had stopped. He wanted her. He had not had her since before the birth, and he was going mad with need.

But their son slept between them in the night, and in the day, they were both bound by the responsibilities of their lives.

This was why Leif had built the cradle.

Olga went to pick Magni up from the cradle, meaning, Leif knew, to bring him into bed with them, where they slept all together each night.

But Leif caught her arm and pulled her around to face him. "Not yet."

His wife smiled up at him. "No?"

"No. I want you. I need you."

"*Jah?* You do?"

"Of course I do. I go mad with needing you."

Her smile widened, and she came close so that her body was flush with his at every point. "I worried that you would not find me…desirable any longer. I don't look as I did."

"You look better. The changes in your body brought my son to me. I see the marks he made, and I want you. I see you holding him, feeding him, mothering him, and I can scarcely stay in my breeches for want of you. You have brought me everything I want in my life. You *are* everything I want in my life. When I am with you, my spirit is full, and my heart is at ease. I love you."

He bent down, tangled his hands in her glorious hair, and kissed her as deeply as he could. When her arms came around his neck, he lifted her and carried to their bed.

While their perfect son slept quietly in his new cradle, Leif showed his wife exactly how much he wanted her.

EPILOGUE
SPIRIT

THE WAY THAT IS

On a gloomy day when the sun stayed hidden behind a shield of grey clouds, Olga stood on the pier and watched the ship carry away her friends. Twice in such a short space of days she had been given the gift of unexpected time with people she loved, and twice she'd had again to bid them farewell.

She was glad, so glad, to have had them close for any time at all, but standing here watching Brenna and Vali—and little Solveig, walking and talking now—sail from her again, mere days after Mihkel had been torn from her again, she could only feel the ache of melancholy.

Leif stood at her side, cradling their son. He put his hand on her shoulder, his arm across her back, and pulled her close. "We will see them again. And you will see your brother again, as well."

Always, he seemed to know her thinking. She laid her head against his broad chest and picked up Magni's little bare foot.

"He's cold. We should take him back inside." She folded his light woolen blanket over his legs.

"Yes," Leif said and shifted to bring Magni even closer to his chest. "Another summer begins to wane."

She sighed. "Winter is hard here."

"Not so hard here as in Karlsa, I promise." With a curl of his finger under her chin, he tipped her head up. "I will keep you warm. Mayhap we will make another child while we keep each other warm." This light in his eyes told her that he was teasing more than planning.

"That is unlikely." She didn't understand how she had been able to have Magni, and she didn't expect such a boon again. "I don't want you to be disappointed."

"I could not be. I have all I need right now. You and our son fill my life." His expression became serious, and his blue eyes darkened. "And you, my love? Do you have all you need?"

Olga turned and faced the sea. The karve had headed to the north and was nearly out of sight. Her friends were gone. Her brother was gone. All she had in Geitland was Leif and her son. Was that all she needed?

It was. Leif's love centered her. His steady spirit and faithful heart gave her a mooring. It was when she'd thought she'd been wrong about him that she'd been lost. Their love for their child centered her, too. Their small family was her home, and it was here. So she needed nothing more to be content.

But she had so much more. She had this town and the people in it, who came to her with their troubles and questions and trusted her to help them. She had lost her calling as a healer, but she had found—had retained—her purpose as a counselor. A leader.

She had dear friends, closer to her in spirit than any other in her life. Vali and Brenna, and Frida and Dagmar, and Jaan and Georg, might all have lived far from her, but they were close always, in her heart, and she knew she was there with them, as well.

And she had Mihkel, returned to her. She didn't know whether she'd ever see him again, but at the least she knew that he had been well, that he was having a life he loved. He had found the adventure and the fortune he'd long ago struck out in search of.

She had lost much in her life. But she had also gained more than she had ever dreamed.

Loss and gain. Dark and light. Pain and joy. Such was life. It was the way of things. The world kept its balance.

Olga smiled up at her golden giant holding their mighty child in his arms. "Yes. All I need and all I want. My heart is at ease."

Susan Fanetti is a Midwestern native transplanted to Northern California, where she lives with her husband, youngest son, and assorted cats.

Susan's blog: www.susanfanetti.com
Freak Circle Press blog: www.freakcirclepress.com

Susan's Facebook author page:
https://www.facebook.com/authorsusanfanetti
'Susan's FANetties' fan group:
https://www.facebook.com/groups/871235502925756/

Freak Circle Press Facebook page:
https://www.facebook.com/freakcirclepress
'The FCP Clubhouse' fan group:
https://www.facebook.com/groups/810728735692965 /

Twitter: @sfanetti

The Northwomen Sagas Pinterest Board:
https://www.pinterest.com/laughingwarrior/the-northwomen-sagas/

Printed in Great Britain
by Amazon